COME SPRING

Charlotte Hinger

SIMON AND SCHUSTER
New York

Copyright © 1986 by Charlotte Hinger
All rights reserved
including the right of reproduction
in whole or in part in any form
Published by Simon and Schuster
A Division of Simon & Schuster, Inc.
Simon & Schuster Building
Rockefeller Center
1230 Avenue of the Americas
New York, New York 10020
SIMON AND SCHUSTER and colophon are registered trademarks of
Simon & Schuster, Inc.
Designed by Jacques Chazaud
Manufactured in the United States of America

3   5   7   9   10   8   6   4

Library of Congress Cataloging in Publication Data

Hinger, Charlotte, DATE–
Come spring.

I. Title.
PS3558.I534C66   1986   813'.54   85-18477

ISBN: 0-671-55429-8

IN MEMORY OF MY FATHER,
CHARLES FRANKLIN SOUTHERLAND,
WHO WAS KANSAS

But my servant Caleb, because he had another spirit with him, and hath followed me fully, I will bring into the land whereinto he went; and his seed shall possess it.

Numbers 14:24

Prologue

She had fallen twice now and her breath was coming in hot, ragged gasps. Terror gave her the needed strength and her only thought was to reach Daniel.

She slowed to a stumbling walk when she saw him, relief flooding her body. She was safe now. Just a few more moments and she would be in his arms.

He dropped his hoe when he saw her and quickly closed the distance between them.

"Someone's coming." It was all she needed to say.

"Christ, Aura Lee. I wish—oh, Christ." He held her to his chest and stroked her hair until her body stopped its terrified trembling.

"Daniel, I'm so sorry," she whispered. "You don't know how miserable this makes me."

"It's all right, sweetheart. If you're scared, you're scared. It's not your fault." *It's mine,* he thought gloomily. *I must have been crazy to bring Judge Lombard's daughter to a place like this.* His wife's unreasonable fear of strangers was a fact of life he would not be able to change. He knew that now. They had talked about it several times, but no amount of reasoning changed her heart.

He squeezed her hand. "Let's go back to the house. It's probably some poor cowboy wanting a meal."

The lonely hoofbeats of a solitary rider echoed over the prairie. Aura Lee stared through the dirty pane of their soddy at the speck on the horizon that was becoming more discernible with each beat of her heart.

She was a frail watercolor of a woman, very slight, with yellow hair and pale, sensitive blue eyes that could become pridefully unreadable in an instant. In another setting she would have been lovely, but the prairie sun was too strong for her. It bleached her out—her hair, her skin, her very soul—with its harshness. Her white complexion required the softness of satin and fine fabrics to reflect its translucence.

She swallowed excess acid saliva and willed herself to remain calm. The rider could very well have murderous intentions, for it was impossible to tell on the prairie what the appearance of a stranger meant. Death and celebration alike approached boldly, and if the rider was dangerous, there was no place to hide anyway. There was not a single outbuilding on their claim. Not even a windmill. Just she and Daniel in their soddy, surrounded by acres of nothingness.

A sudden hiss of scorched liquid made her turn from the window. She was not a good cook. She lacked the single-minded precision that managed to put everything on the table at the same time. She darted quickly to the overheated pot of parched rye coffee and with the corner of her apron deftly removed it from the burner.

She poured the coffee into a tin cup and, after handing it to Daniel, turned back to the window where he stood. She gently stroked his back as he gazed intently at the approaching rider. His outstretched arm was braced carelessly on the window frame. His other hand curled gingerly around one of their three cups.

She could feel the tension in Daniel's muscles despite the casual posture. She knew he too was thinking of everything the rider might represent, and was readying for the challenge. Although they stood side by side, they were miles apart in attitude.

Her face softened as she studied her husband's handsome profile, radiantly lit by the setting sun. His dark complexion made him look like an Indian. He had penetrating, nearly black eyes and a heavy, beautifully shaped mustache that was his single vanity. He was built with a depth of chest that invariably gave people the impression that he was a very large man, although he was not actually as tall as he appeared. He judged people, situations, and animals quickly and with devastating accuracy.

Sensing the effort her stiff-backed control was costing her, he drew Aura Lee to him protectively. He did not speak, nor did his eyes swerve from the approaching rider. She stood quietly, tucked under the shelter of his arm, and blinked back sudden hot tears.

Daniel had come here a year before her. He had staked his claim and built this soddy and then sent for her two months ago when he considered it sufficiently comfortable for a woman to live in. Their soddy was relatively luxurious. He would never have asked her to live in a dugout.

They had been married six months now. She had continued to live with her parents for the first four months of their marriage, until Daniel had prepared this proper place for her. She was still in awe of this man, still lovestruck and anxious for contact. She yearned to be touched, spoken to, stroked, bedded. And yet from the time Daniel had brought her here,

10

his eyes quietly evaluating her every reaction, she had not dared allow herself to think about the life she had left behind.

He had sent for her at the beginning of summer. Her excitement had been unbearable as they approached their claim.

"Just a quarter of a mile further, Aura Lee."

"I can't wait, I've waited for so long." She felt like a small child anticipating Christmas.

"You'll see it soon enough, and for longer than you want, I expect." His eyes were briefly troubled. "Honey, it's not a palace, you know. I've told you that. It won't be easy."

She kissed his cheek.

"I don't care Daniel, as long as I'm with you."

He sighed deeply, then laughed.

The horse and wagon continued to make its way across the prairie. There was no road; only the faint swath of the resilient buffalo grass, where he had traveled the day before to meet the train, revealed the way.

"There it is, darling."

Her body stiffened with shock. She had imagined their soddy on a hillside, in a grove of trees with a carpet of prairie flowers. There were no hills, no trees. Only the prairie flowers were a reality. He could not be expecting her to live in this place. From the back of her mind came a distant voice mocking, "You were warned, you were warned."

She saw a dismal clump of a building that Daniel had proudly declared in his letter to be eighteen by twenty-five feet, one of the largest in the area. She had pored over the description so eagerly. She knew the arched roof, curiously curved like a bent bow and secured with sod, was a "car," unique to Kansas. The windows were real glass and set back a full eighteen inches from the wall. Daniel had described the ordeal of getting them from Wallace. The only thing that was as she had expected was that her home was square with the world, for Daniel had said the first row of sod had been laid at night in alignment with the North Star.

There were tools neatly propped against the sod walls. In front was an old rain barrel, a chair, washtubs, and several buckets. What appeared to be a pile of gigantic thistles lay on the ground south of the house.

"Daniel, what's that?"

"Elkhorn, Aura Lee, for drying your wash. It'll have to do until we have a fence."

She did not talk, and beat down a wild birdlike desire to fly, to rescue herself. She was barely under control and the last bit of it went when her young husband squeezed her hand. Through a haze of tears, she saw the muscles working in his jaw as he awkwardly patted her. He pulled up in front of the house that seemed to Aura Lee to be growing right out of the ground. They sat side by side without speaking, without touching. She was overcome with shame at the effect her reaction was having on Daniel. His head was bent. He did not move.

Aura Lee wiped her eyes, took a deep, steadying breath, and resolutely entered into the prairie lie, the belief in the myth that had enabled thousands of other women to endure—that the world could be transformed into one's vision of its potential. If you worked hard enough, prayed hard enough, and never ever even once doubted, then anything was possible. Was not the state motto "To the Stars Through Difficulties"? The trick would be never to allow herself to see anything but stars, for Daniel's sake.

She decided she would never acknowledge again, not to her husband, to herself, to anyone, the ice water shock of despair she had felt when her life on the prairie kaleidoscoped before her eyes, in shades of gray. She concentrated on an intense inner circle of white light, a total clearing of her mind of all feeling. "You were warned, you were warned," the voice gently mocked again.

Though the horseman was still very distant, he had covered enough ground for Daniel to judge his pace, and as he watched the desperate lunging toward the soddy, he realized the man was literally riding his horse to death.

Christ, he thought. *There's trouble here and I don't want Aura Lee to be any more upset than she already is.* Her heart was beating a rapid tattoo where his fingertips rested on her arm. He quietly kissed the top of her head, inhaling deeply of the faint lilac scent of her hair. Her total trust in his judgment and ability to protect her touched him deeply. Judge Lombard's daughter. The most pampered debutante in Saint Jo. Out here. His wife. He had realized the first night how terribly hard this environment was going to be on a woman of her breeding.

After supper she had gone outside for a few minutes, then came in and sat with a look of strained bewilderment on her face. Her hands nervously twisted her apron.

"What's the matter, honey?"

"Daniel, where is the outhouse?" She kept her eyes on the floor, miserable with embarrassment.

"Uh, we don't have one, Aura Lee. But of course you know that," he said stupidly. "I forgot to buy a chamber pot. Christ, I thought I had taken care of everything. And we bury the other."

Her lips thinned and she did not speak.

"A sod outhouse wouldn't be any good. They have to be moved from time to time, and since there aren't any trees, we can't build a wooden one."

She disappeared out the door in a prim fury. They never mentioned it again, but the shame of these living conditions hung between them. It was an ever-present daily reminder of what had been left behind.

"That man wants help, Aura Lee, or he wouldn't ride that way. It's all right." He could feel her relax.

She was too worried all the time, he thought. *Too nervous.* Judge Lombard's daughter. He thanked God her parents could not see her now. Her mother would faint dead away.

The thumping of the hoofbeats grew nearer. Their steady rhythm was muted by the carpet of short, tough buffalo grass. Sounds Aura Lee rarely paid attention to now seemed unnaturally loud. Their horse was nuzzling a pan of oats and the halter ring ticked against the tin. She wished he would stop it. The wind moaned down the stovepipe as though trapped, and with its eerie whistle, it seemed to beg for release.

She swallowed nervously, and even that seemed to make a vulgar echo.

The man reined in just short of their doorway. He was not carrying a weapon.

"He's in bad trouble," said Daniel. "Look at his horse. No man does that unless something is really wrong. Good animals are just too hard to come by." The horse's flanks were covered with sweaty foam from being pushed to the brink of endurance.

Quickly he drew the bolt on the wooden door and hurried outside. Aura Lee followed, her fear lessened by the man's unarmed and panic-stricken approach. He dismounted and in a thick guttural rush of an alien tongue seemed to plead with Daniel.

"What's he saying?"

"I don't know."

"Daniel, he's frightened to death."

The man tugged at his hat and desperately repeated the words in heavily accented English. He looked alertly for some sign the couple in front of him understood.

Frantically, he reached inside his breast pocket, pulled out papers, and showed them to Daniel, who glanced at them briefly. This man was no tramp. These were legal homestead papers, same as his. The mystery of the language was cleared up also by the way the consonants were run together and the way the accents fell over certain words.

"He's a homesteader, like us, Aura Lee. He's Bohemian, a Czechoslovakian. No wonder we couldn't understand him."

The man brightened at the word Czechoslovakian. Daniel handed him back his papers, and the man pointed to the name at the bottom.

"Smrcka," he said flatly. "I speak pretty good English when—" He could not find the words to complete the thought.

"I'm Daniel Hollingworth."

Smrcka pointed to Aura Lee and gestured for her to follow. He wanted her to come with him. That much was clear, even though he could not explain the nature of the trip. She looked at Daniel in astonishment.

"He wants me, Daniel. Not you, but me."

"I know. That's very obvious." He glanced at Smrcka's hand. It was bare, but that was meaningless for someone of his class.

"Let's go, darling. I have a feeling you've got some work cut out for you."

Quickly he ran to the small corral and began to bridle their sorrel gelding. They would have to ride double.

Aura Lee stood shyly in front of the man. His fine dark eyes shone with intelligence and there was a curious dignity about him that was at odds with his threadbare clothes.

He tucked his precious papers back into his pocket and waited tensely beside his horse, his eyes never leaving Aura Lee.

Daniel saddled the horse with his usual economy of motion. He mounted quickly, and reached down for Aura Lee. She clung desperately to him, her frail body slapping miserably against the pounding rhythm of the horse. Smrcka's exhausted mount was panting heavily with the effort to lead the way.

Layers of clouds gently stacked on each other like wool batting held the hues of spilled watercolors and delicately descended to a sharply defined horizon. This evening, the beauty of the sunset was lost on Aura Lee. It passed by in a rush toward the flat, treeless horizon.

Smrcka was beginning to slow up, but Aura Lee could not see any change in the landscape at all. They stopped just three feet short of a pipe sticking up from the ground and dismounted. Swiftly, Smrcka led them down the grassy bank to the entrance to his dugout. They had approached it from behind, so there had been no sign of it, except for the stovepipe.

They hurried toward what was literally a hole in the side of the hill.

Near the dugout's door were a stove, a chair, a table, and several boxes, for space was so precious inside that all the furniture was carried out at night to make room for bed ticks, then brought inside during the day, and the ticks in turn carried out.

In the dismal light of the fading sun, so faint as to be nearly invisible in the filthy nine-by-twelve room, Aura Lee saw a wide-eyed boy, about five years old, weeping silently as he stared into a corner.

Smrcka rushed toward the bed, which was a feather ticking laid on the floor. Suddenly the room was filled with his anguished moans. Aura Lee moved toward him, her hand on her throat, her face white with despair.

On the bed lay a young woman in a pool of slime and blood. Her hair had come loose during a long and difficult labor. Her eyelids were closed and there was a feathery tracing of blue veins above the dark brown lashes. She was dead but still warm. Between her legs lay an infant still covered with the damp, waxy membrances of birth, sealing him into a gelatinous shroud.

"Julka. Julka." Vensel Smrcka slammed one fist into his other hand over and over again. "Alone," he sobbed. "She died all *alone*."

"She wanted me to come close, Dad, and I—" The words jerked from Anton Smrcka. "She kept crying, asking for you, and I didn't know what to do. She kept saying your name—saying your name—" He gritted his shaking teeth to stop his trembling. "Saying your—and—then she was hurting so bad she couldn't talk and I was afraid I was going to be sick, and then she talked real soft like when she tucks me in, and she wanted me to come over." His head hung down as if his slender neck was too frail to support its weight. "I couldn't. I couldn't. I didn't want to hear her, and then I—I couldn't hear her at all."

"Daniel, my God, my God." Aura Lee reached for her husband's arm, her face drained of all color. "How could any just God permit a boy to see this?" she whispered. "You poor, poor child." She reached toward the boy, but he flinched, suddenly wary as a cornered animal.

"Anton." Torn between the needs of his living son and the grief for his dead wife, he turned again toward the bed.

"Julka." Smrcka's shoulders shook as he knelt beside the pallet and fumbled for her lifeless hand. He stared at his wife's nakedness and began to cover her, then stopped. In trembling haste, he began to claw at the birth sac, never stopping a mysterious litany of words.

At this, Anton curled into a little ball and squeezed his eyes shut as though he could shut off his hearing too.

Aura Lee watched with horror. "Oh, Daniel, my God, do something."

Daniel laid his hand on Smrcka's shoulder. "Stop it," he said sharply. "The boy. You've got to be strong for the boy, and he's scared to death already. You've got to get yourself under control." He looked helplessly at Aura Lee, who quickly knelt beside the man.

"Mr. Smrcka, the child is dead, as well. I'm afraid there's nothing we can do."

The man raised his eyes to Aura Lee, all hope leaving his face, and tears began to course down his cheeks. His shoulders slumped and with a curse he twisted away from the bed. He flung himself on the floor and drawing his knees to his chest lay convulsed with sobs.

Aura Lee's heart turned over as his words exploded from Bohemian into English.

"I want her back. God, please give her back."

Immediately, Daniel pulled him to his feet.

"You *must* think of your son," he said firmly.

Anton made himself even smaller. He did not open his eyes when Vensel scooped him up and carried him outside. The familiarity of his father's arms let him relax enough to remove his hands from between his knees. Desperately he grabbed for Vensel's neck, clinging to his chest like a little monkey.

"Stay outside for a moment, while my wife and I—take care of things," said Daniel, fumbling for the right words. He stood for a moment looking at the father and son, unaware in their grief of anyone but each other.

He ducked back through the doorway and crossed over to his wife. She had not moved from the dead woman's bedside. He drew her up and pulled her body full-length against his, as though he could infuse her with some of his strength.

"Daniel. My God."

"I know—sh—" He patted her and kissed her as he would soothe a child.

"We've got to clean up," he whispered. "Lay out the body."

"Daniel, I don't know how. I *can't*. I've never done any of this before." She was panicky in her dismay. In Saint Jo they would simply have called the undertaker.

"Of course you haven't. I haven't either," said Daniel. "But we've *got* to. There's no one else. We're all these poor people have to help them."

She drew away and, wiping her hands on her apron, turned once more to the bed.

"Don't let them come in again until I'm done, Daniel. You stay outside too. All of you. You shouldn't be seeing her like this either."

"All right." He touched her cheek, his eyes moist with relief, then awkwardly drew back his hand at the cold withdrawal in her eyes. He left the dugout, and Aura Lee had never felt so utterly alone in her life.

She started with the baby. Gingerly reaching between the woman's legs, she lifted the child and then after a sight tug, realized the infant was forever connected through death to its mother's body. Her tears were stopped by horror and instinctively she laid the child back down and located a knife by the wash basin. She approached the bed as though in a trance and with trembling hands sliced through the umbilical cord.

She found a linen runner wrapped in a newspaper and used it to swaddle the tiny bundle of flesh. She laid it on top of the dresser. She did not want ever to have to look at it again.

16

She searched all over for another sheet, then realized the family did not own one. The body would have to lie in its own lifeless drainings until she or Daniel could bring one of hers back from their soddy.

But for now she could at least arrange the woman's limbs and cover her decently. She moistened a cloth and began to wipe up the blood. When she finished washing her, she found a clean dress, and removing the worn batiste nightgown, she managed to slip the fresh garment over her shoulders. Aura Lee's hands shook. Julka was already growing stiff and cold. She found a comb and twisted the hair back into its coil. She pulled the worn patchwork quilt up to the woman's neck, then went outside.

Aura Lee gestured to Daniel to come to her. She spoke softly, out of the Smrckas' hearing.

"Please go back to the soddy, Daniel, and bring me back a sheet and some more water. I want to make this place spotless. It's the least we can do for her."

"I don't want to leave you here, Aura Lee. Vensel and the boy need to be away until we're all done. They need to eat."

"Leave me alone with her, Daniel."

He shook his head. "It's not right. I know this is woman's work, but a lady like you shouldn't have to do this. I'm sorry, Aura Lee."

He walked over to the father and son, who had not moved, and asked them to go for supplies.

"I won't leave her," said Vensel. "I left her once. I left her." His voice broke.

"My wife needs these things. Besides, the boy must be hungry. Aura Lee had supper ready. Feed him and then come back. He's got to eat, and he must not see his mother again until we make things right."

Smrcka nodded, still not attempting to pry Anton's hands from his neck.

"Take my horse. Yours is worn out."

He watched silently as the man mounted awkwardly with his precious bundle. Anton never once loosened his grip and kept his face buried in his father's chest.

Aura Lee watched the slow progress of the horse, then turned to Daniel. She shook with rage.

"This never should have happened. Did you look at her? Really look? She was beautiful, just beautiful. How could he have expected her to live in this hole, this cave, like an animal?"

"Sweetheart, no one plans to live in a dugout forever. Come spring, I'm sure he would have built a proper house."

"Come spring, come summer, come winter. It's always sometime ahead, never *now*, out here. Never, never now. Doesn't anything ever really happen, or is it always imaginary and around the corner? Where was the doctor? Where was the *doctor*, Daniel? Tell me that!"

Daniel was shocked to find Aura Lee's fury directed at him. He looked away from her tear-bright blue eyes, blazing fiercely with her strong sense of injustice.

"There isn't one yet. The closest is in Wallace. We'll have one someday soon, Aura Lee, I promise. In the meantime, we take care of our own."

"Take *care* of our own? Even if I had been here all the time, I don't know anything about having babies. Absolutely nothing. What good would I have been? She needed a doctor. Tell me how something like this could have been allowed to happen."

"Aura Lee, get ahold of yourself. We have work to do. You can't let yourself go like this. Not out here." She had to be made to face this responsibility. She had to understand the danger of abandoning hope. She had to know the sure destruction that would follow a loss of nerve on the prairie.

"I don't want to get ahold of myself. Oh, Daniel, that could be *me* lying there."

"It won't happen to you, Aura Lee, I promise," he said softly.

She stared at him in wonder, then threw back her head and began to laugh. No plan, no system, no doctor, just a promise, and it was supposed to suffice. It was not enough to stop her hysterical laughter.

Daniel slapped her across the face. She had to be brought to her senses. Aura Lee went rigid with humiliation, and held herself perfectly still. Her face began to streak with the acid trickle of hot, bitter tears, which she did not bother to brush aside.

"Oh, my God, Aura Lee, I'm sorry, darling." Daniel gathered her into his arms and began to stroke her hair. She sobbed into his shoulder and he rocked her back and forth in an attempt to comfort her.

"I promise you, darling, by all that's holy, this will never happen to you."

She pushed him away and would not look him in the eye.

"Just leave, Daniel. Right now. Leave me alone for a little while."

"Christ, Aura Lee. I'm sorry. You know I would never hurt you in a million years."

"Go somewhere, Daniel," she said. "I don't care where."

Daniel's face twisted in dismay. "All right. We can use more water than they will bring back. I'll walk to the creek. It's just a half mile from here. We'll talk when I get back and you've settled down."

She nodded coldly, ice encrusting her heart at the chilly instructions to "settle down."

She turned and willed herself to enter the dugout and began straightening Julka's pathetically few possessions. Her thoughts ran in a swift caustic stream and she was helpless to stop them. There had been another woman out here just a couple of miles away. She had a neighbor she never knew about. They weren't very far from each other, and Julka would have been another woman to talk to.

She picked up a piece of carefully folded needlework. The workmanship was exquisite. The intricate crewel work was mute testimony to the dead woman's hunger for beauty. She must have been a lovely person.

She glanced about to see that everything had been done decently and properly before the Smrckas returned. All traces of blood had been scrubbed clean. The tiny baby had been laid by its mother's breast. It was all she could do.

Aura Lee carefully folded the newspaper that the runner had been wrapped in, and then as she glanced at the contents, her features froze, then thawed in a torrent of tears. It was the same paper her friend Samuel had been reading the night she met Daniel.

"The West," proclaimed the headlines, "is a land of milk and honey. Come to this undiscovered paradise where the mockingbirds and cockatoos warble musical challenges to each other amid the rich foliage of sweet bay and mango trees. Come discover the joy of homesteading, the wonder of one hundred sixty acres, to be had for the asking."

Julka Smrcka was buried the next day—her husband, son, and the Hollingworths in attendance. Prairie funerals were held as soon as possible after the death, due to the lack of any embalming facilities.

A faint breeze rippled the grass in soft blue waves. The sun shone relentlessly overhead in a sky as bright as hope. Aura Lee searched the horizon for some sign, some deviation, as though nature owed Julka Smrcka some sort of acknowledgment of her passing. But it was a sweetly warm, ordinary summer day.

"How did you know where to find us?" Daniel had asked Vensel that morning as they dug the grave. Vensel started when the man spoke, as they had been working in a companionable silence.

"Your horse," Smrcka said, "and some days, the smoke. We were going to come—" He groped for the word visit, then shrugged his shoulders. Daniel's curiosity was satisfied. Horse droppings were a trail anyone could follow.

"Now we build," said Vensel.

"What?"

"The" —again the proper English word eluded him and he substituted as best he could—"the box."

"You have wood?" asked Daniel.

Vensel did not reply, and walked firmly over to his only wagon, and with a heavy wooden mallet began to loosen the sides.

Daniel's jaw tensed in protest.

"Don't you have other wood?"

"No."

Daniel stroked his mustache, his mind racing, knowing that this was what people did in wagon trains. But those people had been pressing on to a part of the country where wood would be available at the journey's end. Here on the plains, there were no trees at all to furnish lumber.

"You can't afford to give up your wagon sides. It's not practical."

Vensel Smrcka did not speak. His shoulders stiffened for a moment, then he continued to work as though Daniel had not spoken. Daniel stared helplessly, then seeing that nothing he could say would dissuade the man, he began to help dismantle the wagon. But the men lacked the proper tools to pry the old wood apart with the care that was needed to keep the boards from splitting, and ended up with a ruined wagon, and not enough usable boards for a coffin.

Now the open grave yawned before the handful of broken-hearted mourners. Julka and the baby lay wrapped together in a mended sheet on a single wooden slab.

Aura Lee trembled and looked at Anton, who huddled against his father's knees with a death grip on his trousers. He had not spoken all morning.

She looked at Daniel. Could he save them? He with his unerring instinct for the right thing to say or do? Could he bring order out of this chaos?

Daniel cleared his throat and even Anton's eyes were fastened on him. He held a worn Bible and turned to the Book of John.

"In my Father's house are many mansions," he began.

Aura Lee stiffened. A *dugout, Daniel? A cave? A black hole in the side of a hill? Is that the mansion waiting for Julka in heaven? Will she have to make do there too?*

"If it were not so, I would have told you," he continued grimly, averting his eyes from the faint mockery flickering on his wife's face.

I have been told many things, thought Aura Lee. *God says, and so we have to believe him? Does God lie too? Is this all? This deterioration of flesh and a faint stench and people hurrying to get the body in the earth?*

Daniel's voice trailed off and he looked at Aura Lee with mute appeal for support, as though he could read her mind, and winced at the twisted meaning she was hearing in the words. His black eyes brimmed with unshed tears and suddenly, with a shudder, he closed the book.

"I'm sorry," he said simply.

Oh, Daniel, she thought with a quick surge of pity. *I'm sorry too. Please* forgive me, my darling. None of this is your fault. You're doing the best you can and I'm blaming it all on you.

She moved to his side and he took her hand with wordless gratitude.

"Let's just pray in silence," she said. As they bent their heads, they were unified in grief.

Please understand, Julka, she prayed. *Please God, help Julka understand we are doing everything in our power to make this ceremony decent. There should be music and flowers and food, but this is the best we can do.*

She squeezed Daniel's hand and was touched by his naked need for her forgiveness.

Daniel looked at Vensel Smrcka and reluctantly nodded. Together the two men grasped the ropes looped under the board supporting her body and eased her toward the side of the grave. They worked silently and coordinated their movements in a pathetic attempt at ritual. Together they gently lowered her body into the arid earth.

Daniel felt as though he would choke with shame. His despair over the ugliness, the primitiveness of the burial ceremony was so overwhelming he could not look his neighbor in the eye.

The silence of the melancholy morning was broken by the dull thud of clods being thrown on the young woman's body. Aura Lee winced at each shovelful.

The hole was quickly filled, and suddenly the desperate keening of the young boy, wild with grief, split the air. Tears glinted in Vensel's fine eyes as he clasped his son to his side.

From their first distracted meeting, Aura Lee had had a bewildering sense of having seen Anton before. She knew it was not possible. But as he tipped his pale pointed face toward his father, yearning for consolation, she knew in a flash why the boy seemed so familiar. He reminded her of her kitten.

Anton had lovely, incredibly large, gray hazel eyes and long black lashes and an aura of innocence and perfect trust. The feelings of protectiveness and tenderness he evoked in Aura Lee had first been given to a cat many years ago.

Aura Lee met Vensel's glance across the grave. She thought her heart would break at the stern composure that was beginning to mask his face, and she knew he would never speak of this death again. The depth of his torment would be reined in behind a silent, stoic facade. She recognized and understood this type of pride.

Oh, yes, my friend, I can tell you all about pride. Not vanity-pride. Not the first deadly sin of peacock puffed-uppery, but the desolation of making a wrong choice that can never be corrected and then never mentioning to a soul the weight of the cross that has been assumed.

It was this kind of pride that made her send her parents airy little letters with charming descriptions of life on the prairie. It was this kind of pride that made her reassure her mother all was well, very well indeed, in spite of Professor Brock's dire warning. And it was this terrible, fierce pride that would never let her write or visit Professor Brock as long as she lived. He knew her too well. At a glance he would know all, and his despair over what might have been would destroy her.

She would pull herself together as Daniel expected her to do. Get ahold of herself. Her mother must never come for a visit.

Aura Lee's mother, Elinor Lombard, was a thin, dark-haired woman with anxious brown eyes. All her life she cunningly resisted health through a shifting series of illnesses.

It was generally agreed by her family and friends that her health was delicate, but there was no clear consensus as to what that term actually meant. She was prone to colds and headaches and endless infections. No one doubted the intensity of her migraines, as she quietly withdrew to the peaceful blue solitude of her silken bedroom. An endless parade of doctors confirmed the validity of the ever-present wheeze in her chest. They firmly overcame her feeble objections to still more medicine. Her dresser was lined with tonics and elixirs to coax the elusive bloom of health promised on the labels.

Nevertheless, her husband, Elton Lombard, knew, through an intuitive process he never could have explained, that his wife was one of the strongest women he had ever met.

At the beginning of their marriage he wooed her with limitless patience. His wife gave herself dutifully and serenely and never let their love-making arouse her feelings. He brought her gifts, purchased with her fastidious tastes in mind. They were sweetly received with the same faint disapproval that Elinor expressed toward his body. In time, the bewildered young husband learned to live with thousands of humiliations so slight they were barely there, yet so painful they made his life intolerable. He began to approach their marriage bed with an uneasy sense of shame.

When Aura Lee was born, after an abnormally long and painful labor, Elinor needed a long period of convalescence. The doctor explained to Elton that in time she would be as good as new, but in the meantime, well . . .

Elton smiled wryly and assured him with a hearty clap on the back that he understood. He felt as though a weight had been lifted from his shoulders. Rescued at last from the obligation to consummate the physical, the Lombards bonded their marriage with long discussions about the best thing to do for Aura Lee. It was clear she would be the only child they would ever have.

Her nursery was lined with dolls and stuffed animals and tea sets and blocks and books and boats and toys of every sort. They decorated her room in storybook colors. Her sheets and pillowcases were lovingly embroidered with intricate patterns of butterflies and flowers. Her dresses were pure white with little ruffled aprons of the finest lawn and nainsook. Her bright yellow hair was curled every day into long, perfect ringlets. Her breakfast was recommended by the most prominent physician in Saint Jo. She got just the right amount of fresh air and sunshine. Her skin was very white, but her cheeks had a lovely flush. She looked as fragile and as pretty as a piece of pastel-painted porcelain.

By the time she was five she had sweetly accepted the burden of being responsible for the entire happiness of her parents. She was so sensitive to their feelings she could tell at a glance just what words, what behavior would be required of her that day to set their world right. Seeing the pain fade from her father's eyes and the tension go from her mother was reward enough for laying her own feelings aside.

Sometimes when she lined up her china dolls for tea parties, for they were her very best and only friends, she would gaze wistfully in the direction of children playing outdoors. She never asked to join them. Ever since she could recall, her wanting to play with others, and risk "catching" something, was the most upsetting request of all.

The kitten came on a dreary October day when the weather was beginning to turn. It had been raining off and on, and by the time the cook discovered the damp little ball of fur mewing softly on the porch, it was more dead than alive.

It was immediately deposited in a cozy, blanket-lined box behind the cookstove, and coaxed back to health with sips of warm milk. It had been there a week before Aura Lee discovered it.

The kitchen was forbidden territory, as her parents did not want her exposed to the coarseness of the household help. Nevertheless, she sneaked opportunities to talk to Cook and was happily munching a sugar cookie and dangling her feet off a high-runged stool when the kitten clambered over the edge of the box and playfully swiped at her shoe.

Her hand trembled with wonder as she reached for the wide-eyed little tabby. She softly stroked its gray-striped fur and her ears could not believe the steady purr the tiny little animal made in response. It lifted its pointed face and gazed at her with candid gray eyes, softly licking her hand with a raspy tongue. Totally she gave her heart to the kitten.

Her days were filled with a secret joy, since it was always waiting for her. She never grew tired of their play. Most of all she coveted the times when it would lie blissfully on her lap and fall into contented sleep.

But it was through her love of the kitten and the kitten's love of her that she began to doubt the quality of her parents' love. She was beginning to realize that the anxious concern her parents displayed was not really love, and that real love was not conditional upon behavior.

The day her parents found out about her visits to the kitten was one of the most miserable of her life. Her mother had come to investigate the source of the happy laughter. She reacted with white-faced rage.

"Where did you get that *filthy* animal?"

Aura Lee hastily put the cat back in the box and stood before her mother in bewildered shame.

"It's not filthy."

"It is, Aura Lee. It is. God only knows where it's been and what diseases it's carrying. I forbid you ever to play with it again."

Aura Lee reached for a strength she didn't know she had.

"It's mine and I love it and I want to keep it. It loves me, Mother."

"Nonsense, it would love anyone silly enough to take it in. I want it out of here and that's final."

"I'm keeping the kitten. It loves me. If I can't keep it, if I can't keep it—" Intuitively she grasped for the only weapon at her disposal, their concern for her health. "If I can't keep it, I won't eat."

Elinor looked at her in amazement.

"Your father is going to hear about this."

All it took was one day of refusing food. She lay in bed and sobbed bitterly, and in frantic dismay her parents accepted her devotion to the cat.

Elinor had a deeper concern that this stubbornness was signaling a permanent change. She was afraid Aura Lee would no longer be their biddable, perfectly mannered little girl. Her fears were groundless. All Aura Lee wanted was her cat, and in fact she redoubled her efforts to be the daughter they desired her to be. But Elinor never forgot that single steely display of will.

Then came the music. It was expected, of course, that a young lady her age study the piano, for the nineteenth century was a period of unparalleled keyboard development. The great European pianists such as Chopin and Liszt had attained the status of romantic heroes.

Her teacher, Professor Brock, summoned from the nearby university, rang the doorbell one fall morning, and gloomily cursed the financial circumstances forcing him into tutoring spoiled, untalented brats. He nodded reluctantly in acknowledgment of the Lombards' enthusiastic, overly flattering greetings. A tiny, composed little ten-year-old was presented to him. Her parents beamed with pleasure at her charming manners as she solemnly curtsied.

He politely shooed the Lombards away, and led Aura Lee to the piano. He settled the child on the bench.

"Why do you want to play the piano?"

Most children would turn their heads at this point and awkwardly murmur, "I don't know."

"Because it is expected of me, sir," she replied serenely. "It is part of a young lady's education."

He lifted his head in surprise and looked at her sharply. Had there been a note of self-mockery there? Yes. Her lips were lifted in a wry little smile. Her slender hands still lay peacefully in her lap. An enormous bow had been carefully pinned upon her yellow ringlets.

Professor Brock threw back his head and laughed.

"Do you always do what is expected of you?"

"Yes, it's really not important to me not to. I like to do the things I'm expected to do. I would choose to do them myself."

Someone was burning leaves that fine September morning. The odor mingled with the delicious scent of cinnamon and apples drifting from the kitchen. A door slammed somewhere upstairs. The black and white parquet tiles gleamed under the piano, a Bechstein, imported from Germany. The Lombard household hummed with the organized activity of the day.

"Well, then, let us begin."

By the third lesson her scales were played with each note having equal weight, equal value, equal importance.

"Teach me more," she begged. "Oh, teach me more. Please."

He listened once again in amazement to the scales. The instinctive timing, the inner ear, the sensitivity to subtle sounds that marks the true musician, all this was there in the simple scale: the monotonous, all-important exercise that told so very much.

So it was to be she. He had waited all his life for such a student. He had so much to give and there was so little time.

He stood motionless, staring at a distant spot, his mind a tumult of memories. A single leaf drifted from a tree and made a glorious sunlit descent to the earth below. One bird sang a brief melancholy note. *If His eye is on the sparrow,* thought Dr. Brock, *if even the hairs on the head are numbered, then who am I to question His plans for her or His placement of talent of this magnitude on such an unlikely little girl?*

With great humility, he began, trusting that the meaning of their coming together would be revealed to him in time.

Aura Lee did not see the grayed cuffs or the taped earpieces on his glasses. She was totally unaware of the ridiculous impression he made on people with his pot-belly and his torso supported by spindly, bandy legs. She worshiped him.

The old man in turn gave the wisp of a girl his heart, his very soul, which was his passionate love of music. The techniques she was learning were unusual for a young lady of her time. The complexity of this type of instruction was immeasurably beyond what "was expected." She had asked for a drink of water and he brought her the ocean. All of the feelings she had kept repressed for years poured into her music. She practiced incessantly with a relentless, self-imposed discipline.

They worked in a perfect rapport that was never expressed in words. Aura Lee became painfully aware of the inadequacy of language. She knew that music alone was the perfect expression of all feeling.

She had a deep empathy for all people; a total acceptance of human beings without the slightest desire to inspire or change them. This ability to look with complete openness at the range of human emotions, good and bad, enabled her to achieve a brilliance of interpretation that many a more mature musician had not achieved. She continued to hide her depth of feeling behind a composed facade. But she never lied to herself.

Her remarkable ability developed at a breakneck pace that left even Dr. Brock stunned. Each passing year brought a higher level of competence.

Aura Lee paused one morning as she heard her name coming from the parlor and tip-toed closer to overhear her parents' conversation.

"We've got to do something, Elton. This has gone far enough."

"We wanted her to have lessons."

"I wanted her to have an accomplishment, not an *obsession*," protested Elinor. "Do you realize that playing the piano is all the child wants to do, day in and day out? It's not natural. It's time she was preparing in other ways to take her place in society. This house will be hers some day. She should be learning to manage it and she should have more respect for her proper station in life. I honestly think she would be perfectly happy to hobnob with the help forever."

"If she's happy playing, what does it hurt? And as for hobnobbing with the help, what other contact have we allowed her? And you too, my dear, have strong interests." He did not risk referring more directly to his wife's passion for art. Their home was a showcase for exquisite paintings that Elinor collected without regard to the artists' reputations.

"You have me to thank for what we're worth today," she snapped. She had an unerring instinct for the valuable, and their wealth had increased tremendously through the years because of her instinctive eye for art.

The judge nodded and extended his hands toward his beloved fire. Year after year his wife's coldness assaulted his very bones, and he turned to the flames for strength.

"I think Aura Lee shares our love for our home," he said finally. In a rare display of courage he added, "And I think it's high time she begins to make friends, my dear. Long overdue. In fact, I would be surprised if she even knows how."

Aura Lee stood silent and stricken, too outraged to interrupt. How could they possibly doubt her love for their home? It was the one common bond she shared with her parents and her sole inheritance, in addition to a trust Elton had set up for its maintenance. The house was a magnificent three-story structure, one of the finest dwellings in Saint Jo, with its vast collection of rooms and turrets and porches accented with gingerbread fretwork. The white paint always sparkled and the lawns behind the austere iron fence were immaculate. It was kept in exquisite condition by her mother's vigilant sense of order. Each room was so well decorated that Elinor had become an informal consultant to women who lacked her eye for beauty.

Hot tears stung Aura Lee's cheeks. She was finally going to be allowed friends after being denied her heart's desire all her childhood days. After it no longer mattered to her now she had her music and Professor Brock. Long after the chances for tea parties and shared secrets had passed. Her anguish was so intense she steadied her hand on the doorknob and put her rage into a center of white light, willing her trembling thoughts to stop churning until her mind was cleared of all emotion.

She froze as she seemed to hear a voice filtering through the blood pounding in her ears.

"You hate them, you know," it said softly. *No, no, no,* she thought in horror. *I love my parents. I just don't want them to take my piano away. Oh, please, no.*

She went up to her room and, after washing her face and composing herself, went down to the parlor and asked her parents to allow her to attend a party at the Suttons' the coming Saturday. She was always invited to such entertainments because of Judge Lombard's position, but the hostess always took it for granted that the pale, aloof child would not come.

"Why, yes, Aura Lee," said Elinor. "Yes, your father and I were just talking about your need to see young people." Preventing Aura Lee from "catching something" had been the household priority for so many years that the subtle pattern of isolation had been established long after its usefulness had passed. Elinor felt uneasy in spite of her relief.

Because she had long ago given up her yearning for friends, and was indifferent to the reception she would receive, the girls were instantly drawn to her that weekend, as adolescents are to any genuinely mysterious personality. Aura Lee had exquisite manners and a lovely wardrobe, and as few of them had ever been inside the Lombard home they were thrilled at the possibility of an invitation. In time they all became genuinely fond of her wry, gentle sense of humor, and some argued passionately in her behalf when she was referred to as being "stuck up." One, Marie Sutton, a gregarious, carefree girl attracted to Aura Lee as total opposites often are, became the long-desired very best friend.

Aura Lee was then left to practice in peace for as long as she liked. Her relationship with her parents was restored, with her making any necessary compromises for their happiness as she had always done. In time it was the Lombards' home that became the favorite gathering spot and Elinor glowed with satisfaction at her wisdom in handling the whole situation.

The onset of puberty brought no real interruption in Aura Lee's playing, but rather an increased intensity. She went through a period of extreme agitation and Dr. Brock watched warily. *Dear God,* he prayed over and over, *don't let her be like her mother.* There were days when she was red eyed and trembling, but she always regained a serenity after long sessions at the piano. He was aware of a massive struggle going on in her soul. By the time she was fifteen, her private demons were laid to rest and she was free again.

Dr. Brock decided when Aura Lee was seventeen that he had never heard a finer pianist. She was lovely now, sweetly and slightly curved, with a curiously dual personality. He considered talking to her parents about her future. But just the thought of trying to tell the aggressively banal couple of their daughter's extraordinary ability made him wince. They were so proud already, and it was the shallow misplaced pride that one has for a reproduction of a Michelangelo. The glory of the real thing was totally beyond them.

Aura Lee and Dr. Brock had a brief conversation one day that left him even more puzzled about the purpose of her gift.

"My dear," he said gently, "you need to be heard."

"I am, sir," she replied. "I play often for my parents and friends. And then too, there was my recital."

"That's not what I mean. I mean heard by people who will understand and appreciate what you have become."

"That would mean too many changes. It would be too hard on me. I don't have the—I don't know what. I just can't," she said sadly.

Dr. Brock nodded in silent agreement. She lacked the emotional force to endure. There was no place for a woman on the concert stage other than as a novelty. Her playing would be regarded as a parlor trick. Once again he marveled at the deep instinctive wisdom Aura Lee had always possessed about herself.

By the time she was nineteen, she had an abundance of beaus. She received them all equally, with the exquisite manners that had served her so well for so many years. Eventually her suitors, unsuccessful in their attempts to win any real attention from her, gave up with the miserable realization that others were identically favored.

Many of her former admirers came back with their current lady friends to enjoy the delightful summer evenings spent talking on the Lombard porch. Aura Lee manipulated these conversations as deftly as any mistress of a European salon. With just a word or a glance she directed the discussions of the bright young intellectuals who lived for this spirited exchange of ideas. Their laughter floated over the languid Missouri evenings.

Many young ladies of Saint Jo, yearning to be included in this magic circle, would pass by the Lombard home in their carriages and glance wistfully at the galaxy of young people. They puzzled over Aura Lee's ability to attract so many friends.

She was sitting on the porch swing when Jimmy Herriot brought Daniel over for his first evening at the Lombards'. Although several young men were arguing fervently about the Great American West, one of her favorite topics, tonight she found her mind wandering. She wore her favorite lacy white dress and idly followed the talk with her chin cupped in the palm of her hand.

Daniel and Jimmy clanged the gate to the iron fence surrounding the yard and Aura Lee looked up at the sound.

She would always thereafter associate Daniel with the energy of the sun, for as he strolled up the walk he was lit from behind by its last rays. The beams highlighted his black eyes and hair and outlined the hard male lines of his physique.

Jimmy introduced him and Aura Lee met his eyes with a sudden electric thrill far more than physical. In that instant they acknowledged their match, their soulmate, their own equal. Aura Lee lowered her eyes in an uncharacteristic flurry of confusion. She invited him to have a seat and self-consciously turned her attention to Jimmy.

She was aware of a pure exhilaration that before she had experienced only in music. There was a sudden soaring inside her, a sharpening of the senses, and no matter where she turned she was filled with the presence of this coppery, wood-hued man with the heavy mustache.

She who always knew what to say now found herself struggling for the words to begin a conversation with him.

"We were talking politics as usual, Mr. Hollingworth. Is this a subject that interests you?"

"Certainly it should," piped up Jimmy. "I've yet to see a budding young shyster who did not have political aspirations."

"Are you an attorney, then, Mr. Hollingworth?"

"Not quite, yet," he replied with an amused glance at Jimmy. "My Missouri bar exam comes up next month, and then, perhaps."

Jimmy snorted. "Perhaps, hell. He was at the very top of his class."

Daniel shrugged off his friend's admiration, and easily turned the conversation back to politics.

"Who is dooming the country now?"

"We were talking about the Great American Desert. A friend of Samuel's went West last week."

At this, Samuel produced a worn paper from his breast pocket.

"Listen to this. We're fools, I tell you, for not doing the same."

He read of a glowing land of milk and honey, described as a place where mockingbirds and gorgeous parakeets and cockatoos warbled musical challenges to each other amid the rich foliage of the sweet bay and mango trees.

Daniel threw back his head and laughed.

"*Mango* trees? In the desert?"

"It's not a desert, I tell you. Would men of good judgment be leaving settled territory for a desert?"

"But, Samuel," said Marie Sutton, "it has always been *known* as a desert. Remember our geography lessons? The plains have always been barren. Nothing will grow there. Everyone knows that. Besides, there are all those horrible Indians. Just waiting." She shivered with a toss of her glossy brown hair and a child's attraction to danger in her moist dark eyes. So keenly was her fear felt by her friends that the sound of tom-toms seemed to echo in the night.

They were mesmerized by the tales of death and mutilation reported by those who had come back from the Far West. And the fate of women

31

captured by the savages! The men stared in horror at Marie's soft curves and gallantly declared they would die before they let this sweet young thing fall prey to the lust of the vicious redskins.

All except Daniel. His sudden, arrogant laugh infuriated Marie, who thrilled at being the center of an imaginary tragedy.

"You find it amusing, Mr. Hollingworth, that whole families should be tortured?"

"I find it improbable, Miss Sutton. The truth of the matter is that the redskins are a pathetic handful of people. This is, after all, 1880, and they have been bullied and subdued and lied to for so long now, I can't imagine anyone regarding them as a threat."

"Oh," Marie replied coldly, "and where do you get your information?"

"From the most accurate source of all, Miss Sutton. Personal observation. It is the only basis for judgment that I trust. I have seen lines of Indians being herded onto trains, their spirits quite broken."

"You regard these savages as people?"

"Yes, Miss Sutton," he said evenly. "I regard the Indians as people."

"So do I, Mr. Hollingworth," said Aura Lee quietly, "and I'm sure there are others here who do so as well."

With an apologetic glance at Daniel, Aura Lee quickly restored harmony.

"What were you saying about the land, Samuel?"

"There are other newspapers, I tell you, reporting riches to be had for the asking. Untold wealth. The land is a paradise."

"Our textbooks couldn't be *that* far off," argued Jimmy.

"A Western Kansas newspaper reporting it as a paradise certainly doesn't alter the facts. My God, you would think it was better than dying and going to Heaven."

Samuel flushed and pulled yet another clipping from his pocket. "There have been changes, I tell you. Lots of things have happened since the war."

"Like what?"

"Like railroads, for instance. It's easier to bring supplies in. And some chap has come up with a windmill that can stand up to the winds. There's water there now. And a way to mill the wheat those Russians brought over. Why would all these newspapers report it, if it weren't true?"

"Doesn't it strike you as a little peculiar," said Daniel, "that there are suddenly all these newspapers out in the middle of nowhere? Some counties have as many as five and yet their population is just a mere handful. The stories are being written for people back here."

"Why would they write papers for people back here?"

"To attract settlers to the area," said Daniel. "But one thing's for sure, the land is free and that's a fact. You should always grab for the land every chance you get. Always. It's the one thing in this world that can't be manufactured. And with hard work—" His voice trailed off. He was keenly aware of Aura Lee's eyes on him.

"You have been arguing the disadvantages of the West, Mr. Hollingworth, yet you seem attracted to the region. Would you like to go West?"

"Yes, Miss Lombard, I would. But not as a fool expecting mango trees and parakeets—as a man, not afraid of hard work and smart enough to recognize and seize opportunity. It's there, right enough. But not as many people see it."

"I see," she said.

"The railroads are the key. Give Western Kansas farmers a means of transportation for their goods and they will be rich." Daniel's eyes sparkled with ambition. "I'm not going West, you understand. I intend to practice law right here in Saint Jo, but yes, Miss Lombard, I'm definitely attracted to the region."

"Aura Lee, I hope you're not going to encourage that dreadful man to come back," said Marie Sutton, the next day.

"Why not?" asked Aura Lee. "I thought he was a stimulating addition to the group." She smiled over her friend's petulance. Marie was terribly spoiled. Daniel's attack on her attitude to the Indians was a new and unsettling experience for her.

"Well, I think he's vulgar and very, very rude."

"I think he's a man, Marie." The others seemed mere boys by comparison.

"He's stubborn and disagreeable."

"So? What's wrong with that? If a man knows what he believes and knows he is right, why should he compromise his opinions just to please a group?"

"He reminds me of those Indians he insists on defending," said Marie. "He's too—"

"Virile?"

"Well, yes," said Marie. To her dismay, she found herself blushing furiously. She lowered her eyes.

"And as to the stubborn," said Aura Lee, "since the beginning of time, great men, men who amount to something, have lived and died for ideas. I believe Daniel Hollingworth is such a person, and I would consider it an honor if he joins our group."

"Aura Lee!" Suddenly Marie was aware of the delicate rose flush in her friend's cheeks. "Aura Lee! You're falling in love with this man, aren't you?"

"Don't be silly, I hardly know him." But the yearning in her eyes gave her away, and Marie clapped her hands with glee, delighted to see Aura Lee's heart engaged at last.

"Well, I suppose he does have some good points after all," she said softly.

That evening, Aura Lee's eyes misted with anxiety. There were, after all, other literary groups in Saint Jo. There was no reason for Daniel to return to hers. She made no pretense of concentrating on the conversation. Her heart rolled over in her chest at the possibility of his not coming back. She was furious with Marie, who obviously had wasted no time in informing everyone of her feelings. Everywhere she turned she found her friends watching her with knowing smiles.

When at last he came up the walk, again with Jimmy Herriot, as Daniel greeted everyone with his deep, rich voice, she could hardly manage a relaxed hello.

Self-consciously she settled back in her usual seat on the swing. She knew everything had changed in one day's time. She knew Daniel Hollingworth was the one man on earth she would love. Now she had seen him, there would never be another. The feeling was as sudden and as total as when Professor Brock had introduced her to music. Without this man she would die.

Night after night, Daniel returned, and the group was thrilled with the courtship. Aura Lee listened with a strange, shy pride as he debated. He plunged fearlessly into each evening's topic.

One night the subject was "True Man and True Woman: Their Role in Our Society."

"True man," said Daniel, "the true Adam as the Creator intended him to be, is by nature the hunter and protector."

He stopped in front of Aura Lee and hooked his thumbs in the watch pockets of his vest. Slowly his eyes found hers and her heart began to beat so quickly she feared it would leap from her body.

"True man," he continued, "will make any sacrifice for his home, his wife, and his family. For his loved one, flesh of his flesh." Aura Lee's cheeks stained a deep berry color. "And this woman, this good gift from God, this marvelous rib of Adam is taken from the bone closest to his heart. True Man will bring to this woman every creature comfort he is capable of acquiring and he will love her and cherish her and protect her as long as he lives."

No one spoke. Even the stars overhead seemed frozen, not daring to wink for fear of breaking the spell. Aura Lee felt her very bones melting inside her. She and Daniel were the only two people on earth.

She lifted her eyes, brilliant with devotion.

"True Woman," she said softly, "true woman rejoices in the protection her husband gives her. She endures every hardship with a smile. She fills

her hours with the ordering of her household to provide comfort for him as long as he shall live. She never falters in her duty or complains of the lack of material goods, but instead joyfully manages the resources her husband provides and remains as constant and steadfast as a warm fire all the days of their lives."

Marie Sutton thought she would faint from excitement right there on the spot.

"Neither one of them has a lick of sense," said Jimmy Herriot later. "They're word people, both of them."

"Word people?"

"Yes, they will live and die, both of them, for words. Honor, duty, country. Just fill in the blanks. They're *dangerous* together."

"Oh, Jimmy, you don't have a romantic bone in your body," said Marie. "You just don't know True Love when you see it."

Daniel passed his Missouri bar exam the last of May. His future was assured in the firm of his uncle, who had made a generous offer that would promise a lifetime's security.

Daniel's uncle, Justin Hollingworth, beamed as the young man appeared promptly at his office two weeks after the bar exam. He had been watching him approach from the window, and the pride he felt in this young man's progress was beyond measure.

Daniel was the cream of the crop. Justin's hands trembled with enthusiasm as he straightened his papers. What a rare opportunity. He did not have a son. This nephew would be the natural heir to the brilliant practice he had developed over the years. Yet as he watched Daniel come up the boardwalk, he was surprised at the twinge of jealousy he felt.

Daniel's stern face would have a positive effect on juries. He had already acquired an aura of quiet authority. It was a quality of personality Justin had seen men vainly try to emulate with clothes and grooming. Added to Daniel's poise was a keen analytical mind. He had been at the very top of his graduating class.

He knew the boy had moral courage. Daniel's father had told a series of stories collected since his childhood, revealing how Daniel had taken up this or that cause. More often than not it was against impossible odds and frequently over issues so minor the risks were not worth the effort. From early on, his fierce sense of right and wrong led him into strange alliances. This would not be a bad trait, mused Justin. He would have to learn to compromise, of course, but all in all, this protege was more than he had dared imagine would come his way.

Daniel's first case was over the rights of a desperate young immigrant threatened with deportation. The young lawyer was charged with his defense, and to Justin the case was very clear-cut. It would be an easy victory for Daniel and a splendid introduction into the courtroom.

The man had been caught stealing food for his family. The circumstances were pathetic. He was out of work. His wife and five children were pitifully in need, and what little money he had had been stolen. Even with the prejudice the jury would have against an immigrant, it would be easy to get him off entirely.

Justin was surprised at the length of time it took Daniel to question the man in the preliminary interview. When the door to Daniel's office opened much later, the little Italian emerged ashen, with tight white lips, and left without saying a word.

"Well," said Justin, when Daniel appeared in the doorway, "how did it go? Anything you want to discuss?"

"No," said Daniel. "There is nothing to talk about. The man committed a crime against society. He stole. It's as simple as that."

"Simple? My God, Daniel, you're talking about a man who had starving kids. He had just had his money stolen. He was desperate. You're charged with his defense," blurted Justin. "How the hell can you not see *his* side?"

"He doesn't have a side," said Daniel evenly. "He was wrong. The man is a thief."

"What about his children, God damn it? They were hungry."

"Yes, what *about* his children? Just how was he actually helping them in the long run? Was committing a crime just to put food in their mouths for a day or two worth it? Was he really insuring their survival in the long run? His circumstances were not a bit better after he fed them. They would still be hungry the next day. What then? More theft? He wasn't saving his children, not really."

"What should he have done then?" asked Justin in a clipped, angry voice. "Can you give me a single workable alternative?"

"Hell, yes. He could have gone to his neighbors and asked for help, or his church. He's a Catholic. His parish priest would have some resources. The man is a thief, Uncle Justin. He stole because he was too weak to admit he needed help. He put his own pride before his family. If you put yourself before your family, and your family before your community, your community before your country, you will surely put your country before your duty to civilization as a whole, and therein lies certain and absolute destruction."

Justin's knuckles were white where both fists clutched his pen. Daniel actually believed what he was saying.

His uncle chose his next words very, very carefully. Daniel had to understand the impossibility of his statement. He had to have more empathy, more compassion for human nature or he would never be able to practice law. He drew a deep breath.

"Daniel, what if the man does not understand this?"

"Everyone understands. God's laws are written on our hearts from the cradle on. We know ourselves well enough to recognize the consequences of any evil done to our neighbor. Our own hearts flinch at the wounds we inflict on others. No matter how hard we try to deny it, when an evil is done, we know. The man took what was not his. He was taking his children down a path that would be disastrous in the long run. He is a thief."

Grief rippled through Justin Hollingworth like a poison. Daniel would never be able to live with compromise. He had no heir to his practice.

"What if the man is not strong, Daniel?" he asked with quiet contempt. "What if he cannot make himself do what is right?"

"He could have *found* the strength. It's there for all of us to draw on."

"Everyone? Under any circumstances? At all times?"

"Yes. We all have free will, free choice."

Justin slowly ran a hand through his hair. He rose and stood, staring gloomily out the window.

"The man deserves a fair defense. I don't believe you can provide it. I'll take over the case."

"Thank you, Uncle Justin. I'm sure that would be for the best."

"And, Daniel, circumstances such as this will come up again and again. Are you certain you want to practice law?"

"I'm not sure I can, if it means defending people I know are in the wrong."

"I'm not sure you can, either. Think about it."

As Daniel's hand reached to turn the knob on the door, Justin asked him one more question.

"Have you never failed yourself, Daniel? Never disappointed yourself? Never been able to do what you knew you should?"

"Of course, Uncle Justin," said Daniel with quiet amusement. "Many, many times."

"Well, then."

"Well, what?"

"Well, God damn it, why can't you understand this in other people?"

"Who said I didn't *understand*? I'm weak too, once in a while, but I pay the consequences, just as they do and should."

"One more thing, Daniel, do you intend to marry?"

"Of course," he said. "In fact, I'm proposing this week to Judge Lombard's daughter. Why do you ask?"

"Just wondering. Women have a funny way of changing our point of view."

"She shares my point of view, sir, on nearly everything. In fact, it's her

37

ideals that attracted me to her more than anything." Daniel's face softened at the mention of his future bride.

Justin nodded his head, then solemnly shook hands with his nephew. It was goodbye and they both knew it.

God have mercy on her, thought Justin. *Because this man won't. She had better be made of steel.*

Daniel closed the door firmly behind him, knowing that this early confrontation with his uncle had been fatal to his law career. He could not say he regretted it. He immediately decided to go to Kansas and file for a homestead. It had long been in the back of his mind and this encounter with his uncle only hastened the decision. He wanted room, and space, and a chance to show what could be accomplished by men of ideals.

Daniel called on Aura Lee the next morning. He twirled his hat around on a finger as he waited for the maid to respond to his firm knock. His black eyes were solemn. He wished his parents were alive to share his joy. He was aware of the seriousness of his breach with Uncle Justin and equally sure time would restore their relationship. They both carried the Hollingworth name and that still meant a great deal in Saint Jo. He straightened his shoulders and knocked again. Given a little latitude he would set everything to rights. He would win Uncle Justin's good will by his certain success on his homestead. When the wily old lawyer became aware of the vast amounts of money to be made in Kansas, the man would soften. It would take time, and a lot of hard work, but it would be done.

An old honeysuckle vine supported by an equally aged trellis broke the sunlight on the porch into shaded patches. When the house was repainted every three years, the vine was carefully lifted and a small paint brush used to restore the brilliant white flashes of lattice work. Daniel appreciated the sense of order this careful tending required.

"Miss Aura Lee is practicing, sir," the maid stammered in response to his untimely call. "The family does not disturb Miss Aura Lee when she practices."

"Well, I do, Clarissa, and I'm not family yet," Daniel said with a grin.

He paused at the doorway and stood entranced, listening to the magnificent sound of her piano. Her eyes met his and she continued the complicated rhapsody. See, her hands and her eyes seemed to say. See what I'm like, the woman who is yours for the asking.

The melody rose to a storm of notes and chords, then gently subsided. He crossed over to the piano and tenderly lifted her from the seat. He bent his head toward her lips and as he took her frail blue-veined hand into his own blunt-fingered one, he kissed her gently.

This was their first kiss, their first touch, and yet the agreement to a lifetime pledge was there in that instant.

"Darling, I want to marry you."

"I know," she said with a smile. Suddenly she laughed. Everyone knew. It had been the most ridiculously open courtship imaginable.

"I knew that you knew," he countered. "The perpetual Eve. Aura Lee," he said solemnly. "I want to go West. I want my own land. I want to be my own man. Sweetheart, in spite of what all those lunatics have been saying, it's not an easy life, but it *is* the chance of a lifetime."

"I know," she said, her eyes suddenly filling with tears. "I know." It was impossible for her not to have realized months ago the direction Daniel's ambition was taking.

"You'll enjoy the challenge, Aura Lee, I know you will, and we'll have each other, forever." Daniel's voice was vibrant with restless energy.

"Yes," she said. "Yes, I know I can make a home for you."

"Let me call on your parents this evening."

"Oh, Daniel, I—"

"What, darling?"

She had started to tell him of her parents' neurotic need for her presence and then, with a sigh, changed her mind. It was done, sealed. She would marry this man and no amount of resistance would make her change her mind.

"Just be kind to them, darling. I'm all they have."

"I'm taking their treasure. Don't you think I know that? I'll do everything in my power to let them know how much I love you."

She sadly lowered her eyes. He could not know, would never know the depth of the wound he would cause. But it didn't matter, she would see it through.

She saw Daniel to the door and pressed his hand in a tender goodbye. She slowly climbed the stairs to her room. Her heart was full of joy and thanksgiving, but at the core of her was a knot of sorrow over the grief that would be inflicted on her parents if she and Daniel left Saint Jo. That Daniel would never understand.

She lay on her stomach on her silk-covered feather comforter and traced the grain of the polished cherry posts on her headboard. The soft pale yellows of her room cheered her and filled her mind with light. Satiny tiebacks looped the curtains to one side and she breathed deeply of the heavy Missouri air, so laden with the intoxicating odor of plants that the atmosphere seemed to have a life of its own. There was a hint of Eden in the greenery she saw outside. She fell into a troubled sleep and in her dreams she was paralyzed by inaction. She awoke with her arms clasped about her stomach as though to cradle the dull pain that was beginning.

Daniel arrived promptly at eight and by eight-thirty had so charmed her parents they were convinced he could succeed at anything he chose.

Aura Lee saw them both stiffen with bewilderment at Daniel's explanation that they planned to go West to homestead. Skillfully he assured them they would be back soon. They would return to Saint Jo for frequent visits wealthy beyond all imagining.

Elinor Lombard delicately dabbed at her eyes with her handkerchief and nodded proudly at the plans this fine young lawyer was making. Their household would be allied with the Hollingworths' and that was enough for her.

"I will bring your daughter back often," Daniel promised solemnly, "and with grandchildren, God willing."

Aura Lee blushed. Her sense of relief was so deep it was making her giddy. Her parents were going to be fine. They too would love Daniel. All eyes were upon her, and she did not try to divert their attention. Her gown of pale blue georgette billowed sweetly from her tiny waist. A soft flush illuminated her face. Daniel's love, so potent a force as to be nearly tangible, would protect them all.

Judge Lombard's face was composed as he studied the man who had come to ask for their daughter. It was as though fate had arranged a solution to his problem. The house was an enormous burden financially, and Elinor could not seem to grasp the meaning of constantly draining the dwindling trust for its maintenance. His wife blithely assumed that money enough would always be there, but he knew it was not so. And now this splendid warrior had unwittingly come with a grand plan for redemption.

Cheered by their good fortune, Elton Lombard proposed a toast. The doorbell rang and the four of them turned, their glasses midway to their lips, as Clarissa ushered in Professor Brock.

"Byron," Elton greeted him happily, "come join us on this wonderful occasion. You should be the first to know of Aura Lee's engagement to Daniel. Come toast the happy couple with us."

Professor Brock lifted his shaggy head and curled his fingers around his wine glass. He was deeply touched by the depth of happiness in this room. His eyes shone with tenderness.

"To this young love," he murmured humbly. "May it always be as it is tonight."

They solemnly lifted their glasses and sipped the rosé. Aura Lee welcomed the spreading warmth that was diffusing the nervous joy she had felt all day.

"Well, young man," said Professor Brock, "so it is to be you who will capture our prize. Where do you plan to practice?" His eyes were moist. His voice was resonant with emotion.

"I do not plan to practice," Daniel said casually. "At least not for a number of years. Aura Lee and I are going to homestead out West. There is a great deal of land opening up in Kansas. Later, perhaps, a law practice will open up too."

Aura Lee felt the chill that crystallized in the room before the old man even spoke.

"You fool," the professor stammered. "You utter fool."

"Beg pardon, sir?" The blood drained from Daniel's face and he stood totally motionless.

"You God damn fool. You'll *kill* her." The old man's hands shook with fury. His face was so flushed that a vein in his temple throbbed visibly.

Aura Lee pressed her fingers against the base of her throat as though to slow her racing heartbeat. Tears of dismay welled in her eyes. Her usual ability to deal with people vanished. She felt a gnawing core of pain in her stomach, and did not know where to turn, or whom to talk to first.

"You fool," Professor Brock repeated. His face was even redder, mottled with white patches. "You are taking her to filth and physical labor where her very life will be in danger. *This woman cannot live without beauty.* Don't you know anything about her? Don't you know anything about the West at all? My God, man. It's killed strong women. Killed them, I tell you, with the work. She's had a maid all of her life. And her music—" his voice dropped now to an anguished pleading— "what do you intend to do about her music?"

"I can live without my music," said Aura Lee. "Daniel will take its place. I love him so terribly much. And we won't do without forever. My love for Daniel will take the place of my music. There's bound to be other women like me and we'll create our own culture. We will endure."

"You cannot, my dear, and the effort will kill you. By your own admission you did not have the will to pursue a career on the concert stage. You know in your heart you are not that strong. Think how much more stamina this life will require of you. For one moment, Aura Lee, try to imagine your life without any music. Don't you see it's what permits you to survive? It's the reason you have the strength you have now. It's your lifeblood. *You see too much and feel too much.* Your piano is what keeps you sane."

The others listened intently to this peculiar conversation between the old man and the girl. It was as though the two communicated in a secret language that excluded the rest from any real understanding.

"My love for Daniel will take the place of my love of music," she said again with an attempt at firmness, but her agitation was evident in the quaver in her voice. She turned to Daniel for deliverance. Only he could set the world right again.

He stood quietly and waited for emotions to ebb. Carefully, and with a deep sense of compassion for the people who loved this woman so much, he tried to set their minds at ease. He spoke to her parents first.

"Do you think," he began quietly, "I would ask a woman such as your daughter to live under circumstances that would destroy her? I know what a rare person I am marrying. I will treasure her very soul. The hard years will be very few, and together we will transcend them. There are qualities of the prairie that are never mentioned. Everyone is instantly aware of the grandeur of the mountains, but only the finest sense the beauty of the Great Plains. Only they can appreciate the shadings in the landscape, the color of the sunsets."

"I just want her to be happy," sniffed Elinor, her eyes dark with anxiety.

"It is for people such as Aura Lee, whose appreciation of beauty is keener than most, that the prairie is intended," Daniel assured her. "God reserved this land for his very best. Men and women with more steel. Men and women with courage and honesty and decency and integrity, who are not afraid to live by their wits."

"He reserved that land for God damn fools like you," replied Professor Brock stonily. "God reserved that land for people with the most incredible capacity for self-delusion since Adam and Eve. You deserve the prairie. *She* does not."

With a stiff bow toward Mr. and Mrs. Lombard, he turned abruptly and left the room. He did not look at Daniel and Aura Lee, and as his footsteps echoed through the silent room, she gazed at the departing figure of the proud, stubborn old man and felt as though her very soul were being wrenched from her body.

Daniel was the first to speak.

"Professor Brock is wrong," he said. "But he does not have to explain to me the protectiveness he feels toward you. How could any man feel otherwise?"

But with all his oratorical skills, Daniel could not restore the former joyful mood. They finished their wine, and by unspoken consent, he left early. Elton ran his hand through his hair and with a brief apology left the room for one where the fire was already burning brightly, afraid that he would never in the rest of his lifetime be really warm again. He needed time to think. What if the old man were right?

"Sweetheart," said Elinor. "It's not too late to change your mind. What if everything Professor Brock said is true? Are you positive Daniel is the right man for you?"

"Oh, yes. Daniel is my life. He's the right man. There could never be anyone else."

"You can always come back here," said Elinor. "We want you to remember that this will always be your home if things don't work out." Her face was strained, yet beneath her agitation was the budding of a sly pleasure in the thought that Aura Lee would be back. If so, her little girl would be hers to keep forever. She and the judge would own her totally. In her heart she allied herself with Daniel Hollingworth. He would break her daughter's will in a way she had never been able to.

Aura Lee looked fullsquare at her mother, seeing all, feeling all with a curious lack of judgment.

"I'm going to be just fine, Mother," she said. "Just fine." *And if I'm not,* she thought, *if I'm not, I swear to God you will never, never know it.*

Elinor pleaded with Aura Lee to change the wedding date. "No one, absolutely no one, gets married in January. At least give me the satisfaction of planning a Christmas wedding. It would be so lovely."

"I'm sorry, Mother, but Daniel can't come back until the first of the year. He doesn't want to take a chance on anyone challenging our claim, and residency requirements are very strict."

"He could bend a little, what with all he's asking *you* to give up."

"He's not asking me to give up anything, Mother. I'm choosing to live in Kansas, and it will only be a short time until our living conditions will be every bit as comfortable as they are here. Besides, he *is* bending by coming back in the dead of winter just for a wedding ceremony."

Daniel had left immediately, fired with the intent to get the best possible claim.

"The ones nearest a creek are always taken first," he said. "I don't have a moment to waste."

Aura Lee was touched by the devotion of a man who would discipline himself to write every single day. The mailman's steps made her heart proud with anticipation. Usually there was not a letter for her at all, however. For in spite of Daniel's faithfulness in writing he explained that he simply did not have time to ride often to the flimsy hut that had been designated an official U.S. Post Office.

"And besides, when I can go, I can barely stand the smell or the attitude of the old geezer who runs the place. I don't know how much longer he's going to be around here anyway, and good riddance as far as I'm concerned." In spite of Daniel's disdain for the postmaster he continued to write each evening and in his letters he lovingly and frankly described his day's labor. Occasionally, she permitted herself the tiniest of smiles at the glimpses of the boy she was seeing in his eager phrases and joyful descriptions. She was charmed and yearned for the vigor of the prairie.

"It will be hard in some ways, my darling," he wrote, "but worth every bit of our striving. I only wish I could bring you here immediately after the wedding. But I want our home to be worthy of you, and I know how important a decent ceremony will be to your parents. So plan away, sweetheart."

Aura Lee sighed. She was tired of others deciding what would make her happy. Determined to settle the issue once and for all, she went to her mother's bedroom.

"Mother, a Christmas wedding is out of the question. You might as well accept it."

"Why can't you wait until spring, then?" wailed Elinor. She was propped up on a pile of feather pillows encased in the palest blue silk and had been crying for days over her daughter's stubbornness.

"Mother, he can't leave our claim for that long during spring and summer. We've been over this a hundred times," she said, exasperated with the attempt to make Elinor understand. "It's only during the winter that he can get away long enough for a trip back here. He wants to break enough ground for three acres of corn this year, and he'll be lucky to get that much land ready in time for planting even without any interruptions."

"Couldn't he get someone else to do the manual labor?"

"Mother, honestly!" Aura Lee rose in disgust, weary with the effort to make her understand the realities of homesteading.

"No one gets married in January," said Elinor again.

"We will," snapped Aura Lee. "You have a choice, Mother, between a large wedding in January or—we will be married by a justice of the peace when I get to Kansas."

"You'll do no such thing, young lady," said Elinor, sitting bolt upright. "What would people think? You're our only child. It wouldn't look right for people in our position to let you sneak off like some runaway serving girl."

Aura Lee checked the urge to laugh. Oh, Daniel, she thought. I wish you were here to see this. Trust Mother to put everything in the right perspective.

"So you'll agree to January, then," said Aura Lee. "Why don't you do all the planning, Mother?" she said, suddenly inspired. "Daniel and I will cooperate in every way." This would be her farewell present to her mother— letting her be in charge of her life one last time. Encouraged by the spark in Elinor's eyes, Aura Lee continued.

"Look at it this way, Mother: a January wedding could be the ultimate test of your artistry."

"I can plan the whole thing?" sniffed Elinor. "Motif and all?"

"Completely," said Aura Lee. "My dress, the colors, the flowers, you can decide everything. There's just one thing I ask of you."

"Yes?"

"Please watch the expenses on Daniel's side." Daniel's parents, Roland and Esther Hollingworth, were once counted among the town's socially elite, but most of their money had gone into a failed manufacturing venture years ago. Some said it was the wasted effort of trying to recoup his losses that had caused Roland Hollingworth's death at such an early age.

"That's not what killed him," Daniel had explained to Aura Lee. "He just lost his will to live when my mother died. But you need to know, darling, that I don't have very much money to fall back on. I have enough to get us started and tide us over until our first crop, and that's about it. It was Uncle Justin's idea to invest what little money they left me in my head. He insisted that I go to Yale, and I've never regretted it. Who knows—I might yet start a practice out West."

Elinor nodded haughtily in response to her daughter's request. "I don't need you to lecture me on manners, young lady. After all, you didn't get yours out of the blue."

Aura Lee Lombard's wedding day was still and clear and as white as the fur on a newborn snow rabbit. It was as though nature had decreed that light alone would be used to adorn the day; the rest of creation was silent. The sun's rays lit up icicles and tiny crystals of snow and highlighted frost patterns until the town sparkled with rainbowed prisms that winked away as suddenly as they had appeared.

The church was packed. The heavy air was weighted with the scent of candles. Their soft flames flickered as wedding guests settled in hushed silence.

"Aura Lee, it's perfect," breathed Marie Sutton, "absolutely beautiful." She alone was reckless enough to peer out the door of the small anteroom.

"It should be," said Aura Lee. Elinor had immersed herself in the wedding plans with a vigor that surprised everyone, her ill health momentarily forgotten.

Marie softly closed the door and gave her dress a last-minute check. The other bridesmaids fidgeted impatiently, waiting for the change of music by the organist that would signal the procession.

Even Marie fell silent when the subtle transition of chords began and at last, with a nod from the usher, the four bridesmaids began the measured tread to the altar.

Their gowns were a deep orchid crepe de Chine with sweetheart necklines just high enough for decency. The basque bodices emphasized the wasp waists which had been cinched tightly and without a shred of mercy by Elinor herself.

"Of course you can breathe," she snapped at the girls' yelps of pain. "The whole effect will be ruined if you go out looking like peasants."

The skirts were a triumph of design. Three full tiers were draped individually on the bias with the folds hiding all the seaming. The bridesmaids carried massive bouquets of orchids. More of the waxy blossoms with their exquisite purple centers were used to decorate both sides of the altar.

When Daniel and his groomsmen filed out, even Mrs. Carmichael, president of the Altar Guild, momentarily stopped talking to Mrs. Schipper.

"He doesn't look *civilized*," she whispered critically.

Daniel's Prince Albert coat and striped pants were cut to perfection and, being the gentleman he was, he was perfectly at home in formal attire. But his normally swarthy complexion had been sunburned to a bronze that seemed brutish and coarse for one of his class. The muscles in his arms and shoulders were barely concealed by the lines of the jacket. An aura of power and vitality emanated from Daniel that seemed to fill the church.

"Penny for your thoughts," said Mrs. Carmichael slyly.

Mrs. Schipper blushed furiously and as she flopped the cardboard pew fan back and forth she gave her friend a withering glance.

The organ was silent for a few seconds, then, as the chords triumphantly rang out the beginning of Mendelssohn's "Wedding March," the congregation rose to its feet.

Elton nodded at Aura Lee and solemnly extended his arm. As she

accepted his protection for the last time as his little girl, she gently leaned over and kissed his cheek, then together they walked down the aisle.

Three-fourths of her dress consisted of snow white heavy satin. The edge of the skirt and the yards-long train had been overlaid with expensive reembroidered European lace that Elinor had finally imported after searching the local shops in vain. The same lace traced a sweetheart, off-the-shoulder neckline, with a closely woven netting that discreetly covered her bosom and connected the highbanded circle of satin around her neck.

Aura Lee's hair had been arranged into a mass of curls and waves by a hairdresser personally coached and bullied by her mother.

Elinor was triumphant as she watched her daughter and her husband. The wedding guests were clearly awed, thanks to her meticulous planning.

The layers of veiling created a misty barrier to Aura Lee's vision. The forms of the guests were softened but she knew, before her eyes even found the vacant seat reserved for the guest of honor, that the one she loved second only to Daniel was missing.

The pain was so sudden and unexpected that her father looked at her with alarm as her hand trembled suddenly on his arm.

Professor Brock isn't here, she thought, with a quick fierce stab. She yearned for the blessing of her devoted friend. She wanted him to say all would be well. All at once she was furious with him for casting this pall over her perfect day. What did an old bachelor know about love, anyway?

She steadied her trembling hand and lifted her head with proud disdain; there was no turning back. In a moment this marriage would be sealed on earth and in Heaven.

Her eyes never wavered for a moment as she fixed her gaze on Daniel, her Daniel, guided by his cold, sure star.

Aura Lee awoke with a start when the Pullman car lurched and she looked up at Daniel with dismay.

"Oh, Daniel, I couldn't have slept. I'm sorry."

"Sh, darling. I'm glad you were able to relax." He wanted her to rest from the day's draining rituals. The faint dark smudges under her eyes from attending to the jangling press of people were gone now and he lightly traced his finger across her feathery brows, then laughed gruffly at the slow blush that rose to her cheeks.

The elaborate wedding trip had been a gift from her parents. When Elton had delicately offered it, Aura Lee looked at Daniel eagerly, yet she was determined to yield to his quick pride if he thought it wrong to accept.

It would be the only time they could take such a trip, Daniel reasoned. He agreed with swift delight to the journey on the plushest car available from Saint Jo to Kansas City.

They would arrive at their hotel in good time this evening.

"Daniel let's eat in our room. I don't even want to have to talk to a waiter."

"All right." His dark eyes, restless as fire, were diverted from the rushing landscape to the petite body of his young wife. She was dressed in a cerulean blue velvet traveling costume with a sparkling white jabot cascading down the front of her blouse. A collection of blue feathers floated jauntily from the band of her wide-brimmed hat. He was drunk with adoration as he looked at her sweet, pale face shadowed by the sooty lashes that were in such stark contrast to her eyes.

"Oh, Daniel, it's absolutely wonderful." Aura Lee turned to him in delight after the bellboy set the last of their bags in the room. "I don't think I can bear to leave it at all, no matter how much there is to see in Kansas City."

A blaze glowed softly in the marble fireplace and she knelt to trace the outline of a rose in the Aubusson carpet. The enormous four-poster bed was covered with a rich rose velvet spread.

And it was Daniel, the cosmopolitan man of the world, who first averted his eyes from the bed with a deep flush.

And it was Daniel, with desire hotter than a kindling fire, who lingered at the meal, determined not to rush her with his need.

"Daniel!" He looked into the amused eyes of his wife as she set down her coffee cup and looked at him with sudden perception.

"You're worrying about me, aren't you? Sweetheart, I'm not made of glass."

She slowly walked around to his chair and settling on his lap gave him a long, lingering kiss that left no doubt as to her longing. With a deep, trembling breath, he pulled her to him.

And it was Daniel, with his quick hot blood, who lost all control and received the first guiltless fires of her eager virginity in dazzled wonder.

Aura Lee hands shook as she unfolded the bundle of letters. She had read them so many times they were in danger of coming apart at the creases. Some days she read them in a certain order and on others she made a game of shutting her eyes and reading the first one her finger touched.

When Daniel had first brought them to her she opened them eagerly and pored over every word. Now she found herself hiding them when Daniel was around, sensing his stern disapproval at the unhappiness on her face. The ones from Marie depressed her as much as the ones from her parents.

"We miss you terribly, Aura Lee. The town is still talking about the wedding. Last week, when I was at the dressmaker's, she showed me a piece of blue silk that made us both instantly think of you. It would just be perfect made up for the dance sponsored by the Women's Relief Guild next month."

Aura Lee had not been prepared for the unhappy jolt she felt at the memory of the dances she was missing.

Oh, why, oh, why didn't it dawn on me what an intolerable burden the lack of a post office would be? she asked herself for the hundredth time. Daniel had explained it all to her before they were married. And to think this batch of letters would be the only one she would receive for God only knew how long. He had come back from his last trip to post her letters at her insistence, irritated at having used the horse for nothing.

"Guess the son-of-a-bitch just took off," said Daniel. "Knew it was going to happen."

Aura Lee was incredulous.

"You mean we don't even have a place now to get our mail?"

"Don't know where it would be," said Daniel gruffly. "Come spring, when there's more folks here, the government will probably set up a permanent one. In the meantime, I guess we can make do. You read them too much anyway, Aura Lee. I've been meaning to talk to you about it, but I didn't want to hurt your feelings."

Fall was fully in the air. Aura Lee was relieved that summer was over, even though there were no fall leaves to color the landscape, no quickening of the social season with the accompanying fashion changes, and oh dear God, no music. She sat paralyzed with grief at the one thought she ordinarily never allowed herself.

Lately she permitted herself only the thoughts she could bear. The others were instantly banished into the center of white light that enabled her to endure.

Ever since she was a little girl, the light was there. She could not remember when it was not present. When the pressure her parents put on her became unbearable, she used to escape to her room, and by squeezing her eyes shut and willing her troubled mind to calm down, the light came and obliterated her thoughts, steadied her breathing, and restored her tranquility.

One day when she was playing the piano, in the space of a few notes she felt herself enter the mind of the composer. Her fingers faltered a second at this strange empathy and then she soared into the elation that had inspired the song. When she reached the last measure, she was fully back into her own mind.

It was real. It had happened. She had entered another person's mind. She wanted to ask Professor Brock if this was normal, but she was afraid his reply would be "no." She suspected that her thoughts were very curious and not like other young ladies her age. She knew instinctively that none of her friends would understand her light, or her need for it. There was a mystery to it, as though there were more she needed to know. She knew entering the composer's mind had actually happened, and she knew the warmth and help afforded by the light were actually real, but the two phenomena were linked in her mind as similar occurrences, best not talked about. Yet, through her music she knew that every emotion she had ever experienced had been felt as deeply by someone else; the compositions told her so. So through the years, she continued to trust that there would surely be someone, some day, safe to ask about the mystery of the light.

Aura Lee swatted at a fly that kept buzzing around the soddy. Yes, fall was welcome even without all its remembered splendors. For it brought with it a briskness to the air, a lessening of the swarm of insects, and even a respite from combatting the body odors that were a constant plague with such a limited water supply. Would there ever be a time, she wondered, when a change of seasons on the prairie brought something of itself to look forward to instead of just the sense of relief at not having to put up with this or that?

Her housework had evolved into a bearable routine. She cooked, she cleaned, and she washed their clothing. She moved restlessly about the soddy during these subtly invigorating fall days. Back home, the cook would be putting up food in a frenzy of activity.

Here, there was no way to can. Everything had to be dried. Even her green beans had been pierced with her quilting needle and slid down the cotton thread to form a chain. At first she had pretended it was fun, for it reminded her of stringing popcorn and cranberries for the Christmas tree. But a lump formed in her throat when she realized these pathetic withered beans would be her only supply of green vegetables for the winter. Her rhubarb, started by Daniel that spring, was cut in slices one inch thick and hung by a thread in the sun. Pumpkin meat, dark and leathery, would be soaked for rare precious pies at Thanksgiving and Christmas. Her winter stores were meager and unappetizing.

She spent long hours working calico quilts, with intricate designs of her own creation, and she thought about Julka and her life in that miserable dugout, and realized again how well, in comparison, Daniel had provided for her.

Her disposition had changed since her experience with the Smrckas. A hint of melancholy, barely suppressed in her under normal circumstances, was beginning to dominate her personality. She felt a recurring bitterness at the thought of Julka Smrcka having lived just three miles from her house. It was the most heart-rending thought of all. Just three miles. Within easy walking distance. She could have gone there every day if she had wanted to, while Daniel worked. Sudden tears, unbidden and far too frequent lately, overwhelmed her again. There had been another woman just over the rise. They could have talked. She would not have felt this terrible frightening loneliness with a neighbor three miles away. She was certain Julka had spoken English. Anton had spoken it well on that tragic day.

The prairie silence waited for her like a wolf this morning. It waited to devour her if she spoke. She moved her chair outside the soddy to read the letters from her parents in the bright sunlight.

"My darling daughter," her mother began. "We pray for your welfare daily and rejoice to hear that your new home is living up to your expectations. Your father feels your absence keenly and is particularly anxious for your first visit. We keep your room in constant readiness even to the point of placing fresh flowers on your dresser every morning. How we long for your return. *When* can we expect you back for the first visit? The judge has literally kept the home fires burning for you."

Aura Lee examined her hands, once smooth and white as alabaster, and wondered how she could ever let them be seen again in civilized society. Would it even be possible to look a lady again? Her ears were filled with an uneasy vibration, almost as though the silence itself had a sound. Tears came suddenly again and, as the salty drops hit the top sheet of paper and caused muddy little splotches on the ink, the flood gave way. She buried her face in her hands and sobbed helplessly, all pretense of

51

pride gone. It didn't matter anyway. There was nobody to see her.

A shadow fell across her chair. She looked up and there stood Daniel, his hoe held across his shoulder.

He propped the hoe against the side of the house and held out his arms in a gesture of accepting sympathy. Aura Lee rushed into them, basking in his gentleness.

"I've tried to tell you that reading those just isn't good for you," he scolded mildly. She bowed her head in shame at having worried her husband yet again.

He was always exhausted lately, always short-tempered, and there was a new grimness, a tension to his mouth. She did not want to add to his problems. She wanted to be a worthy helpmate, but only when she was in his arms, only when he was soothing her did she feel normal. Only then did mind and body and soul seem to belong together. The rest of the time she felt so terribly strange, and she could not keep her hands off her letters.

She felt a strange, frightening force stalking her. She yearned to tell Daniel of this, but did not know how to begin.

When he left in the morning, her mind went with him. It split cleanly into halves. The part of her that stayed behind in the soddy, the part that worked under the protection of the circle of light, that part was like a ghost that moved from task to task, tip-toeing fearfully and breathing slowly and carefully lest she antagonize the silence.

But here in Daniel's arms, she was brought back to life again. In Daniel's arms she was almost happy. He held her at arm's length and clumsily smoothed back a tendril of hair. He solemnly studied her face and his eyes began to twinkle.

"If you aren't a sight, now."

"Oh, Daniel, just hold me some more."

She clung fiercely to him. He looked more like an Indian than ever and his body had become rock hard. The prairie was tempering him into fine steel. She kissed him over and over and strained against him with the sweet painful eagerness that made their lovemaking such a joy. His arms tightened around her and he scooped her up and carried her inside the house. He laid her gently on the bed and fumbled with the buttons on her bodice. Aura Lee smiled up at him, her heart pounding. She let herself drift into pure feeling. Then, against her will, maddening in its intensity, the image was there again, and she stiffened abruptly against Daniel's embrace. This was the second time it had happened. Just as Daniel was loosening the string on her bloomers, she saw Julka Smrcka again, lying white and waxen in a pool of blood and slime.

As before, her reaction was immediate and irreversible. She shuddered and shoved at Daniel's chest. She darted from the bed and drew her dress around her. Her hair tumbled down her back in damp ringlets. She stared with apprehension at Daniel who lay propped up on one elbow in the bed.

The only sound was Daniel's ragged, uneven breathing. They did not look at each other. Aura Lee stood poker straight, desperate in her inability to find words to tell Daniel how terrified she was at even the thought of having a baby. She yearned for a child, but not for pregnancy and child-birth.

How could a child be raised decently out here? She could not even teach it to be clean. Not here, where every swallow of water was so priceless she hesitated before she took a long drink. She would never bring a baby into this desolation. And in addition to the impossibility of rearing it, she would never knowingly risk her life and that of a baby during an unattended birthing.

Yet this man, dearer to her than life itself, guide, protector, lover, her husband, was being diminished by her fears. She had to make him understand.

"Daniel."

He did not look up. A patched quilt was pulled up to his waist and he thoughtfully pulled at the tufts of tying thread over and over again. His powerful shoulders gleamed with a faint sheen of perspiration.

"Daniel, it's not you, it's me and—" Her voice trailed off helplessly. She knew he would not understand, could never accept the terror of the images in her mind. Like a drowning person fighting for survival, she knew she had to get back in Daniel's bed if they were to retain the bond, the spiritual union, so inexplicably tied to the physical, that made their marriage so solid as to seem predestined. But her feet were rooted to the floor. Again the silence had a life of its own.

Daniel swung his legs to the side of the bed and rested his elbows on his knees. His head drooped and he sat motionless. At last he rose deliberately and pulled on his trousers. With a deft sure motion, he buttoned his shirt.

Aura Lee stood paralyzed with grief and shame. Quietly he crossed the room, went outside, picked up his hoe and left for the field again. The quiet contempt in his departure, the absoluteness of his acceptance of her terror was as rejecting to her as a slap in the face. Physical abuse, angry words, anything would have been easier to bear than that silent acceptance.

She settled her dress back over her shoulders and combed her hair, twisting it into its usual bun at the nape of her neck. She looked at herself in the mirror. The cornflower blue of the calico enhanced the color of her eyes. The thick black lashes, her best feature, had not changed. It was only on the inside, only in her mind that the blackness lived.

Tears streamed down her face and she laughed morbidly at their coming. Crying again! Sometimes it seemed as though she had shed enough tears to irrigate the whole prairie. But she had to stop this time. Had to get ahold of herself or the tears would cost her her Daniel. Something inside her warned her she was going too far.

There was some water in the basin. She poured it into the pan and put it on the stove to heat. Through the window pane, dirty again in spite of frequent scrubbing, she saw a jack rabbit run an erratic path across the grass. Daniel was a speck in the distance. She saw the rhythmic rise and fall of the hoe.

She was determined to pull herself back together. She poured the water into the basin and scrubbed her face vigorously. She assessed the water supply, always too meager; it had to be hauled a distance of three miles and was precious beyond all imagining.

Daniel had assured her that the very first time a well-digger came by they would have a well dug. And with the well would come a windmill, and with a windmill a pump, and at long last a supply of water.

With a constant water supply they could have animals. She would have a cow to milk, and perhaps even chickens. An egg sounded an unbelievable luxury. She would have a garden and maybe, maybe even some flowers. She was desperate for any type of beauty.

She looked quietly at the water supply again and made the decision. Even though it was not time, today she would wash her hair. Even if it involved making the trip herself to the creek to replenish the supply.

It was important to her to be scrupulously clean. She wanted to scrub and scrub and scrub, her hair, her skin, her mind, until every dark corner of her black soul shone again. She would even change dresses. Perhaps she could scrub away her attitude and replace it with the homestead optimism that buoyed Daniel.

Kansas was "next year" country and she knew she had to believe this. That "next year" there would be water. "Next year" they would harvest a decent wheat crop. If they could just endure the first year on the plains, then "next year" their troubles would be over.

Toward evening, after the soddy had been put to order, she sat quietly on a chair and waited for Daniel. He came slowly across the field, his powerful legs moving easily across the clods. Her heart ached at the slight droop of his shoulders.

She was going to change. She could feel the resolve within her. She too would become a "next year" person. And she would learn to lie and lie and lie to herself. She would pretend she was able to endure any affliction, even the terror of childbirth. She would scorn those weaker than herself and ridicule the women who "couldn't take it."

Tears threatened again and her hands trembled in her lap with the effort of self-control. Self-deception did not come easily to her, but she was certain this course would lead her back to Daniel and that was the only thing that really mattered.

Daniel stopped when he saw his wife waiting. An uncertain expression flickered across his face.

Oh, Daniel, mourned Aura Lee, drawing a quick trembling breath, what have I done that even you can lose your sureness, your absolute, pigheaded, infuriating conviction that you and you alone know the right thing to do at all times. What have I done?

Slowly she rose to her feet and went to meet her husband.

"I've got supper ready," she said. She wanted to say so much more, but could not find the right words.

He nodded and followed her into the soddy, taking in at a glance the tidied room and the newly bathed freshness of his wife. His eyes softened.

"The place looks very nice."

"Thank you." She was warmed by his cautious approval. "It didn't take all that long," she said, "after I set my mind to it."

She was furious with the quick approval she saw in his eyes.

"It's all in attitude, Aura Lee," he said, encouraged by the change in her. "People can do anything they want to, if they just straighten out their thinking."

"Yes," she said, sickened suddenly with loneliness. She flirted with the beckoning blackness, dimly aware of the dangerous bleak peace it offered. She was attracted to the darkness. The voices there were becoming warmer, helpful, like the very best friend she yearned for.

"Yes, Daniel, I must work on my attitude."

"There now," the voice cried triumphantly. "That wasn't so hard, was it? See how proud he is of you? Just say what you're supposed to say, and do what you're supposed to do."

Stop it, she screamed silently, touching her fingers to her temples. *Just stop it.*

"Are you all right, darling?" asked Daniel. His brow wrinkled in concern as Aura Lee swayed for a moment, then steadied herself, her hand groping for the back of the chair.

"Yes, Daniel, I'm just fine." Her tongue thickened on the words.

"Good. Let's eat. Nothing like a hot meal to set everything right."

"Yes," she said woodenly. "I'll dish it up." *Oh yes, Daniel, nothing like a hot meal, and hours of cooking, then dishes, heating water, carrying in buckets that leave white marks on my hands. There's nothing quite like it.*

After supper, he pulled her onto his lap and inhaled deeply of the faint perfume emanating from her freshly washed hair. He softly kissed her blue-veined lids, and stroked her hair in soothing gestures, as though he were comforting a child.

"Oh, Daniel, just hold me." He cradled her against his giant chest and she was blissfully warm, safe from terror, all the night things gone, shielded by Daniel's strength. Then the rhythm of his breath quickened and she felt his heartbeat through his chest, and the steely tension in his arms.

She longed for the sweet joy they had once had. The laughter, the eagerness.

"Are you laughing at me, Daniel? Am I doing something wrong?" she once asked, suddenly anxious over his secretive smile.

"God, no, Aura Lee," he said, instantly sober. "It's just that when I come home at night and find you waiting, wanting me, I'm so pleased I don't know what to say. It makes me feel ten feet tall and so damned lucky that I can't imagine anything else I could ever want in this world."

"Sometimes I wonder if other wives are like me—you know, just loving to make love?"

"I don't know," he said, eyes sparkling. "I've never been married before. I doubt it, sweetheart. How could anyone else be your match for feelings? You're deeper than anyone I've ever met, and that comes into bed with you. It has to make a difference."

But that was months ago. A whole world ago. And this was now.

I must, she thought, I must get back in Daniel's bed for his sake. It's not fair. Her jaw locked in determination and she willed her body to stay still and her tongue to say the right words as he lifted her onto the bed.

Afterwards, Aura Lee drew a long slow breath and then carefully expelled the air. She lay beside Daniel, one hand touching his leg.

He only cares about himself. He couldn't even tell how much I hated it. He, who always knew her heart of hearts. How could he not tell the difference? She felt a sense of loss so deep she wondered if she could ever forgive him. A deep proud rage was beginning to possess her and she winked back the icy tears that were her body's way of expelling poison. Daniel was upset when she cried? Very well, then, she would never cry again. He wanted a wife who was eager to go to bed? Very well then, she would yield in a moment.

She lay motionless, absorbed in her grief, and longed for sleep. Then to her troubled mind came the haunting notes of a violin. The music seemed to float over the prairie and give voice to her anguish.

"You were warned," the music reminded her. "The professor tried to tell you."

In spite of her resolve, the tears began again.

Aura Lee froze when she saw herself in the mirror the next morning. It was as though an unfriendly haggard stranger stared back at her from the glass. Judging her. Mocking her. She traced the deep lavender circles under her eyes in wonder as though they belonged to someone else. Surely the loss of one night's sleep could not have caused the paleness in the mirror. No, more than one night. Many more now. So many she had lost track. It was this stranger who was stealing the sleep from her.

Aura Lee willed the morbid fantasy to stop. *I've got to get out of here today,* she thought. *If I were home it would be so easy. I would just go downtown. But then again, if I were home, I wouldn't be in such sad shape.* Determined to get a grip on herself, she knelt down beside her wardrobe trunk and began to sort the contents. Under her best satin lay her riding costume. It was a heavy maroon velvet with a row of tiny covered buttons up the tightly fitted basque bodice. Back home on a fine day like this she and Marie would have an appointment at the stables. Daniel had laughed when she showed him the outfit one evening.

"We don't hold with such nonsense out here, sweetheart. I'll bet there's not a sidesaddle within a hundred miles, and besides, you just don't go riding for no good reason. It's a waste of horseflesh."

Aura Lee had just nodded, schooling in her feelings. She had been so mortified when she was expected to ride astraddle the night they had gone to the Smrckas' that she did not how to explain the sense of shame to Daniel. It was as though Daniel had handed her a man's undergarment to wear. Suddenly she buried her face in her hands and swallowed painfully, furious that every single thing had to be to suit Daniel. She got up and quickly found the acre of corn where he was busy hoeing.

"I want you to hitch up Toby for me," she said. "I'm going for water. I used too much yesterday when I washed my hair."

"No need, sweetheart. I'll tend to it as soon as I get through here this evening."

"I want to go now, Daniel. By myself."

He wiped his hand across his brow and squinted into the sun and then back at the weeds and buffalo grass that still needed to be culled out of the corn. His wife's mouth was trembling, and measuring, weighing all, he decided.

"All right." His tone was abrupt. It was an unnecessary waste of time in the middle of the day to have to harness the horse and never good to have Toby work in the heat, but this was the first time Aura Lee had asked to go anywhere alone. She could surely manage the horse and wagon for the three miles, but he knew she could not handle the barrels.

"Sweetheart, there's no way you can lift the barrels. Why don't you wait until evening and we'll go together."

She shook her head, barely trusting herself to speak.

"No, Daniel, please. I want to go now. I can fill the barrels by using a bucket. It will be just fine." She lowered her eyes silently, pleading for understanding.

Daniel's throat constricted with pity as he studied the top of her bowed head and saw the tension in the tightly clenched hands she held before her as if in supplication.

"All right, then. I appreciate it. Save me from making the trip myself," he lied. He flushed when she raised her eyes and he saw the tender mockery there. She knew and understood the motive behind his words, and gently squeezed his hand in appreciation of the gesture.

"We're going to be all right, Daniel," she whispered. "I swear we are."

He moved quickly to harness the horse and to lift the heavy iron-banded barrels into the bed of the wagon. He waved cheerfully, but his face was lined with worry as she disappeared over the rise, and his hoe rose and fell with short choppy strokes at the burden this trip would place on their poor horse. The demands of the work on the homestead were already too much for the animal.

Aura Lee firmly grasped the reins and with a sharp cluck flicked the harness traps over the back of the horse and headed toward the creek. She inhaled deeply of the crisp fall air. Here and there clumps of goldenrod lit up the pastures.

Her throat began to constrict and she swallowed painfully as she drew closer and closer to the Smrckas' dugout. The underlying despair began to tug at her mind again, as though mocking her new spirit. It seemed to tease her. "See, no matter how hard you try, I am always here. I will always be with you. You can't lie to me."

She wanted to see Anton, but she could hardly stand the sight of the place where Julka had died.

This was the most direct route to water, she scolded herself. It was the sensible way to go, and the kind thing to do would be to look in on Anton Smrcka as she passed.

They had offered to keep the child. Aura Lee yearned for his company.

"I would not burden you," Vensel said.

"It's no burden, Mr. Smrcka," she pleaded. "Anton is so quiet and sensitive. It would be a joy to have him." *He's like me*, she thought. *Oh, why can't you see he's like me and it's not fair to ask him to take on this harsh life. He can't. I know he can't.*

"He's my boy," said Vensel simply. "We belong together."

"What will he do all day? Who will feed him?"

"We will manage," he said. His face was polite and grief-lined, begging her not to ask questions for which he had no answer.

She had seen the sudden tightening of Anton's body, the fear of being taken from his father.

"Of course, you will," she said soothingly. "Of course, you can." The little hand had lost its whiteness where he gripped his father's arm. The animal wariness disappeared from his eyes as he looked at Vensel in grateful adoration.

"I want to thank you, for everything," Vensel said.

"Don't mention it," said Daniel.

"If there's anything I can do," said Aura Lee, "anything at all, please come and get me."

Vensel nodded and ruffled his son's hair.

"We can be friends, Anton, would you like that?" asked Aura Lee, tears brimming. "I think we both need one."

The boy looked at her, gray eyes wide with concern, as though he were seeing her for the first time.

"I would like to be your friend, Mrs. Hollingworth," he said formally, son of his father, full of old world courtesy. "I had one once before we came here. The only thing is, I forget what they do."

Of course he didn't remember, Aura Lee thought. *Alone all day with this tragic, solemn man. How could he bear it? An empty dugout, or worse, days in the field. No children to play with. Just sky and wind and unbroken days, one exactly like another. How could he possibly bear it?*

"There are no rules for being friends, Anton. We'll have to find our own way."

He nodded, brightening.

"The important thing is for you to remember that I'm always here. Would you like to call me Aura Lee?"

A rare smile split his face. Yes, yes he would.

They had left then, and just before they reached the top of the bank, Aura Lee turned for one last look at the father and son; Vensel with his head bowed and Anton looking straight at her.

"Aura Lee," he called, the wind snatching away his defiant blaze of words, "Aura Lee, my dad takes good care of me. You'll see."

Aura Lee twitched at the dull jingle of the harness. Every revolution of the wagon wheels brought her closer to the dugout.

Suddenly the air was split with a joyous greeting.

"Aura Lee! Aura Lee!"

The small, dark-haired boy ran up to the wagon, elated to see her. She stopped the wagon and stepped down to the ground.

Anton was surprisingly clean and she was baffled at his high spirits. He did not look like a child in mourning for his mother. He even had a well-fed look.

"I've got a surprise for you. Hurry." His eyes beamed his excitement. He tugged insistently at her hand, and she laughed as she allowed him to pull her along. They went down over the rise and then she stopped abruptly.

Framed in the doorway was a tall, beautiful woman with a snowy apron wrapped around her homespun dress. Aura Lee had never seen a more gorgeous head of hair. It was the color of an old cello, and was pushed forward in charming natural waves. The remainder of what seemed to be its great length was wrapped into a bun at the nape of her neck.

Aura Lee was so astonished she could not speak.

"How glad I am right now to see you. My first visitor," the woman said in a rich, controlled voice.

Even apart from her accent, Aura Lee knew she was Czechoslovakian by the curious positioning of her words; a struggling for the correct American order of sounds that so charmed her about Vensel's speech.

The woman lifted her proud head and extended a hand toward Aura Lee.

"Come inside, Aura Lee. I am glad to have you. I am Lucinda, Vensel's wife."

Aura Lee gasped.

"I know your name, you see. Anton and Vensel have told me. Come, let us talk. Eat some good bread. Rest a spell. Anton," she said crisply, "tend to her horse."

Aura Lee was shooed down the steps and promptly seated in a cane-bottomed chair. She did not know a dugout could look so orderly. No elusive dreamer, this woman, this Lucinda, with sun-kissed skin and apricot cheeks. She bustled with a vitality and optimism that completely captivated Aura Lee.

Once when her school had toured an art gallery, Aura Lee had stood spellbound in front of a painting of a woman in a field, and now as she watched Lucinda move confidently about the dugout, never stopping her talking as she deftly sliced the bread, Aura Lee recalled the feeling the woman in the painting gave her. She, with her sterile, privileged life, had envied the strength, the flash of joy the painter managed to capture in the woman's expression.

Lucinda Smrcka's lovely face was rounded with high Slavic cheekbones, and like the woman in the painting, her arms were firmly muscled. Dazzled, Aura Lee could see her baking, lifting, wringing wash, plunging into the task at hand. Singing, laughing, running into the wind. This Lucinda, with life abundant, seemed destined for the prairie.

"This bread, it's delicious," Aura Lee murmured. She looked around the room and in the corner stood a violin case.

"It's *real*," she cried. "For two nights now, I've heard you. But I thought I was dreaming. Oh, how wonderful." A neighbor to talk to, and not only that, she was musical.

Lucinda poured Aura Lee more of her carefully hoarded coffee, real, not parched rye, and shrewdly glancing at her guest, began to answer unasked questions.

"I became Vensel's wife a week ago. I am Julka's cousin. He wrote the family of her death and of his great grief for the boy. I decided to come, to offer myself, that he and the boy should not be alone. Vensel should not have married Julka and brought her here. It was foolish. He needs guidance. A woman to shape him. Julka did not apply herself well to her task. There were many things undone here, when I arrived."

Aura Lee checked a sharp stab of anger and drew a shaky breath.

"She was terribly sick, I think, with the baby coming and all, and maybe lonely."

Lucinda eyed her coldly.

"She did not take herself in hand. She stayed in bed too much. She could have been well."

Aura Lee struggled for control. She lowered her eyes and drank slowly from the cup, but a tiny corner of her soul grieved for the blue-eyed Julka who had died before her time. She suppressed her irritation. It vanished as quickly as it came, and soon they were chattering away.

"And now," Lucinda said merrily, "now I play for you."

She tucked the violin under her chin and deftly tuned the strings. She tested the tone with a rasp of the bow and then began her little concert. The room picked up the vibration of her soul, and Aura Lee's lip began to tremble. No backwoods fiddler she, but an accomplished Czech musician, educated in her country to appreciate the finest quality of music, with the Czech people's natural affinity for strings.

The notes quivered with unbelievable clarity and, as she played, Aura Lee marveled at the subtlety of her interpretation.

Aura Lee was drowned in pleasure. Oh, I wish, I wish I played the violin. It would make all the difference in the world. A piano would be ruined in a soddy. There was no way to control the moisture, let alone the dirt. But a *violin!* Such a small, wonderful instrument, and it would have a case to protect it. It's not enough to have her play for me. I want to do it myself. Oh, God, how I want to. If I had this, I could get through my work in a flash. I know I could. It would be enough. Not like my piano, but enough to still the voices. I could stand it here. I know I could.

She sat quietly with her hands in her lap. I'm healed, healed, healed. This is what I must do. It is laid to rest. She will teach me and we will be friends. I'm sure she doesn't realize how harsh her opinions sound.

Lucinda stopped as abruptly as she had started. She threw back her head and laughed. Then tapping her foot, she began to fiddle an exaggerated rendition of "Turkey in the Straw."

"Come join life," her fiddle intoned. "I scorn the timid, the weak-willed. Come wrestle with God and the land. It is here you see what stuff you are made of. Come to the prairie. Take the ultimate test, but live and do not falter, and you will find your salvation."

Lucinda stopped and laughed again. A dark, moist curl sprang from her auburn waves and there was a hint of malice in her eyes as she inspected Aura Lee again.

"And now we will take care of you. You are too thin, too nervous. Like Julka, you need to be built up."

Aura Lee started to protest, then laughed and allowed herself to be enfolded in the care of this outrageous woman.

Lucinda laid the violin carefully in its case, as Aura Lee studied her hands with wonder. They were larger than normal for a woman, but beautifully shaped, with long tapering fingers, capable of any undertaking that required dexterity. They were strong and competent. Yet she felt a slight uneasiness at her recognition of this woman's strength.

By the time he was eleven years old, Graham Chapman had discovered that dreams and illusions were the most important things in the world.

His father, Theodore Chapman, ran a small general store in the lazy, obscure little town of Lucerne, Missouri. It bravely competed with other towns around it for leftover commerce from the motherlode city of Saint

Jo. Theodore was an affable man with a preacher's instinct for people's troubles and triumphs. He did not hesitate to put this information to use. Thus, through his little business, he brightly kept his fingers on the pulse of the town.

When Mrs. Olsen came in one day with her face strained and a slight drag to her normally sprightly step, he shrewdly decided that their strong-willed daughter, Elvira, was giving them problems again. Theodore put out sensitive feelers.

"Morning, Mrs. Olsen. Fine day today."

"Morning, Theodore."

"What may I help you with this morning?"

"Just a satchel, please. A soft bag that's easy to carry."

Oh, yes, the tension was there. He noticed the deepening of the lines in her forehead. A furtiveness that was not like her at all.

"Going on a trip?" he asked casually and with great delicacy. He did not want to seem to be prying.

"No, it's for Elvira. She's the one who's going. She's leaving this week to go back East to spend time with Hiram's sister."

"Fine traveling weather. Hope she has a nice trip," he said, dropping the topic.

The lines in Mrs. Olsen's face relaxed. He knew then. Why did parents send their adolescent daughters on extended trips? To bear an illegitimate child, of course.

Well, well, well. Must be a terrible blow to such a stuffy family, thought Theodore. Bound to be. But he could have told them the girl was headed this way. He had seen the shy glances she gave Leon Riordan when they passed on the street and he had noticed the man's quick hot stare in return. Well, well, well. He kept his eyes inscrutable. Never could tell when a little tidbit like this would come in handy. Old man Olsen owned a lot of land and while Theodore didn't need real estate now, still you never could tell. Thus, for Theodore's canny mind, chips of facts fit carefully together into little mosaics of information that formed patterns of opportunity. In the meantime, he generously lowered the price of the satchel by fifty cents, which he could not afford to do.

Mrs. Olsen blinked back tears, head straight.

"That's mighty generous of you, Theodore."

"You're the one who's doing me a favor, Mrs. Olsen. Don't know why, but satchels are slow movers."

With his usual unerring instinct, he had bought her good will, and she would always thereafter declare him to be a very kind person, although she could not for the life of her explain why. But Theodore knew. He had allowed her to keep face.

Elvira Olsen came back to town seven months later; her face bleak and without hope. Even her bright brown hair seemed to have lost its luster.

Theodore saw Elvira and Mrs. Olsen on the street, and in the girl's eyes was the weight of lost virtue. He greeted them politely and passed by quickly. He needed time to collect his wits. What did they want more than anything else in the world? He suspected that a chance to feel respectable, honorable again was their hearts' desire.

"Can you do some knitting for the church auxiliary, Elvira?" he asked the next day. "It's for orphans and homeless youngsters."

A sob caught in her throat, but she turned in time to hide the tears and compose herself. At last, a chance for penance. Redemption. Turning back, she nodded quickly.

"I swear that Elvira Olsen is the workingest girl I've ever seen," said one of the auxiliary ladies to Theodore about a month later. "She's going to knit up enough wool to keep socks on every man, woman, and child in Missouri."

"She'll make some man a wonderful wife, won't she?"

"Land sake's yes. She's a real jewel."

With just a word here and there, just an occasional well-placed remark, Theodore managed to plant the idea in the minds of the unsuspecting people of the community that Elvira Olsen was one hell of a good girl. As a result of his benevolent interference, the Olsen family would have died for one Theodore Chapman.

Graham's mother, Belle Chapman, was known as a fine figure of a woman, with Junoesque proportions and a feverish gaiety that infected all those around her.

When Belle walked into a room, the air fairly crackled. There was a constant tension about her, a peculiarly electric quality. Her hair was piled high and was suspiciously blond for someone her age. If she had been a madam at the local bordello, where she really appeared to belong, the townspeople would have known it was dyed. As it was, it was attributed to luck, as was the high, high blush to her wide cheekbones and the color of her berry red lips. Her waists were immaculate and her skirts crackled with starch. She had impossibly high standards for maintaining a household.

She was an organizer and a people person. She could get a quilting bee or a dance together in nothing flat. All it took was the blithe assurance that "it'll be fun."

"Going over to Ted and Belle's tonight?" their friends asked each other. Are you one of the magic included ones? their faces implied. I am. They asked me. Do you count too? No one ever refused.

"Well, son, I hope you realize how lucky you are to have such wonderful parents," a visitor said one night.

Graham pinked with pleasure. Yes, he knew.

"Gets you off to a good start."

Theodore and Belle glittered like stars, never tiring of compliments.

"Mom," said Graham that night, barely able to keep his eyes open, "Mom, you know something funny? No one ever tells you and Dad you're lucky to have me. Aren't you lucky too?"

Belle's hand faltered. "Of *course* we're lucky, Graham. What a strange thing to say." She frowned. She wished he weren't so serious, and really, he was different. She bit her lip. He watched too much. Thinking, always thinking.

Belle blew out the lamp. "Put those silly notions out of your head," she snapped. "It's late, go to sleep." She remembered several nights ago, when he had been watching her.

"Mom, why do your eyes get such dark circles under them? Are you sick?"

"Just tired, son. Not sick."

"Tad's mother doesn't scrub the floor every night. Why do you?"

"I can't stand filth, Graham. I hate it."

"Tad's mother just scrubs once a week. I know, I asked him."

"Well, I like things spotless."

"Can I help? I don't mind." He eased his toe toward a bubble of soap. "Your skin looks like it's too big for your face," he observed.

"Oh, for God's sake! That's the last straw. I've worked my fingers to the bone all week, and now to be insulted by my own son."

"I didn't mean nothing, Mom. Honest." Why were things never as they seemed? He knew she was tired just the same, just as he knew she was ashamed of having even him, her own son, see her at a disadvantage.

Graham knew another secret about his mother. He also knew, son of his father, with Theodore's instinctive wariness, that he should not tell, either. Some days the lines in Belle's face would deepen and the cords of her neck would tighten and as soon as the last customer was whisked out of the store with a lively "you come back, now!", she would go to the dresser in her bedroom; back of her waists in a pink satin box was a precious bottle of elixir.

Belle would carefully measure out two spoonfuls, swallow the liquid, and in a short time she was all soft again, and the lines in her face relaxed. Sometimes she would sink onto the bed and tears would trickle down her cheeks. Being able to gauge the fury of his mother's responses very well, Graham kept quiet.

Some nights he wondered if he was an orphan or a changeling. He did not feel as though he belonged in this family. He had Belle's blond hair and Theodore's fine gray eyes, but something in him was out of place.

Only the world of adults interested him. Because the regard of children his age didn't matter to him, his cold contempt for insults was misinterpreted as weakness. It had just taken one incident, however, one surprising victory, for his playmates to see him with awed eyes.

Graham had stopped in the prairie, the grass bending before him and the wind ruffling his fine blond hair as he watched Tommy Baalman approach the schoolhouse. Tommy was a terror. Beefy, hostile, the type of unchecked bully who made school an ordeal. He was so quarrelsome that even the schoolmarm, a spinster long seasoned in dealing with disciplinary problems, had given up. He wore her down. Miss Dodson settled for an uneasy truce that permitted her to get through most of the classes, most of the time. Even a talk with Tommy's parents had not produced results. They were glad enough to send him off to Miss Dodsen each day. The boy was a surly, irresponsible worker and therefore no help to his father and cold comfort to his mother.

To Tommy, Graham was like antagonizing smoke. The most reaction he had ever gotten from him was a withering glance. As he had been goading Graham for over a week without getting a rise, Tommy waited for a better victim, his favorite.

Lucy Fenton started to weep the moment she saw the older boy. Her mother had lied when she said she would just love school. The little first grader could hardly make herself go. Her great blue eyes filled with misery when she saw Tommy waiting for her again.

"Come on, kid. Let's see whatcha got."

Silently, without a word of protest, for she had learned very well by now, she extended her skimpy little lunch. It was poor enough, but lovingly packed by her mother. Lucy's stomach knotted in protest and a tiny whimper escaped her trembling lips. She was so hungry. Breakfast was so scant that some mornings she felt light-headed and had to pinch herself to keep from drifting into sleep, and especially to keep the numbers in arithmetic class from swimming before her eyes.

"Oh, please," she begged.

Tommy's eyes brightened with delight.

"Please what?"

"Please leave some for me."

"Say pretty please."

"Pretty please." Her voice quavered. It was useless. No words would help. This was a ritual he went through every morning. He loved to bring her to the brink of hope then hurl her down again. He ate the cold corn bread while Lucy watched, swallowing hard. There was a tiny bit of dried plums today. Would he eat them too? Slowly Tommy examined the precious fruit. He held it in the palm of his hand and then before Lucy's horrified eyes, he threw her mother's wonderful gift onto the ground and mashed it with his foot, bare now, during these warm spring days. Sobbing, without a speck of pride left, Lucy turned toward the schoolhouse. Tommy would let her go now. There wasn't another thing he could do to her.

She stopped abruptly as she looked into the cold gray eyes of Graham Chapman. He didn't say a word to Lucy as she brushed past, but stood watching, watching Tommy Baalman as though seeing him for the first time.

"Why don't you mind your own business, you queer son-of-a-bitch?" Tommy blurted.

Graham did not respond and Tommy snorted. Damn coward. Damn white-handed, scrub-faced coward.

Graham's eyes were as silvered as the underside of cottonwood leaves and Tommy felt an uneasy prickling on the back of his neck.

The bell rang then and the children filed into the schoolhouse, with Tommy and Graham the last to enter.

Shortly after Miss Dodson turned toward the board, Tommy took a sling shot and four sharp pebbles from his pocket. With an arrogant glance at Graham, to make sure he was watching, Tommy took slow careful aim and grinned as little Lucy Fenton jerked in her seat, her six-year-old mind numb with terror. He shot Graham a triumphant look and began to fumble for another pebble.

Graham slowly looked around the room, weighing, measuring, then rose to his feet.

"Miss Dodson."

"Why, yes, Graham," she said, turning from the board in surprise, as he was a gifted student who rarely raised questions over the lesson.

"Miss Dodson, you need to know that Tommy just hit Lucy Fenton with his slingshot and also that he steals her lunch from her every day."

The room was so still, it was as though the children had stopped breathing. Miss Dodson's scalp pinked through its wispy covering of graying hair. Even the bun at the base of her neck seemed to tighten.

How *could* he? How could he possibly put her on the spot like this? Of course she knew. In their hearts, teachers always know. Now Graham was forcing her to make some sort of response. What?

"Is that true, Tommy?"

The children's eyes were filled with confusion as they looked at Tommy. Graham had broken the cardinal rule; thou shall not snitch.

"No, teacher," Tommy said cheerfully, "it's not."

"He's lying," said Graham. "I saw it all." The very air in the room stilled. The children exchanged worried glances. This was going too far. Tommy would kill them.

"Well, now," said Miss Dodson. "Those are awfully harsh words, Graham. I—"

"I have a right, Miss Dodson, to study. The others do too. I'm tired of his bullying. Are there others here too who are fed up?"

Eyes quickened in agreement. A few of the older ones even nodded their heads.

Miss Dodson was very, very quiet. What did he expect her to do? Whip him? She couldn't and Tommy knew it. Expel him? She had tried that once and he had just come back like the seven demons, worse than ever.

"Miss Dodson," Graham persisted. "I believe that an eye for an eye, a tooth for a tooth is fair, don't you? It's in the Bible, isn't it?"

"Yes," she said, sensing a trap, but she was unable to side-step it. "Yes, an eye for an eye." Her voice trailed off.

"It's not your lunch he takes away, Miss Dodson, it's ours. Lucy's isn't the only one. And it isn't you he hits with rocks, it's us. So *we* have the right to get even, don't we?"

"Yes," said Miss Dodson softly, weary beyond all words. Sick of the one child who made learning impossible. Sick of the grief he inflicted on the weaker ones. Sick of seeing the rights of the whole sacrificed for the rights of the one. Her voice was steady now. "Yes," she said. "You have the right to get even."

"What's going on here?" asked Tommy. "What does he mean?"

"Just what I said, Baalman. We're getting even, all of us." Graham stood as straight as a poplar, his arms folded confidently across his chest. In an instant the strength was transferred; the mantle of power was bestowed upon another. Tommy was dethroned.

"What are you going to do?" Tommy asked.

"Why, hit you with little rocks and eat your lunch, of course," said Graham softly. "I said an eye for an eye. Why? Are there other things we should be doing?"

Thus, with the teacher's blessing, the children waited for Tommy Baalman every day like little cannibals. The older boys held his arms behind him, while the younger ones stung his flesh with stones. His lunch was divided instantly.

The children were hesitant at first, then eager; feeding on the desperation in Tommy's eyes.

Miss Dodson watched from the window, ashamed and unhappy. She had actually given her permission for this. She had let a boy, not even into puberty, persuade her to be a party to sadism. She saw her pupils changed into barbarians in a flash, by one person's words.

In a week's time, Tommy was no longer a student at the Pleasant Home School. Miss Dodson was relieved when the children's swift savagery went back to the depths where it belonged.

She could not put the charisma of Graham out of her mind, however, and one day she asked him to stay after school.

"Do you know what you want to be, Graham? When you're grown?"

"No, not for sure. I just know I want to make a lot of money."

"The thing with Tommy Baalman," she said carefully, "how did you know just what to say? To me, to the children?"

"I don't know. I just do."

"It's a rare gift, Graham, and very unusual. It will give you tremendous power over people, and can be used for good or evil. You must be *very*, very careful with this trust."

"I will," he said politely, keeping her at a distance with his voice.

"Since you quoted from the Bible, Graham, I hope that you become familiar with its teaching." He did not respond.

"Thank you, Graham," she said. "You may go now."

For the rest of the week, she found herself looking at the slender youth as he bent over his studies, and old troublesome Bible verses came into her mind, one in particular: "And He hardened Pharaoh's heart." Did the good Lord create such people as Pharaoh or a Graham to bring about a higher good? Miss Dodson sighed. One thing she knew for sure. Tommy Baalman was gone and her students had never been happier.

In time the children called him Gray Man as often as they did Graham, because of the warning in his eyes and because of his aloneness, which reminded them of the great gray wolves they read about. Sometimes Graham would pause in the schoolyard and his eyes would focus on a thousand prisms turned inward, and visions would bounce off the mirror hall of his mind and he would see wonderful things that he dared not speak of. He knew he was very special.

In adolescence, however, he was diverted from the world of adults and ideas by a yearning to be included in his own age group. He noticed the ease with which the other boys flirted with the girls and then went on to dating.

His nights were spent in deep, disrupting, conquering dreams, in which he was always riding. Riding females, riding horses, riding the wind, but always high, aloof, admired, and in command, and moving rhythmically toward some unknown goal. The feverish shades of dawn, gaudy and mockingly real, jarred him back to reality and the shame of his semen-stained bedclothes.

He was not relieved of his burden of loneliness until Annabel Schoeffner decided to help him out. Annabel was a natural, dyed-in-the-wool shrew at the tender age of fifteen; a sober-minded, scolding little sparrow of a girl.

She was the first girl Graham had ever asked for a date. He asked Annabel because, he reasoned, she was so brittle and contrary that no one else would and his chances of being rejected were much less. The big event was the community box supper.

Annabel heard his invitation with a sniff. "Well, I s'pose—won't hurt me, I guess."

Graham gnashed his teeth at the audacity of this undesirable female, then asked her out again because it had been so easy. After that, it was as though they were tutoring each other in social skills. They learned and they practiced with no thoughts of romance whatsoever. They needed each other and depended on each other. There were no secrets between them. She corrected him constantly.

"Graham, why are you always so polite?"

"Why shouldn't I be?"

"I don't know," Annabel said earnestly. "I just don't know. But it makes people nervous somehow. It makes you different, and, Graham, I don't think people *like* it when people are different."

Her face was lined from the strain of finding the words for this statement. It was as close to philosophy as her practical mind could come. She smoothed the wrinkles in her calico dress and patted a tendril straying from her thin braided hair. Her pale, colorless face was highlighted by a dull raspberry flush on her cheekbones.

Graham became very quiet and listened so intently that Annabel struggled again to find the right words.

"You're not *that* different, Graham. Just different enough to, well, you know, just enough to make people not want to be around you."

"Different how?"

"Too clean or something. Too polite. Too perfect."

Graham looked at her with amazement, knowing she had just given him a priceless bit of the puzzle. He would have to think about what she said, but he knew it was important. He fumbled for her stubborn little chin, and tilted it upward. He looked into her troubled blue eyes and, flushing deeply, kissed her thin pale lips. Annabel blinked rapidly, then, planting her hands on his chest, pushed him away.

"Why, Graham Chapman. Shame on you." She patted her hair into place again and scurried off toward her home. Graham smiled to himself.

He too started for home, taking a long thoughtful stroll, and slowly kicking a rock from one side of the road to the other. I'm better than they are, he thought. They know it, too. That's all that's wrong, just envy. I'm smarter and I work harder. It's not fair to have to lower myself to be just like they are, so they don't hate me. Their names for him kept going through his mind. Gray Man. Wolf Man. At one time he had had an intense interest in religion. But where had his striving after holiness gotten him?

Plop! The rock hit a bed of Queen Anne's lace and a grasshopper leaped for the next weedy haven.

There are ways to be different that are acceptable, thought Graham.

Even as people abhor saints, they adore royalty. Folks chuckled and whispered about the sexual escapades of the town banker, but the gossip didn't hurt his social standing. The key was money and power. He knew in that instant exactly what he wanted from life: enough wealth and influence to live exactly as he damn well pleased, forever.

For a second, he had a heavy, frantic sense of loss, of something supernatural being withdrawn, and he stopped and looked uneasily around him as though he had forgotten something he was so used to having with him that the removal brought tears to his eyes. He looked up at the sky. There was nothing there; no sign, no altering of light. Just a void. He was never troubled by another religious thought again as long as he lived.

What his parents were took root in him in a dimension that Theodore and Belle could not have predicted in their most optimistic plans for their son. From Theodore, he acquired an unerring instinct for manipulation, but his father's ability was pale beside his own. The crowning touch came from Belle. Through her tutelage he had acquired a deep respect for the power of appearances. Through the homage paid to Belle by the community, he became aware of people's yearning for the Nephilim, the giants of the earth. The average man *wanted* to be led.

Creating his new image began with breaking off with Annabel. He could not afford to be seen with such a little prig. Nevertheless, it cost him something he could not put a name to, to set aside this small, brittle person who had taught him so much.

When she asked him to take her to the next ice cream social, Graham looked her squarely in the eyes.

"Annabel, there are others who want to go out with you, and if we are always together, no one will ask you."

"Oh, Graham, I don't think so. I truly don't. You see, before you, no one paid very much attention." Her voice trailed off and her color deepened with the embarrassment of confession.

"Oh, but it's true. After all, I'm the one who hears what the boys say. I know for a fact that Joe Newland is sweet on you. It's just that you have such high standards compared to the rest of the girls that you're seen as a prize."

Annabel knew she was quality. She had always known this in her fierce little bones, and to think this was keeping the boys at bay.

Graham pressed his advantage. It was perfect. Now even if Joe didn't want to take her out, there was an escape.

"If Joe doesn't ask you out soon, remember sometimes it takes a while for a man to come forward for the girl he really wants. You'll have to be patient with those of us who are shy."

Her homely heart filled with hope and she batted her sparse eyelashes in bewilderment. To know she was so highly regarded by so many was almost more than she could bear. She would wait. The smile she gave Graham was almost beautiful.

He was sad and triumphant at the same time. He had always known Annabel wanted to be popular, wanted to be courted in spite of her priggish, banty-hen ways. In later years, he used this uncanny feel for the yearnings in a woman's heart to stoke banked fires. Dazzling beauties decorated his arm and his parlor, but he delighted in seeking out the spinsters with the tightly anchored hair twisted into hard little buns that suggested passion kept severely under control in order to be contained at all.

"What do you want to be, son?" Theodore asked.

Graham looked up, puzzled. Be? Then he understood. It was *the* question adults had been asking ever since he could remember. It was usually followed by "when you grow up," but not this time. He had just turned sixteen.

"Rich," said Graham. "I want to be rich, beyond all counting or imagination."

Theodore looked at Graham with a spark of interest.

"That so?"

"Yes. That's what I want."

Theodore chuckled. "Any idea how you plan to do this?"

"No, not yet. Hard work doesn't do it. I know that. I've watched and sometimes the people who work the hardest end up the poorest. In fact, they usually do."

Theodore was more than interested now. "You can have it given to you," he said. "That's the best way."

"But there's not too much chance of that in my case, is there, Dad?"

Theodore flushed. No, he and Belle were really just big ducks in a small pond and hadn't done too well financially.

"No, son. We don't have that much to give."

"Another way is luck," Graham continued. "Blind, silly luck. That's the way the great fortunes are made. But you can't count on that."

Well, well, well. There was more going on in the lad's head than Theodore had dreamed.

"Go on."

"The only way left for someone like me is to get a good idea for something people need terribly, and then get it for them before someone else does, and make them pay through the nose."

Theodore grinned. His son had perceived the genius of the American capitalistic system and summed it up in the most simple, comprehensive terms he had ever heard. There was a fair chance the lad would amount to something after all. In the meantime, thank God, it didn't look as though he were going to have to pay for more schooling.

"Just one more thing, Graham. Make them think they're happy with it after they've gotten it."

Theodore was seeing his son with fresh eyes. "Why don't you come into the store with me now, Graham? The business will be yours some day anyway."

"I want to be rich, Dad."

"Well, by God, now. We make plenty of money, your mom and I."

Graham's eyes didn't waver.

Theodore's face flushed with anger. "Don't need no kid looking down on us, especially our own. We're well thought of here, your ma and me, and don't you forget it. Don't need no stuck-up kid putting on airs. Just try it outside of Lucerne and see how far you get."

"O.K. I will some day," said Graham. He spoke softly to defuse his dad's temper. "I've got to get to bed now. Old Man Minkler's been riding me to death lately." He worked before and after school as a carpenter's apprentice. It was one of his secret pleasures, but he enjoyed Belle's concern when she thought he was working too hard.

The day he turned seventeen he left Lucerne for Pinkerton, Kansas, without telling a single person goodbye—not even Belle and Theodore.

The town had been picked far in advance on the information a drummer had given him. It sounded as though it were growing and there would be demand for his carpentry skills. Any other expanding town would do just as well, but it made him feel secure at night to be able to name the place where he was headed, and to know exactly just how much he had to have saved to get there.

He wanted to be a totally new person, with no parents and no past. Most of all, he did not want Theodore and Belle visiting and contaminating other people's perception of him. He was very short of money, and it had taken several nights for him to dream up a plan where he would be assured free room and board for as long as he liked, and it was essential that his parents not try to get in touch with him.

Graham was shocked by the squalor of the surroundings when he stepped off the stage. It had rained recently and the streets were muddy and cut with deep ruts where a teamster had flogged his horses out of the mire.

The narrow planks perilously placed above the mud just barely deserved the name of a sidewalk. Nevertheless, there was a briskness to the trade area that pleased him. It was what he had hoped he would find, and from the amount of building going on, the people intended to stay.

"Hotel Pinkerton" was crudely labeled on a pretentious fake front. Hotels existed to draw immigration. They were public improvements, like parks or schools, and were usually paid for by the town company that was promoting the town.

Graham walked inside and headed for the makeshift two-barrel desk held together with a plank board. An old Indian was huddled in the corner next to a cold pot-bellied stove. He was so still he appeared to be asleep or dead.

He was looking about for a bell to summon the desk clerk when suddenly a frail old man in filthy trousers and a greasy eyeshade came from the back room. He stared at Graham as though he had no right to be there and said nothing.

"I want a room," said Graham nervously. "My father and I, that is. He'll be arriving later."

The man continued to stare and Graham felt perspiration start on his upper lip.

"May I have a key," Graham blurted. The clerk snorted and rubbed his nose with contempt.

"God damn foreigner, hell no, you can't have no key. You'll have to make do like everyone else. No keys to any of the rooms. This ain't no whorehouse and God damn sure ain't no private room. There's just three kinds of rooms. One for married couples, one for women, and one for no-good, whiskey-drinking hell-raisers like you. You'll sleep with everyone else. First person to a pillow gets it. Same as for the covers. That's three bucks up front."

Graham's mouth fell open and his ears reddened with fury. The price was outrageous. He would think of something else tomorrow, but for now the main point was to get into a town, find a job, and figure out some way to make ends meet. He was determined not to let this foul-tempered little son-of-a-bitch undermine all his plans by causing him to lose his temper.

"My dad needs a room," he said evenly. "I don't want to quarrel with you. He'll be here tonight and we'll take whatever you've got. If we have to double with others, we will."

Graham wheeled around and went back to the sidewalk for his luggage. Hotels on the prairie were supposed to be hubs for business deals along with a place for community dances and occasional funerals, but he would be surprised if this one survived at all. His good humor returned as he clutched the valise, and he began to whistle. He had a place to spend the night.

Upstairs, he found a filthy room partitioned off with brown paper. A used chamber pot reeked in the corner and he clamped his teeth together in revulsion at the idea of spending even one night in a place like this. The bed was unstable and had a single hay-filled pillow. The wash basin was grime-rimmed and set next to a cracked pitcher. He sat down on the bed and put his head on his hands. He could not afford to be seen on the streets tonight. He had to stay in the nauseating room at all costs, because he would attract too much attention otherwise. He would make other arrangements tomorrow.

In the meantime, he would save the price of supper. The stench had ruined his appetite. Fully dressed, he flung himself across the bed and slept immediately. He roused only when two drunken cowboys stumbled into the room. They shifted him to make more space, and then they too fell into a deep sleep.

He was up at sunrise the next morning. This was the day he needed to be remembered.

He approached the desk clerk.

"My father did not come last night."

"So?"

"So, did you see him?"

"Jesus Christ, sonny. I wouldn't know your father from Adam's off-ox. So how would I *know* if I seen him or not?"

"Did any strangers come here?"

"Hell, yes. Strangers are here all the time. This is a hotel, you know."

Graham clenched his fists. He wanted to slug him. He wheeled around and went out onto the perilous boardwalk and began canvassing the town, going from one store to another.

"Have you seen a man about five foot ten, carrying a brown valise?"

He made it a point to be seen in each store, and all the while he watched for a place to stay. There had to be somewhere besides the stinking hotel. The first night was the only one that was important. It would seem strange to everyone to sleep out in the open to begin with, but now it would work to his advantage if he pleaded finances.

Conversation stopped when he entered the general store. One of the men continued his whittling and pretended not to see Graham; a mark of delicate prairie etiquette.

"Have you seen a man about five foot ten, with brown hair and a mustache? He's probably wearing a blue jacket and brown pants and carrying a brown valise."

"Can't say as I have," the merchant replied.

"I'm looking for my father. He was supposed to come last night from Omaha. I got a room for us in the hotel and he never did show up."

Several of the men grinned when he mentioned the hotel.

"Any man who can stand a night in that stinking flea trap can take anything."

"Who said I stood it? It nearly killed me. If I hadn't promised Dad I'd meet him there, I would have gotten out. God, the smell. Dad will probably be along tomorrow, but I'm not staying there again. I'll take my chances with the horses tonight."

A large red-headed man with a straggly beard nodded his approval. They had all slept in a stable at one time or another. It was clean and it was cheap. A covering of prairie feathers, two blankets to slip between, with a warming layer of hay on top was not bad sleeping. It sure as hell beat the hotel.

"Well," Graham said briskly. "Thanks. I'm sure Dad will be here by night. He's bringing in some lumber and we want to start doing a little building. Ma died last year and she had never wanted to move. After she was gone we decided to try making a living in a town that's going someplace, and looks like this one knows where it's headed for sure."

He was understood, right then, as being one of them. Decent folk trying to make an honest living. He and his father would no doubt be a splendid addition to the community. And bringing in lumber to boot. Wood for building was in such demand that Pinkerton just couldn't get enough.

Graham tipped his hat to the group, and hitching his thumbs in his pockets, he turned and walked out of the store. He grinned at the thought of the discussion he knew they would be having after he was out of earshot. He went to the combination eating house and saloon and ordered ham and eggs.

That evening he peered up and down the street, pretending to be on the lookout for his father. He plunked down his thirty-five cents for a corner in the livery stable that night, then counted his blessings.

76

By the third day, most of the citizens of Pinkerton were sharing his concern about the whereabouts of his father and uneasily scanning the horizon for a wagon.

That noon, the westbound Wells Fargo wagon drew up to the hotel. There were no passengers, and no one to be picked up, but the driver put off some freight and the mail. Graham followed the driver when he came out of the saloon and called him aside.

"Mister, can I talk to you for a minute?"

"Sure, kid." He was used to being approached for jobs and he supposed this was another hand that wanted to sign on.

"Mister, can you tell me what it costs to send something on out West?"

"Sure. Twenty-five cents for a middle-sized box and fifty cents for a large one." The driver scratched his head in bewilderment. The kid could have gotten this information from anyone.

Graham was careful to keep their conversation from being overheard. It was important just to be seen talking to the driver.

Impatiently, the Wells Fargo man hopped onto the seat and with a flick of the reins, pulled out. Graham watched him leave, then with a deep sigh, headed for the general store. Inside, he approached the cracker barrel crowd.

"The Wells Fargo man, that man. I just found out. Dad's dead. He was killed loading lumber at Omaha."

"Christ," someone said softly.

There was a silent shared sympathy for this proud, handsome boy who was already accepted as one of their own. "I can't leave," said Graham. "I haven't got any money."

He sat down on a seed sack and buried his face in his hands.

"Where's Pa's money? He had to have some when he died. Either that or lumber. One or the other. He took out all of our savings to make a start here."

"Probably long gone by now," piped up Ed. "By the time those thieving sons-a-bitches in Omaha got through. Probably picked cleaner than a whistle."

"The Wells Fargo man said that nobody knew what to do. They found my name and the name of this town on a scrap of paper. But he didn't know what I looked like or nothing when he came in this morning. Good thing I went up and asked him about Pa. They buried him anyway. Without me. Had to."

By that evening, every housewife in town knew there was a penniless orphan boy forced by cruel fate to sleep in a pile of hay in the livery stable. There was not a good woman among them who was not moved by Christian charity to do her duty for the lad.

Thus, Graham Chapman was assured of a bed and a hot meal, free, in practically any house in town. Most important was the community's acceptance of the presence of a young boy among them, without kith or kin, with no danger at all of anyone snooping into his background.

Finding a job came next. He had to get one fast. Having already established himself in people's minds as a serious carpenter, it was just a matter of approaching the right person. Building was going on at a feverish pace and he had all too many places to choose from. But he wanted more than just a job hammering nails. He needed information about buildings and towns and layouts and, most of all, a way to get rich.

One morning, he found himself watching a sweating giant of a man. He was heaving planks in front of men who were sawing as fast as they could work. He had a heavy black beard and under the open neck of the roughly woven homespun shirt was a filthy set of underwear with the top collar button gaping. He swore savagely at his hard-pushed employees and was made all the more formidable by a slight cast to his left eye that did not permit him to look at anyone perfectly square.

Graham studied him for a few minutes. He was everywhere at once, and for sheer volume, he could not be matched. He oversaw every detail of a huge crew of men. They were erecting new false front store buildings as fast as they could be slapped together.

Hiram Rosler, the owner of the local livery stable, joined Graham as he watched.

"Quite a sight, ain't it?"

"Damned if it isn't," said Graham. "But I don't get all of this. I've been in this town over a week now, and I know there's not enough people here for all these new buildings. What's going on?"

"Town fever," said Hiram. "It hits just about everyone out here. They think it's going to make them rich. They're not too far from right, either. The man who starts a town, lays it out and plats the lots, sure as hell doesn't die a pauper. The trick then is to lure settlers out here. You've got to have someone to sell the lots to."

"How do you get people out here in the middle of nowhere? It doesn't make sense to me," said Graham.

"Doesn't make sense even if you understand it. Only the ones at the top get rich. But if you can get a railroad to come through, or get your town to be the county seat, the town will live forever. It's a known fact. There's just one town in a county that will survive."

"How do you get a railroad or a county seat?"

"By getting enough people to come to a town. Everyone wants to settle where there's a railroad. It's only natural if they homestead that they want a place that's handy to ship things from. They don't want to haul grain for miles just to get to sell it."

"O.K.," said Graham, "but who cares if a town is the county seat?"

"Everyone." Hiram took careful aim and spat tobacco at a dog lying against the side of the feed store. The dog opened one eye in annoyance and Hiram laughed and hooked his thumbs under his suspenders.

"Hell, man. *Everybody* wants a county seat. If you have to pay taxes or file papers, no one wants to drive a team fifty miles just to do a little business."

Graham pursued the conversation with mounting excitement. He needed to know more.

"How do you get a county seat?"

"By having enough people to vote it in. Besides, the railroads like to go through county seat towns. Usually the people there are serious enough about staying to finance bonds to pay to get the tracks laid."

"How do you get people to move here?"

"Lie like hell," Hiram explained cheerfully. "After all, you're here. Ain't you read no paper yet? Come on. I'll buy you one."

He and Graham walked over to the *Prairie Crier* and pushed open the door. Inside was a bandy-legged man with a green celluloid eyeshade scribbling furiously on a piece of paper.

"Morning, Hiram," the editor called to the livery stable owner as they walked in. He acknowledged Graham with a nod.

"Morning, Ethan."

"Be with you in a minute. Let me finish this sentence," said Ethan Wheeler, turning back to his work.

Graham took advantage of the "minute" to look over the office. There were law shingles hung on one wall. The editorial office was also clearly the bedroom and the kitchen. The bed was a jumble of coverlets, towels, and cooking utensils with a huge pan of rising dough plopped right in the middle. A half-eaten ham bone lay next to it. On the wall was tacked a string of onions and corn. A saddle hung from a wooden peg.

Wheeler scratched his eye and with a flourish finished what he was writing. Laying down his pen, he clasped his hands behind his head, cocked one ankle over his knee, yawned happily, and stretched.

"Whew. I've been writing more than five hours now. I'm glad for a break. The editor of the *Muleskinner Daily* is spreading the most vicious lies I've ever heard about our fair city, and they need to be stopped. It usually works to fight fire with fire. He'll have a hard time getting out of this." He picked up a paper and began to read.

"We will protect the reputation of our fair Pinkerton as a lover would protect his sweetheart from the horde that would despoil her.

79

The paper of our rival editor, Colonel Palmquist, has been distributed over the county for the purpose of misleading the public and injuring our city.

"There were never lies so black as these, and the miserable rascals who spread them will reap the whirlwind of indignation and destruction which they so richly deserve. Colonel Palmquist, as residents of the county are well aware, is a man who died influentially, mentally, financially, and politically, in Omaha, Nebraska, and now has been transplanted to Pinkerton where he sells old and shelf-worn goods in his miserable little store. To subsidize this failing adventure, he spreads lies through his little paper, which is seldom purchased and then is instantly recognized for the low-class scandal rag it is, by people of breeding."

Graham suppressed an impulse to laugh out loud. He could not believe the man was serious. It was the most inflammatory rhetoric he had ever heard. Hiram grinned. Ethan was also the mayor of the town as well as a practicing attorney and the holder of a homestead claim. His writing style was not unusual for pioneer editors. No holds were barred to lure people to a town. The sampling was mild compared to some of the columns Ethan Wheeler had turned out.

Graham picked up one of last week's papers.

"Do you do these ads yourself?"

"Oh, hell, no. I do well to think up enough copy for the two blank sheets. The insides are printed by a ready-print company in Chicago or Saint Paul, then shipped here. It's full of high-falutin' advertising, with left-over blank pages for our town's news."

The paper was full of so many inaccuracies that Graham was speechless. Pinkerton was off to a splendid start, but it was hardly an established town.

Graham knew the new brick hotel mentioned did not exist and the pure clear water the editor bragged about had such a high alkali content that it would eat the commas off his type. The climate was miserably unpredictable and not the consistent eighty-five degrees, give or take a little, that Ethan Wheeler reported. It was crazy.

Ethan beamed. "What do you think of our city by now, young man? It's something, isn't it? People and businesses coming in every day."

"Yes, it's really something," Graham said. "I'm glad I landed here."

The editor grinned his approval. This was the type of attitude that thrilled his soul.

By the sincere gleam in Wheeler's eyes, Graham realized he actually believed the lies reported in the paper were future truths—events so close to being already accomplished that in his mind they were practically history.

"Well," said Hiram, "we should be going. Graham here lost his father and he needs a job. Won't be any trouble finding one, of course, but he wants to get started as soon as possible."

Wheeler nodded in sympathy.

They left the office and headed down the sidewalk.

"How can he live with himself?"

"Old Ethan? Hell, he's one of the best. We're lucky to have him. Some newspapers are just fronts for town companies to steal homesteads. They're the sons-a-bitches. That's what happened to old man Cornwall. He busted a gut for five years trying to do something with that place of his. Proving up came at a bad time, anyway. He was trying to get his corn picked and supposed a couple of weeks wouldn't make no difference. Besides, it was one hundred miles to Oberlin, the nearest place to pay up. Now you can see why everyone wants a county seat near them."

"One hundred miles just to file a piece of paper?" said Graham.

"Yeah. Anyhow, he sold his corn and had enough money to finish processing his claim and when he finally got to Oberlin he found out that town companies were just waiting for men like him. The minute he was late, they arranged for a legal notice of the claim being forfeited to be published in the paper and after it was published three times, that was it. Someone else bought it for a song."

"Sounds like a good deal for someone."

"Hell, yes," said Hiram. "And you can just bet it's the railroads backing the town companies, not the poor bastard who came out to this godforsaken country for nothing. Anyhow, some papers are just started to publish these legal notices. No one else ever sees them or gets to read them, and that's why forfeitures are published in them. At least Ethan's paper is legitimate."

"He's sounding better all the time," said Graham.

"Old Ethan's not bad. You just have to learn to read between the lines, is all."

"Has he been here long?"

"Sure. He was here before Pinkerton. The paper *always* comes first, ahead of the town. It's the only way to get a town started."

Graham watched the building being done with rising excitement. This was his opportunity, he was sure of it.

Suddenly his thoughts were interrupted by anguished screams as a young man, no older than himself and standing just ten feet away, made a horrible miscalculation. His ax had slipped in his sweaty hands as he cut the plank and he laid open his foot lengthwise from the third toe back to the instep.

Graham fought back nausea as the man drew up into a tight raw ball of pain. Hiram knelt beside him immediately.

"Get a doctor," he yelled. "He's hurt bad."

He ran toward Dr. Brummeyer's office, but someone else was there first and the doctor was already reaching for his bag.

The old doctor's shoulders drooped as he examined the mangled foot. He sighed and reached for a vial of morphine to put the man out of his pain. It was probably the only thing he would be able to do. The gaping wound was slit through the bone, no doubt about it, and he would be lucky if gangrene didn't set in and cause him to lose his leg, if he lived at all.

He and Hiram grabbed his shoulders and legs and carried him into his office. He would keep it clean and pray. If it didn't kill the lad, he would surely be a cripple.

The black-bearded giant supervising the crew treated the accident as a mere interruption in the day's work. "You there," he bellowed at Graham. "Want a job?"

Graham hesitated for only an instant, then walked forward.

"Yes."

The man looked him up and down and nodded.

"Two bits a day and no time off."

"It's a deal," said Graham.

Hiram looked at him sharply and took him aside.

"Christ, kid, you don't want to work for him. That's Black Jack Tucker. He'll kill a kid like you. It takes a hell of a man to work alongside of him. Pick somebody decent who'll treat you right."

"I don't want someone decent," snapped Graham. "I want to work for

the man who can teach me the most. And it's him. I've been watching. He's the man who gets things done."

"Everyone hates his guts," said Hiram. "He's town company for one thing and for another he don't let nothing stand in his way. For God's sake leave him alone. There's plenty of other places to hire on."

They argued briefly, then Hiram shrugged his shoulders as he watched Graham roll up his sleeves and join Jack Tucker's crew.

It was typical of Graham's allure that his friends never did see him as being one of Jack Tucker's men. He was always looked upon as a young man who had been taken advantage of and not really one of the town company at all, when actually Graham was one of Jack Tucker's most loyal employees.

The sun was shining directly overhead when he began and there was no breeze. The air rang with the rhythmic thump of axes and the rasping irritation of hand saws as the teeth serrated the too-green wood. The occasional shouts of the men coordinating the work disturbed the cadence of the crew.

Graham exalted in the feel of the ax as he bent to the job. All his frustrations and the burden of the decisions he had been making were chopped away with the ax. He felt an enormous release of nervous tension with the demand of physical labor. A hint of a smile played at the corners of his sensitive mouth. He knew no one expected him to last. He did not have the look that suggested a capacity for this killing work. Well, they didn't know Belle, and he had learned well from her. Certainly no one suspected the depths of his pride.

His shoulders ached miserably by the time the sun went down. He was so sore he felt like just dropping his ax there beside him, and his legs were like numbed tree trunks. He struggled to control a spasmodic involuntary trembling. He placed the ax carefully in the supply wagon and anchored his hands under the rim of his waistband to still the fatigued shaking that would betray to all the toll this day's work had taken.

Jack Tucker grinned and clamped down on his cigar as he watched Graham neatly line up his tools. He watched the lad try to hide his tiredness. That alone signaled a quality he had been looking for for a long, long time. Time would tell, but this one surely bore watching. Time, and the work ahead, would test the worth of any man.

By God, but he was proud of this town, Jack Tucker decided. It had well-constructed, decent buildings that would not fall apart, and that was more than most town companies could say.

Tomorrow he would start the hotel. A good hotel was crucial to the town's ability to attract speculators. Men of breeding and money could not be expected to stay in that fleabag. It always made a good impression on the people back East to be able to read of a hotel in the paper and when prosperous men passed through, trading in lots and claims, there was always a better chance for a town to persuade them to leave their money there if they had a decent place to stay.

Jack Tucker did not leave the type or order of buildings to chance. There was a logical sequence of additions that were the most likely to attract people. However, just any buildings at all were welcome to most of the harried settlers, who were often so disheartened at the exaggerations in the brochures that lured them out that *any* sign of civilization was a wonder.

One town builder cheerfully reported later in the *History of Kansas and Emigrant's Guide* that "no man was considered a hero unless he could describe Kansas as a paradise."

Jack Tucker scoffed at other town builders so lacking in skills they had to rely on prefabricated structures. Mail order architecture offered buildings of every description from one-room dwellings to four-hundred-seat churches. The prefabs were shipped West in freight wagons, boxcars, and riverboats.

One summer, when the caliber of man Jack had attracted had been outstanding, he had even beaten Leavenworth's spectacular record of a steam sawmill, two brickyards, one three-story hotel, four boardinghouses, five dry goods stores, five groceries, five saloons, two boot and shoe stores, two saddlery shops, one tin shop, two blacksmith shops, and one hundred tenant houses—all constructed in a mere eight months' time.

The financial stakes were tremendous, but he was limited because he could not trust anyone but himself to do a good job of overseeing his crews. But now Graham had come along.

In one month's time he watched the boy become a man. Graham's long muscles lengthened into stringy cords and became rock-hard, but still with slender proportions. His face darkened under the relentless glare and his ash blond hair became handsomely streaked.

At last the town was a respectable size. Even though it was far from complete, it was there, and it was a genuine attempt at a town, not just a series of lots platted on paper with no real attempt to make it go. Jack was proud of it and now the work would be up to everyone else.

Pinkerton sponsored a celebration to attract homesteaders and other potential customers to the auction of lots. Graham wandered down the main street and studied the changes that had occurred since he first stepped off the stage. The street was faced with buildings—a new hotel, a saloon, a blacksmith shop, a dry goods and general store, a drug store, and a combination barber and bath house, along with fifteen rental houses.

Jack Tucker came up behind him and laid a hand on his shoulder.

"Something to see, isn't it?"

"God, yes," said Graham. "Doesn't seem possible."

People were beginning to trickle into the town. They had come for miles and miles. Some were lucky enough to have horses, but others were on foot. All were eager to see if the town really existed. They enjoyed the extravagance of a free oyster supper supplied by the town company. It was served with such generous hospitality that the luxury-starved homesteaders looked upon the company as the right hand of God Almighty, rather than the right hand of the railroad.

One small boy clung to his mother's skirts. The sounds and colors were so strange after a life of total isolation that he was too bewildered to let go.

Some of the business buildings were already occupied. They had been sold at a low price to get people established before the celebration, thereby increasing the worth of lots. Their wares were all displayed to the very best advantage today. The dry goods and general store was loaded with pots and pans and flour and shoes and marvelous bolts of calico that drew the women like brightly colored magnets.

The woman Graham had noticed coping with the clinging little boy earlier fingered some of the calico wistfully, then quietly wiped away a tear. She found her husband outside the barber shop and beckoned him to one side. Graham saw the pair begin to argue and he moved closer to hear what they were saying.

"It wouldn't be giving up, Robert," the woman pleaded desperately, "no one in their right mind could call us quitters. We've stuck it out for three years now, and it just ain't worth it."

"Just two more years to go, Sharon. Just two years and it will be ours."

The woman began to cry.

"*What* will be ours? Just what? A house made of dirt that's crawling with bugs when it's not freezing to death, and ground so hard it's killing you. *Bob*, it's killing you. I can see it. For God's sake let's move to town before we put in another crop."

"We can't afford it," he said bleakly. "We just can't."

The woman continued to beg. She smoothed her patched and faded dress over her work-weary body. Her thin colorless hair was drawn into a pathetically small bun under her bonnet.

"We've got to be able to. We've got to find a way. Surely there's something you can do. At least there's water here and food and people." She started to cry again.

"People are coming in every day. If we had a business here, I know it would work. I just know it."

"Damn it, woman. What do you expect me to do? Just march right up and buy a lot?"

She shook her head slowly and continued to weep. Those nearby had turned their heads in embarrassment, pretending not to hear, and in some of the women's eyes was a leaping flicker of bitterness in sympathy with the woman's predicament.

Graham watched Jack Tucker study the couple. Tucker looked debonair today in his tailored pants and jacket. The cigar clamped between his teeth and the heavy gold watch fob set him apart from the homesteaders. He came up behind the couple and discreetly cleared his throat. When they turned, he immediately swept his hat off his head and began to speak.

"Pardon me, sir and madam. The press of the crowd was such that I was within earshot of your conversation and I believe I can be of some assistance. I believe you would like to move to town, but do not at this time find it possible financially."

The man moved protectively toward his wife and child and the three stood quietly, waiting for him to continue. Robert slowly nodded, the shame of imminent failure in his eyes.

Jack Tucker continued, "It is apparent to even the most casual observer that you are a family of uncommonly high caliber. In fact, just the type we want to have settle in our town, and perhaps my company can be of some assistance."

A sudden ray of hope lit the woman's eyes.

"My company is prepared to offer to people such as yourselves a lot here in town that you will own outright, along with a modest home. And if you would like, sir, we could arrange terms for a business building."

Tears of gratitude began to well up in the woman's eyes, and she reached for her husband's arm.

Robert looked at her. It sounded too good to be true. A second chance for them, and in a town to boot. Even his wife did not know, could never begin to understand the gut-wrenching depths of his despair when he faced a field, bone-tired, scared to the core of his soul, with the immensity of the prairie taunting him. In some places breaking the sod was nearly impossible. And in the corners of his mind, he felt like the biblical Jacob, who had wrestled with God, sometimes winning, sometimes losing, but always emerging changed and crippled.

He knew in his heart that it was not worth it, and had been too proud to say so. The land was just not worth the price it exacted. And here, like a blooming miracle he was being offered another way. It *had* to have a hitch someplace.

"I don't understand, sir. What is the price for all of this?"

"The price is nothing. Practically nothing, when weighed against all the benefits. The price is simply your homestead."

The woman laughed with bitter amusement. They could have it and gladly. It held no joy for her, no lovely memories at all. She shook her head in wonder. A mere hundred sixty acres of untillable soil, in exchange for this Eden. It was the chance of a lifetime.

Robert flushed with confusion. A warning bell was sounding in his mind. Mingled with this was a strong sense of gratitude for the balm that was being offered. There was a way out. But God—his homestead. A full one hundred sixty acres that had some improvements on it now. It was his *place*. However, there was another thing to consider. If he went back, it would surely cost him his Sharon. Already she drifted over the house like a wisp of smoke, distant, seldom speaking. But his homestead. For a little dot of a lot.

Sharon watched his face and realized that Bob was hesitating. He couldn't possibly be thinking of refusing. She squeezed her son's hand so tightly he gave a sudden yelp of pain.

Jack Tucker did not press.

"This is a big decision," he said, "and not one to be taken lightly. Why don't you think it over. There's no need to decide right now."

He bowed to each of them, then strolled over to Graham.

"Is this going to be a *lasting* town, Mr. Tucker?" Graham asked quietly.

"Who knows? They're all a gamble. At least it's an honest try here. That's more than some can say. If we get a railroad or a county seat, we've got a winner. Or sometimes just selling enough lots will do it."

"What happens to the kind of people you were just talking to, if the town doesn't go? They'll have a tiny worthless lot in the middle of nowhere and have lost all their land to boot. One hundred sixty acres can be a hell of a lot of ground."

Jack Tucker shrugged.

"If they play their cards right, they could just as easily be stinking rich. All depends on how it goes. They may have just traded their homestead for a prime lot in a town that's going to be an inspiration to the whole prairie. And where's the crime in that? Maybe they're just not farmers by nature, but merchants. If the town folds, they'll just move their business to another town. It's done easily enough."

Graham nodded. It was not illegal and in its own way actually made sense. But whether or not town companies were a boon to the West, the fact remained that an enormous number of homesteads, nearly two-thirds of them, ended up being owned by the railroads, who were usually sponsoring the town companies to begin with.

The day sparkled with sunshine and hope, and was a great success. The visitors to the town were so exhilarated by the presence of others that they were receptive to any type of propaganda. By sundown, a full three-fourths of the people were ready to locate in Pinkerton.

No one was more delighted than Ethan Wheeler. The editor was everywhere at once, urging people to settle in this town that had just been an idea some six months ago. By evening the price of lots had risen beyond anyone's expectations. Bob and Sharon Doolittle had signed their contract that noon, deeding their homestead for a town lot, and were well-to-do by nightfall.

It was impossible not to catch each other's enthusiasm. The bidding accelerated with fierce competition for prime locations until all three hundred twenty acres were sold.

The lines in Sharon Doolittle's face softened. With a trembling hand she touched the calico in the dry goods store. For three years now, she had strictly denied herself the luxury of even looking. *I can have a new dress*, she thought with amazement. I can have a new dress, and there's three colors to choose from. And she promptly burst into tears.

A trio consisting of two fiddles and a French harp was tuning up, and the women were hushed with the wonder of merriment so long overdue.

The children's eyes shone. Some had never been off their homestead before, and this was the first time some had ever heard a musical instrument. They did not know how to make friends. With great shyness, which was overcome by a yearning for playmates, they moved from furtive peeks from behind their mothers' skirts to solemn little questions.

"What's your name?"

"Jim. And I've got a frog."

By evening, with the instincts of migratory birds, they seemed to have been born knowing that children were supposed to chase one another and drive adults to madness.

Several days after the wonder of the celebration had faded, Jack Tucker asked Graham to come by after work.

"Chapman, how would you like to be my assistant?"

"I can't think of a greater accomplishment than to start towns and fill them with people."

Jack nodded. "I'll show you the ropes, then in a couple of years, we'll talk about a more profitable arrangement. You've got the kind of brains—and business instincts—that are hard to come by."

"Mr. Tucker, I just don't know what to say."

"Don't try. Just get cracking. I'll soon be done here. We need to be moving on to the next place."

"Where will that be?"

"Anywhere we want. Congress passed a law in 1844 for townsites. Three hundred twenty acres can be set aside for a town. Just pick your spot, pay the fee, and start building. Our town company, which is the Hamilton Cranston, by the way, is backed by the Union Pacific itself. They will supply us with everything we need. You're young, Chapman. That's another reason I want you to work under me for a while. The men need to know that you're my right hand man. Don't want no smart aleck testing your mettle till you get more meat on your bones. You're looking better every month."

Graham flushed.

"Well, that's all. Tomorrow morning we'll head out. Oh, and, Graham, just one more thing." Black Jack frowned as he delicately flicked the ash of his cigar. "We find that it's best not to mention the name of the town company or even the railroad. Better politics to name a town company after some local citizen or a nearby river or something like that. Makes folks feel more at home. Big money makes 'em edgy. We want 'em trusting."

Graham understood. "Like my daddy used to say, 'People, like trout, can be had for the tickle.'"

Black Jack grinned. "Finding the right tickle is damned important, boy. You'll find out just *how* important in the months ahead."

Graham returned to Pinkerton two years later. He had mastered as many of the details of town-building as possible, and he was worldly to a degree that Black Jack would never be. Whenever they were near a town of any size, he indulged his fondness for clothing and women. The ladies adored him, flirted with him, trusted him blindly and completely because of the pains he took to flatter them and let them save face.

Just as he never lost his temper or displayed an inappropriate emotion, he never allowed entanglements with women to develop to the stage where they were messy. He left them happy, confused, and with a feeling of being privileged to have experienced one great love in their lifetime. As Graham developed an awareness of the marks and trappings of culture, he began to admire the fine, noble women he occasionally found along the way, and he knew they were as rare as a four-leaf clover.

Jack Tucker had told him to stake off a town wherever he wanted to, as long as it did not compete with any existing town that he owned. Graham applied all the expertise he had acquired. This was a chance to become Tucker's partner.

There had to be water. After investigating sites within a forty-mile radius of Pinkerton, he found a spot near a grove of trees with a creek nearby. He looked it over and then pulled out his stakes. The perfect place. No doubt about it. He was a townsman. He was going to be rich. He filed at the nearest land office, then reported back to Tucker.

"Where do I find an editor?"

"What's wrong with yourself?"

"I'm no editor."

"You can write your name and know the alphabet, don't you?"

"Sure," said Graham with a laugh, "but that doesn't make me an editor."

"It does out here! That's all it takes. Just start writing and another editor will come. There's always journeymen leaving some town that has folded, looking for work. In the meantime, you're the town. So get out there and do a good job, and I'll send off for your printing press."

He set off two days later for the new town of Brookline City, which he and Black Jack owned in partnership with the Hamilton Cranston Town Company. It would be known as the Brookline City Town Company here. He and Black Jack would split the profits from the sale of lots and the Union Pacific Railroad would have another organized county ready to vote bonds to finance the laying of tracks.

When he arrived at the site, he climbed down from the wagon and unloaded his supplies. He stacked his belongings in an orderly pile beside the gentle rise of a hill that would do for his dugout. He had a decent if unappetizing supply of food, one extra horse, a tripod cooking pot, matches, some tools for digging, an extra change of clothes, perhaps enough covers to keep from freezing to death, a deck of cards, and the rude makings of a printing press.

The type for his press had to be set by hand and then inked with a messy, uneven roller. A lever was then yanked to make an impression, then the job press was kicked by foot. The weights and levers were heavy. It was exhausting, primitive, physical labor.

Ethan Wheeler had given him information on the mechanics and also supplied him with his first patent sheets. With some reluctance, he dug out an old press and showed Graham how to operate it.

"Don't start a town near here. I'll ruin you if you try it."

"No chance of that," said Graham. "A man would be a fool to try to compete with Pinkerton."

"The type's not all the same size," warned Wheeler, "but it will have to do, until you can afford to send for something better. People like to read about themselves, so talk up what they do. Don't forget, Graham, you're starting a real town. Some days that's the only thing that will pull you through. The whole thing will get to you sometimes. For instance—" He did not complete the thought. His normally direct gaze faltered. He started to say more, then clamped his teeth together. Graham had been charged with beginning a town, and the things he would have to do would stick in his craw from time to time. Either he would be able to do it, or he wouldn't. It was that simple.

Graham spread his feather tick out on the prairie, and pillowed his head on his saddle. All the subtle colors of the sunset were before him, but he didn't see a thing. He was too busy counting houses in his mind.

He tackled the dugout at first light. After two hours his arms began to ache, but he felt a quiet exaltation at the pile of dirt that was accumulating.

He ate just enough beef jerky at noon to quiet his stomach, not wanting to lose any more time than he had to. He had brought everything he needed for a primitive dugout. Digging the hole was easy enough. All he really cared about was housing himself and the printing press.

Cutting sod by hand was impossible. By the second day, he decided the long trip back to Pinkerton to borrow a grasshopper plow was even worth leaving his belongings unguarded.

He returned two days later with the sod cutter that was coveted on the prairie. It shortened the time it took to build, and made uniform blocks. He also brought back real panes of glass for the windows. It was important his dugout look as impressive as possible to the citizens. In his mind, this town had already become a city; elegantly platted and inhabited by charming, genteel people.

He hitched the grasshopper plow to his horse and watched the long, continuous strips ripple up. The blade was very sharp and did not turn the earth over like a regular plow, but gouged out a twelve-inch-wide strip that was three inches deep. Later that afternoon, as he broke the strips into two-foot-long blocks, he wished he had burned off the grass first. He had been advised to do so, but had hesitated for fear the fire would get away. Now he was afraid the blocks would settle unevenly as the grass dried.

He pounded short timbers that would support the door frame firmly into the floor, then began laying the sod strips. By noon, he was ready to insert the casing for the window. He laid a strip of wood on the sod, then short planks on the sides where the window would go and laid sod up to the opening. The frame was holding easily, and he nailed the side to the ends of the short boards he had laid between the sod bricks.

By evening he had made a good start. He decided to call it a day and had just rolled out his feather ticking when he heard glass splinter. He turned and saw his precious window had shattered into tiny slivers. The weight of the top layer of sod on the window frame had settled to put tremendous pressure on the glass. He was so disappointed he could have bawled, not only for the delay, but for the glass itself, which had come dearly and was not always obtainable. The wall had collapsed just before sundown, so he had to wait until morning to begin again.

He was up at dawn and began carefully searching out each fragment of glass. It was sure to be useful for something. Then, with great care, he pulled down the rest of the wall and began to lay it again. He was midway through the second layer when he realized there was no way to rebuild a single wall as now the corners would not interlock. He walked off several paces from the dugout and his hands trembled with anger. Stoically, he turned back and began to take down all of the walls. It took him until noon to get everything apart, but he did not dare waste any of his lumber. It had to be done. That night, the whole structure had been rebuilt.

Wearily, he stretched out on the ground and slept. He awoke forty-five minutes later from hunger and began to gnaw on some jerky. Still tired, he lay back down and rested his head on his saddle. An abrupt boom catapulted him to his feet. His house had collapsed, again. He ran over and looked at the damage. He picked up a piece of sod brick and examined it. It crumbled easily to the touch. Once sod had been used, it could never be reused. And as his instincts had warned him, not burning the grass first resulted in the structure settling unevenly.

He was too tired to curse. He lay down and slept, totally exhausted. In the morning he was overwhelmed with hopelessness. He was so tired he could hardly force himself to begin. This time, however, he applied everything he had learned so far. He plowed a firebreak and burned off the sod, then cut his strips. By evening, he had a fine dugout. Like most settlers, although he had begun in total ignorance of the methods for building with sod, except for some instructions and advice passed on by others, by the time he finished, he had learned everything there was to know.

He came very close to having an accident when he set the ridge pole. The thought of lying injured and helpless, totally alone in the middle of nowhere, depressed him. The window, which had been reconstructed from the salvaged wood, was now covered with a buffalo robe. It wasn't glass, but it would do. At the sight of his printing press, sitting in a corner, his spirits revived. Suddenly the room seemed cozy and comfortable.

The next morning he started to work on the blank white pages of his patent sheets, pure and empty and ready to be imprinted. Finally he settled beside the light coming through the door and began to write. He was exhilarated by the sense of power, of the potential for creating and controlling.

"The great Eden of the West," he began,

transforming the Great American Desert to an area of fertility and plenty, was begun last week by a colony of merchants and bankers, unsurpassed in their ability to evaluate financial opportunity. The new town of Brookline City, in the lush state of Kansas, has been platted by experts for maximum growth. Although settlers are arriving daily, there are still lots available for those with vision to appreciate opportunity.

Graham stared thoughtfully at the floor. There ought to be something for the ladies. Inspired, he continued:

The ladies of Brookline City were entertained last week at a literary tea and recitation day at the home of Miss Abby Kindrick, a recent arrival to Brookline City, who intends to start a school.

He worked hard on his first issue. He carved out wood blocks to advertise an imaginary bank willing to loan money for building, and in fact all sorts of essential goods and services that newcomers might be interested in.

It was evening before he had his copy written, and yet another day before he had set the wooden type. When the first copy had been inked and printed, he read the pages through, made the necessary corrections, and then began to print the blank papers.

When he had accumulated a respectable pile, he saddled his horse and rode back to town with the stack carefully packed. They were shipped back East from Pinkerton. He replaced his supplies and headed back to his dugout. He wanted to be around when the people started arriving.

Before he began to work on the next issue of the paper, he decided to plat his town. He did not have the type of pencils necessary to produce the lines he liked, but he made do with what he had available, and mapped out his streets, with names.

He provided for schools: one elementary, one normal, and a good academy for female education. There was a park, a fairground, and a variety of churches. He then began to measure and stake the land. All three hundred twenty acres were divided in two days' time, and he winced at the contrast between the picture he had portrayed in the paper and the reality. All that was really here was himself, two horses, and some shop-worn equipment. It would all *be* true in a short time, however.

He waited for the rush of people, and spent his days dreaming up intriguing items for his blank pages.

One morning, a wagon lumbered over the horizon. In it was squeezed the Flynn family and all their worldly possessions. The woman perched tenaciously on the seat, clutching a nine-month-old baby to her bosom. Three somber, red-headed children peered through the puckered canvas opening. The man pulled up beside the orderly stakes and spoke curtly to the young man sitting beside him.

Graham stepped forward to greet the family.

"Welcome, stranger, to Brookline City."

Grenelda Flynn looked Graham coldly in the eye and returned his greeting.

"You lying, thieving, egg-sucking son-of-a-bitch. God damn you whoring God damn bastard to lie like this."

All the color drained from Graham's face. He had never heard a woman swear before, beyond a simple damn, and her invective was delivered in such measured, even tones that every word stood separately. She continued in the same quiet monotone, using phrases Graham had never even heard men use. The children sat with stony faces and did not lift an eyebrow. Their mother's cursing did not alarm them or even attract their attention.

Her husband, who had not shown a bit of interest in the conversation, suddenly slapped his hands on his knees as though he had come to a decision.

"It could be worse, Mother. It's a damn sight better than anything we've seen so far, and we've got to light somewhere. At least this place has water. The last two so-called towns ain't even had water. We can stop long enough for us to rest up."

Grenelda's face twitched, showing the first signs of feminine vulnerability. She took a long, trembling breath, and the lines on her face deepened with despair. Graham had the good sense not to defend himself at this moment. He knew he would be hopelessly drawn into a losing argument with a person who already disliked him intensely.

He lifted his arms to the first freckle-faced chubby red-headed girl.

"Come on down, sweetheart."

She jumped forward eagerly, and the little boy did the same, but the older daughter stared at Graham with suspicion. The older son had a shock of dark auburn hair and cold green eyes. He did not smile as he studied Graham. Nearly a man, he turned and looked at his mother with an adult's concern.

Graham studied the silent family. By God, if this wasn't something. Grenelda was no gentlewoman, for sure, but by the sound of her, she was a stayer, so he hid his momentary disappointment at the caliber of people he had attracted, and briskly began to hand down their meager supplies.

The evening passed in wary silence. Graham was at a loss for words. Too much of an attempt to cover up would only result in furthering their contempt. The Flynns knew what was going on by now, as well as he did. But it was absolutely true there was going to be a town here. He had to convince them of that.

He saddled up the next morning and left for Pinkerton. It was still too dangerous to try to talk to the Flynns at this point. They needed to see

94

some action. He knew he didn't have to worry about their leaving. Their supplies were so scant, and their exhaustion so total, the family was immobilized.

Jack Tucker did not need any persuasion to call on the newcomers. Brookline City was located a healthy forty miles from Pinkerton, and he had a large financial stake in this new town also. He piled his wagon full of lumber right away and struck out with Graham, who had asked Ethan Wheeler to go with them.

The team drew up in front of the Flynn family, and Tucker nodded at them, as though he could barely be bothered with introductions. He jumped from the wagon, as did Ethan, and they hurried over to the townsite; the conglomeration of stakes on which all their hopes were pinned.

"O.K. Looks like everything is in order for the builders," said Tucker.

He suddenly wheeled around to Graham.

"We'll begin in three more weeks. I understand the banker's family will be here in just ten days. You'll just have to do the best you can to make them comfortable," he said for the Flynns' benefit. "Tell them we'll be coming right along. That other family didn't say what they planned to do, so there's no point in worrying in advance. There'll be plenty of buildings here, and they can take their choice. Oh, yes, and signs. We'll bring a load out with us, for all types of businesses."

The Flynns stood open-mouthed, and listened to this powerful man in his handsome brocade coat, as he whirled from stake to stake, barking comments at Graham. He confirmed the delivery of every item on the lithograph that had lured them here to begin with, and then shook hands all round.

"You folks are very fortunate," he said heartily. "Very fortunate indeed, to be in the hands of this kind of man. My, but there are some rascals dealing in townsites right now, and very few indeed who have the character of Mr. Chapman here. Fine hands indeed."

With that, he looked at Ethan Wheeler.

"Ready? If we're lucky, we can be back by the end of the month."

Ethan had not been idle either. While Jack Tucker was dazzling the Flynns with the news that this was going to be a bona fide legitimate town, he had been judiciously commenting to the family on the qualifications of Graham himself.

The bandy-legged little editor sighed and looked guilelessly at Grenelda.

"So sad, really. He was actually orphaned when he was but a lad of twelve, and had made his dying father a promise on his deathbed that he would carry out his daddy's goal to begin decent cities for people to live in. You've heard of his father, of course, Senator Chapman?"

The Flynns nodded eagerly. They hadn't actually heard of Senator Chapman, but Ethan was casting such a hypnotic spell they believed they had.

Grenelda's eyes brimmed with tears. The son of a real senator, charged with such an important task. And so young. So noble too, and the *things* she had said to him! She turned scarlet with embarrassment. She would make it up to him if it was the last thing she ever did in her life.

The two men left, and the Flynn family, with a reverent look at Graham, rolled up their sleeves and began to work.

The next day brought two more wagons, and Grenelda Flynn was the most passionately effective ambassador for the town that Graham could ever have found. The women were reassured by her frank, cheerful optimism. Clearly, Brookline City was destined for greatness.

True to promise, Jack Tucker arrived in three weeks, and through word of mouth, the townsite was soon dotted with so many tents it looked like an overgrown cotton patch. The air was filled with the sounds of frenzied building.

Later, historians would agree that the speed with which towns sprang up on the Kansas prairies was one of the most amazing social phenomena in America's history.

Graham was so exhilarated at the progress that his rhetoric was unsurpassed. The trouble was, however, that it was only slightly more flowery than what he had been publishing before. The only difference was that what he was writing now was *almost* truth. People *were* arriving daily, and it was just a matter of time before people would start gravitating naturally toward their rightful occupations.

This was the American dream—to seize unlimited opportunity and fulfill one's destiny. This was Kansas, and these were its people. *Ad Astra per Aspera*, "To the Stars Through Difficulties," was their motto. With it came a perverse contempt for anything that could be acquired easily.

11

Graham grinned as Grenelda Flynn waved him over to the newly constructed dry goods store. The woman glowed now. She baked pies for him, insisted on doing his washing, and never missed an opportunity to praise him. Even the older son, Tim, had mellowed toward him, and displayed respect by immediately putting down whatever book he was reading and paying attention to the editor's words, a courtesy he awarded very few.

"His name's not really Tim, it's Tem," Grenelda explained once. "It's short for Tecumseh Spangler Flynn. Ain't it pretty? That's why we choosed it. Our Tem is going to be real special. I can feel it in my bones."

A smile split her face as Graham approached. "Look here, Mr. Chapman. My Jed fetched me some calico for stock, and we've done planned everything we're going to need to start a store. You'll be plumb proud of us, Mr. Chapman. It bothered Jed some, but we sold our team and wagon yesterday to buy this lot and building from Mr. Tucker. Jed brooded some. Said it didn't seem right for a man not to have a horse. But like I told him, we ain't going nowheres. We'll have another team back soon enough out of our profits from the store. We just want you to know how much we believe in you."

"What a wonderful thing to do, Mrs. Flynn."

"And another thing, Mr. Chapman. I guess I've told you often enough how sorry I am that I was so mean to you that first day. But I want you to know that all of my life, I've wanted a store. I've always thought that was the grandest, happiest place in the world to work, so I thought it might make it up to you somehow to know you've made my dream come true. I reckon I would just die if something happened."

Graham was sincerely touched. "Don't worry about that, Mrs. Flynn. Just hang on and as more folks start coming in you'll have more people to sell to. Are you going to be helping your folks out?" Graham asked Tem. Then he noticed with surprise that the boy had been reading a volume of Shakespeare's tragedies. He wondered where the lad would have acquired such sophisticated schooling.

"Yes, sir," Tem said, "but just until the girls are old enough to give Ma a hand." His green eyes were calm and watchful underneath the pointed brows that gave him a Satanic look. "I would like to be a writer some day."

"Well," said Graham, suddenly at a loss for words, "well, perhaps we can work you in at the paper one of these days then."

"Thank you very much, Mr. Chapman," he said. But Graham noticed his eyes had not responded at all. He tipped his hat to the Flynns and continued his stroll.

Soon Brookline City would be able to vote bonds for a railroad. The rails were magic. They would make the town. Any sacrifice was worth obtaining a railroad line. He had promised his citizens that in a short time they would have one, as soon as they got enough people to finance its construction.

Graham frowned as he saw Clark Henson disappear into his blacksmith shop. Henson was one of the few who doubted the merits of the railroad.

"Why should our town have to pay for building a railroad?" Henson argued fiercely.

"Because *we're* the ones who will gain the most from having it go through our town. We owe it to them."

Clark snorted. "Nobody owes them a damn thing. The government gives them land just to coax them to build. We *are* the government. It's our land. A section of land every five miles should be payment enough. We shouldn't have to pay for the construction too. It's like someone stealing your horse and wagon and then charging you ten dollars a mile to haul you back home in them. Thieving sons-a-bitches."

"No," said Graham, "you're wrong. It's your goods they'll haul to markets we need. It's our men who will have extra jobs and work."

Graham had no forewarning that morning. No uneasiness, no premonitions. In fact, he was warmed by quiet pride in the wealth he was accumulating. He strolled back and forth down the imaginary streets. The paper was finished for the week, and he decided to join the carpentry crew. True, the big cash flow essential for building had not materialized yet, but it was just a matter of time.

Two men rode toward Brookline City. Their jaws were set in tough, angular lines as they reined up in front of the general store. They stood in the middle of the group that was beginning to form around them, and then began to speak.

"Friends, you are being swindled," one of them said. The crowd became so quiet even the crickets could be heard from a far field.

"Friends, the people you are listening to in this town, the very ones you are giving your money to, are evil. Get out now, while you can, I beg of you. Not far from here, just fifteen miles on west, there is a *real* town, Morganville, being created. I, like yourselves, once settled in a place like this, bought a lot, a building, and then got wiped out because it was all built on lies."

The women glanced uneasily at their husbands. They had been waiting, waiting for so long now. Most were still living in tents. There were many gaps in the essential services. Where was their doctor? And a real teacher? Even the bank had not materialized.

"Come to our town," said the man. "Look it over. Think about it. There's a railroad coming through. See for yourselves, and here—this is the most important of all." With a flourish, the man unrolled a petition for a county seat. There were two hundred signatures on it. The crowd was deathly quiet. This man had an unmistakable ring of credibility.

Clark Henson stepped forward and headed for his blacksmith shop. "Wait till I get my horse," he called. "I want to see this for myself."

The stranger looked quickly around to gauge the people's reaction to this volunteer.

"That all right with you, folks?" he asked. "Is this the man you want to look things over? To represent you?"

Heads nodded. Clark's judgment was as solid as the anvils he worked on. There was not a better man in town.

"Frank, come with me to bear witness," called Clark to his apprentice. "There needs to be someone to back me up."

Graham stood on the fringe of the group, white-faced and impotent at the shock of this bizarre turn. Why in the hell hadn't he found out if there were towns being built near here? He had checked for other townsites north and south, but it had not even occurred to him that another town would be started further west. He knew it would be best to say nothing until he could meet with Jack Tucker and plan some strategy, but his anger outweighed his usual prudence.

"Clark," he called. "For my proof, when you find that railroad, bring me back the pigtails of one of those almond-eyed devils, will you?"

There was a snicker from the citizens, and when they turned and saw Graham casually leaning against a hitching post, relaxed and nonchalant, they began to doubt the motives of the strangers.

When Clark and Frank arrived in the other town, they slowly rode their horses up and down the street. In the distance, clearly visible, was the gleam of silver rails and a crew working in furious rhythm.

"No flim-flam here, Miller. I've heard so many lies about railroads going through a town that I was beginning to wonder if they ever went

99

anywhere at all. Looks like this one is for real. I just want to check out one more thing," said Clark Henson. "Give me that petition for a county seat."

The men handed him the paper and their glance never wavered.

He picked out a name at random on the sheet.

"I want to meet this person."

The two men looked at each other and grinned.

"Art Smith? You could ask to meet better, but come on. He's for real all right. We'll take you there."

"No," said Clark quietly, "just tell me where he lives. I don't need no one telling him what to say."

The older of the two men nodded his head in approval. He understood this type of suspicion. It was well founded. He pointed down the street. Clark knocked on the door.

"Are you Art Smith?"

"Yes."

"Is this your name on this petition?"

"Yes." The man looked puzzled.

"That's all I need to know." Clark's face was lit by a wide grin.

"It's real," he told the people who surrounded him back in Brookline City. "There really is a railroad under construction, and the people who signed the petition for the county seat really do exist." He answered their questions as quickly as they could ask them. Yes, he had seen the railroad and it was going to go through Morganville. Yes, there was a doctor.

At this last statement, a young pregnant woman burst into tears. Her husband patted her comfortingly on her shoulder. She would probably be just fine, but still the pending birth of their child was a worry to them both.

"No," Clark said, "there's still no law yet." There was a disgruntled buzzing over this. Organized law enforcement would come later when a county was formed and attached to a territory.

The crowd was silent for a moment. The tension was broken when a hat was tossed up in the air. A great cheer went up from the people.

Graham's mouth was as dry as cotton. His dreams were vanishing in one day's time, as the result of a blunder so senseless he still could not believe he had made it. Why in the hell, he thought, didn't I check further west? He turned and left quickly, broken and humbled—even his bones were sickened by this colossal error.

"Wait, wait. You've got to stop them," a woman's voice called after him. He turned and stared at Grenelda Flynn. "You can't—" Her voice trailed off. Her shoulders slumped and she turned and walked toward their family's tent, clutching the hand of her younger daughter.

"Are we going to the new town, Mommy?" she asked.

"We can't," the woman said. Her voice did not hold a trace of emotion. "We don't have no team and wagon no more."

The residents of Brookline City behaved as though they were possessed by a fever. The rush was on to get to the new location. Those still living in tents were the first out. Their canvases and supplies were loaded onto wagons as soon as everything was collected.

Those who had bought houses had to content themselves with taking a little more time. The moving of buildings on the prairie was done regularly by putting them on log sleds and pulling them with teams to a new location. When the first tent dweller arrived at the new townsite, there were a couple of men in the business of moving buildings who immediately wanted to know the exact location in order to contract to move other settlers' houses.

By the third day, Graham Chapman was once again looking at a prairie empty of buildings and now littered with debris. Even the commercial buildings he and Jack had sold on speculation had been moved. Only a few tents were left. The Flynns were still in theirs.

Graham sat on the ground in front of his dugout and stared at the sunset. He repeatedly slammed his fist into the palm of his hand. He went inside and got the bottle of whiskey he had been hoarding. He uncorked the bottle and gratefully swigged down the stinging liquid. Tears came to his eyes as it singed his tissues all the way down, and he gasped at the shock to his system. He had not eaten since breakfast and was quickly numbed by the alcohol. He drank himself senseless, and the moon and stars that he glimpsed through a bleary, mindless haze mocked his dreams with an unmerciful light. He fell beside his doorway in the chilly night air.

When he awoke the next morning, he reached for his bottle again. He looked up as shadow loomed on the ground in front of him. He turned and looked into the cold green eyes of Tem Flynn.

"Can I help you, son?" he asked.

"No. You can't."

Graham was stunned by the hatred he heard in his voice. "What's the matter?" he asked.

"It's Ma. She's dead. Killed herself. Her blood is all spilled out on the ground like a butchered hog."

"No. God, no. I don't believe it." Guilt and grief penetrated his alcoholic fog and seared his brain.

"God, no. Why? I would have helped her get a new start. It's not the end of the world."

"Was for *her*," said Tem. "She didn't have no more starts left in her.

101

She'd used them all up. I'm going to get even with you if it's the last thing I do. Sometime, someday. Right now, I've got a no-count pa and a whole passel of little kids to look after. But someday, sometime, Mr. Chapman, I'll be waiting for you."

12

Lucinda Smrcka looked at her freshly swept floor with satisfaction. Even the corners had been cleared out with nails, and the cheesecloth on the ceiling that caught the drift of dirt that trickled down had been taken outside and shaken. Her feather ticks were lying out in the hot sunshine and her bread was rising in the blue enamel bowl on her little cupboard shelf. It was very, very good, this day, her life.

The dugout was not the best, of course, but it would do fine. It would just be a matter of time before her Vensel would build her a house above the ground—a fine house, with a wooden floor perhaps. She smoothed her dress, newly made, over her hips. It was softly gathered with a buttoned bodice and constructed from the brilliant blue calico she had brought with her to Kansas. The apron covering her bosom was snowy white and tied in an ample sash in back.

The sky was so blue it made her eyes ache. She breathed deeply of the pure light air. The prairie seemed to hum with life, with a constant vibration that echoed inside her. She had brought a geranium plant with her when she came and it was struggling for life on her windowsill. She did believe it was going to live. She would make it live by sheer force of will.

As she stood outside, she thrilled to the call of the day, and the tasks that lay before her. Her impatience to be at her work was checked momentarily by a response to the wildness of the elements. Like called to like and the soil had met its match.

The flash of blue from her skirt, the ancient smell of yeast rising and working, the insects, how she loved the sound of little creatures doing the job for which they had been intended—all these things stopped her this morning. Her oneness with nature made her soul surge with blissful energy and she tilted her head and burst into a song of jubilation. Her work, her day, the pleasure of it all!

She went back inside. The dugout was much neater now. She had stacked old crates for shelves and at last even found room for their bed to be brought inside permanently. Everything was spotlessly clean, so she began to quilt, to prepare her nest for the coming winter. A frown wrinkled her brow as she thought of her little Anton off with his father; off as usual lately. She was doing her best by the boy, but by God, it wasn't easy.

Quickly she smoothed out a wrinkle forming in the square she was piercing. The tempo of her rocking chair increased with her growing agitation as she thought of her failure with Anton. Her frown deepened. Failure was too strong a word. It was ridiculous. The boy was perfectly obedient. Still, there was something there she could not put her finger on. It was stubbornly elusive. He would not look her in the eyes and murmured, "Yes, ma'am," at all her instructions. Perhaps she had taken over too quickly with the boy. She shrugged her shoulders. It did not matter. It had to be done or he would grow up weak, like his mother, and never learn to be a stayer.

Most of all, he had to be strong. And already there were signs of Julka's frailties. There was a fragile quality about him, and his coloring remained wan, no matter how many hours she made him play in the sun, or how much tonic she forced down him. She had yet to see an illness her tonic would not help. Perhaps she needed to double the dosage. Still, it came very dear, and perhaps should not be wasted. After all, she too hoped to have a child someday and it would best be kept for that time, and not poured down the boy.

She was too restless to enjoy sewing this morning. Too full of exuberant energy. She would rather be spending her time in hard physical labor, but everything she could think of had already been done. So even though it was too early in the day to be still, she sat doing handwork and her mind raced with plans.

With each piece of the quilt she imagined her house, her farm, and her children. Such pride she would take in her abilities to keep her house sparkling and her cellar laden with all manner of food to see them through the winter. The barn would be filled with hay, neatly stacked for their sleek animals. At the last thought, she pricked her finger and then quickly sucked at the blood before it could stain the white in her square. Crossly, she waited to resume her work.

Spreading her fingers, she slowly examined her hands as though they were somehow separate from the rest of her body. Her fingers were square-tipped, and the veins in her hands were well defined. Her hands were the one part of her that kept body and soul together. Through her hands flowed her whole philosophy of doing: whether through shaping bread, executing complicated movements of her violin, or strongly grappling with steaming piles of laundry. Without hands, you could not do, and if you did not do, you were nothing, below contempt. Even sitting for this short a time without movement made her uneasy.

It was the thought of the barn that had caused her to prick her finger. For the barn, the farm, brought her thoughts around to Vensel and the annoyance she was beginning to feel with him. Such mistakes as he made and how unnecessary. If he would only listen. She sighed and resumed her sewing. The fact of the matter was, her Vensel did not work hard enough. He should be training his mind to stay in the here and now, instead of whiling away the time dreaming.

In late afternoon, she abruptly arose and put away the sewing. It was time to begin supper.

She cut down strings of rhubarb and started soaking it. Tomorrow she would make a pie. In the meantime, for tonight, she began to fry ham and then stirred up thick gravy to pour over her bread.

Vensel and Anton wiped their feet carefully before entering the door. Vensel hung his coat on a peg and quickly washed his face and hands. Shyly he kissed Lucinda on the cheek, but she blushed and said quickly, "Vensel, not in front of the boy."

He blinked in bewilderment. Not *what* in front of the boy? He had kissed her cheek, that was all—just that and nothing more. He felt a quick surge of anger. The woman who exhausted him with her demands at night, how dare she affect outraged modesty? He thought of his Julka and coming home in the evenings to his wisp of a wife and her adorable bumbling ways. His little Julka. The pain was so intense it was still physical. A deep, unspeakable grief was there that he carried about with him like a stone. How his Julka would fly out the door in the evenings when she heard him coming, and throw her arms about him and with tears or laughter, tell him about her day. Together they would reach down for Anton and hoist him up between them, then kiss him back and forth until he shrieked with laughter.

The sun used to burn the window panes in the evening with a brilliant glow and then his whole world was ablaze with light and hope, and at the center was his wife and boy.

He blinked again and then sighed. Vensel Smrcka was a patient man and he did not want to cause trouble with this new wife.

He took his place at the table. He was worried about Anton. Since the boy's mother had died, he wasn't himself. At first he had been jubilant to have a woman around. Now he was too quiet and picked at his food. Ah, well, reasoned Vensel, his appetite was no longer normal either, and he too was quiet.

"You make the best bread I have ever eaten," he said to Lucinda truthfully. "The very best bread of all."

Her lively brown eyes beamed with pleasure. She talked about his next trip to town and the goods she would be needing, correcting Anton all the while, without stopping to draw a breath.

"Then I will be needing muslin for domestics. Anton, don't play with your food. How many times do I have to tell you. And if we have the extra money to spend, some real needles. The bone I have been using is wearing out. Anton! You're not *listening* to me again. I said don't play with your food. You're wool-gathering. You should be learning to pay attention. Perhaps we will have a school here someday if we can find a teacher, and then where will you be?"

Now she turned back to Vensel. "Although I doubt that we will ever have a school, and even so, Anton is so dull it would hardly do him any good to go anyway. How many times a day, I wonder, do I have to repeat the same thing over and over again in order to make him hear it?"

Vensel Smrcka laid down his fork and said carefully, "Anton is not dull."

"The boy is not smart, Vensel," she said coldly. "He learns slowly. I have to tell him everything over and over."

"Shut your mouth, woman," he said furiously.

She finished her supper in silence, too astonished by Vensel's blaze of anger to reply.

Vensel rose from the table and gestured to his son to follow him outside. They sat wordlessly in the cool evening air and looked up at the stars. What his woman had said was nearly unforgivable and so false. His Anton's mind darted like a hummingbird. He used to talk incessantly, skipping so quickly from subject to subject that he was like a stone skimming across a brook.

He sat with his arm around Anton's shoulder, and without a word spoken, he comforted his son.

From inside the dugout he heard the clatter of plates being done up, for Lucinda never allowed them to sit for a moment. Suddenly tears sprang into his fine brown eyes and he buried his face in his hands. Anton did not look at his father. He gazed clear-eyed at the stars overhead.

Ah, well, Vensel thought gloomily, he had made a bad bargain with fate, although he had used his very best judgment at the time. It would have been better, perhaps, if he and the boy had remained alone. Would there ever be any way to repair the damage she had done the boy by telling him he was stupid?

He spread his thick stubby fingers and studied the dirt-stained knuckles. They never really came clean. He sighed and clapped Anton on the shoulder.

"Time for bed. Let's go inside." Brooding would do no good. He would have to make the best of it, and in time, when Lucinda had children of her own, she might become a kinder person.

105

Lucinda liked washday the very best of all. She was up when day began to break, heating the water for the laundry. She liked the briskness to the morning air and the grayish light that subtly began to quicken and move toward the dawn. Different birds sang too, at this time of day, and always the sky contained the unnatural light of a few stars being overwhelmed by the sun. Her soap had been rendered weeks before by running lye through ashes.

When the water was boiling, she threw in the towels and other white clothes and, with a touch of bluing, let them boil in the water to remove every last trace of dirt. Then came her colored dresses and finally Vensel's work shirts and pants. When the rinsing was done, she spread the clothes over bushes and elkhorn to dry. She dipped out a bucket of scrub water and dampened every surface she could lay her hands on.

That done, she washed her abundant mass of long auburn hair, and picking up her mending, sat outside in the sun. She was putting patches on Vensel's pants when she saw Aura Lee and a man she supposed was her husband coming across the prairie.

Company coming. Oh, wonderful. It was the perfect time to have her first visitors. She had baked yesterday and would be able to offer some refreshments. She folded up her mending and darted inside. Vensel and Anton would be here soon, and they would all have a wonderful time, laughing, talking, eating together. Her house was in perfect order. Quickly she picked up her hair at the nape of her neck, and shoved it forward, and it fell of its own weight into beautifully arranged waves. She twisted the remainder into a knot.

Aura Lee stopped for a moment to catch her breath.

"I can't wait for you to meet her, Daniel. She's wonderful. I'm going to have a woman to talk to just a couple of miles away, and oh, Daniel, I do hope she will play for us."

Aura Lee was being so careful in what she said. Every cent she and Daniel had was so precious right now, so dear. But if he could see Lucinda's joy, perhaps he could understand her yearning for an instrument, and a violin would be perfect. It would never replace the piano in her heart, but a violin would be on the same level. There were only four instruments, she decided, that were on an equal basis for solos: piano, violin, harp, and flute. Well, maybe the flute. It was as good, but it still wasn't a stringed instrument.

Lately her thoughts had been neither weird nor bizarre, but filled with her old passion for music. He would see, he would see how like her old self she could be again, if she only had a violin.

Lucinda came to the doorway and waited.

Aura Lee quickly looked back at Daniel as his firm stride faltered and then turning, followed his gaze.

He did not, could not speak, and for a moment, for just a single agonizing moment, Aura Lee was seeing Lucinda through Daniel's eyes. The rich auburn hair, high Slavic cheekbones, the round lush breasts, and the raw energy.

She doesn't have the right, Aura Lee thought hotly, she doesn't have the right to look like that. Not out here. Oh, Daniel, she's like you. She's just like you. Look at you both. Just look at you. The two of you are even a different color than other people.

Daniel was rock-hard now, and ramrod straight; his high bronze coloring united him to the earth. At home, back in Missouri, he would match the rocks and the fall leaves like any other animal that acquires adaptive coloring, but here there's just the grass and the sky and the wind and nothing to blend with, but still, oh, just look at you both. You seem to belong together like hues of the same value and intensity. And look at me. I'm too pale. Too sickly. And far too tired all of the time.

With a stern shake of her head she stopped this dangerous line of thought. What in the world is the matter with me? We are visiting our neighbors for the first time. That is all. A simple visit.

"Lucinda, I want you to meet my husband, Daniel Hollingworth." Aura Lee flushed with pride as her husband removed his hat and inclined his head.

"How do you do, sir? My husband and the boy are coming home now. Do come in and set a spell."

Lucinda's eyes did not waver from Daniel's face for a single second, as though she were in a trance.

Don't look at him like that, scolded Aura Lee silently, now seeing Daniel through this woman's eyes. Daniel with his pine-straight back and his hawk-quick eyes. He's my rock, my mountain, my man, my husband. Please don't look at him like that.

Daniel smiled at Aura Lee with a quick tender glance as though he could sense her awe of Lucinda. The expression in his eyes was guarded as he looked at his neighbor's wife.

Aura Lee drew herself to her full slight height, proud of Daniel, and suddenly and gleefully aware of the surge of envy she had felt in Lucinda. Secure, oh, blessedly secure, in her husband's sense of right and wrong. There would never be anything more between Lucinda and Daniel than this first exchange of admiration and that simply could not be helped.

"Aura Lee, Aura Lee." She turned to receive Anton's hugs. The boy had run the last quarter of a mile and was out of breath.

She laughed at his exuberance, as he flung his arms around her neck and squeezed with all his might.

"Goodness, you're getting strong. I think someone has been feeding you very well."

She inhaled the clean out-of-doors scent he had brought inside and was warmed by his frail flesh. Still kneeling, she glanced across his shoulders into his stepmother's eyes and was jolted by the disapproval she saw there. Lucinda did not say a word, but Aura Lee immediately regretted her own thoughtlessness.

How could I have been so careless, she chided herself. Of course Anton has not had time to warm up to her yet, and here I am, completely taking over. It must be very difficult for her to find her rightful place in a family that has been this close. I must remember to be more considerate.

"Anton, here, let me go," she said gently. "I've walked a long way, and I need to rest a while. Then I will help your mother get supper."

His eyes flared with pain at the word "mother" and Aura Lee sighed. Just as she suspected. Now that the new had worn off, this little boy was putting his stepmother to severe tests.

"Here, Anton. Why don't you look at my new quilt squares? Wash your hands first and be careful with them. It's very important not to get them dirty."

He took her basket and searched for a place where he could lay out the scraps of fabric. The dugout was so crowded with the things needed for daily chores that he had to settle for the bottom of a chair.

Aura Lee smiled as he soon became absorbed in arranging the patches. She watched as a variety of patterns developed from the bright triangles and squares. The boy's quick grasp of the possibilities for design intrigued her. His face was intent as his fingers shuffled the bits of material.

"See how this one is like the sky, and this one is the same, the same— as the grass." He frowned as he grasped for the word.

Of course, how could I have been so stupid, thought Aura Lee. No one has taught him the idea of colors. He's never been to school. She bent over and began pointing to the bits of calico.

"This one is red, Anton, and this one is blue, then yellow, then green."

He recited the names after her and then began chanting them as though his life depended on learning every single one.

She listened absently to Lucinda's chatter as they finished putting the meal on the table. She was distracted by what she was hearing from Anton.

"And this is how I feel when I wake up in the morning, and this is how I feel when I go to bed at night." He had grouped together little squares of yellow and blue. "And this is how I feel without my mommy," he whispered, as he carefully picked up a square of black.

Oh, Anton, she grieved, time will take care of things. Then the other implications of all the child had been saying struck her.

"Your child has a wonderful artistic sense, Vensel," she said. Her voice was tense with excitement. "He's outstanding, and at such a young age that I can hardly believe it. He must have careful schooling. A talent like this must not go ignored."

For a moment she was puzzled by the look on Vensel's face. His quiet pride was to be expected, but the smug triumphant lift to his smile puzzled her.

"There's no school here," said Lucinda, "and no chance for one."

"Of *course* there's a chance. We'll see to it," said Aura Lee. "Anton has to go to school." What was the matter with these people? And what had she said to provoke such a quarrelsome note in this woman's voice?

"We will have a school," said Vensel flatly, "and soon. There will be others here before long."

"Time to eat," said Lucinda, slapping a pan down on the table.

They finished the meal, contented, glad to be together, their faces softly lit by a kerosene lamp. The precious oil was usually hoarded, but the Hollingworths were Lucinda's first visitors, and it was important to her to treat them well. There was a definite chill to the evening and they were saved from being uncomfortable by the lingering heat of the cookstove.

Both of the women worked on quilt squares and listened to the men talk.

"When the railroads come," said Daniel, "the desert will bloom like a rose. We have to have one soon. You know how desperately we will be needing coal. We can't count on cow chips forever for fuel. Then too, we need the Eastern markets for our grain. It will involve money, of course."

"I don't know," said Vensel heavily. "It seems when money is needed, a lot goes wrong for the farmer."

"The money won't come from the farmer," said Daniel. "The money will come from the men building the railroad. They need the farmer to make the line profitable. There will be a constant exchange of goods between the East and the West."

Lucinda listened in awe to Daniel. His face was firm and intense. His magnetic voice mesmerized Lucinda with its resonant timbre and the words she did not understand.

So *these* were quality folks, then. Not like herself and Vensel at all. She could tell by their words. The moment she had met Aura Lee, she had felt the same separation she had felt from her employers in New York. When the letter arrived from her mother, telling of Julka's death, she decided to leave. Being an indentured servant was like being in a prison. It was not the work she minded, but being perceived as a servant by the type of woman she had come to despise. In fact, at times her cousin Julka had reminded her of these women, and Aura Lee certainly did. There was a faint-heartedness to them, as though they knew from the moment they were born that they were to be waited on.

"All we lack is imagination and vision," said Daniel. "If we speak with one voice, we can exert enormous influence over the building of the roads, and the rates they will charge."

Lucinda didn't know anything about farm problems and shipping rates, but she knew it had taken every cent she could accumulate, a coin at a time, slipped from purses and possessions of visitors to her employers' household, every last cent to be able to afford the ticket to Wallace. She smiled for a moment, wondering when her employers had first missed her. This venture had been far less risky than shipping out as a mail order bride, however. She had known much about Vensel before she came, just from her mother's habit of relaying Julka's letters. She knew he was a decent man. Well, she had not been misled there. Decent, but dull, dull, dull. Not like this man, Daniel Hollingworth, at all.

The lamplight was reflected in Daniel's eyes, already sparkling with the inner fire of his ideas. He hooked his thumbs in his suspenders and his granite features were unyielding.

Lucinda's hands were still for a moment as she looked at Daniel. Vensel was nothing compared with him. *What she and this man could not do together.* What a team they would make. How glorious it would be in every way. She had watched this type of man before, and his power was wonderful. With enough power and confidence, you could own the earth. She was this man's match.

Suddenly Lucinda was aware of Aura Lee's scrutiny and she flushed deeply, lowering her eyes to hide her thoughts.

Lucinda was acutely miserable in the space of a few seconds. She had seen the way Daniel looked at Aura Lee, this lady, with her careful words and haughty airs, and she was sick with jealousy over the adoration she saw there. No, she knew in her heart that the Hollingworths were the natural match; not herself and Daniel at all. From the two years she had spent in New York, watching, always watching, she knew that people with position were very different from herself and Vensel. It showed in the ideas they were willing to tackle, and even out here on the prairie, Aura Lee's bearing, even the way she walked, announced her social superiority.

Why, she moaned inwardly, why, oh why? And this is Kansas, not New York. Why can't we all be equal out here? Her head snapped up at Daniel's next words.

"I don't agree," he said. "We must have railroads to survive. How much can we buy from each other? You'll buy my wheat, if I'll buy yours? And as others come it will be worse. We have to get our wheat to those who have none at all. How do you expect to do that? With pony carts? Railroads are the answer."

"The farmer will end up getting cheated," Vensel argued stubbornly. "It has always been so."

Lucinda was weary with the strain of following this talk, talk, talk.

"Enough," she said, rising quickly. "Enough of this for tonight. I will play for you."

She unsnapped the clasps on her violin case and blinked in surprise at the tips of Aura Lee's fingernails where her hands were resting on Anton's shoulder. They were pale, without a trace of red. She glanced at the rims of the lower lids of her eyes while she was so close, without appearing to examine her. They were nearly totally white and her cheeks gleamed like pearls, lovely, translucent, and pale.

So that's it, then, thought Lucinda in amazement. My tonic would do wonders for her.

"Do you folks have any livestock yet?" she asked carefully. Chickens, perhaps? Eggs? She knew at once that the yolk of an egg, daily, would do wonders for Aura Lee's health. Her mother had trained her well when she was growing up and she was far ahead of her time in her understanding of the importance of good food.

"No," said Aura Lee. "We have all we can do just to keep our horse in water. But we will have a well soon. Daniel has promised."

Lucinda nodded, keeping her face expressionless. They too would have to wait for a well-digger before they bought animals. But in the meantime, she had her tonic. Perhaps she should share, or at least tell this woman what was wrong. But the elixir was so precious. She would have to think about this a bit.

She tuned the strings, then paused for a moment. There was a respectful hush in the room as she lifted her elbow, the bow held firmly in her long, strong fingers.

With narrowed eyes, she played a simple, merry tune. Anton was lulled and at peace. He would soon be asleep. Vensel's grave smile of quiet pride in her ability amused her. Stupid man. He did not own her talent. It was no credit to him that she played so well.

She stopped abruptly and then in a lightning switch of theme and intention began the most poignant of rhapsodies she knew. She saw with satisfaction Aura Lee's face tighten as she stiffened against the melancholy tug of her uprooted soul, yearning, yearning for relief from the weird wavering images that stormed against her again in a single dreaded instant. For Lucinda had known since the foundations of the world were laid, the agony that could be evoked by a single note.

Then she turned to Daniel, watching his face respond to the first thrilling notes with a shudder of fierce surprise. Flushing deeply, the man carefully, stubbornly looked at the floor. The notes quivered in the warm air. Lucinda leaned forward, coaxing him, willing him, with her sweet wild strains to look her fully in the face, until at last he squared his mighty shoulders and looked up. Lucinda's pulse leapt. She smiled and wrenched his soul from him with a single final note. She had dealt with men of honor before and it was simply a matter of time.

Vensel plodded home, his day's work done and his head filled with Daniel Hollingworth's ideas about the railroad. He envied Daniel his quick wit and his words, especially his words. The wonderful way he could say exactly what he wished. He was so often handicapped by his inability to find the ones he wanted. The thoughts were there, but their expression was blocked. He looked across the treeless plain. The light, the time of day, the hues in the sunset, all reminded him of the night Lucinda had come to them.

Vensel Smrcka had been looking across the prairie when he saw her in the distance. He drew in his breath and shook his head as though this were some apparition. Her dress was a deep maroon, and her bonnet had fallen off her head to reveal the most beautiful head of hair he had ever seen.

She was taller than the average woman, and with just a little extra weight would be too plump. She looked like a goddess with her rounded curves and hair ablaze, queen of harvest and fertility. He watched as she studied the prairie, and then turned quickly toward the man in the wagon who had brought her. Vensel saw her shake her head as she reached for her possessions.

Even after a cross-country trip that would have exhausted most people, there was a radiant energy about her. She approached the dugout with her suitcase and her violin case in hand. He did not wait for her to knock, but went outside to greet her, with little Anton shyly peeping from around his leg.

She greeted him softly in Czech.

"Hello. How are you, Vensel? I am Julka's cousin, Lucinda."

So, she spoke Bohemian, this prairie goddess. With this one who stood before him, he would be able to speak his heart and not have to stop with the pitifully inadequate words he knew of English, which only reflected a fraction of the meaning he felt so deeply inside.

Vensel was stiff with despair. Julka's cousin. Of course she did not realize Julka had died. What was there to do? It was impossible. There was no way to get her back to town, and she could not stay here. "Wait," he stammered. "The driver—call him back."

"It is too late. I told him to go on. We were afraid there was no one here, and then we saw your smoke." He shrugged helplessly. There was no point in worrying about what the neighbors would think, because other than the Hollingworths there were no neighbors at all who would think anything. Still, surely the man from the livery stable who brought her out must have wondered. Then Vensel realized that there was no one who would have any reason to know or to care about Julka's death. She had come in innocence for a visit, this cousin, and now he must explain.

"Julka, my wife, is dead."

"No," she said, pressing her hand to her heart. He was lonely, lonely, lonely. She could see it in his eyes and nothing would stand in her way now.

"How did this happen?"

"She died in childbirth," he said simply. "There was no doctor." He spread his large hands and studied his thick fingers.

Shrewdly, Lucinda stood outside and did not make a move. Inviting her into the house must be his own idea.

"You must come in," he said awkwardly. "We were getting ready to eat. You must be hungry."

"This is terrible," she said. "I had planned to visit for some time. See, I brought her a present, Vensel." She showed him the half-dead geranium slip tied to the handle of the suitcase. It was wrapped in cheesecloth and she rewet it each time the train stopped. "Now I have no place to go."

Drawing a deep breath, she plunged into a semi-accurate explanation of how she had gotten here, omitting the fact that she had already known of Julka's death. All the while she was whisking about the kitchen. In a flash she located some flour and lard and made some biscuits. The oven filled the room with a homey glow.

She augmented the pathetic meal they had been prepared to eat with all the culinary skill she possessed. Once everything had been cleaned up, she turned to look the boy over.

He was small to the point of frailty, and had enormous gray eyes. Under his unwavering stare, her eyes at last faltered. He was very polite, but the only time she was able to evoke any emotion was when she tuned her violin and began to play a simple melody so smooth it hung in the night air like a benediction. Then and then only, tears began to trickle slowly down Anton's cheeks.

Vensel carefully turned toward the fire as Lucinda began to dress for bed. He was rigid with humiliation for her. Such a wonderful woman to be put in such a position. He slept restlessly that night. This woman's sudden appearance had stirred too many old memories and heartaches.

The next day he began to make plans for taking her back. Then he was brought up short when he realized she had no place to go. She had already said it took her last cent to get here, and God knew he did not have any money to give her.

A plan was beginning to form in his mind, and he trembled at his own boldness. He had no wife, she had no husband, and little Anton needed a mother. Could it be possible such a creature would consent to marry him? To agree to live in this place that was actually little better than a cave?

Lucinda feigned surprise when he asked and pretended to think it over. Her heart skipped a beat. It was done. They would be married properly when the next circuit rider came through, but in the meantime, they simply began living together as man and wife, and Vensel was stunned by the sexual intensity of the woman. He felt consumed by her. Used up.

The wind was coming up and with it the dirt from the land Vensel had overturned. Lucinda jumped when a bucket blew against her laundry kettle. Where the sod had not been disturbed, there was no blowing dust, as the thick network of grass had enormous roots that would bind the soil for decades.

What difference did it make anyway, she thought angrily, if dirt blew into a dirt house? She looked around with dissatisfaction, and impulsively decided to go see Aura Lee. Everything was done here. She would take food. Suddenly cheered, she even tucked her iron-rich tonic into the basket, although she was still undecided about sharing.

She began to hum. It was only right to return her neighbors' call, and maybe, just maybe, Daniel would be home, inside, for some reason. Not likely during a working day. But still. . . .

Lucinda stared as she approached the homestead. There was a small sod stall that Daniel had built to shelter their horse and a wagon was parked next to the sod corral. Next to the wagon was a real grasshopper plow for cutting the sod, and next to it, a breaking plow.

The Hollingworths' horse has a better place to live than I do, she thought, suddenly ashamed. Even his horse gets to live above the ground.

Lucinda walked past the improvements. She smoothed back her hair and stood resisting the wind, envy seeping from every pore. This man, this couple who had so much already, who were so blessed with advantages, had two plows? And both with steel beams. One just for breaking the sod into continuous strips, and the other for preparing the ground for planting. Oh, not fair, not fair. Her Vensel had just one, with a wooden beam. The beam often broke and had to be repaired or replaced.

Back East, some farmers were even able to use wooden blades, which would have suited Vensel. It worried him to put something into the soil that had not come from the soil. But here a steel blade was essential. Its invention was one of the reasons it was now possible to settle the plains.

The wind bent the grass before her in sudden outraged gusts and the deep, blue green waves flashed silver, then inky depths. The wind was bunching the clouds into dark pillows, then tossing them about. The restlessness of the air matched Lucinda's mood. She was tossed and at odds inside.

She knocked on the door of the soddy. There was no answer. She knocked again and boldly put her shoulder to the door and shoved. It was locked from within.

Aura Lee was numb with terror at the first thump on the door. She listened and tried to still her breathing. Afraid the intruder would hear, would know she was home by herself. She lay huddled under the covers, where she had fled after the worst morning of her marriage. She and Daniel had fought bitterly.

For three weeks now, she had been preoccupied with dread. Something was terribly wrong. This eerie feeling was even stronger than her attraction to morbid thoughts and had begun in the middle of one night, when she sat bolt upright, her eyes wide with alarm. She had been paralyzed with a sick certainty that something was terribly wrong. Daniel lay by her side, sleeping deeply. She had listened carefully but could not hear a sound out of place. Her lips trembled; she knew she was inviting the voices to fill the void. Willing herself to listen and not to listen. There had been no easing of her apprehension since. And this morning she had begged Daniel to find out where their mail was being delivered.

"Please, Daniel. Please. It's such a small thing to ask. Just see if there are letters waiting."

"I can't take a chance on going to Wallace," Daniel had argued. "For nothing."

"Daniel, mail is not nothing."

"I know it's important, Aura Lee. I don't mean to minimize your problems and I know you're having a hell of a time out here. But the point is, it's a trip that can wait. Now, can't it?" he asked. Furious with his insistence on settling the matter by sweet reason, Aura Lee began to cry.

"Please, please. Daniel. I'm begging you. If you need a decent reason," she mocked, "how about getting me some coal?"

"There's no point in spending—oh, well, hell. I'll go check where the old trading post used to be. We damn sure won't be able to get any coal there, but maybe there'll be some mail waiting."

Fuel too had become a bitter issue. The woman of the house, in her free time, was expected to pick up cow patties off the prairie. The chips were stacked in a corner of the soddy and further dried, and when they burned they gave off an odor of fresh hay. Most women approached the task of collecting the cow chips gingerly at first and would use the corners of their aprons to pick up the droppings. Normally they all adjusted, and then approached the task with a saving measure of humor, but Aura Lee was still not able to conquer her loathing for this domestic chore.

She had just had a fit when Daniel first told her what she was expected to do.

"You can't be serious, Daniel. I won't do it. I can't believe you are expecting this of me."

"What did you think we used for fuel?" he said hotly. It was their first quarrel and was fueled by their mutual shame and had upset them both terribly. "Didn't any of the letters I wrote you educate you at all for what you would be facing? I told you there were no trees at all, and no railroads bringing in supplies, so what did you think we used for fuel? And while we're on the subject of not thinking, didn't it really register with you that there was not a post office? You knew my letters came in batches. I told you I didn't go to town very often. Oh, damn it, honey."

He saw her eyes brim with tears and held out his arms.

"Just bear with me, sweetheart, just for a little while longer and things will get better. Just wait until—"

"I know until when, Daniel," she whispered in a soft voice so heavy with irony he thought his heart would break. "Come spring."

When Daniel had left this morning she was relieved as his horse disappeared over the rise. Some days, bearing up under his sharp scrutiny was more than she could stand.

She squeezed her eyes shut tight when the knocking resumed and she knew she would give anything to have him beside her right now. She would go without mail for a year at a time and burn grass for fuel before she would ever let him leave her alone again.

"Aura Lee, it's me. Lucinda."

Aura Lee's heart leapt with relief. "Oh, thank you, God," she whispered. "Thank you, thank you, thank you."

She threw back the bar and tried to still the quaver in her voice. Willed herself to sound normal and composed.

"Lucinda! Come on in. Sorry it took so long to answer the door, but Daniel's gone for the day, and I wasn't sure who it was." She stood in the doorway, now ashamed of the mess her neighbor would see. The pans from dinner had not been done up. In fact, supper hadn't even been started. There was no point in taking the feather tick out to air today. Not in this wind. But it could have been plumped and straightened. *But I wanted to lie on it,* she thought.

Her house had an untidy, uncared-for look, and it was not fair that Lucinda had chosen today to come calling. She was so terribly, terribly tired, and today with Daniel gone for the very first time since they were married, she had not even tried to get any work done. In fact, it could possibly be tomorrow when he got back, and she had planned to make an evening meal of biscuits and a bit of dried fruit so there would not be any dishes to do.

Lucinda's skin glowed from the walk over. She swept into the house, bringing with her a clean, cottony, fresh air smell in her starched skirt.

"I will help you set your house in order," she announced firmly.

"Nonsense," said Aura Lee. "Let's just visit." Her voice was stiff with anger. This woman had no right to come in here and take over her house. Then her shoulders slumped. It was her own fault really, she thought. She should have been up and about ages ago. She was just so tired.

"Thank you," she said, blinking back tears. "Thank you very much. But before we begin, I have some tea I've been saving. I would like to fix you a cup." Aura Lee proudly raised her chin, determined to adhere to some standards of decency. She crossed over to her trunk and brought out the precious can of Oolong-Formosa.

"You are my first guest, Lucinda. My very first. This calls for a celebration."

"Let's enjoy," said Lucinda, suddenly cheered at being this woman's companion. It had taken the great leveler, the prairie, for her to achieve this type of equality. She was as good as anyone.

Aura Lee walked over to the stove to heat the water. Lucinda was by her side in a flash. "Oh, my," she said. "You have a stove such as this?"

Aura Lee nodded. The Acme steel range was her wedding present from Daniel. She still had not mastered the techniques for controlling the flow of heat in its six burners. It was intended to burn coal or wood, but easily handled their only source of fuel: the droppings of cattle herds or the increasingly rare cache of buffalo chips. The stove was heavy enough to handle the hot blaze of twisted hay cats, hanks of grass that burned in a flash, or corn cobs after the crop was harvested.

"Next year," Daniel had promised, "there will be a railroad through and we'll have a pile of coal right outside our house, and it won't be necessary for you to gather the uh, other," he mumbled, looking away from the scorn in his wife's eyes. She still absolutely hated gathering cow chips. Although it was woman's work, after their quarrel he did it himself when he had time, rather than endure her martyred silence as she grimly stacked them in a corner.

The range was heavily plated with nickel and the doors and shields and trimmings were scrolled with burnished curlicues, and Lucinda thought she had never seen anything so wonderful in her entire life.

"Your stove has a reservoir for hot water too?" asked Lucinda. "All you have to do is cook a meal? And you have hot water, for your dishes, and for your hair?"

Aura Lee nodded, ashamed at not being more grateful for the blessings she and Daniel had.

Lucinda's eyes swept over the soddy. She saw the cupboard for storing dishes. This woman did not even have to have her household goods on open shelves where they would collect dust. She had seen the clothing packed in the trunk, when Aura Lee got the tea out. She had noticed many other luxuries. But most of all there was the stove. She decided in a flash. If this woman had all of this, had it this cozy, she did not deserve to have any of her tonic. Not one drop.

Lucinda went back to her chair and put her feet on the footstool they were sharing.

"Thank you," she said, as Aura Lee handed her the tea. It was served in a delicate cup that Aura Lee had stored in her trunk. It was the only one she owned. She herself was using one of their tin cups. Lucinda savored every drop. In the corner of the room was a quilt Aura Lee was putting together and she marveled at the blend of colors.

"Let us begin," said Lucinda abruptly. Aura Lee joined in behind her neighbor, and it was like trying to keep up with a small whirlwind. In no time at all, her house was set to rights, the dishes done up and even a yeasty dough set to rise.

"There now," said Lucinda, "don't you feel better?"

Aura Lee looked around, pleased with the order. It would have taken her all day to accomplish what had not consumed even a good hour.

As the two women sat down again, Aura Lee was trying to find the words to ask Lucinda about the violin. Would it be possible that on afternoons such as this, they could play together? Wouldn't it be heavenly? She delayed a moment longer, mysteriously heavy at the thought of being under further obligation to this woman.

Lucinda stopped in mid-sentence at the sound of a horse outside. Someone was here. The two women were suddenly motionless. Aura Lee sat like a person who has just seen a snake and has become too paralyzed to act at all.

Lucinda was fascinated by Aura Lee's reaction. Her face, normally pale, now had a definite grayish cast and her lips were a thin, blue, trembling line. Lucinda had never seen such stark, naked terror. Helpless tears sprang to Aura Lee's eyes.

Lucinda's every sense was heightened. The adrenaline immediately raised her natural combativeness to a new pitch. Her nostrils flared slightly, and she rose and with a nod at Aura Lee to be quiet, crept to the window and peered out. She quietly brushed back the heavy homespun curtains and her eyes widened in an effort to keep from sneezing from the faint puff of dust that drifted out.

It was a single man, a lone rider. He stayed on his horse and looked about.

"Hallo, the house," he called finally, in the classic greeting to keep from getting one's head blown off. When there was no answer, he dismounted, warily approached the front door, and knocked rapidly.

Lucinda and Aura Lee looked at each other. Hospitality should be extended to any stranger who came hungry or thirsty, or in need of a bed, but they did not want to let someone in who could be a danger to them. Lucinda peeped again at the man and then decided. He was probably just tired and hungry. There was almost an animal's instinct within her that was able to evaluate people. A sensitivity to another person's aura that was nearly one hundred percent correct. She never could have explained this primitive intuition, as she was not aware of her ability to make judgments on this basis. When he knocked the first time, she was already at the door.

"Hello," she said warmly.

The man stood awkwardly twisting his hat. Even Aura Lee relaxed. A smile tugged at her trembling lips at the thought of being afraid of this awkward, tubby little man.

His blue work pants were held up with suspenders, and a red kerchief circled his thick, short neck. His face was pleasant and mild.

"I'm Jeremiah Keever," he said. "We're going to be homesteading on west of here, and it's getting too dark for me to see where I'm going. I wondered if I could get some water for my horse?"

"Of course," said Lucinda. "The tank is out back, so help yourself, and then do come back in, and we'll get you a bit of supper."

He grinned.

Biscuits were put on the table in short order, and Lucinda quickly browned lard and flour together in a frying pan to make gravy.

"Elvira and Agnes will be out here as soon as I get things in shape to fetch them," said Jeremiah. "Agnes mostly just gets in her mother's way, but she's the apple of her eye anyway. My wife's going to be mighty glad when I write and tell her there's neighbors close by. It's been a-worrying her."

"Just set her mind at ease, Mr. Keever," said Aura Lee. "We will do everything we can to make her feel at home." She was thrilled at the thought of having another woman within walking distance. It would take more time to get to the Keevers', but sometimes Lucinda made her feel just terrible, and it would be wonderful if there were someone less challenging to visit.

"Do you hear something?" As the three of them listened, there was another knock at the door. Aura Lee's thoughts whirled. This was to have been her day by herself, and now look at it. Lucinda rose to answer, as though it were her very own home. With a man in house, now, to protect them, she did not even hesitate.

She opened the door to find her husband and stepson standing there.

"Come in," she said grandly, as though their appearance were the most natural thing in the world. Her brown eyes sparkled, and the room was filled with her rich laughter. With a mock bow she waved them in.

"We was worried, Anton and I," Vensel Smrcka began in his halting English. "We came home from our work, and you was not there. We was worried. We hoped to find you here."

Lucinda's eyes danced with cheerful malice, suddenly enraged by his awkward ways, his lack of grace. Her husband's large hand dangled helplessly below the bottom of his denim work coat. His fine, dark eyes patiently expressed the words he could not find to tell her of the anguish they had felt when they came home to the empty dugout.

She did not help put him at ease, and his sense of shame deepened. His old felt hat flopped over his brow, and his mustache drooped like his soul.

"You will come home, now," he said slowly. "My Anton and I, we was worried."

"Nonsense. There's nothing to worry about out here. I just came over to see my neighbor and lost track of time. That's all."

"Anton." The boy flew to Aura Lee's side, as she rose from the table.

His smile faded as he looked back at his father. With a single glance, Aura Lee was keenly aware of the depths of Vensel's despair. His face was deeply lined and strains of a bass violin playing a minor concerto came to her mind when she looked at him.

"Come in, Vensel. I want you to meet our new neighbor. He will be moving here soon and bringing his family. Anton will soon have others to play with."

The men shook hands and then they all sat down to the table. Vensel ate quietly and with simple dignity, and Aura Lee's heart went out to him. His stoic forbearance of Lucinda's high-handed treatment of him and Anton wordlessly revealed their marital problems.

After doing the dishes, Lucinda deliberately delayed getting her things together. She forced Vensel to ask her to come home, once again.

Then as she walked briskly toward the dugout, easily keeping pace with her husband and her son, her mind was on Aura Lee's terror when the stranger came. In the days to come, she would pull out this image at will, and gleefully go over each memory. She would recall her friend's pallor, the clenched fists, the sickly wan smile, and the prominence of her tiny blue veins, made even more visible by tension.

There was no moon, but she walked confidently, sure of her footing, toward her home. The day had turned out to be very, very good after all. Who would have thought the high-falutin' aristocrat would turn out to be such a frightened mouse?

Daniel smiled as he called out to his wife. She flung open the door and waited as he unsaddled the horse, then hurried toward the house with his precious bundle of letters.

"Good news, sweetheart. I think you're going to be occupied for a while."

"Oh, thank God, Daniel. Where was the post office this time?"

"Well, that's quite a story, but for now, just be glad I found it."

Aura Lee quickly untied the letters. There was a whole stack of them, as she knew there would be.

"Look, Daniel, there's even one for you from Uncle Justin."

She turned up the wick in the lamp and moved closer to its light. Daniel watched her face glow as he ate a leftover piece of the cornbread Lucinda had fixed. Aura Lee murmured to herself as she read the first letter from her parents. From time to time she looked up at Daniel and shared snatches of information, and occasionally a smile lit up her face.

Daniel washed his hands and, smoothing back his hair, he too joined her at the table. He carefully slit the crease of the envelope containing Justin Hollingworth's letter, and pulled out the sheets of paper inside.

An arrow of pain shot through his heart as he read the words and was suddenly sickened by the God who delighted in giving his children stones.

"Ah, sweet Jesus."

Aura Lee looked up, her sweet face flushed in alarm with soft, fragile color.

"Why, Daniel, what's the matter?"

For an instant he could not bring himself to speak the ancient words to the woman who so desperately needed water for her parched heart.

"Aura Lee, I have some bad news."

"What? Who is it?"

"It's your parents, sweetheart."

"Mom and Dad both?" The boundaries of the room faded. "How?" she asked at last, confident it would soon be morning and she would wake up. Daniel's voice sounded as though it were coming from the bottom of a drum.

"How?" she persisted.

"It was a fire, sweetheart. Your home burned to the ground."

"My father, my father," she grieved. She had robbed him of his warmth.

"They have no way of knowing what happened, Aura Lee."

"I do know. I do know. He was just trying to stay warm. When, Daniel? When did it happen?"

"Justin doesn't say. He was very upset, I'm sure, when he wrote this."

Chilled to the bone, Aura Lee was sure it was the night she woke so full of the terror that had not abated. Suddenly the other meaning scorched through her body like wildfire. Her home, her beautiful home. Her beloved Bechstein grand. And she fainted from the heat of the torched dark remembrance.

Vensel ached in every fiber of his body as he moved wearily toward the dugout. He had spent the entire day breaking sod and his arms were still numb from the pain of guiding the plow through the unyielding soil.

Maybe it's wrong, he thought, to fight this network of roots that has been here so long. Maybe we're going against God's purpose for the land, or He wouldn't make plowing this hard. He felt as though he had committed a crime by tearing the centuries-old grass from the soil. The earth herself was pitted in a furious battle against his blade.

He turned back and stared a moment at the ground. He had so little to show for his day's labor, but what he had done could never be undone. Tomorrow, another row would join this one and he would eventually have another three acres prepared for seed.

He scraped his heavy brown shoes against a rock and slowly raised his foot against his knee to examine the soles. They had to last until he could bring in a crop and they were already dangerously thin.

He turned, and bracing his shoulders and his soul, went down the steps through the open door of the dugout.

"Vensel? You're back? While there's still light to work?"

He nodded.

"Supper will be ready soon. But I thought you would work longer, so I didn't hurry it. Let me see what you've done." Lucinda wiped her hands and quickly moved off into the lingering rays of the sun.

Vensel sank into a chair in uneasy exhaustion. He covered his face with his hands. He trembled with fatigue and waited nervously for his wife to return.

It wasn't long. She burst through the doorway in a scolding explosion.

"That is *all*, Vensel? *One row?* All you have to show for a day's work?"

He nodded, too ashamed to reply.

"You move too slowly. You don't plan your work. You don't work hard enough. See, even now, all you can think about is resting when there is an hour's light left."

He closed his eyes and endured. Dear God, he prayed silently, give me the strength to stand this woman. He had discovered that he had two choices in coping with Lucinda; quarreling, which made him miserable, or not quarreling, not answering at all, which evoked a cold fury within her and led to even more tension.

"Where's the boy?"

"Outside. I sent him off to play. I can't get a thing done with him underfoot. The boy is slow, also. He could be helping me. Carrying water and making himself useful."

"My God, woman. He's only five. He can barely lift an empty bucket, let alone a full one."

"He could do more if he would try more to build up his strength."

The flush of combat was gathering in Lucinda's cheeks. So, he was going to do battle with her after all, instead of sitting motionless like a meal sack.

"Anton is not strong."

"It's your fault," she said spinning around, pouncing on the opening he had provided her.

Suddenly Vensel rebelled against the trap that was being laid. This would go on all night. He got up and went to the doorway and called for his son. There was no reply.

"You might check toward the creek," said Lucinda, as though the boy's whereabouts was not any of her concern. She shrugged, and quickly turned to the stew she was cooking.

She gasped as heavy steel hands clasped her shoulders and whirled her around. She clenched her teeth to lessen the impact of the violent shaking. Her head snapped back and forth as though it were a thing apart from the rest of her body.

"I swear to God, woman, if anything has happened to my son—" His words trailed off and he stood clenching and unclenching his fists, every muscle quivering with the effort of keeping himself under control. He whirled toward the door, energized by his anger, and set off to look for Anton.

Lucinda raised her hand to touch the aching cords in her neck. She bent over and began to pick up her precious hairpins that had cascaded from her now disheveled hair. As she gazed into the tiny mirror she kept above the wash basin, she unbuttoned the bodice of her dress, and, slipping the coarse muslin off her shoulders, she stared with disbelief at the bruises on her creamy flesh. Her eyes were bright with exhilaration. How strong he had seemed. *How manly.* She had never been so aroused. She hummed a little folk song and slipped the biscuits into the oven with a new surge of vitality.

Vensel's voice was snatched away by the wind as he called for Anton over and over. His apprehension mounted as he approached the creek.

"Anton, Anton, can you hear me?"

The boy darted abruptly over the bank.

"Dad, look what I've found. Look what I've found." His eyes were wide with excitement as he showed his father a piece of charcoal he had unearthed from an old campfire.

"Look, Dad, it makes a mark. I can draw with it." Proudly, Anton showed his father pieces of bark he had gathered and the clumsy beginnings of little pictures. Vensel's hands shook as he reached for his frail son and hugged him slowly to his body.

"I was afraid something had happened to you, Anton. You know I've told you not to come near the creek," he said solemnly.

"She said—" Anton bit his lip in confusion. She told him to come here. When he reminded her his father didn't let him play at the creek, she crossly said that she was his mother now and had just as much say so as Vensel.

"Has she got supper ready?"

Vensel winced. After all this time, Anton would not call Lucinda by her name, just "she."

"Look at this one, Dad. It's the best of all."

Vensel reached for the awkward drawing of their dugout. There were three stick people standing in front of it. The man was drawn to scale with the dwelling, the boy was pathetically small with his mouth an unhappy straight slash, and the woman towered like a giant above the others.

"Can I take my things home, Dad? Please?"

Vensel nodded, his face gray with despair. "Let's hurry, we don't want to keep supper waiting."

Joyfully, Anton gathered up his treasures, carefully stacking the bark with the charcoal on top. He began a happy stream of chatter, but Vensel didn't hear a word. He was too distracted by remorse to concentrate on the boy.

He had come within seconds of striking a woman, and his wife at that! His great soul pleaded with God to grant him forgiveness and to relieve him from his sense of shame. He would try harder. He would work harder. He would look for his wife's good qualities and not be so critical.

Anton stopped talking when they came within sight of their dugout. His ragged black cap of hair seemed to accent his widening pupils as he followed his father with an animal wariness. They wiped their feet and went inside.

"So you're back," said Lucinda gaily. "I'll dish up supper in a moment." Briskly, she slapped down their tin plates.

Vensel looked with wonder at his unpredictable wife. It was as though nothing had happened. Nothing at all. She was not going to use this against him. All his remorse drained with the quick rush of pure gratitude.

"What do you have there, Anton?" she asked sharply.

"It's—it's—something to draw with. Dad said I could keep it," he said, his eyes pleading with her.

She hesitated. "Good. It will give you something to do around the house."

Vensel did not see the instant tightening of her jaw, but Anton did, and he hurried over to the section of shelving where his change of clothes was kept and carefully placed the bark and charcoal beside his shirt.

With each spoonful of the savory rabbit stew, thickened to a lumpless perfection, Vensel's nerves were soothed. He could hardly stay awake. Immediately, when supper was over, he fell asleep in the chair, all his aches forgotten.

He jumped with fatigue when Lucinda touched his shoulder.

"Bedtime," she said cheerfully. "Help me bring things in." They moved in unison to carry in the straw-stuffed pallets, and she swiftly began to collect their blankets from the shelf. Anticipation quickened her movements.

Vensel was asleep again the moment his head hit the pillow. He was aware of the familiar tightening of his stomach even before he was sufficiently awake to be conscious of her hands, stroking him, exploring him, wanting to touch places no decent woman ever touched, and wanting to do things no decent woman ever did—things his Julka would never have dreamed of doing.

A yearning for his lost wife's sweet body swept over him in a fire wave of pain. He missed her shy modesty, the lowering of dark eyelashes and the soft maidenly blush to her cheeks as she slipped her nightgown about her shoulders and removed her clothing layer by layer from under its voluminous folds. He had never seen her nude. She had never once initiated lovemaking. It would not have been seemly.

With Julka, there was shared passion and warmth that was strong and superb. Yet he was restrained from time to time by his grave natural courtesy, which enabled him to sense subtle shifts in her moods. With Julka he had felt like a man, sure of his place in all areas of his life. With this woman, however, his days were spent in lonely confusion, with a heavy sense of ineptness, and it was carried with him into bed every night.

He was limp in every muscle, and with proud stubbornness kept his back to her. He breathed slowly and evenly, feigning sleep.

He can't be asleep, thought Lucinda. She knew none of her attempts to arouse Vensel would bring a response. He's lying, lying, lying. Furiously she withdrew her hands and moved away. She lay on her back and stared into the blackness, aching with desire. She shook with rage. It was hours before she slept.

The wind was waiting for her when she got up in the morning. It had searched in vain over the vast prairie that night, for just one tree to uproot, just one object to buffet about. Only the eternal grass was there to receive its force, and it bowed and swayed obediently to the wind's bidding. Dark clouds swirled and gathered, then broke again in the shifting currents of air. Only the deep bending of the grass was there to show the strength of the wind. The sound was muffled by the earth of the dugout.

Normally, Lucinda looked out the window immediately to gather the thrilling sense of creation she received with the dawn. But this morning she moved mechanically and without joy. Her eyes were bloodshot from lack of sleep. Her lids were swollen and heavy.

She picked up the chamber pot, always her first task of the morning, and drew the piece of wood that secured the door at night. The wind pounced on her. The door slammed into her unsuspecting body, and sent the contents of the pot sloshing across the floor, down her dress, and even into her hair that she had not yet put up. The china container was smashed to smithereens.

Her frustrated cry of rage woke Vensel and Anton, and the room was filled with her curses. Some in English and some in her native Bohemian.

Although Vensel was up and at her side in a flash, her tears were so unexpected he gaped in amazement. He had never seen Lucinda cry. Her features were coarse and ugly, splotched from the salty tears.

The dirt floor had been sprinkled with water and packed and swept until it was now rock hard and shiny, but nevertheless, some of the urine was already beginning to soak in.

"My floor," she wept, "my floor." She snatched a dish towel from the washstand, then could not bring herself to use it as she realized she would not be able to wash today because of the wind. She needed to keep the already dirty towel for her dishes. Frantically, she grabbed a shirt of Vensel's and began to sop up the mess. Vensel pulled on his clothes and grabbed the trousers she had intended to wash and knelt beside her, trying to help.

"I can't carry water today. It's impossible. I can hardly move outside. The wind is too strong."

Vensel did not reply. It took her five trips of one-half mile each way, with a bucket in each hand, to get enough water to wash. His horse could not be spared for domestic tasks at this time of year. Besides, there would be no way to keep a fire going under their huge iron kettle in the yard, and no way to keep the clothes from blowing off their elkhorn into the next state.

"I'm going to have to stay inside all day, with my floor stinking, and your sniveling kid. When are we *ever* going to get a well? If we had water on our own place, I could take care of this right away."

"In a couple of months, Lucinda, when the well-diggers come by. You know that's one job I can't do by myself. We're lucky as it is to have water so close by."

She placed the soaked clothing under a bucket outside, trusting its weight would keep the trousers and shirt from blowing away. She grimly began to sweep up the pieces of china.

"How long will it be before you will be going to town? I expect you to part with a few of your precious coins to replace this."

"I've got to keep at it, Lucinda. I've got to keep on with my work." Going to town would mean missing a whole five days' labor. They bought all their supplies in bulk and he would not need to go in for another two months. He could not afford to go just for the sake of acquiring another chamber pot.

She changed her dress without replying, then bent over the wash basin and washed and rinsed the hateful odor from the tresses that had been contaminated.

Coldly, she slapped down last night's leftover biscuits in front of Vensel and started the coffee.

Vensel looked gloomily at his plate. It was not enough food. It was going to be a terrible day. For him, for her, for the boy, and for their single workhorse, whose strength would be severely taxed by the wind.

Deprived of the release of her favorite household job, Lucinda substituted her quilting for physical labor.

Anton was forced to stay inside. Cautiously, he took his charcoal and bark over to his pallet. He sensed that today she was too distracted to say the cruel things to him that drove him outside the dugout. In a few minutes, he was so absorbed in his drawing that he didn't give her presence a thought.

"Don't hum," she said sharply.

He swallowed nervously, for he was usually careful not to make a sound that would annoy her.

The creaking of her rocker and the keening of the wind seemed eerie to them both. Anton worked on in an unnatural silence, swallowing frequently as his mouth filled with saliva.

"Stop making that funny noise."

"What funny noise?"

"In your throat. You're just doing it to aggravate me."

Slowly he began to take deep even breaths, fearful that the beating of his heart, conspicuously loud to him, would make her mad.

"Stop that panting," she snapped. "If you can't play quietly, then don't play at all. Put up that stuff. Your father should never have let you bring it home in the first place. He has no consideration for me at all."

Anton headed for his shelf. He would have to cross in front of her. Balancing his precious bit of charcoal on the bark, he slowly started to walk across the crowded dugout, moving as carefully as possible.

When he stumbled, he reached instinctively for his stepmother's knee to check his fall. As he slowly lifted his head he saw the terrible black streak his charcoal had left on her quilt. On the white part, filled with thousands of tiny stitches, now ruined forever.

The blood rushed to his head and frantic tears began to silently trickle down his cheeks as he slowly began to back away from this giant of a woman who already filled him so full of fear he could hardly sleep at night.

She did not speak, but calmly began folding the quilt, with neat, careful movements. Her deliberateness was so ominous he thought he would faint from terror.

"You must be punished. You've ruined my quilt. On purpose."

128

"I didn't mean—"

"Shut your mouth, boy. You did mean to."

He threw up his hands to protect himself from the first blow. Instead, she crossed over to the cookstove and reached for the poker she used to stoke the cow chips. She threw open the grate and slowly heated the piece of iron.

Anton was frozen to the spot.

She withdrew the poker and examined the heated metal. It was not red hot, but would serve her purpose well.

Anton watched her advance slowly toward him, his eyes darting in panic for a place to hide. He trembled as Lucinda reached for his hand and turned the palm down. He was afraid he was going to vomit.

She raised the poker and then laid it across the back of his hand, taking care not to sear through the blood vessels. The scorched smell of his flesh filled her nostrils. It was no more than he deserved for ruining countless hours of labor. A simple spanking would not have been enough.

Anton's wild cry of pain turned into convulsive sobs and he crawled onto his pallet.

"I want—I want—I want my *mother*." He tore the words from his body in hot, airy gasps.

Lucinda did not reply.

After an hour, she approached his bed again. He lifted his head with helpless resignation at the sound of her footsteps. She reached for the burned hand, and after a brief glance, applied some ointment, then swiftly wrapped his fingers in continuous strips of white rags. She spread her own hands, deprived now of every scrap of work this day, and studied the long capable fingers.

"I didn't burn your palm. See, I spared you, Anton. Palms don't heal well, because they get too dirty."

She listened to the constant whining of the wind. All her anger was gone. She stared bleakly at the boy, her face flat and colorless, and waited for him to speak.

"I'm going to tell my dad."

"He won't believe you," she said quickly, sensing Vensel might at that. "He doesn't love you any more. He has me now."

Anton began to sob again, in lonely despair. His knees were drawn up to his chest. It was true. Everything was changed now. He was completely alone.

She made him get up before his father came home for dinner.

"What happened to the boy?" asked Vensel, glancing at the bandage.

"The stupid child tried to reheat his charcoal in the stove, then reached in while it was still too hot to take out. I warned him he would get burned," she lied calmly.

Anton choked back a little cry of protest, shocked by his father's weary nod of acceptance. For a moment, Lucinda's eyes challenged his, and he swallowed, trying to get up his nerve to tell, knowing his father would listen. But they would quarrel, and he didn't think he could bear it. Besides, even Aura Lee had warned him the day she taught him his colors, never, never to get a quilt dirty. And he had.

He had learned very well from his father how to endure in silence. With the righteous dignity of the wrongly injured, he looked squarely at Lucinda and said nothing.

"It's not too deep," she said. "I put some salve on it so it won't become infected. It will heal in no time at all."

"Sometimes we have to learn the hard way," said Vensel. "Let's eat."

Anton did not lift his eyes to his father again. His frail shoulders drooped, and he ate just enough food to satisfy Lucinda.

The three of them sat at the table. Wordless, wind blue and miserable. There was no out from each other, none at all.

Graham Chapman glanced at the man sitting across from him at the plush green table. He coolly assessed the cards in his hand. Not a flicker of heightened interest showed in his face. He reached for the cigarillo he held between his teeth and thoughtfully flicked the ash into a heavy glass tray beside him. With an annoyed movement of his hand he brushed aside a dull spark that had fallen on his dove gray brocade vest. His ruffled white shirt gleamed in the stark glare of the overhead light, and his elegant hands easily fanned the cards out before him.

He had not bothered to take off his hat, and the rich beaver brim cast a shadow over his eyes. Carefully, carefully, he hid the exultation he had felt when he first glanced at Nester's hand. He knew the reckless effect it would have on the man. He had been waiting for a chance like this for a long, long time now. This hand, this town, the wealth of the man sitting here before him—yes, by God, but he had been waiting. He had just dealt the fourth round in five-card stud. Nester had two aces showing and one jack. Graham had two kings and a six. He raised an eyebrow as the man looked at his hole card and tried to appear calm.

"Five," said Nester.

Graham had left Brookline City dead broke, with a modest debt for the lumber he had contracted for. He managed to pay this off and clear his name in a reasonable length of time. A bad reputation with bills had a peculiar tendency to follow a man, so he made it a rather showy point to pay off all debts, legally contracted or not, as quickly as possible. Therefore he gained a reputation for honor with all sorts of people. Less easy to square with himself was the death of Grenelda Flynn, and he was haunted by it for many months.

Since the fiasco at Brookline City, six years ago, he had drifted over the western half of Nebraska and finally back down into Kansas, all the time observing how fortunes were made and the workings of the world of speculation. His intense feeling of personal failure dimmed with time when he saw over and over again how easily towns folded for other men as well.

He was much wiser now. There were only two sure ways to establish a town. Make it a county seat or get a railroad going through. Brookline City had been based on the first way. It hadn't worked. People were too whimsical to be counted on to vote in a county seat. The second was surer, and the more dependable, as it was based on money. He understood railroad men. They were only interested in the bottom line.

"Raise you five," he said to the man across the table.

"See you five, and raise you five more."

Graham had discovered his natural knack for gambling a couple of years ago, and he was able to build a good stake in a very short time. People's eyes reflected very clearly the nature of the cards they held in their hands. Theodore had taught him very well.

Sooner or later, as he hung around saloons, someone would ask him if he wanted to be dealt in, and then he would accept. The trick was to strike just the right chord when he first came into town. He must appear prosperous enough that he would seem to be worth inviting to join the game, yet not appear to be so professional that people would be wary of him.

Graham was definitely a professional. He rarely cheated. It was not so much that it was against his ethics as it was that for him it was simply not necessary. Through his instincts, winning came honestly and easily. Tonight, however, he planned to use every card-switching trick he had ever learned.

Normally he settled for modest increases in his bankroll, and deftly manipulated the opinions of those in the town he was in in such a way that he was usually remembered fondly, if with a trace of confusion, even by those he had fleeced. But he was always remembered. He saw to that. The slim, elegant man dressed in gray stayed on people's minds for a long time.

A couple of feet from the table, Shirley, one of the town's three dance-hall girls and occasional prostitutes, stood with her arms folded across the skimpy black bodice of her flounced dress.

"Another round, boys?" she asked, swallowing hard as she glanced at the two kings and the six Chapman had on the board. It didn't stand a chance against the hand Nester was already showing. She went behind the bar and stayed there, too nervous to watch.

"Stay the hell away when I'm playing," Graham had warned when he first came to town. "A man would have to be blind and deaf not to know what I have in my hand just by your snorting and squealing. Just stay the hell away."

Shirley narrowed her eyes as she looked around the room. Tonight was different from the other nights Nester and Graham had played. She could feel it in the air. There was a tension to Graham's movements, however casual they appeared to others. And there was money, money, money behind Graham Chapman. She just knew it. Too many other gamblers had passed through for her not to realize the man was in another class. She didn't know what he was up to, but something big. There wasn't a chance he would ever fall for her, but still, she didn't want to make him mad.

"That five, by the way, was five hundred, not five dollars," said Graham.

The man standing at the end of the bar was close enough to their table to hear the last words, and he nudged his friend. Quickly the word spread that there was big doings going on right before their eyes, and suddenly the room became quiet and ears became sensitive to every sound. Not a man there had seen a game played for this high a stake before.

Hank Nester was not a favorite of anyone here. If this stranger who had just been in town for a week now managed to take the little son-of-a-bitch, it would not wring a tear from a single one of them.

Old Hank had taken advantage of every homesteader that was in trouble for miles around.

"Five hundred?" Hank tried to keep his voice steady. The fool must think he was bluffing. But he had three aces with his hole card, and the gambler was clearly a goner. Chapman had to be bidding on the strength of two pairs, kings high, with a six in the hole. It was the only thing that made sense. "See you five and raise you five more."

"I'm staying," said Chapman. The tension crackled in the room. There was just one more deal remaining. A fine sheen of sweat gleamed on Graham's forehead as he considered the stakes. It wasn't a question of money. He had the resources of the Union Pacific Railroad in back of him. It wasn't a question of the cards. He knew what Nester had on the board, what he had in the hole, and what he would have by the time the deal was finished. This game was the ultimate test of Graham's ability to evaluate people. The problem was seducing Hank into staying in the game. If Graham won, he would control the most valuable piece of property between the Rockies and the Mississippi. This particular game was the culmination of many poker hands he had played with Hank Nester. Carefully, carefully he had brought this man along.

Graham had met a depot agent for the Union Pacific one night who had sworn, in a state of drunkenness, that a certain strip of land in this county was destined to be a railroad division point—the magic factor that literally assured the success of a town. This time, by God, he wanted a town that was successful and not a facade.

Graham went immediately to the surveyor's office to learn the name of the owner of the favored piece of land.

No one would have suspected that the man who had shown up in the saloon six months ago in shabby work clothes and a month-old beard was the same person they saw before them now. He had casually drifted into town and then faded into the general atmosphere as adeptly as any other bum who liked to drink too well. He did not ask any more questions than were absolutely necessary.

The third night, his ears perked up as he heard the name he had been listening for. A cowboy at the bar stood with an uplifted beer stein, slopping suds over the counter-top and cursing Hank Nester.

Graham had not looked at the two men at any time, so they were not aware of his intense interest in their conversation. After the homesteader had left, he sidled up to the man's friend.

"Anyone know where I can get ahold of Hank Nester?"

"Why in God's name would you *want* to?"

"Need a job. Hear he's looking for a hand."

"More'n likely," said the man with a snort. "He goes through enough of them."

"His place must be big, then."

"Hell, yes. It ought to be. He stole every damn acre he could get his hands on, the son-of-a-bitch. Poor farmers never even see the foreclosure notice, let alone the newspapers. They think it don't matter none, if they mess around a month or two when it comes time to prove up. No hurry, in their mind. They'll go to the county seat when they can, and pay the fee. Well, it does matter. First thing you know, some s.o.b. from the territorial land office rides up and tells them Hank Nester has bought their claim. Five years go down the drain. For nothing."

"Does he farm at all?"

"Not as much as he could. Some folks think he's just gambling that a railroad will go through his holdings if he can get enough ground. He's probably right. If you own it all, there's little way it can miss."

Graham frowned. No doubt Nester knew the land's potential value.

Getting it would be more difficult than he thought. He would not offer to buy it outright. That in itself would be a sure tip-off something was going to happen.

He began the long walk out to the Nester homestead, comfortable in his conviction he would not be recognized. He did not ride, because the possession of a horse by the type of person he wanted to appear to be would be cause for suspicion. Nester lived in a frame house on a claim some ten miles from Fredricksville. The house alone put him in another social bracket from his neighbors. Although sod houses were much more practical and provided excellent insulation from the climatic changes of the prairie, a frame house was reserved for the elite and was every woman's goal.

He "helloed the house," and when Nester came to the door he meekly asked for a job, all the while twisting his hat in his hand and keeping his eyes downcast.

Nester coolly looked him over and dismissed him.

"No jobs here. Move on before nightfall."

Room and board were normally offered to anyone. With the curtness of his voice, this beefy-faced man had told Graham everything he needed to know. Nester, then, was a very small person who could be counted on to underestimate others' abilities—the type who always overplayed his hand.

As he left, Graham slowly kicked a rock in front of him, his childhood habit that persisted when he was deep in thought. This would be like shooting ducks in a bucket, and he was looking forward to every minute of it.

He left the next morning and came back to town six weeks later. He was impeccably turned out in a gray brocade vest, tailored dove gray broadcloth pants, and a ruffled white shirt. His horse was a splendid black stallion with a high-stepping gait. His saddle was decorated with engravings of silver that flashed in the sun. There was no mistaking his occupation. They took one look at his handsome blond face and steely gray eyes, and word went quickly about that there was a professional gambler here, ready to try his skills against the local population. He lost no time in following through on their image of him.

One fall evening when the sun was setting and there was a single bird singing from the cupola on the livery stable at the edge of town, Hank Nester came riding in, perched on the seat of his wagon and flicking the reins with unnecessary frequency against the sweaty backs of his pair of roan workhorses.

After picking up his supplies he headed for the Caged Bird Saloon and with swaggering authority ordered a round for himself and the other two men at the bar.

He picked up his mug and surveyed the room. One foot was cocked casually on the brass rail, and his huge belly hung over his sweat-stained belt buckle. Graham did not meet his eyes but simply went on dealing to the four men still left in the game.

Again Nester ordered a round of drinks, in a loud tone of voice, as though he wanted to attract Graham's attention.

Another hand was played without so much as a glance in Nester's direction. At last, Nester strolled over to the table and stood casually watching a friend's hand. After the round had been played, Graham looked up and said pleasantly, "The game's open. Do you want in?"

"O.K.," said Nester. He crowded a chair into the circle.

They played quickly, with wins and losses being dealt evenly about, and Graham noticed Nester was annoyed at the minute stakes. Graham smiled. He had a lot more money.

"Kind of penny ante, ain't it," grunted Nester finally.

"I'll play for any stakes you want," Graham said. "The choice is yours."

"O.K. Two dollars, then."

Graham shrugged.

"Whatever you say."

Two men dropped out at the heightened stakes and the other two stayed in with Graham and Nester. Graham felt the cords in his neck tighten slightly, but his voice did not betray his increased interest at all.

He let Nester win, deliberately not calling him, when he knew intuitively that he had the better hand. Carefully, Nester was duped into thinking his abilities were better than the professional's. At the end of the evening, Nester pocketed a pile of coins, and as he swaggered out the door, he condescendingly called back to Graham, "Better let me give you a chance to win it all back. Hate to see you leave town like a plucked chicken."

"O.K.," said Graham. "I'd appreciate it. We'll try another game anytime you're in town."

He grinned and slowly started to deal himself a game of solitaire. There was no doubt in his mind that the sucker would be back.

He didn't have long to wait. Just three days later, Nester came in and challenged Graham.

"Just one thing needs to be understood," said Graham. "I want the money on the table for whatever stakes we play, or real collateral in writing. Not just a promise to get money. It's got to be setting right here on the table for each and every game."

"Done," said Nester impatiently. He rubbed his hands together and blew into them. He could not wait to get started. Already the town was buzzing about how he had cleaned this gambler out several days ago.

Most saloons in rural areas were little more than trading centers for gossip and information. Beer, crackers, and cheese were the staples for those lucky enough to be able to afford them, so the clientele at the Caged Bird that night gasped at the glamour and uniqueness of seeing a game played for high stakes.

Nester began with table stakes of twenty dollars, and Graham was careful to let the man see a hint of alarm in his eyes, as though he were already beginning to regret his own rules. At last Nester was dealt an exceptional hand. His triumph as he glanced down at the full house was clear. Two pairs were showing on the board, and his eyes gleamed as he studied his hole card.

"See you twenty and raise you fifty," he said gleefully. His hands were trembling as he reached into his money bag.

Graham gritted his teeth. Raising as much as fifty dollars was the stupid mistake of an amateur. It was a sure tip-off to the importance of his hand, and only a total idiot would try to stay in after this. He was even going to have to teach the damn fool to play first, before he could lure him in deep enough to fleece him.

"Can't see you," said Graham. "You've got better than me showing on the board."

Nester's mouth went dry with chagrin, and realizing his own ineptness, he swore in his mind this kind of blunder would not happen again.

Finally Nester had another good hand. Graham let himself be lured upward. Then as Nester bid another prudent amount, Graham declared in an annoyed tone of voice that he did not have enough money to see him again. Nester raked in a healthy pile of coins, and his shrewd mind was beginning to realize the potential for backing people into a corner who did not have the stakes to stay in the game. It was a practice he was very familiar with. After all, on a larger scale, it was how he had acquired nearly all his land. But for tonight, the handsome stranger was out of money, and he got to take everything he had.

On the way back to his house, Nester plotted his strategy. He would lure the man in and then make sure he had all of his money and raise the bet far beyond the amount Graham had on him.

Graham smiled at the memory of the past games, and the effort he had expended to bring this man along. Tonight when Nester walked into the saloon, without speaking or even nodding his head at anyone, Graham was waiting. It was as though he had sensed that tonight would be special from the very beginning.

"Before I deal this last card," said Graham quietly, "I just want to remind you of our table rules. The money has to be up front or solid collateral put in writing."

"Yes, yes," said Nester impatiently, "that's all been decided. Just deal, damn it."

All eyes were on Graham. He reached for his cigar and slowly took a deep puff, to hide his nervousness. There was not a breath of air in the saloon, and what he was about to do required superb concentration. He looked at Nester, wanting to remember every last detail of the man's expression, then flicked over a jack to match the one on the board.

Nester's scowl deepened in an attempt to hide the triumph in his eyes. His first by-God, genuine full house, with aces high.

Graham dealt his last card, and the on-lookers gasped as he turned over a third king to join the two on the board. His hand brushed against a pile of chips, and all eyes were briefly diverted as he switched the king of clubs remaining in the deck with his hole card. He now had four of a kind. He carefully restacked the chips. He was too professional to do anything as blatant as knocking a chip on the floor. Just a flicker of disarray was all it had taken.

Nester was sweating heavily now. He was attempting to hide his glee over the full house. He did not want to alert Graham to the real strength of his hand.

He was counting on Graham's believing he was bluffing, as the two pairs were hearts and there was a possible flush. It was the last bet, and his move. He took a deep breath.

"Bet a thousand," said Nester, sure Chapman would not stay in. The crowd gasped. This type of money was unheard of.

Graham sat very still. He was well prepared for this move. He had come to the table with all the money he needed. Still Graham did not speak.

"If you don't have the money," Nester said, "your horse is O.K." He had coveted the black stallion ever since Graham came into town.

Graham nodded and motioned for Shirley to bring him a pen and paper, and he signed his horse over as collateral for the hand.

Nester did not try to conceal his surprise, then grinned as he looked again at his hand. His face froze as Graham said, "See your thousand with my horse as collateral as you requested and raise you one thousand."

The color drained from Nester's face. Graham's move was so stunning that the people in the saloon found themselves holding their breaths to hear every word.

"I don't have that kind of money on me," he stammered. Graham had always dropped out before when the stakes got so high. I could borrow, he thought wildly. Anyone would loan him money on this hand, for Christ's sake. He still didn't understand just how this had happened.

"Let me give you an I.O.U.," he pleaded. "I can get you the money, but let me stay."

"You can stay," said Graham, "but there will be no I.O.U.s for money.

We agreed on that from the very beginning," he said. "Just acceptable collateral."

"What do you want? Name it. You can have everything I own." Nester was so sure he had the winning hand that at this moment he would have pledged anything.

"I want the five sections along the bank of the Little Beaver." Graham looked him in the eye and gave an exact description down to the latitude and longitude. "Plus the southwest quarter of section twelve, township thirteen, range thirty-six, and the southeast half of section eleven, township thirteen, range thirty-seven."

Nester's mind was functioning in a confused haze. The type of description he was hearing could only be gotten from a land office. He was in so far over his head that he wasn't sure of his next move. What in the hell was going on? It was all up to him. There was no doubt in his mind that he had the winning hand. He didn't dare lose the thousand dollars. He was land poor without much cash, and the money was earmarked for the interest due on just the five sections Graham had named. He had to stay in. If he quit and forfeited the thousand, he would lose the land to the bank.

Three of a kind showing on the board beat two pairs. Graham must think he was bluffing, as he had been the other night when he raised the stakes too high for anyone to stay in. He hesitated and then drew his red kerchief from his back pocket and mopped the sweat from his brow.

"You're on," said Nester. "I'm calling your bet."

Graham reached inside his coat pocket and pulled out a thousand dollars' worth of gold coins. He could have produced even more money if necessary. The officials of the Union Pacific Railroad Company had learned a great deal since the Credit Mobilier scandal. He was well financed. If he was successful in acquiring the land, he had been promised shares of stock in the railroad itself and the possibility of becoming rich beyond all imagining. Fulfilling his childhood dream was nearly within his grasp.

Nester, in turn, reached for a slip of paper and carefully wrote down the legal description of the land. There was a small chance Graham had a full house too, but it had to be kings high and his aces would have him beat.

Nester snorted like a blacksmith's bellows losing air and wheezed out his challenge.

"O.K. Let's see 'em." His hands trembled as he held the cards. Why in the hell would this man just happen to know the legal description of his best piece of land? He felt as though he had gotten into a game with the devil.

Graham Chapman looked squarely across the table at the petty huckster and smiled inwardly. He would remember this night for a long, long time.

Without a flicker in his expression, Graham laid the other king out on the table. Not wanting to miss one moment of Nester's anguish, his eyes did not swerve.

Nester laid his hand, the hand of a lifetime, down on the table. Three aces and two jacks, and it wasn't enough. He had just lost the most wonderful package of land in the territory. Chapman had to have some inkling of its worth, to have had the exact legal description. The man had to have cheated. It was the only thing that made sense. You could play forever and not get four of a kind and a full house in the same evening.

Nester's rage grew. The bastard had ruined him. His grief increased with each passing beat of his heart. He had no friends. They were all glad to see him fall flat on his face, he realized. Well, he would show them all.

He groped for his revolver, and Shirley screamed. Graham dropped beneath the table, and a split second after Nester's shot had ricocheted across the room, Graham took careful aim and shot Nester through the heart.

The sheriff was among the observers.

"I saw everything," he assured Graham. "You were acting in self-defense." If he privately thought that Nester's shot was the clear miss of an amateur and that it would not have been necessary for Graham to return the fire at all, he kept it to himself. They were finally rid of a notorious bully. The town had been done a big favor, clear and simple.

Graham nodded curtly at the sheriff, collected the winnings, and walked from the saloon, head held high, with slow, deliberate steps.

He went to the telegraph office and sent a wire to E. H. Huttwell, vice-president of the Union Pacific Railroad.

CAN DELIVER LAND AS PROMISED. WILL BEGIN TOWN IMMEDIATELY AND SECURE BONDS.

The next week, he surveyed his holdings. Suddenly, as the land swept before him in its incredible potential, he had a vision of what his town would be like. It would be real this time. He would see to that. He knew every single detail, now, of creating a town.

The railroad would insure its success, but he wanted to play every angle. He wanted his key people to be here first. He wanted a doctor, and a blacksmith, and a first-rate hotel. This time, when people came, they would find more than a set of stakes driven into a plot of land. They would find the people and services they wanted most.

He vowed that this would be the most stable and popular town west of the Mississippi, and it would be his own creation.

There were only three claims that had been filed in the area: a Daniel

Hollingworth, a Vensel Smrcka, and a Jeremiah Keever. None of the families had been here for long. No doubt by the time he got the town started and the railroad going through, they would be more than glad to sell out. He, in turn, would then sell their land back to E. H. Huttwell. He whistled cheerfully, and then turned and headed back to town.

Daniel's face was lined with worry as he hitched Toby to the wagon. He had expected three acres of corn to yield more. The scarcity of the harvest had frightened him as nothing else had. Yet there was enough seed sacked and propped against the walls in their soddy to plant the three acres he had broken out plus enough for the additional three acres he would have ready next year. Their cash needs were minimal and the profit from the corn he was taking to market would see them through the winter.

He spent every waking moment from dawn to sunset trying to break out more sod. At least the three acres he had worked this year would be more receptive to grain. Next spring, when he planted his corn, it would simply be a matter of punching holes in the soil with a stick, then covering the seed. He would not ever again have to go through the first process of hacking at the massive grass-bound clods with an ax to cut a slash for the precious kernel that had to compete with the grass roots for nourishment.

He had rejoiced when he was finally able to plow the field decently and could actually work a row. The stubble was plowed under and would deteriorate to enrich the soil. The earth had given up and was at last resigned to losing her grass. He had won. But at times, when he thought about fighting her for additional acreage, his heart sank. They now had a pile of cobs for fuel. It was certainly not enough to provide heat for the winter, but it would help.

Aura Lee stood in the doorway, her hands hidden under her apron, her eyes solemn and bright with tears. Since she had learned of her parents' death, she dogged Daniel like a shadow. She would not speak of the tragedy for days at a time and then her need to talk would be so overwhelming words would pour out of her.

"They buried them *without* me, Daniel. It seems so unreal, like they can't really be dead. It's just not possible. Some days I just can't believe it."

Most of the time he was at a loss for words and the situation had been made to seem even more abnormal by the other two batches of letters he had fetched from the trading post.

She wept hysterically when he brought the first bundle back. As she read the ghost letters written before her parents' death she swayed back and forth in her chair, then turned to Daniel for comfort. The next batch also contained letters of sympathy from her friends and she read these over and over again, and grieved until her heart was wrung dry of all emotion.

Daniel had read her the second letter from Uncle Justin in which the old man expressed his dismay that so little money had been left in Aura Lee's trust.

"Every spare nickel was poured into that house," he wrote. "God only knows why, but the remaining funds are in the First National Bank here in Saint Jo, and there is a very small amount of stock in the Union Pacific Railroad. I believe it is sound, and I will leave everything as it is unless I receive instructions to the contrary."

When Daniel had asked Aura Lee if Justin's financial arrangements met with her approval, she looked at him blankly and shrugged.

"You decide," she whispered.

Daniel checked the trappings and turned to Aura Lee and hugged her one last time.

She had not asked to go with him, but he still felt guilty she would not be making the trip. All he had to go on to locate the new town of Little Beaver was a flyer left at the trading post. He had been given vague directions to the location by the postmaster. He had not even considered risking Aura Lee's precarious health in weather that was already nippy. If there were not a hotel available, she could never stand sleeping in the open.

"Little Beaver embodies the most liberal and advanced ideas of what a town can be," the flyer read.

Begun by merchants of matchless vision on the banks of the most benevolent body of water this side of the Nile, this booming metropolis boasts of the most generous prices outside of the Chicago markets for goods produced by our noble husbands of the soil.

"Well, I guess it's time," said Daniel. He gently kissed Aura Lee and resolutely turned away. "Are you sure you'll be all right?" he asked foolishly.

"I'll be fine, Daniel," she replied mechanically, and her eyes flickered with chagrin. They both knew it was a lie, and they both knew how she would be did not matter. There was no choice. The wives stayed home, and the husbands went to town.

Daniel pulled into the primitive town mid-morning of the third day. He grinned at the inconsistencies in the flyer, but was limp with relief that Little Beaver actually existed. There was a market for his corn, and that was all that mattered.

He pocketed the money for his grain, then went to investigate the hubbub on the outskirts.

"What's going on?" he asked.

The man standing next to him could not restrain his laughter.

"Circus folks. Claim they've been conned. They're all madder than hell. They came by rail as far as Wallace, and then when they saw the flyer about Little Beaver they decided to take a chance on coming here to give a performance. Thought there would be more people."

"What's so funny about that?"

"Take a look at their flyer."

Daniel read the brochure the man handed him.

Ten big shows rolled into one. Thirty-one chariots. Twenty-five hundred costly and rare animals, including a three-headed calf. See the authentic Indian chief reenacting the blood-curdling raid that made his tribe the terror of the plains. See the most beautiful woman in the world suspended by a slender thread in mid-air as she risks her life in a death-defying spin. See the harem rescued from an Indian Sultan, determined to keep them in bondage. See Attila hurled one hundred feet by the ancient Roman war machine.

Daniel's laugh echoed across the crowd.

"Now which one do you suppose is the most beautiful woman in the world?" he asked.

"Don't have any idea," the man replied. "Couldn't say right off hand."

The two men studied the tacky menagerie in front of them and chuckled.

The chubby little manager shook with rage.

"This town has been misrepresented," he said. "The lies are a disgrace." With a self-righteous attempt at humiliating the townspeople, he shook his fist in the air, and continued dramatically, "Laugh if you will, you perverse and viperous collection of people, but through your willful deception of your fellow man, you are forcing these fine people with an ancient and honorable tradition of showmanship to disband and seek employment as they may find it. Their blood is on your hands. We will be conducting an auction at noon tomorrow, as this—this—booming metropolis," he jeered as he waved the flyer promoting Little Beaver, "this booming metropolis clearly cannot generate enough funds to pay the rail fare back to our winter quarters."

The men immediately began to prowl around the equipment and tentatively set prices in their minds for the wagons, ropes, wires, buckets, poles, and other circus trappings. This was a rare chance to acquire goods not normally available, and some items, such as the canvases for the tents, were extremely valuable.

Daniel walked around a light-weight wagon, pulling at its wheels. He stopped abruptly at a whinny and whistled when he saw the most magnificent team of Clydesdale draft horses he had ever seen. They grazed contentedly and did not look up when Daniel stretched a hand out to caress the powerful haunch of the one nearest him. Circus broken, they were used to crowds of people, and capable of incredible feats of labor. Their medieval forebears were used as knights' chargers; protected by their heavy metal skirts the great horses once mowed through enemy lines.

Daniel Hollingworth, with his princely gifts of a towering intellect and an iron will, whose pride in his own abilities had always protected him from the other deadly sins, suddenly was consumed with longing to own these horses. He was burnt up with the coveting of them. The one on the right suddenly shuddered its coat and with a proud swell of its graceful neck looked into Daniel's black eyes. The animals had bright bay coats accented with snow white stripes on their faces. Their feathers, the fine white hairs on the bottoms of their legs, were as soft as powder snow. The white extended beyond their knees and hocks. They represented perfection for their breed.

Daniel lifted a hoof and ran his finger around the circular outline of the wall. The soles were properly arched and the frog, the triangular fleshy pad, was full and elastic.

His mind whirled in protest against the fierce twang in his heart. The money from the corn could not *possibly* cover their purchase price.

One of the horses gently stamped a huge hoof and tossed its magnificent head. Daniel's hands passed upward in his examination, marveling at their strong grace. There were no lesions or abnormalities.

I need these horses, by God. I need them. His thoughts were fueled by the return of his dreams for his homestead. The sheer practicality of owning these horses was overwhelming. Think of the sod that could be broken, the improvements that could be made on their land. The magnitude and wonder of the work that could be accomplished. As he continued to stroke the horses, he fought against the one possibility that to him was unthinkable. He could invade Aura Lee's trust. Uncle Justin had said the money would be made available at any time.

He gave a quick jerk on the brim of his hat and resolutely began to walk away. A gentle snort from one of the Clydesdales made him turn back. Indecision assailed him. In a way, it would be the best thing for Aura Lee too. After all, he wanted to make a go of their place for her sake as well as his.

The circus manager watched from a distance, and called to Daniel as he started to walk away.

"You need to see them in motion to know their real worth, mister." He loosened the horses from their tethers and led them to a clear area to put them through their paces.

"Walk them toward me," said Daniel. His sharp eyes could see no signs of the slight lameness that could be disguised by faster paces.

"Now a trot." Many men were watching now. The horses obediently trotted with a high, springy gait, covering the ground in long, proud strides.

The crowd was unusually silent. Most draft horses in the area were the far less spectacular Percherons, and the incredible grace of this team seemed incongruous. When the demonstration was over, there was not a man there who questioned their worth or their soundness, but few had the cash to seriously consider bidding.

Still undecided, Daniel wired Uncle Justin for the money. Sell the stock in the Union Pacific as well, he had instructed. If he went ahead he needed to have the funds on hand; if he backed out, he could replace the money as easily as he had obtained it. By evening he had the necessary letter of credit on the First National Bank of Saint Jo, but was no closer to deciding if he had the right to use Aura Lee's money this way.

That evening he strolled into the bar and was sipping his beer when the Indian who had been billed as the Authentic Chief in the circus came in and sat down on a stool. His long hair was braided into a single pigtail and was topped with an old black felt hat. Like most Cheyennes he was tall and his large frame was carried with rigid straightness.

The bartender hesitated at taking his order, then shrugged. He grinned broadly when the redskin ordered a sarsaparilla.

The bat-wing doors flew open and three men paused in the entrance. Their eyes, perennially suspicious, quickly swept the room. Their hands were poised on empty gunbelts; they had surrendered their weapons to the sheriff in compliance with the town ordinance against firearms.

Now to a man they wished they had not given in so easily when they saw the Indian and a chance for a little fun. They would have enjoyed a war dance.

"Hey, you there. Noble savage. Well, now, looky here, boys. Just look what I've found." The scar running from Deke's ear to his mouth gleamed under the soft lamp light. As his face split into a wide grin it distorted his features into a grotesque lopsided mask. "Now just looky here. I've found a noble redskin with no hankering for firewater. What do you reckon it would take to make him change his mind?"

"Don't know. Ain't hardly polite now, is it, to turn up your nose at a white man's drink?"

"How much persuasion do you s'pose it'll take?"

Charlie Stone Wolf tensed his shoulders, beneath his buckskin shirt. He steadied his fury with deep even breaths.

Deke slipped out the door and returned in a moment with a coiled whip. Charlie swung around on the bar stool and his eyes glittered with contempt. To him it was no weapon at all. The manhood rites he had endured at puberty had inflicted more pain than this piece of hide ever could. Deke was infuriated by his lack of response.

"Oh, a smart-ass, huh? Let's see you shrug this off."

Faster than Charlie could move, Billy had roped his arms to his sides, and Willis, the man on the right, pulled a knife from his boot.

"Now, God damn it. You're going to have a drink."

"No," said Daniel, rising to his feet like a strong tower. "No. He's not."

"Well, damn, boys. Looks like we have a genuine first class Indian-lover. Stay out of this, hayseed."

"Turn him loose," said Daniel in a quiet, dangerous voice. "Right now." Deke snorted.

Daniel crossed the room and slammed his steel fist into Deke's mouth so quickly the cowboy's face mirrored his shock as he thudded to the floor. With a sure, deft movement he crushed the wrist of the man holding the knife, and slashed the rope constraining Charlie Stone Wolf. Now there were two against three, and just as suddenly there were none, as the two drifters sullenly dragged Deke out the door.

"I would be honored, sir, if you would join me at my table," Daniel said solemnly.

Charlie quickly scanned the man's face for sarcasm at the unaccustomed "sir." As he looked into Daniel's clear eyes, fierce with jubilation at having achieved justice, Charlie knew he had met a man.

Ousting the three men could have been done by anyone who liked to fight. It was the fact that Daniel had aligned himself with an Indian over an issue involving human dignity that was rare. He had seldom found others with this quality of courage. The Cheyenne glorified integrity above all other virtues. But even among his own people it was a rare chief who commanded this sort of respect. Occasionally he had observed the trait in some white men while he served the United States Army as a scout. In that long glance, his kinship with the homesteader was sealed, and Charlie proudly moved his glass of sarsaparilla to the table of his friend.

. . .

The whole town attended the auction. As he stood watching the sale of goods, Daniel was startled to find Charlie standing at his side. The Indian's approach was so quiet he hadn't realized he was there.

"What will you do now?" Daniel asked.

Charlie shrugged. "I'll find work," he said easily. "I know the ways of white men."

Daniel nodded, reluctant to pry. The man obviously had a good command of the language.

Then they announced that the Clydesdales would be auctioned. Daniel's eyes were drawn again to the huge, feather-legged draft animals. Having decided to replace Aura Lee's money, he stifled his longing and reviewed his arguments. They would eat too much. Horses required care. He did not have any place to put them. There would be the additional expense for harnesses and trapping.

The man from the livery stable placed the first bid and grinned good naturedly at the hooting from the crowd. Others picked it up, and then the bidding began in earnest.

Daniel swore softly, stunned when he realized the last bid had come from one of the cowboys he had tangled with.

Suddenly all the arguments for buying the horses came to mind. He could do more work in less time, make more money. He could easily build a barn for them if he had them to cut the sod. There were used harnesses available. His unbroken land would furnish all the pasture they needed. But the most compelling reason was that he knew the men would not be good to the horses. If it were his own money, he would not hesitate for a moment. The team was his best chance to break out enough land to make a living.

His voice rang out clearly and he topped the bid, exhilarated at having decided at last.

"Two hundred dollars."

The bidding was quickly over. He soon located some used equipment for his horses.

When he went into the general store he noticed an advertisement for a dance, and promised himself he would take Aura Lee to one as soon as possible, as they were held in Little Beaver every month. He hummed to himself while the clerk cut the fabric he was buying to surprise her. When they came to town again there would be an abundance of money for the goods he wanted to buy for his wife. His eyes danced over the dishes and fancy vases. His horses would help make it all possible.

As he flicked the reins he marveled again at the strength of this team. They were pulling his wagon as though it were a toy, and at last Toby was getting a well-deserved rest. He would make Aura Lee understand how immeasurably the horses would improve their lot. And he had made sure there was enough of her money left for the well she yearned for.

Aura Lee laid down her quilting and rushed outside. She had sat by the window with her work all morning, watching, waiting, listening, yearning for Daniel's return. At last she could see a shape on the horizon. Her husband was coming home. She was limp with relief. She could feel the tension melting away. When the team came closer to the house, their giant hooves sounding like muffled thunder as they pranced smartly in the bright, high air, Daniel stood up and waved his hat joyfully at his wife. She ran to meet him and he sharply commanded the horses to stop as he jumped to the ground and swung Aura Lee off her feet in a quick embrace.

"Daniel, what on earth have you done?"

"Bought us a team, Aura Lee. Going to make progress, by God."

"Where did you get the money?" she asked in bewilderment.

"Well, that will take a bit of explaining," he said, groping for the right words. "Sweetheart, I know this is going to sound a little drastic to you. But I cleared out your trust."

"Cleared out. What does that mean?" Her heart sank as she pressed for an explanation. "Does that mean I don't have any more money, Daniel? Does it? Not for anything? We'll just have to live on what you make on this godforsaken place in spite of whatever happens?"

"Well, it just means we're going to have to wait a little while longer to buy some things I know you would like to have."

"Like to have? Need. I *need* things, Daniel." Her voice rose in fury. "How could you, oh, how could you have done such a thing to me after all I've been through? You didn't have the right. What about water? You promised me a well, or does *that* fall under the category of needless luxuries?"

"There's money for the well, Aura Lee. I made sure of it. I would like to remind you that you did give me permission to decide how your money could be best used. And believe me, these horses will be the best possible use in the long run. Let me tell you why."

"Never mind the reasons, Daniel. I don't want to hear them. I'm sure each and every one is beautifully, flawlessly logical." She whirled toward the soddy, her hand covering her mouth to muffle the sobs. Daniel got back on the wagon seat and hung his head as he rested his hands on his knees, his jaw muscles working. Abruptly, he slapped his hands, clucked to the team and tethered them outside the corral.

"Welcome to our happy home, fellows," he said ironically, as they immediately began grazing.

Daniel Hollingworth completed plowing under the last row of stubble, then leaned against the side of one of the Clydesdales. Every last muscle of his body had been strained to the limit this past month. The weather would be turning soon. There was a heavy, brooding quality to the air that quickened his blood and infused all the farm work with a sense of urgency. Such a short time before winter set in.

Maybe next year, he would have a riding plow. But he groaned at the thought of having to learn how to use anything different from the equipment he had assembled to utilize the team. His wife's attitude had not helped at all. But he always put her first. She was usually unaware of the sacrifices he had made for her welfare. He had wanted to ask her for several lengths of the fabric he had brought back from Little Beaver because after he had worked the horses for a couple of weeks, their necks had grown a little thinner and their collars were no longer a perfect fit. He needed Aura Lee's material to pad the collars' inner circles. He knew better than to ask this of her, however, and had instead made an unnecessary trip to the trading post where he exchanged the old collars for new ones, taking care they fit so snugly that just his fingers, held flat, could be passed between the rim and the sides of the neck.

Back home, he put the leather collars in lukewarm water in Aura Lee's wash kettle to soak for an hour. Afterwards, he would work the horses lightly and as the damp collars dried they would adjust to the exact shape of the horses' necks and shoulders.

"Whatever are you doing, Daniel?" she had asked.

"I had to buy new collars for the team," he said, not looking up. Too proud to let her know how her feelings had been protected. Her lip trembled but she did not reply. He kept his eyes on the kettle. The old collars would have done just as well, with a little padding.

Other problems and expenses had come up in relation to the horses. The rings on the hame were not at the right location for hitching his plows correctly. They had been placed for pulling the circus wagons. As a result, there was an up-pull on the plow causing a too-shallow furrow. He added a stop at a blacksmith shop to get new hame rings attached to the growing list of goods and services that would require another trip into Little Beaver.

Now as he rested for a moment his heart leaped in triumph in spite of his fatigue. Today's work was done down to the very last bit—everything he had set out to accomplish. He frowned as he realized he would be late for supper and flicked the reins across the horses' backs. Dapper, the huge Clydesdale on the left, stamped impatiently before he responded to the command. Daniel grinned, knowing the draft horses understood they had finished. He had a nearly psychic rapport with this team. His pride in owning these magnificent animals was boundless.

He reached the barn just before dark. The last rays of the sun highlighted his heavy masculine features as he looked proudly at his homestead. By God, but it was something. Expansion of the corral was the first improvement he had made, and just this last month he had added this sod barn so he could properly house his animals this winter. He had been reluctant to ask Vensel to help lay the heavy blocks, weighted with the guilty knowledge that it would be many years before his neighbor made this kind of progress. However, Vensel's gratitude at being offered the use of the horses for a day in exchange for helping build the barn quickly laid his doubts to rest.

No matter how tired he was at the end of a day, Daniel was always renewed when he looked around and took in the results of his work. It was a neat place. Patiently each morning he set everything to rights. Sometimes this meant just lining up a milk bucket blown over in the night or freeing a tumbleweed that had blown in the yard.

Tonight he did not waste any time admiring his work. Tomorrow would be a big day for them, and there was still much work to be done in spite of Aura Lee's protests.

"You don't need to help me get ready," she said stiffly. "I'm perfectly capable of cooking for a little company, Daniel."

"I know that, honey. I didn't mean to hurt your feelings." He sighed. He never seemed to say the right thing. "I just want to do right by you, Aura Lee."

But the offer to help had been made in the morning, and this was tonight, and even he was drained. He had driven himself too hard today and his team too. He eyed the Clydesdales critically. He needed food and a rubdown nearly as bad as they did. He dipped up the measure of oats. Then when they jostled each other for position and started nibbling, he walked the long yards to the water tank and carried back the water they needed. With the doggedness that tapped his physical strength over and over again, he picked up a gunny sack and began their long nightly grooming ritual, taking care to brush off any dirt or caked mud that might cause a skin irritation. Insects and parasites were not given a chance to breed in the coats of these glorious horses.

Aura Lee slipped out to the barn and paused in the fading light. Daniel's back was to her. She smoothed back her hair and folded her arms across her chest and listened to Daniel with wonder.

"There now, boy," he crooned. "That's a fine boy. Just let me see your other leg, now." Gently Daniel lifted a hoof and examined it, all the while caressing the horse. His deep voice was whisper-low as he stroked the Clydesdales.

"'At's a good boy," he continued. "Time to rest, now."

Aura Lee's heart broke with the longing to be included. Oh, Daniel, Daniel. You never sing to me, never talk to me like that. Never pet me, never praise me. And I swear to God you've never once in your whole life worried about my getting enough rest. My heart is cored out from the trying. With grief beyond tears, she slipped back out as quietly as she had come in.

When their coats shone at last, Daniel looked around with satisfaction. All was taken care of, down to the last detail. He turned them out to pasture for the night, securing long ropes to the tethers.

The odor of beans and johnny cake drifted through the open door. He hung up his jacket on the peg in the wall and warily looked over at his wife. Her face was tighter than usual this evening—a sure indication she had had another bad day.

Nevertheless, the house was in order for once and the cheerful squares of their patchwork quilt brightened the room.

Hesitantly, he held out his arms and without a word, in spite of her injured soul, Aura Lee walked over to him and leaned against his shoulder. He was like iron now; it was literally like embracing a tree. He gently stroked her hair and ached with sympathy he did not know how to express. She no longer struggled for words to explain emotions she herself did not understand. He relaxed and held her less stiffly as she rested with powder softness against him. She welcomed this contact tonight, but he was never sure in advance. Sometimes, under circumstances that to him seemed just the same, there would be flicker of annoyance in her eyes when he held out his arms and with an expression too subtle to be called coldness, she would proudly dismiss his sympathy.

"Just hold on," he whispered softly. "It will get better for you, I promise."

"Oh, Daniel, I love you so. I just wish—"

"Sh," he whispered, and his jaw tightened with self-control. At least he had this tenderness and so did she.

He held her at arm's length and whirled her around, spanking her lightly on the butt.

"Go get my food, woman," he said with mock gruffness.

She dished supper quickly, and they sat down to beans that were too watery and cornbread bitter with the lingering taste of the scorched edges she had scraped off.

Aura Lee smiled apologetically, and Daniel quickly grinned. For a moment he remembered Lucinda Smrcka's heavenly kitchen with aromas that would make Christ himself weaken if the devil had tempted him with her cooking. Along with the memory of the odors came a vision of the woman herself, with her firm, promising body and her tremendous competency. Mostly he wished Aura Lee had some of that. Dangerous to dwell on such thoughts, he decided. Especially when the Smrckas would be here tomorrow.

"Glad the weather's holding," he said. "Well-digging's a bad enough job when things are just right."

"It will be good to see Anton, and of course, Vensel and Lucinda," she added hastily. "What are the well-borers like?"

"I've never met them. Their work is guaranteed, that's all I know. If they don't get a well, I don't have to pay any money. You can't beat that. They're probably bachelors. No woman could stand for a man to be gone as long at a time as they are."

"You can't imagine how wonderful it will be to have water on our own place."

"I know. We're just lucky they're coming before winter."

Well-digging was especially dangerous—a job that was hired out by any homesteader who could possibly afford it. The number of deaths was astronomical. The men who escaped cave-ins and falling objects were often killed by the poisonous gas, damp, that was present at great depths.

Although he was bone-tired and wanted to get to bed, Daniel started to help clear the table. He stopped when he saw the pail sitting by the wash basin.

"Haven't you made the butter yet?"

"I forgot," she stammered. "Oh, can't it wait until morning, Daniel? I've spent all day cleaning."

"No, it can't," he said flatly. "After we get the well dug, maybe it will wait a day. Then we'll lower our cream into the well in a bucket. Cream will hold for a little while inside a cold well, but this will turn by morning. We were lucky to get it."

Tears stung Aura Lee's eyes. She had been truly grateful when Jeremiah Keever dropped the cream off. She had watched his wagon full of supplies until it disappeared over the horizon, touched by this gift of appreciation for the help she and Daniel had given him. She had wanted to get to the butter right away, but she had had so many other jobs to do.

Now she was so tired she could hardly keep her eyes open. She felt a quick rage welling inside her. She hated this prairie that was sucking the life out of her. She hated this house, and for a moment she hated this man who made her feel guilty every moment of every single day because she could not keep up with the mountain of work that was always before her.

She looked at the dishes that needed washing, the endless layer of dust drifting down from the sod ceiling, and then at Daniel doggedly working the churn, and suddenly whirled around and defiantly began to change into her nightgown. She was going to bed and he could stay up and work as long as he liked. Daniel gritted his teeth and the thumping of the churn in his hands acquired a steady, unnecessarily heavy rhythm that never let up until the butter was done.

"They're here, Daniel."

"Smrckas or the men?"

"The men." Aura Lee glanced at herself in the mirror and flushed at the lift of Daniel's eyebrow as he watched her admire herself. There was even a touch of color in her cheeks today, and he prayed this meant the shadow of her parents' death was lifting. Perhaps she was taking the first steps toward greener pastures after all. Her hair was freshly washed and her home was clean and tidy. Her marvelous patchwork designs were beginning to transform the place. Her eyes were feverish with excitement. There would be people about today, and she had drawn on the false energy anticipation gives.

Daniel waved to the men from the doorway, nearly as grateful for the break as Aura Lee. His horses would be used today to haul up an occasional load of dirt, but it would be a switch from their usual grueling labor.

The two men pulled up in front of the soddy and Daniel gave a whoop of delight as he saw who was handling the reins.

"An Indian, Daniel?" asked Aura Lee, ashamed at her sudden fear.

"An old friend, honey, believe me, an *old* friend," he said, squeezing her shoulder reassuringly. He had yearned to tell her about all of his experiences in Little Beaver but had been stopped by the pain in her eyes whenever he mentioned a single word about the trip that had ended in robbing her of her inheritance.

Charlie Stone Wolf jumped down from the wagon, and stood proudly in front of the homesteader.

"So you *did* find a place for yourself."

"Right away." He grinned.

The other man extended his hand.

"Lark Slocum," he said.

"Daniel Hollingworth, and as I'm sure you've gathered, this other fellow and I have already met. The last I knew he was looking for a job."

"Well, I was damn glad to find him. He's the best well-witcher in the whole state of Kansas."

Daniel eyed the wagonload of equipment. Jeremiah Keever had brought word from Little Beaver when he dropped off the cream that their farm was next on the well-borers' list and they would arrive today.

"This is probably the last well we can sink before winter sets in," Lark said.

"I know," said Daniel. "I was getting worried you would not be able to make it."

"We're in demand, all right," replied the well-borer. He knew that even with neighbors helping one another, the homesteaders who could not afford their services could not afford the loss of time from their field work that it took to locate water by themselves.

Lark Slocum was a small man, quick and serious, and seemed to Daniel too frail for work.

"Let's unload, Charlie," he said.

The two men laid an assortment of picks and shovels and a well-auger next to the wagon. The auger was the professional badge of the well-borer. The enormous spiraled bit would be fastened to a buttressed cross-piece of wood and twisted into the ground, then hauled back out, straight up, with the wood attached to a pulley attached to the top of a derrick. Each time five feet of dry earth was extracted, another five feet of pipe would be added. Always, there was the heartbreaking possibility of the pipe twisting off, at a great depth, causing the loss of the bit and the poles, without knowing whether or not water had been reached.

When they had finished, the Indian stood beside Lark with his arms folded across his chest. Deep lines running from his nose to his mouth were etched in his swarthy skin.

"There's the Smrckas, Daniel."

Aura Lee waved at her neighbors. Vensel would help haul up the dirt. She wished she could greet his wife with more joy, but she could not suppress the edginess Lucinda evoked in her. Still, she would have a woman's company for a whole day, and there was always little Anton. Her house was ready, so she needn't be ashamed of it, and perhaps Lucinda would play for her. No matter what, she had decided, today was the day she would ask her neighbor to teach her to play the violin.

Lucinda could not believe her eyes as they came upon the homestead and her heart lurched with misgiving.

"Vensel. What is this? Did you know about all this?"

Vensel was filled with self-reproach. Contrite now, that he had not

153

been able to bring himself to tell Lucinda he had helped build a barn on the days he had gone over to the Hollingworths'. He had let her think his labor had gone to assist with ordinary field work.

Shamed, he nodded his head.

"Yes, I knew, and there are horses also," he said quietly.

At that moment one of the great Clydesdales whinnied and Lucinda darted to the corral and stared with awe at the horses. Dapper tossed his proud head and his white mane floated like a banner in the gentle wind as his coat rippled with power. The horses suit the man, she thought. They are just like him. And our poor miserable creature is as spiritless as my Vensel. She continued to look as though a spell had been cast over her and Vensel watched as her handsome face cracked with envy, her mouth growing heavy and sullen. He sighed. Perhaps he had been wrong not to tell her, but he had known what her reaction would be. Now here it was, and they would pay for days now, he and Anton.

Aura Lee laughed at Lucinda's extravagance as she carried the food into the house. She was determined to pretend to be a gay, charming hostess and enjoy the day, but something within her drew back at the tightness in the woman's mouth, and her greeting sounded more formal than she had intended.

"Let's go watch the menfolks," said Lucinda after they had placed her food on the shelves.

The two women stood to one side.

"How do they know where to dig?" asked Lucinda.

"I asked Daniel. He says one of them can witch."

"Witch?"

"Not witch like an old crone. He says some people can just tell where there's water and oh, look! It's the Indian who can. I guess that's what he's doing."

Charlie Stone Wolf firmly held the two ends of a forked willow stick and began to pace back and forth, carefully working outward from the house. Absolutely nothing happened.

Aura Lee looked at Daniel as the color drained from his face. If water were not available on their homestead, they would have to start all over again. The house, the corral, the barn would have been put up in vain, because sod structures could never be moved. Then the fields he had worked so hard to prepare would have to be abandoned.

The Indian began to pace again, working farther and farther away. Even if he located a vein now, at this distance they might as well be going the three miles to the creek, as it would still involve loading barrels in a wagon.

Charlie came back and the lines on his face had deepened.

"We will try one of the other ones," he said, gesturing at the Smrckas and the Hollingworths and even little Anton.

"Charlie can only witch to a certain depth. If water is close to the surface, he can find it. Always," Lark said flatly. "There may still be water here. Can any of you witch?"

"None of us has ever tried, I'm sure," said Daniel. "I'll go first." He grasped the willow stick with its prong pointing straight up in the air and he began to criss-cross his property. He finished in silence and handed the divining rod to Vensel, who also tried, with no results.

Anton was wide eyed at being permitted to participate in this grown-up ritual, but Charlie insisted.

"Sometimes the little ones are the best."

Lucinda was next and as the handsome woman began to pace, her hair blowing in the wind, Aura Lee just knew at once that she would not be successful.

What a curious thing to be so sure of, thought Aura Lee. But Lucinda's so much of the earth and like the earth that all currents and vibrations coming from it are already a part of her.

Aura Lee was next to take her turn with the willow stick. She set off at a brisk pace, walking north to south. Then as she headed east to west, she stopped in amazement. The stick vibrated and she was jolted by an unmistakable current. Suddenly, the prong twisted so hard in her hands she was unable to control it. It resisted as though it had a will of its own.

"Daniel." She dropped the stick as if she were holding a snake. "Daniel, I don't even believe in this," she stammered. "I don't understand. I don't even believe." She began to back away from the willow stick.

"Just be glad it happened, Aura Lee. I don't know when I've been so relieved."

"You don't have to believe," said Charlie quietly. "The power is given where the power is given. Do it once more and we'll start digging."

With trembling hands, Aura Lee picked up the stick. Again it dived toward the spot it had found.

"Thank God," said Daniel.

"It's very deep," said Charlie, "but the water is here, so let's get started."

The group relaxed and started to praise Aura Lee.

"You've saved the day," said Vensel.

"Glad you were here," said Lark. "This doesn't come up very often, but who knows? Maybe there were lots of other wells we didn't dig because we couldn't witch deep."

"I didn't do anything," Aura Lee protested. "I don't even believe. I'm going inside. There's work to do there."

Embarrassed by all the attention, she turned, and her feet froze to the ground.

The envy on Lucinda Smrcka's face was unmistakable. The woman's lips were heavy and twisted downward. Her eyes were narrowed and her pupils were pinpoints in the full sun. Aura Lee was seized with a chilly reluctance to be in the house with the woman.

"I'll be inside in a minute," she said. "You go on ahead." Daniel and Vensel went to the corral to hitch up the horses. She walked over to Charlie and pretended an interest in his pick axes and sledges. Anything to escape the hostility radiating from Lucinda.

The Indian was squatting on his haunches and he turned to Aura Lee, glancing at the other three men who were yards away now.

"You're *shaman*."

"What?" Aura Lee started backing away. There was no one or no place on her homestead today that seemed even vaguely normal.

"Don't be afraid. You must understand the power or it will destroy you."

Aura Lee turned and walked away, swallowing hard. There were already too many things she did not understand. She did not want to know anything more about the willow stick. Even the early winter sun's rays seemed queer and threatening. She went inside her house to seek the warmth of her stove.

"So you have completed your magic for the day," said Lucinda. She was sitting at the table, the basket of food resting on the cottonwood planks that were already beginning to warp a little from frequent scrubbings.

"It's not magic," said Aura Lee. "And it's none of my doing. I didn't even know I could."

"In my country," said Lucinda, her sly eyes studying Aura Lee, "in my country, a woman has to be very careful of such things or she will be accused of witchcraft."

Aura Lee surprised them both with her fierce blaze of words. "I do not want any mention of this nonsense ever again. Not from you, or that Indian out there. We've got *work* to do. Food to fix."

She angrily crossed over to a bowl of bread dough and began to pummel it. Temporarily subdued, Lucinda began to husk the corn she had brought along. Deftly, she hacked off the ends of the ears and carefully searched the rows for any remaining traces of silk. When she was finished, she went outside to light the fire under Aura Lee's huge laundry kettle. When the water was boiling she would add the corn. She did not speak to Anton as he left the menfolk and went inside the soddy.

Her anger dissipated now, Aura Lee looked up from her work.

"Anton, you can't begin to imagine how glad I am to see you today," she said dryly. "You're the only one who seems to be even slightly familiar. Besides, I've put some things back for you. I want to see if you can remember your colors and—why—sweetheart, what's the matter?"

Great tears were trickling down the little boy's cheeks as he stood wordlessly before her. His frail body trembled like a tiny blade of grass in the wind. He kept his enormous gray eyes lowered to the floor.

"Anton, what's wrong?" She knelt in front of him and anxiously searched his face.

"I can't—I can't tell you." His voice jerked as he began to sob in earnest.

"Sweetheart!" She hugged him in dismay and felt his little heart, rapid as a bird's, beating frantically in his breast. "Sweetheart, we're best friends, don't you remember? And best friends tell each other everything."

Stubbornly he shook his head, and sniffing, he lifted his hand to dry his tears.

Spotting the bandage, Aura Lee took his hand in her own.

"You've hurt yourself. Is that it? You poor little thing."

Still he did not reply, then gave a faint cry of protest as Aura Lee began to unwrap the cotton covering the angry, festering wound.

"Oh, Anton. My God, what has happened?" The blood rushed to her head so quickly she had to reach a hand out to the floor to keep from losing her balance. Her voice was shrill with shock.

"Anton. Tell me. There's no way a burn on the back of your hand could have been accidental. Tell me."

His slender neck was bowed in agony.

"Anton. Just nod your head then. Did—did *she* do this to you?"

He nodded and tears of relief began.

"Oh, my God, why? Why would anyone do this? Does your father know?"

He shook his head. "Don't tell, please. It wasn't her fault," he whimpered. "Just don't tell Dad. It's my fault. I ruined her quilt."

"Anton, listen to me. No matter *what* you did, there's no excuse for this, and certainly your dad needs to know."

His eyes were miserable with alarm. "Don't tell," he pleaded. "Oh, please, just don't tell."

"Don't worry, Anton. I won't do anything to bring any more grief on you. I need some time to think just now." .

At that moment, Lucinda entered. Seeing Aura Lee kneeling in front of the boy, and glimpsing the unwrapped hand, she felt a high blush flame in her sunburned cheeks. Then she shrugged and her eyes challenged Aura Lee.

Aura Lee rose to her feet, sick with pity for the boy, and wary as she had never been before in her life. She was amazed at her own cunning, knowing that for Anton's sake, she must find some way to let this evil woman save face. She must not, whatever it cost her or however much Anton misunderstood, must not let the woman see her horror, or Lucinda would surely take it out on the boy.

She responded to her neighbor's challenge with her own brand of silence. She too shrugged, and patted Anton on the shoulder.

"Run along now. Your mother and I have work to do."

Relief flickered across Anton's face. Averting his eyes, he headed out the door.

Lucinda frowned and continued to watch Aura Lee. Waiting, waiting, for the words that would permit her to attack. They did not come. Aura Lee began to busy herself with setting plates on the table.

Lucinda watched her for a moment, then her face sagged with shame.

"My water is probably boiling," she said heavily. "I'll go see if it's time to add the corn."

"All right," said Aura Lee, relieved she would not be forced to confront the cruelty to Anton until she had time to think.

The menfolks were boisterous and entertaining at dinnertime. It would take many days to finish digging the well, and this was the only time the Smrckas would be here too, so the well-borers devoured the food, enjoying the variety offered.

Charlie's face was inscrutable as he half-listened to the others talk. They were out-doing one another with well-digging stories.

"And there was another man up near Richmond," said Lark, "who got down far enough all right and was just bringing up the last few loads of dirt when the rope broke. Killed him deader'n hell before anyone could so much as call out a warning."

The danger of the rope breaking on the twenty-pound steel-banded buckets was known by all. Many a man had lost his life from a falling object.

Vensel looked solemnly at Lucinda, hoping she was hearing and understanding what was being said so she would appreciate his refusal to dig a well alone. The lines in his face had deepened when he saw the effect the barn and the horses had on Lucinda. And to think that these possessions had been acquired in the short time since he had asked them to attend to Julka. He had watched the Clydesdales with amazement today, admiring their formidable strength and grace. They had rotated the auger with ease, and easily pulled the huge loads of dirt up from the hole. Shyly he looked at the Indian, wishing he too could afford to make arrangements to have a well dug while the men were in the area.

Aura Lee passed the bread to Charlie, avoiding his eyes.

In my tribe, thought Charlie, this woman would be given a place of honor. During puberty rites and ceremonials, her abilities would be discovered. There would be women like my mother to show her the way to keep the power from turning inward. He could tell by her haunted eyes that it was what was happening. Maybe there was a way provided for white people that he didn't know about. But it had always seemed to him that as a people from the cradle to the grave they turned their backs on the gods.

"Tell them about the man over by Vicksburg, Charlie," said Lark. Charlie began the tale, still watching the pale, frail white woman. Something had happened this morning to upset her.

At that moment, Lucinda reached for Daniel's coffee cup and as her fingers brushed his, he saw the man's chest stop mid-breath for just a second and a deep flush stain his cheeks. The Indian's eyes darkened with understanding. Quickly he looked at Aura Lee. She was too preoccupied to notice. It was something else, then, that was upsetting her. Like the currents she had found this morning, the trouble was deep and dangerous.

After they finished doing the dishes, Aura Lee picked up a sock she was darning and sat at the table, silent and edgy. Let Lucinda think of something to say. She refused to. The room was filled with the woman's presence somehow as she worked a patch in a pair of trousers.

Suddenly Lucinda could stand it no longer.

"I'm going outside," she said, leaping to her feet.

"All right," said Aura Lee, meeting her eyes across the table. "All right."

All afternoon Aura Lee's mind had been awhirl. She went over possibilities until she was dizzy. Tell Vensel? He couldn't watch Lucinda all the time, and what purpose would it serve? She knew from the day they had first come over to their soddy that Vensel was already having trouble enough with this woman. Take the boy to live with them? She would love it, but neither Vensel nor Anton would agree. Ask Daniel for advice? Quick tears of dismay stung her eyes and she closed them tightly as she put his sock down on her lap. She brushed back a tendril of hair. Tell Daniel? She knew how harsh Daniel could be sometimes. Would he think somehow that it was Anton's fault, or that he deserved it?

"He might," the voices mocked. "He's cruel to you." *Not true*, she thought, shocked. *Not true, oh, you don't understand him. You don't, you don't.*

The evening meal consisted of the leftovers they had covered with a cloth. It was twilight now and the kerosene lamp made the inside of the soddy homey and pleasant.

After they had eaten, the men visited some more, then Lucinda volunteered to play.

Charlie watched Daniel Hollingworth's face as the room was filled with

159

a subtle Slavic melody. At last the homesteader could not resist looking at Lucinda, and her face was bright with mocking laughter. Charlie's eyes became tiny with knowledge. He had no doubts at all about the woman's intentions. He was not, however, sure of the man's.

Aura Lee reached for Anton and pulled him closer to her as his stepmother switched tempo.

If it was the last thing she ever did, she decided, she would figure out some way to protect this child.

Lucinda stood before them, her linsey-woolsey dress straining over her full bosom as she drew the bow. Her hair was the color of bronzed autumn leaves in the lamplight.

Aura Lee shuddered as if overcome with a chill, and was filled with an absolute aversion to the violin that she would carry with her the rest of her life. She was shaking now with her loathing of this woman and her damnable instrument, the devil's own choice, with its capacity for atonality and imbalance. Like Lucinda herself, it could turn jarring and discordant in a way that was not possible to duplicate with the piano.

Thank God, Aura Lee thought, *I did not ask her to teach me before all of this came up. She must never, never know of my music. She would turn my yearning against me somehow, as she has everything else she has learned about me. I don't ever want to see or hear the violin again as long as I live.*

It was Sunday. A day of rest. But there was no peace in the Smrcka household. Vensel would not work on Sunday. His refusal had caused friction between Lucinda and him from the very beginning.

"Even if the weather is fine? You lose too much time, Vensel."

"I get the time back," he said. "There are small things that heal that day. And for my horse also." He once honored God with this day, and in spite of the work during the week, he made his peace with his Maker and was given a measure of mercy, just enough strength for the week ahead. He lived from Sunday to Sunday. The light was different that day. The air was brighter. At first he had tried to persuade her to do little cooking. She too could rest, and perhaps they could find simple pleasures to share together as he and Julka had once done. It was a fine thing to sit outside on a Sunday evening and pray together.

Now he simply did not work on that particular day and there was no goodness to be found anywhere. No balm given from the Bible that lay spread open on his lap. He blinked his sad eyes and tried once more to focus on the words. It was no use. Anton was curled up on his pallet, driven there by Lucinda's scolding. Vensel squeezed his eyes to check the

160

tears that were trying to find their ways over his lids. He had so little, and now she had even taken his Sundays from him.

She had not stopped talking about the well since they had come back from the Hollingworths', and this morning she had been swarming at him like a wasp since dawn.

"We could dig our own, Vensel. I *know* we could. I watched. I know how it is done. We don't need an auger. Other people have done it. We're closer to the creek than the Hollingworths and surely would not have to go very deep."

"Lucinda," he protested. "Lucinda, didn't you hear the stories? The danger?"

"We have a horse to bring up the dirt," she said, her ears deaf to his voice. "We can build our own derrick from—from the wood on your useless wagon." The ruined wagon was a closed subject between them. When she first asked him what had happened to the sides, her question had been met with one of the stubborn silences in Vensel that drove her wild.

"There are other things that are needed, Lucinda. Things we do not have. A pulley. Enough rope."

"So. Now you are seeing how. Well, Vensel, let us begin to make our plans then."

"I didn't say—" His eyes were grave. Perhaps it would be possible. They could use the wagon tongue and splice the boards to build a three-legged tripod. Perhaps the water was very close to the surface. Perhaps she would agree to a trade. She wanted her well, he wanted his Sundays back.

"Lucinda, if I do everything I can to bring in a well, I want peace in this household on my day of rest. Will you agree to that? No quarrelsome words, no complaining?"

"Yes, yes, yes. I will do this for you, Vensel."

"We will have to borrow."

"Just a pulley. And the Hollingworths owe it to you."

He looked up in surprise.

"Owe?"

"Yes. They have more than their rightful share already. More than is just."

Vensel pounded the last board into place to form the third leg of the flimsy, short wooden derrick and began to dig in the spot Lucinda had selected. He had wanted to ask Aura Lee to come over and find the water for them, but Lucinda stopped him.

161

"What the woman did was nothing, Vensel. I too can find the water. On our own land, we do not need such nonsense. We are close to the creek. You can just dig anywhere. I'm sure there's no need for such witchcraft."

With a pick and a shovel, Vensel began, at first just placing the bucket of dirt on the rim of the hole when it was full and resting when Lucinda emptied it. Then as the cavity grew deeper he hoisted the twenty-pound steel-banded bucket onto his shoulder and Lucinda squatted down to pull it out and take it away. At last he had dug to such a depth that it was necessary to attach a rope to the bucket and use their pulley system, with the weight of the extracted dirt being borne by their horse as he towed the bucket up and down, stopping obediently as Lucinda unfastened the thick wire handle from the hook suspended from the pulley mechanism. Even little Anton had a part in the work. It was his responsibility to lead the horse and control the tension on the rope.

Aura Lee stood by the side of the well. She was tempted to lift the boards off to peer into its great depths, but had learned to be content with just going outside to see it once or twice a day. She could see Daniel in the distance driving his team and himself to break more land. The air was cool this morning and she shivered, feeling foolish at her need to see this proof that there was actually water on their land. It was like a miracle, and if it had not been for the Indian's quiet insistence that it was there, just on the evidence of the diving of a mere stick of wood, they would have given the project up as a lost cause long before they brought the well in. Daniel was jubilant and fired with energy. She had not realized how much the lack of water had troubled him.

A queer thing had happened since the day the Smrckas were over. She was now so intensely preoccupied with concern for Anton that the voices had stopped. For several days now her mind was blessedly free of their haunting, troublesome echoes. But a new demon came to take their place. She spent every waking moment testing possibilities in her mind, imagining the results and discarding one plan after another. Every fiber in her body was involved in finding a way to protect the child.

She hugged her shawl more closely about her and turned toward the house when suddenly she was filled with a spasm of apprehension so powerful she shuddered violently in the pale gray light. She looked about in growing fear for a presence, an unseen force. Her teeth chattered as she ran for the soddy. She flung the door closed behind her and pressed her back against it with her hands outstretched to barricade her home. Her breath was coming in short bursts and her breast was heaving.

In spite of her fear tears began. She had thought she was getting better.

The voices had stopped. Oh, was there no offering, no sacrifice she could make to appease the God so bent on tormenting her? I *can't* be getting worse, she thought. It's not possible for me to get worse. But I never have felt like this before, not once. Her eyes opened wide with the memory. Not true. She had felt like this, and it was on the night her parents died. The blood drained from her head and she slowly crept over to the table and sat on a chair with head lowered between her knees to avoid fainting. Oh, no, she thought with cold horror. Was one of her own in danger? Was this a warning? It had been true before. Daniel? Anton—her heart leaped with sureness. Anton. The sick despair whirled away from her the moment she acted. Fired by urgency, she unbolted the door and ran toward the Smrckas' and at last had to settle to a ragged, stumbling walk. Her heartbeat thundered in her ears. I do not want this—I do not want this—I do not want this.

She came up over the rise just yards now from the Smrckas'. Lucinda stood tall and erect, her skirts whipping about her legs in the wind and her proud head held high. And there was Anton, sound as could be, leading a horse away from the well.

Aura Lee sank to her knees in thanksgiving, laughing and sobbing at her foolishness. Thank God, the boy was fine. She lifted her chin and shook her head to free her mind of nonsense, then with a weak cry tried to rise to her feet, but her strength had been spent.

She saw Lucinda go behind the horse and give it a resounding slap just as it was pulling the full bucket to the top of the derrick.

Aura Lee screamed into the wind. "Anton, Vensel. My God."

Hearing the words the child whirled just in time to see the horse rear.

"Dad," he called. "Dad. Watch out." The horse bolted in the opposite direction and the heavy bucket plummeted downward, the rope breaking as it received the jolt. Vensel flattened himself against the side of the well, his hands stretched above his head to protect his skull as much as possible. But the bucket had been hung dead center and there was enough clearance for it to miss Vensel entirely. He yelled up immediately with a shaking voice.

"I'm all right."

"Dad didn't get hurt. It missed him," Anton shouted. "He's fine, Aura Lee. Oh, no," he said suddenly, remembering. "The horse. I've got to go catch the horse so we can get Dad out of the well." He took off at a trot as Vensel now straddled the lowered bucket and depended on the strength of their horse for the long ascent.

Great sobs of relief washed over Aura Lee in waves. She leaned on one arm, her legs curled under her, brushed her hair away from her face and looked at her neighbor. Lucinda's eyes were fastened on a distant spot on the horizon as though she were in a trance. She broke and covered her face with her hands as her shoulders shook with remorse.

Aura Lee rose to her feet with the wobbly tentativeness of a young colt trying first steps. She steadied herself and walked slowly over to the woman. Lucinda saw her coming from the corner of her eye and stiffened.

"You saw what happened," she began. "The carelessness of that boy. We trusted him with such a small thing. To steady the old horse, and see what he almost did while his mind was off someplace gathering wool, and to just think that my Vensel—"

"Stop it, Lucinda. Right now. I won't listen to another word. I *saw* it all. The whole thing."

Lucinda's eyes were wary, carefully hearing her out before she said a word.

"Now, you listen to me. I *know* what you did to Anton, and I *know* what you tried to do to Vensel. There's no law out here right now. There's no money to leave or God knows I would have done it months ago, so we're all going to have to learn to live together, and if you ever hurt either one of them, I'll—" She hesitated. Do what? Who would believe her?

Lucinda immediately sensed her double-mindedness and continued to listen with a mocking smile. Aura Lee stood tall and she looked the Bohemian woman full in the face.

"I'll know. You can be sure of that. And I have special ways. Ways you do not know about. I can do things to you that will seem so natural to have gone wrong, that you will never be sure if it's my—my abilities— or just the usual course of events." She fumbled as she searched for the words, then her heart leaped in triumph as the woman's eyes wavered in fear. Lucinda was clearly superstitious to the core.

Lucinda raised her eyes to the horizon, and it was a moment before she replied.

"I will not hurt them," she said quietly. She turned and went into the dugout, leaving Aura Lee to marvel at what had taken place.

Aura Lee hurried home to start dinner. Her mind whirled with wonder. But one thought kept leaping like a spring lamb. Lucinda Smrcka was afraid of her. She believed every bit of her claim to special powers. The thought made her gleeful. And planting it in Lucinda's mind—that when natural things went wrong, it would be her doing! What a stroke of genius. Aura Lee laughed out loud. Now the poor woman would think it was she who was in back of every broken bowl, every batch of bread that failed to rise, anything at all that went wrong. It had been so long since she had experienced a good emotion, she had forgotten what a wonderful feeling it was. Flowers were sprinkled across the prairie and the buffalo grass felt like a magic carpet under her feet. She had been able to take some action, and although she knew she had gained control over a situation through deceit, it felt marvelous. She had protected Anton. She herself had been able to stand up to this wicked woman. All by herself.

20

"Ready, Aura Lee?" asked Daniel. They were going to Little Beaver. It would be her first trip to town since their marriage.

She paused beside the wagon and looked around one more time. Everything was put inside the soddy, or secured against the wind. Jeremiah Keever had agreed to look after the place and feed Toby in exchange for their bringing him back supplies.

She smiled at Daniel and nodded her head. Things were better between them. They were not so quick to take offense at small things done in innocence. The voices had been banished for a while now, and she was strangely at peace over Anton. Sure he was safe, if not happy, and if the situation changed she would know somehow. This certainty was somehow mixed up with the light, but she could not allow herself to ponder too long on such thoughts. The mystery was that since the day at the Smrckas' she had gained some control over all the forces tugging at her. She was still too thin, too nervous, but better, and for right now it was enough.

She had decided not to mention the episode to Daniel, afraid to hold the day's event before the scrutiny of his bright logic. Even Anton and Vensel had no idea the bolting of the horse had not been accidental. This dark secret was only known to herself and Lucinda.

"I can't think of another thing that needs to be done, Daniel."

The main purpose of the trip was to bring back a pump, and attach new rings to the hames on the Clydesdales' collars. Daniel had collected a list from the Smrckas and Jeremiah Keever. They all had letters to post and the Hollingworths would bring back any mail that had arrived for the other families. Trips to town were never made casually on the frontier. Requests from neighbors were always accommodated. Little Beaver, still the nearest town to their homestead, was fifty miles away and each family had requested that they purchase the precious goods required for the coming winter. Each and every item had been evaluated against the scant supply of money.

Making her list had totally preoccupied Aura Lee for days now. It was a pleasure to her to be able to concentrate finally on practical matters. It was so important not to forget anything, as Daniel had warned her they would not be going again for many months, until they had the time and money to put up a windmill.

"We'll get seed then too," said Daniel. "Wheat for me and vegetables for you."

"And flowers, Daniel? Please, some flower seeds?"

"If you want them, sweetheart," he said, his eyes softening. "Whatever you want that we can possibly afford, you can have. Anything."

"Oh, Daniel," she said. "You really do care for me, don't you? Down deep inside."

"Of course," he said, wounded and surprised. "How can you not see how much I love you? Do you think I would be busting my guts every day if I didn't? Don't ask things like that," he said. He helped her into the wagon, and the Clydesdales started off under a cloudless blue sky, heading blindly through the grass in the general direction of Little Beaver.

Daniel felt the tension leave his shoulders when their homestead faded from sight. He had driven himself to the brink of exhaustion getting ready for the coming winter. Every fiber in his body welcomed the thought of winter and the chance to repair harnesses in front of the stove. The hope of rest was the only thing that kept him going some days. And Aura Lee's work would be that much less too.

She sat beside him on the wagon, glowing with anticipation, and planned how she would spend her day in town. She did not want to squander one single moment. This trip was such a treat it had had a nearly magical effect on her disposition. It had even drawn her thoughts away from the Smrckas.

She just wished the entire time would be spent in town. Instead, there would just be one day allotted to Little Beaver. The other four would be spent coming and going. She had placed their tickings in the wagon bed so they could sleep comfortably.

A shadow of sadness crossed her mind as she realized that just a year ago she had all the treasures of Saint Jo to choose from. "Town," back then, was taken for granted, with a dazzle of bright little shops to go through. She and her girl friends had spent whole afternoons just browsing, and there had been money. Money for silks and ices after idle afternoons, and money for books and entertainment, and money for jewelry.

She closed her eyes and willed the thought to leave her mind. There was no point in letting the remembrance of past pleasures ruin the delight she had felt in the potential of the days before her. It was wonderful just to sit here beside Daniel with nothing to do.

The stars twinkled in the velvet sky that night as she lay beside her husband. One, brighter and more splendid than all the rest, caught Aura Lee's eye. *It's like Daniel,* thought Aura Lee. *Higher than all the others somehow, and set apart too.*

"Star light, star bright," she whispered fiercely, "first star I see tonight, I wish, I wish—" A tear trickled down her cheek with only the steadfast star to see it. "I wish, I wish I felt the way I used to when we made love. I wish I didn't have to pretend. I wish I could tell Daniel, but he would be so hurt." Weighted by the night, she was quickly asleep in spite of her despair.

In a couple of days, they crossed a little rise and suddenly a town sprang into view. She and Daniel stared in disbelief.

"I can't believe it," he said.

"Is that Little Beaver, Daniel?" she asked, confused.

"It *has* to be, but it's at least five times as large as it was."

"Daniel, it's a town, a real town," she cried in delight. "Look at the stores. There's everything here. Daniel, look at it. It's almost like home."

They both laughed at the exaggeration.

She looked down with dismay at her blue calico dress. If she had only known. She had decent dresses back at the soddy; silks and taffetas she had brought as part of her trousseau. If only she had known there would be decent boardwalks instead of dirt streets to tramp through.

"You'll not be needing my protection, I suppose," he teased gently as they pulled up in front of the dry goods store.

She laughed and Daniel was astonished at the change that had come over her. He wanted to kiss her, but settled for a quick squeeze of her hand instead, as displaying affection openly on the street was unthinkable.

Tears started to her brilliant blue eyes, and the delicate wild rose coloring that had given her subtle aristocratic beauty in Saint Jo was there again. She sparkled like a precious gem.

Daniel lifted her down from the wagon and impulsively gave her too much money to spend.

She stared at the five dollars.

"Oh, Daniel, you've worked so terribly hard for this."

"Don't think about that. Just have a good time, sweetheart. Buy whatever you want to."

Her eyes held his in silent, steady adoration. Daniel watched her walk down the street. Even in her faded calico dress she had the regal bearing of a lady.

Aura Lee proudly looked everyone she met straight in the eye. And every woman she spoke to was taken aback by the brightly spoken "good morning" in cultured tones that let everyone know she was no ordinary farmer's wife. Her fair hair was twisted into a cornsilk bun under her faded calico bonnet. Her blue eyes gleamed under her black lashes, and she glowed with pleasure at the prospect of having so many shops to choose from.

She went into the drug store first and looked at the array of elixirs and tonics on the shelf. She picked up a number in turn and studied the labels with astonishment.

There was one elixir in particular, Vin Vitare, retailing for $1.25 that promised nearly magical results for the very problems that worried her the most.

"For weak women, easily tired, worn out by ordinary household duties," it promised to "renew energy, soothe nerves, improve digestion, induce restful sleep, and bring back former strength."

There are other women who feel like me, then, Aura Lee thought. She stared at the five dollars in her hand. The money was so terribly hard to come by, and yet, if the medicine would set her to rights and help her sleep with her husband again, perhaps it would be worth it.

Her face turned a bright crimson as she handed the clerk the money. She watched him wrap the bottle in a plain brown paper. She stumbled over a few words of small talk, embarrassed that by buying the medication she was owning up to all the ailments listed on the label.

Well, what of it? she thought defiantly. After all, it was true. She did have almost everything wrong with her that was possible. She ached for the presence of a woman clerk who would understand her condition and advise her.

Her next stop was the dry goods store; the ever-present wonder of prairie emporiums. It was filled in every nook and cranny with the most desirable array of goods the owner could possibly squeeze in.

Aura Lee stroked a piece of dusty black velvet, then turned her attention to a bolt of slightly stained creamy satin, then to the rows of laces bound on cards. There were very plain lengths of unbleached muslin and she knew these were the most practical of all. She moved dreamily from one counter to another.

Her heartbeat slowed suddenly and there was a swift rush of blood to her head. The people, the wares, seemed far away and unreal. For there in the corner, topped with a velvet runner and a glass-shaded lamp, was an American Home upright piano. The case was hard rock maple, beautifully finished to resemble burl walnut. A wave of grief swept over her body like a jolt and she began to tremble with piercing depthless longing for the life she had left behind. She moved toward the instrument like a sleepwalker and ran her fingers in wonder over the highly polished surface of the case.

The storekeeper immediately noticed her interest.

"Do you play?" he asked politely.

"Yes," she whispered softly. "I do. That is, I used to."

"Go ahead, then," he said cheerfully. "Try it out. We're always glad to hear a little music around here."

"Thank you. Thank you so much."

She laid down her basket and her bottle of tonic and carefully sat down on the little windup stool. Slowly she pressed the ivory of the middle C and winced at the tone that emerged. It was clear and melodious, but just slightly out of tune. It was a piano! Imagine that here, out in the middle of nowhere, there could be a piano.

The price was posted in a corner of the music stand. It cost two hundred fifty dollars. Actually the storekeeper had ordered it from Sears, Roebuck for $98.50, as it was the catalog house's policy at the time to sell to storekeepers and individuals alike at the same price, and for this reason, the Sears name did not appear on very many goods, in case merchandise was being shipped to a retailer who planned to resell it for higher prices. The price on the piano, like most other items in the store, was open to negotiation.

Carefully, Aura Lee tried a simple C scale, then switched to more complicated runs and technique exercises. After she was familiar with the action and sound of the upright, she played her first piece.

As she bent to the keys, she lost all awareness of her audience, of the people drawn by the sounds, who were now silently coming into the store. Her fingers told a tale of passionate controlled pain, always suppressed, that was understood by everyone. The minor melody articulated their individual loneliness on the prairie, their fear of defeat.

As she played for over an hour there was not a sound. Finally a man pressed forward from the back of the room. The people stepped aside for the tall, elegant gentleman who had come to their new town several weeks ago. No one seemed to know what he did, but he spent whole days watching and studying their activity. He leaned against the piano case and watched Aura Lee's tapering controlled fingers glide across the keys.

She did not miss a note but there was a slight hesitation as she looked up into the unreadable gray eyes of Graham Chapman. She was acutely embarrassed, so overwhelmed with self-consciousness she felt as though she had taken leave of her senses. What had possessed her, she wondered, to show off like this in front of total strangers? What must people be thinking?

"Excuse me, please," she murmured, and rose from the stool, passing in front of the gentleman. The presence of the man before her, clad entirely in gray with the faint odor of cologne clinging to his person, painfully reminded her of her former station in life. He was like her father,

her old beaus. His face was gracious and polite. His shirt sparkled, and his fingernails were clean.

Near the entrance she saw Daniel, standing as though carved out of wood, like a cigar store Indian with his rigid posture and his arms folded across his chest. She walked with stately grace that made her appear far taller than five foot two. There was grief in Daniel's eyes as he extended his hand to her. He put an arm around her shoulders and they went out the door.

She could not speak. The emotions she had just released were too close to the surface to keep them safely under control. He led her into a restaurant and ordered a meal while she kept her awful stricken silence.

Finally, she looked at Daniel and her eyes pleaded for understanding and she said in a trembling gush of words, "Daniel, I didn't know. I didn't even *know* there were pianos out here. Daniel, if I had a piano, it would be so different. I could be like Lucinda. I know I could."

"Aura Lee, you can't mean now. Wait a couple of years and I swear you'll have your piano. But for Christ's sake, sweetheart, you know good and well you can't have one in a soddy. There would never be a way of keeping out the damp. It would never be in tune. And think of the dirt falling from the ceiling all the time. The silt would ruin the keys. God damn, honey. Just wait a couple of years, and you'll have your frame house. Then it will *all* be different." His words were harsher than he intended.

"Oh, Daniel. Can't you see what this is doing to me? I can't last another couple of years. I just can't *take* it. It's too hard on me."

"That's crazy, Aura Lee. You're made of too fine a stuff not to be able to make your way out here. You can't just give up. You know you have more steel to your spine than that."

"In another place, another life, Daniel. But this is Western Kansas, and it's a terrible place," she blurted in despair. "Daniel, out here, it takes a different spirit."

"This different spirit is what will make this part of the country great someday," he said stubbornly. "It's a matter of will, Aura Lee."

"No, it's not," she said sharply. "No, it's not, damn it. It's *not* a matter of will. We're just not meant to live out here. Daniel, I need some beauty, some grace, something to look forward to, once in a while. If there were some hope, maybe I could stand all the chores. But for right now, I just can't take it."

Daniel set his jaw. The waiter brought their food and the two of them ate in uncompromising silence. Daniel was suddenly out of sorts as he remembered the gay note on which the day had begun.

A small group of townswomen came into the cafe. One of them spotted Aura Lee. The lady turned, spoke to her companions, then headed toward the Hollingworths' table. Daniel rose to his feet as she introduced herself.

"I'm Mrs. Upjohn. My dear, we can't tell you how much we enjoyed your concert this morning."

Aura Lee blushed. She had played oblivious to the impression she was making.

"Thank you," she said. "But believe me, I got more pleasure from being able to play again than anyone else did from listening."

"The other ladies and I would like to invite you to join our literary society."

"A literary society," said Aura Lee wonderingly, "out here?"

Mrs. Upjohn glanced sharply at Aura Lee, saw the lavender circles under her eyes and the strained set of her mouth, and understood her perfectly.

"Yes, a literary society, and of course, out here. Where could it possibly be more needed? We meet once a week in each other's home and have lessons and refreshments and those of us who have some small talent perform for one another. It gives us a chance to visit and enjoy each other's company."

She longed to ask the woman questions. What did they wear? Could she wear her taffeta? Would they really like her playing? Could she discuss composers with somebody? Would they understand when she spoke of the crushing loneliness she felt in her sod house? Would they understand the awareness of inadequacy that women like Lucinda Smrcka evoked? And with a deep sense of shame, she wondered if someday there would be someone with whom she could speak of her terrifying fear of childbirth.

"Tell the other ladies I am flattered by the invitation, but our location makes it impossible at this time. We live some fifty miles from here, and of course we can't possibly come into town. We homestead."

"Oh, what a pity," said Mrs. Upjohn. "That you live so far away, I mean. You must come visit me anyway," she added firmly. "Anytime you are in town, please drop in."

"I will," Aura Lee promised, deeply pleased with the social acceptance this invitation implied.

"Daniel," she said, with a sudden flash of insight as she watched Mrs. Upjohn go out the door, "I could take this country if we lived in a town. If there were other women, and schools and churches. Just some kind of civilization."

"I will not leave my land. I can't believe you're asking me. If I wanted to live in a town, I never would have left Saint Jo."

"You're a lawyer, Daniel. A lawyer."

"Be reasonable, Aura Lee. Can you imagine me making a living practicing law out here?"

"No," she said. "To tell you the truth, I can't imagine anyone doing anything at all out here."

"You'd leave our farm for a literary society?"

"No, but for a piano, maybe." Then she was ashamed, in spite of her anger. "That just slipped out, Daniel, I'm sorry I said it, and you know I didn't really mean it."

"It's all right," he said gently. "I understand more about this than you think. Just hang on. And besides, I have a surprise for you." Daniel sat even straighter in his chair. His eyes gleamed like coals and his face split into a wide grin. "I was going to save it for later, but I think you might need something special, right now."

"What, Daniel? Oh, what?" She was pleased with his consideration and eager to put a stop to the quarreling before it ruined their trip.

"I put aside enough money to buy you a violin," he said proudly. "I've been thinking about it for a long time. Just because you can't have a piano doesn't mean you can't have any instrument at all."

Nothing, absolutely nothing he knew about his wife, and he was beginning to think that was damn little indeed, nothing had prepared him for the violence of her reaction.

"I don't want a violin, Daniel. Not now, not *ever*," she said between clenched teeth. She was shaking as though taken with a sudden chill. "Do not ever, ever speak to me of this again."

"Well, God damn. You can bet your life I won't. Case closed."

The color was returning to her face and she picked up a fork and tasted the apple cobbler, the first real dessert she could remember having in ages. Her appetite was gone, however, and she could not call it back, nor her former mood.

Daniel would not look at her. He had had another treat in mind also. There was a dance tonight, and he had planned to take her. Secretly he had packed a dress he knew she favored. In fact, he had planned a whole series of little treats for this trip. But son-of-a-bitch, if he was going to risk taking her to a dance. If just mentioning music or a violin set her off like this, who knew what effect a dance would have. Suddenly he just wanted to get the shopping done as fast as possible and head the hell for home.

The door opened and Graham Chapman came into the restaurant. He scarcely glanced in their direction as he took a table nearby. He wanted to learn everything he could about this couple before he approached them with the business he had in mind.

He wanted their homestead. It was just three miles from the town he planned to start, and was directly in the path of the proposed railroad. Just those three pieces of land, Hollingworths', Smrckas', and Keevers', were all that was needed to round out the perfect package. But in addition to their land, he wanted to acquire this couple for his town. They were the epitome of the quality he hoped to attract. He was acutely aware of the reaction of the women to Aura Lee's playing. There was adoration in their faces. She had given them hope that if a person of her caliber would consent to live here, then perhaps this area would amount to something after all.

His ears strained to hear their voices. Daniel's jaw was rock-hard as he stopped talking, and the woman was wide eyed, almost panicky. They were quarrelsome and he would love to know why. His fingers drummed a little tattoo on the red-and-white checkered tablecloth. The reason didn't really matter. Trouble was trouble, and a smart person could always use it to advantage.

Aura Lee glanced about the room, and as her eyes lit on Graham, she blushed momentarily, then looked at Daniel.

The sudden crimson in her cheeks was not lost on Graham. So she had remembered him standing at the piano this morning. He suspected that the way to Daniel Hollingworth would be through his wife.

Graham consulted his map and decided to approach Jeremiah Keever first. The other homesteader, Vensel Smrcka, might not be able to speak English, so he wanted to start with his best chance.

Graham found Keever working in the field. The man was cheerful and friendly and when Graham told him he had some business to discuss, he stopped his work willingly enough.

This man would make an ideal merchant, Graham decided. He had the pleasant, affable manner that would bring customers back year after year. He would be the perfect person to start his general store. They went into the newly built sod house, and Graham outlined frankly and honestly his plans for the future. He offered Jeremiah a fair price per acre for his homestead, thus acquiring an extra one hundred sixty acres to augment the three hundred twenty he could legally set aside under the government town act. He smiled at the relief on Keever's face.

"I'll write to my wife today. I don't know how to thank you." Jeremiah felt as though he had been delivered from hell. He could not wait to tell Elvira of their streak of good fortune. There had been a heaviness to his letters lately as he tried to prepare her for the tremendous hardship they would be facing, and deep in the back of his mind was the persistent feeling that after all, even if they were very successful, it wasn't really going to be worth the loneliness. He could not say he felt good about bringing Agnes out here. He should be able to offer the child more than mere existence. Jeremiah needed people. The monotony was already taking its toll. Even before Graham came he was beginning to question his right to bring his wife and daughter to this life, with the same routine day after day, week after week, just for the sake of owning one hundred sixty acres of land.

Right now, he just wanted the chance to get out. He signed the paper, gladly turning his holdings over to Graham, and they shook hands on the deal. Although the price Keever had received was fair per acre of farm land, it was ridiculously low per lot, if the town were ever successful.

Graham promised him he would begin building in a couple of weeks. He casually asked about the Smrckas and the Hollingworths, and Jeremiah beamed with the affability of one who sees his fellow man as basically good.

"They're wonderful people, both families."

"Do you think they'll want to sell?"

Jermiah thought for a moment.

"No," he said. "I don't."

There was a difference between himself and the other two men. Keever had felt it to the core when they were putting up his sod house. They had a type of enthusiasm for each improvement, a tie to the land he simply didn't feel. Each time Daniel or Vensel added something to their homesteads, they seemed to regard it as a victory. He glanced uneasily at the signed papers in Graham's hand. He knew the other two men would not understand, and he treasured the good opinion of his friends, but it was done.

When Graham rode out to the Smrckas' the next day, he found a neat homestead, well tended and showing evidence of the common sense it took for survival.

He helloed the house and smiled at the dark-haired little boy who darted from the entrance. His mother followed quickly behind.

Graham caught his breath as Lucinda Smrcka stood framed in the doorway, her dark auburn hair piled high. Even the ordinary homespun dress looked grand on her lush body. He was stunned not only by her beauty, but by her manner. He was used to seeing women beaten down out here, and instead there was an extraordinary vitality about her.

174

Lucinda's eyes narrowed as she studied the elegant man mounted on the coal black horse. She waited coldly for him to state his business, and told Anton to run to the field and fetch his father.

Anton's little legs just flew in the excitement a stranger brought. Lucinda's instincts told her this man was safe enough to invite in. She also knew immediately that she did not like him.

He sat down at a table that had been scrubbed and bleached. It was the most spotless dugout Graham had ever seen. She served him some freshly baked bread, and there was a steaming cup of hot coffee before him in no time.

They looked frankly at each other, without a trace of self-consciousness, and there was a sense of recognition there. They were repelled instantly by one another, as certainly as if two magnets were laid with the same poles together.

Graham did not speak, nor did she, but little moths of memories rushed at him, for Lucinda reminded him of his mother. This woman would put Belle to shame. She had the strength Belle had always yearned for, the strength to match her visions.

Vensel greeted him carefully when he came in the door. He frowned at Lucinda. He had warned her time and time again about letting strangers in when he was not there, and was always chilled when she told him not to worry about it.

"If they intend any harm," she had replied, "I will know."

Graham outlined his offer—a fair price for their homestead, plus a stake in the new town and the guarantee of backing for a business of his choice.

"It is my land," said Vensel simply.

Graham studied the solemn man with the wise, sad eyes, and at that moment Anton walked over to his father and put his hand on his shoulder. Vensel patted the boy's arm affectionately and as Graham gazed into Anton's clear, intelligent gray eyes, noting the slender body and the sensitive mouth, he knew the way to Vensel's heart. Seeing the well-worn Bible lying on the shelf, he chose his words with care.

"True, Mr. Smrcka, it is your land and I believe the man who tills the soil is the closest to God. The blouse of homespun covers a true and honest heart, linked to his Creator by his stewardship to the greatest of God's gifts, but have you thought about your son?"

Vensel waited, sitting heavily, but Graham had seen the alertness in the man's eyes.

"Your son, Mr. Smrcka, may not be intended for hard work. It says in Second Timothy that in the same household there are vessels of wood and earthenware and also vessels of gold and silver. It is a sin to go against

175

God's will for a life, to ill-use a weaker vessel. Are you usurping the role of the Master Potter, Mr. Smrcka, in deciding the shape your son's life must take?"

He settled back in his chair to let the man mull over his words. This would not be a quick decision. He knew it was not the time to push. Smrcka nodded his head to acknowledge that he understood.

"I will think," Vensel said heavily. "For this, a man should think."

"Your neighbor to the north, Jeremiah Keever, has already decided. You need to know this. He's going to start a dry goods store, and frankly, he could not be more delighted with the opportunity."

Lucinda had not said a word. The boy is all he cares about, she thought. Himself and the boy.

"Mrs. Smrcka," he said, "are you happy with your lot out here? With no one—" His words were checked by the animosity in her eyes. As though they were ancient enemies from another time.

Lucinda did not reply. She could be happy if she were not married to this dolt of a man and saddled with this whining boy. She loved this land, this life.

Graham flushed, realizing she was only too aware of the self-serving purpose of his words.

"I will think," Vensel repeated stubbornly.

Graham picked up his hat and said his goodbyes. It would be prudent to let matters rest for a while.

Vensel sat in gloomy silence and thought of the future for his boy out here on this claim. It was no way for a child to grow up. What would he have to look forward to? But would he, like Esau, be selling his birthright for a mess of pottage if he let the land go? Already it had cost him his Julka, and he was not sure he wanted to sacrifice this investment of agony. But if his quick-witted Anton needed the special schooling Mrs. Hollingworth had mentioned, this was a big decision. He needed the guidance of his friend Daniel before he would know. And as always when he was troubled, he went to the shelf and took down his battered old Bible and began slowly to search the Scriptures, hoping for some flash of insight.

Lucinda sat on the edge of the chair and stared blankly out the window. The offer had made her uneasy, but she could not find the words for her thoughts. They swarmed like bats, dark and elusive. She, this land, her life would never amount to anything married to Vensel. As she groped for expression, she finally turned crossly to her violin and began a melancholy serenade.

She loved the excitement, the glamour of towns, the bustle and the confusion, but this was the land. Here the challenge was so much greater. Anyone could survive in a town. Anyone could live decently there. But here she stood out like a shining star in her spotless dugout. Here on the prairie she was the queen.

But on the other hand, she thought peevishly, who was there to see her? What point was there in arranging hair in such glorious waves every morning, if there was no one to appreciate it? And then too, things had a way of not working out right for her and Vensel. The well had come in, just as they had hoped, very close to the surface, and now there was no money for a pump. The dead weight of a bucket of water pulled up from such a depth was so difficult for her to manage she had been better off carrying it from the creek.

It was all Aura Lee's fault that things went so badly. Perhaps her curse would not follow them into a town. It was not fair. She had kept her word. She was good to the man and the boy, but there were small mishaps that upset her. However, it seemed to her the only ones who did well in towns were quality folks. Even here in this area, where there was no pretense of social delineation, she feared the town's scrutiny most of all. There was an awareness of other people's goodness or a lack of it; an evaluation of a person's ability to build or tear down a community. It was the sole criterion for acquiring a good reputation.

There was an abrasive, disquieting quality to Lucinda. Normally she enjoyed the antipathy she aroused, but right now she was not sure if she would enjoy being friendless in a town year after year if there were not going to be a place for her to shine.

She felt curiously passive about Vensel's struggle to decide. Ordinarily she would have known immediately which decision she wanted him to make, but this time, her own confusion was the predominant emotion, and so she let Vensel brood over the offer.

She put the violin back into its case. The one thing she was sure of was that she did not like Graham Chapman. Not even a little.

22

Graham rode out to the Hollingworth claim the next morning. The impact of the piano concert in the store was still fresh in his mind, and never had he been so intrigued by a woman. The range of emotions that were expressed through her fingers was stunning. He smiled at the memory of her hair twisted into the tight bun at the stem of her slender neck and the proud, masked eyes. Banked fires still burned the hottest, and in his many years of wandering he had not seen her equal in controlled intensity. She shone like a clear, pure flame and kindled a yearning in his soul for a presence withdrawn many years before. Normally Graham was too bent on shaping circumstances to allow himself to look inward, but for a brief unhappy moment, he wished he were linked to something higher than the Union Pacific Railroad.

He was surprised at the physical appearance of their farmstead. It was very neat, and he could have sworn the woman did not have the necessary physical stamina it took to achieve this. Buckets were lined up, and even the tools were placed in descending heights at the side of the house.

It was beginning to cloud up and looked as though it would start to rain. He saw Daniel coming in from the field and waited as he came near the house.

"How do you do, sir," Graham called courteously. "I have some business to discuss with you."

"Good enough," called Daniel. "Wait until I finish taking care of my horses and we'll go inside."

Graham followed him out to the barn and watched as he rubbed down the animals, measuring the tireless quality of this man. He would have to proceed very carefully to make any progress at all with him.

At last, Daniel turned his entire attention to Graham. He remembered seeing him in Little Beaver. Graham was not an easy person to overlook. His clothes alone set him apart, and then there was his aristocratic manner.

"Let's go in the house and get some supper."

Graham followed Daniel through the yard and wondered again at the strength of the man who could construct this much order out here.

Aura Lee was standing by the stove when they came in. Her face was abnormally flushed from the steam rising from the pans she was stirring.

She blushed deeply when Graham walked in. She remembered him very well, and the intense interest he had shown in her playing.

It was wonderful to see a man dressed like a gentleman again, and she wished she had dresses that were somewhere between the dressiness of the silks and taffetas and the limp, faded, utilitarian fabrics she wore around the house.

"Mrs. Hollingworth, I'm Graham Chapman."

"I recall seeing you in Little Beaver, Mr. Chapman. Won't you eat a bit of supper with us before you tell us what brings you here?"

"It would be my pleasure, and of course, Mrs. Hollingworth, I recall seeing you, as well as everyone else did who happened to be in town that day."

The strained lines in her face softened, and he followed his comments on her playing with bits of information that he sensed would interest her.

"It was a pity you didn't stay over for the dance, Mrs. Hollingworth. There was an excellent crowd and in fact it lasted until morning. There was just a violin and a guitar, of course, but it was enough."

A dance, a dance, she thought wildly. There had been a *dance*, and Daniel hadn't told her. Had not even mentioned it.

Daniel swore savagely, silently in his mind, and his grip tightened on his coffee cup. Perhaps they should have stayed for the damn dance after all. Hearing the music, dredging up forgotten dreams, could not possibly have upset her more than she was right now.

"I'm sure it must have been delightful, Mr. Chapman," said Aura Lee, standing rigidly, proudly erect.

Graham wove in the type of gossip women treasured, and she was spellbound by the lovely, luxurious details.

"The hit of the dance was Mrs. Noonan's daughter, who was turned out in a reasonable copy of a dress she had found in *Godey's Lady's Book*. It was a bright rose cotton with a full deep skirt and shoulder extensions on the sleeves. Truly, it was a remarkable needlework achievement, and much admired by all the other ladies. Do you sew, Mrs. Hollingworth?"

"What? Oh, yes," she stammered. She was totally engrossed in both speaker and story. "Oh, yes, in fact it's one of the few things I do really well. I love to sit and think in the evening and watch—" Her voice trailed off in embarrassment. What must Daniel be thinking of such unseemly familiarity with a perfect stranger? She couldn't imagine what had come over her.

"Then you must spend some time really looking at the fabrics available in the dry goods store. They have new taffeta in, and wonderful muslin," Graham persisted. "There's going to be theater there next month. A Chautauqua group will be coming through on tour, and actually their entertainment is quite good."

"A theater? I don't believe it. What do the women wear?" she asked.

"Your favorite dress, my dear. Most of the ladies enjoy this opportunity to break out the dresses they don't get to wear at any other time."

Daniel was shocked by his wife's openness. Aura Lee normally had a delicate reserve that kept people at arm's length. Yet here she sat, chatting like a schoolgirl with this damn hustler. He glowered at her.

Graham caught the warning glance, but he stubbornly continued to charm Aura Lee. His instincts were right, he decided. Through this woman lay the way to this man's land.

"The cast has received good reviews, Mrs. Hollingworth. It would be well worth your time to attend."

She looked at Daniel, and was again warned off the conversation by the coldness in his eyes. She would never pressure him to take her fifty miles to see a theater group.

"It sounds very interesting, Mr. Chapman," she said politely. "But it is very difficult for us to get into town, you see, beyond our ordinary trips for supplies."

She was in control of herself again, and leaving the two men to their talk, she finished serving up the supper.

Graham was amused at the aplomb with which the couple was handling the meal. Clearly, they must yearn to know what he wanted, but the Hollingworths' scrupulous prairie etiquette dictated "Don't ask, it's none of your business."

To Graham it was a pleasure to talk with people aware of ideas not confined to the ordinary details of day-to-day existence. Perhaps they would catch his vision. Suddenly it became important to him that they believe. Not because he had discovered their secret strengths and weaknesses, but because they simply *must* believe in the potential that was there for towns.

Aura Lee cleared the table, and the men drew their chairs closer to the warmth of the stove.

Daniel picked up a piece of harness and began to oil the leather.

Graham knew he was among equals here, and he did not puff up his spiel.

"Mr. Hollingworth, I want to start a town in this area. I have bought land from your neighbor Jeremiah Keever. I've approached Vensel Smrcka. He has not decided yet, and now I want to see if you would be interested in selling your homestead."

Daniel looked up sharply, and he carefully laid down the harness.

Graham drew a deep breath and continued. "A town, Mr. Hollingworth. A place of commerce and opportunity, as well as the potential for great wealth. You, sir, would find many outlets in my town that are not normally available. Would you know what line of work would most appeal to you?"

"The line of work that would appeal to me, Mr. Chapman, is just what I'm doing now," he said curtly. "I am an attorney. I have many options. I am a Yale graduate. My wife is the daughter of the late Judge Lombard of Saint Jo, a very prominent and influential family in the area. I was offered a position by my uncle in one of the most promising law firms in the state of Missouri. However, Justin Hollingworth's invitation was based solely on the strength of my abilities, although my wife's social connections undoubtedly had some bearing on the other offers I received. I am here by *choice*."

Graham sat in silent chagrin. He had known from the outset that this couple was from a different cut of cloth, but with their credentials, he did not understand why a man with such a brilliant future before him would choose to grub out a meager existence.

"Can you imagine," Graham said softly, "can you begin to imagine what a person of your caliber could do in a town, in a city?"

"You talk of riches, Mr. Chapman? It is here in this earth, and someday all the merchants who have sold their homesteads for their little lots in town will bitterly regret their decisions."

"Surely you don't believe we should all have the same vocation?"

"No, of course not," said Daniel. "Of course I realize not everyone wants to be a farmer. You would be surprised at how much I know about towns and how they are put together. Something else that will surprise you, Mr. Chapman, is that I'm all *for* your ideas. But the men who are able to stick to their visions and start decent towns are rare. You may be one; I can't say. But regardless, you can count on this. You will do so without my land, and you will do so without threatening my land.

"In a town," Daniel continued with deadly verbal precision, "in a town, your soul is owned by other interests. The common good of the community has to come first. While it is honorable and necessary, I do not choose to spend the rest of my life making compromises for the good of the whole. On this one hundred sixty acres, it is myself and God and the elements. I rise and fall on my own wits and abilities and bear the responsibility surely and by myself for everything I do. I take the credit and the blame. Alone."

You are a fool, thought Graham, *and moreover, you are killing your wife, you son-of-a-bitch.* The words racing furiously through his brain were not spoken, however. He did not want a head-on confrontation with Hollingworth just yet. The man was too powerful to antagonize. Instead he turned to Aura Lee.

"Do you concur with your husband's decision, Mrs. Hollingworth? Is this life agreeable to one of your sensibilities? Are you optimistic about your future?" Graham was aware of her reticence, her reluctance to go against her husband. Her blind devotion. He was envious.

Aura Lee sat stiffly on the edge of her chair. The question made her absolutely miserable. Suddenly conscious of every sound within the room, and without, she carefully kept her eyes averted from her husband's face. She loved this man, her Daniel, with a depth that was impossible to give word to. She loved his goodness, his ideals and honor, but this existence, as Dr. Brock had frantically predicted little less than a year ago, *was* killing her, and she wanted life. She was not rejecting Daniel. She had to make him understand that. She was choosing life, for herself, and for them as a couple. If she did not, "they" would no longer exist. Just him.

She looked Graham squarely in the eye. "Yes, I want a town," she said softly. "I need it for the sake of my soul. I cannot endure long out here." There, it was said. Simply and publicly.

Daniel looked at her long and hard. For just a second there was a flicker of admiration in his eyes, but it was quickly replaced by pain. He rose and hooked his thumbs in his belt as he peered out the window at the stars, his brow furrowed. "I have just one more question, Mr. Chapman. Can you help us get a railroad?"

Graham's heart leaped at his amazing fortune. "Oh, yes," he said firmly, "I can help you get a railroad."

Aura Lee was silent now. She did not want any more discussion to take place in the presence of this man. Did not want him to see any more of their sore, hurtful places, and most of all, did not want him to see her Daniel at a disadvantage.

Graham took his cue quickly and rose to his feet. He thanked Aura Lee and Daniel for the meal and then, tipping his hat, turned toward the door.

"Think it over carefully, Mr. Hollingworth. Towns are inevitable. Why not throw your weight behind one you can be proud of—one that is decent and made to last."

Graham waved to them as he rode off. He had to have their land too, of course, in order to deliver the promised tract to the railroad, but it could be done one step at a time.

Daniel stood gloomily inside the door frame. Then he turned to his wife. He held out his arms almost absentmindedly and as she drew close against his chest, he silently stroked her hair.

"I love you, darling," he said softly. "I want the very best for you, and believe me, it's here. Wheat alone will make us rich someday. There will be money for everything, and you can do as you please. If I can only make you see that. And how important it is just to last. Yes, that's the thing. Just to wait it out is all it's going to take."

"Daniel, you don't understand," she said. "I know that. Believe me, darling, I do understand. The point is, I *can't* last. Darling, I can't even start to tell you where my mind has come from. It was a terrible journey and I—you know what made the difference, Daniel? What brought me back for good and allowed me to hold my head up after all? The day I said to myself out loud that I could not take this life out here. I'm wrong for it. It set me free, Daniel, to say so. It didn't free my body, but it freed my mind. I no longer start out each day blaming myself for not being the perfect pioneer. I'm not a no-good woman, and your insistence that living here is just a matter of will, Daniel, is impossible. You can't imagine how it makes me feel when you say that."

Her face was no longer pale. It was a flame, but her voice was calm and steady.

"I have nearly killed myself trying to be a good wife for you. I love you and admire you more than any man I could ever have married. But, darling, I just can't take it."

"I won't abandon my land, Aura Lee." Daniel's face was pale even under his swarthy complexion, and he stood tree tall, picking his words carefully. "If I did, I would be letting you persuade me to be in the same position you say you are in, leading a life I hate. And by God, I won't do it."

There were tears in Aura Lee's eyes. "There has to be some way. I can't believe we are simply doomed. Do you hate towns so much then, or is it that the land is so precious to you? More precious than I am, perhaps? You said you stood alone, that you didn't need anyone." Her eyes pleaded with him to deny it.

"Aura Lee, of *course* I need you; you're my wife." His voice softened in apology for the curtness of his tone. "You're the reason I want to succeed. No, I don't hate towns. I hate some of them. They aren't fit to bring a dog into, let alone a wife and children. You don't want a town, my dear, you want civilization, and you think a town will automatically have this, and they don't. And yes, I love the land. My joy at seeing the turn of the seasons, the comfort I take in my place. It gives me a sense of thanksgiving that nothing else can equal. But, Aura Lee, nothing on earth, no other woman, no piece of dirt, not even my land, can replace what you mean to me. Not even my land." The air was charged with his love. "But even more important than you to me, is *us*, and sometimes I will have to put your immediate desires aside for what will be the best for us as a couple. And choosing a way that will make one or the other of us miserable is never going to be good for *us*."

Aura Lee's eyes quickened in sympathy. She understood what he was saying perfectly. It was the same concern for their love, their *oneness*, that had prompted her to be so open with Graham.

183

"Daniel, isn't there another way? *Something* we can do?" They talked late into the night about their existence on the prairie.

Finally Daniel decided. "I won't give up my land. Since Keever has sold out, Chapman has all the acreage he needs anyway to start a decent town. But I will help him. We will do our best to see that it's a good town. You'll have your civilization, sweetheart, not more than three miles away. You won't be able to go in in the evening, of course, without me. But you can go during the day fairly often. There's bound to be a piano there. And until we get a frame house set up, having a piano that close should keep you occupied."

"Oh, darling, thank you." Aura Lee kissed him on the cheek and tugged gently at his mustache to clear the brooding reservation in his eyes. "Daniel, there's one more thing I want to know. Why didn't you tell me about the dance? Surely you know what it would have meant to me. Mr. Chapman has just met me, and he knew, I could tell. You're such a funny person, Daniel." Her blue eyes clouded with pain. "One moment I don't doubt your love for me at all, and the next, I find out about being denied something as important as a dance."

"I was wrong," he said. "Dead wrong. When you got so upset over the violin—I was just trying to protect you, Aura Lee."

She believed him and nodded, still unwilling to tell him about Lucinda and Anton. They had had enough troubling problems for one night.

They lay quietly side by side on the bed, their fingers interlaced. Her excitement was like a current running through her body. Daniel's hand was warmed by hers, and he wished with all his heart that he could share her exaltation in the town. It was a long time before he dropped off to sleep. Dark, heavy thoughts kept surfacing. He did not trust Graham Chapman. Not completely. There was something he could not put his finger on. There was no doubt in Daniel's mind as to the man's natural abilities. He could not bear to help a fool, and this, Chapman was not. In the meantime, it was wonderful to see the pleasure kindling in Aura Lee's eyes. He trembled at his responsibility for this fragile soul that could be so easily shattered, and as her heart beat against his chest like a little wren's, he sighed at the heaviness of his burden.

23

Graham clucked to his horses and they began to put forth a little more effort to pull the wagon up the incline through the heavy grass.

All traces of the gambler were gone from his attire now. He still had the chameleonlike ability to change his personality as easily as most people change clothes, and he was gearing up for the job ahead.

His team reached the top of the rise, and he pulled back on the reins. Somewhere a meadowlark called clearly to its mate, and a vast wave of bluestem grass, heavy now with its eternal reseeding, bowed in the wind and dipped and swayed to the rhythms of the earth.

It was sundown, and the light was ebbing through a cloudless aura of mauves, golds, and roses. Only in Western Kansas, with the sky forming a huge inverted blue bowl over the land, only on this vast expanse of treeless horizon was it possible to see such matchless sunsets. Jeremiah Keever's soddy was just a quarter of a mile away now. The man had offered Graham the full use of his home. Keever was still assembling supplies at Little Beaver and Graham had come ahead of his men. He halted his team. Quickly he unloaded the grain for his horses. It was too late to set up his press tonight, and he was reluctant to sleep inside on such a fine evening. He made his bed on the ground, and with his hands clasped behind his head, he gazed up at the stars.

Far to the west, the magnificent town of Denver had already begun. It was a constant inspiration to townsmen. But his town, Gateway City, with its abundance of water and limitless horizon would surpass even Denver some day.

The next morning he set up his press inside the soddy. There would be no temporary dugout this time, as there were no bluffs or valleys here. Gateway City was located on a gentle rise that sloped easily to a creek two miles away. They would be far from any danger of flooding if the townsite began here and yet there was room for unlimited expansion. Having the creek nearby would provide water for construction until a well could be dug.

Graham removed the patent sheets from the wagon. These had been carefully protected with a tarp in case of an unexpected shower. He felt like God, present at the creation. He began to assemble all the components. This piece of equipment was the vanguard, the forerunner of civilization, the opinion maker, the dictator of tastes. As a surge of power coursed through his veins, he was in awe of the shaping force he possessed.

Graham scanned the preprinted sheets that had been supplied by the patent companies. In the short story "Golden Fetter," the heroine came to realize she had turned her back on paradise for an old man's riches. There was a poem about making up after a quarrel, a column of jokes and quotations and a bit of obscure information about bee-keeping in Australia.

He had been thinking a long time now about the tone and temper he wanted to establish for his townsite. The type was small and difficult to work with, but he soon finished his first ad, which would take up a full quarter side of the page.

> Gateway City is a government townsite, in the finest portion of northwest Kansas. It is rapidly building up and is the best place to make money fast.

He frowned. The last statement would be true by the time the paper reached Daniel Hollingworth.

> The water is sparkling and cool and delicious to the taste and the facilities are far in advance of any place in this part of Kansas.

That surely was true, whereas most townsites did not have water anywhere near them. The little stream sparkled in the distance as though it shared a joke with Graham.

> The water is pure and clean and free from lime, and wells are easily hit in just twenty-five to forty feet. Railroad prospects for Gateway City are excellent. It is on the direct route of the Union Pacific. It is also on the proposed route of the Missouri Pacific and the Kansas Texas. As Gateway City is in the best and soon to be most thickly settled portion of Western Kansas, the chances for prosperous business ventures cannot be better. If you want a farm, come West and get one free and save your money for improvements.

The ad was attractively laid out and eye-catching. On the opposite left side of the double page, he prudently began listing business cards for goods and services he knew prospective settlers would be looking for.

The first need would be for food and lodging, so he made up the name of a lady furnishing room and board. The animals came next, so he added a livery stable, promising plenty of warmth and grain and hay at all times. He mentioned a real estate dealer and a justice of the peace, and a dry goods store furnishing everything necessary for settlement. That would be Jeremiah Keever's department.

He advertised a lumber dealer whose stock was increasing daily, selling lumber, lathe, shingles, and lime; a carpenter builder and contractor, J. E. DeBois, who declared himself to be a practical and competent workman.

> Have followed the trade for years. Have a full set of tools— saw filing a specialty.

In bolder type yet, he set up ads for legal services. The management of claims was frightfully complicated, due to the lack of comprehensive territorial organization. So he threw in his own name as that of a real estate agent willing to buy claims or relinquishments or to file for homesteads. He promised to improve timber claims, and if the person filing had never seen the claim, he promised to look it up and send the owner a plot of its surface. If they wanted a house, he would build it. He promised to contest cases and he made restoration of rights and changes of entry a specialty.

The business section was complete. He went to bed that night exhausted, but confident. Not one essential service had been neglected, except a doctor. In his heart, he did not consider what he had done dishonest. He knew that by the time the first person had arrived, it would all be nearly so. Truth on the prairies was mostly a matter of timing.

The next morning he looked over the remaining blank space. The back page was the "patent" page, advertising medicines for every ailment known to man or beast. There was even a promotional for the Buyer's Guide, the early publication of Montgomery Ward and Co. It sold to dealers and customers alike at wholesale prices and was a most coveted possession by those fortunate enough to have the ten cents to mail in.

Graham thoughtfully reviewed his copy once more and when he realized that nothing of any social importance had been mentioned, he added the following:

> The young people of the town gather almost nightly and spend the entire evening singing. Several are accomplished vocalists, and the occasions are very enjoyable.

He was satisfied at last. He was sure there was not a finer town in existence in the whole state of Kansas.

The first of the wagons carrying the building crews arrived the next morning. The men swiftly began to unload lumber and tools. Graham's papers were collected and sent back East. Most men would arrive later in the day to begin building in earnest. In the meantime, after sending the driver on his way with copies of the *Gateway City Gazette*, Graham dug out his precious blueprint for the town and studied its layout. He did not have a compass, but the night before he had laid his wagon tongue toward the North Star in the time-honored way of the prairie for determining direction.

He had verified the order of the stakes according to the plan he had devised months ago. He wanted the building to proceed in an orderly fashion.

The men worked as though driven by furies, and by evening three buildings had been framed in, and temporary tents for the workers were strung over the prairie like bales of cotton.

The next day would bring in prefabricated buildings which would go even faster. Graham was everywhere at once, directing and correcting. He worked tirelessly, a man obsessed. By the second day, the place had been transformed beyond all his expectations. So self-assured and confident was Graham that some of the men in the building crew, tired of being constantly moved around, were looking at this town above all others to settle down in.

Already three had approached Graham for chance to start a business. He soon had a blacksmith, a carpenter, and an owner of a lumber yard as promised in the business cards in the paper.

The ears of the Clydesdales pricked and the muscles in their shoulders quivered with alertness at Daniel's sharp command to stop. With a furious gesture he wrapped the reins around the plow handles, and grabbing his hoe he rushed at three head of cattle that had strayed onto his property. The cattle wheeled and scattered and then began to graze again just a hundred yards from Daniel's plow.

Daniel was shaking with anger. He had not set aside enough cash to fence his land. His cheeks were bright red from the crisp morning air and his quick puffs of breath lingered like gloom in front of his face. Ah, hell, he thought, wouldn't do any good anyway to have money for barbed wire without a railroad to bring it into the area. He might as well be living in China. He was capable of making do, or going without, back-breaking labor, unpredictability, but he was suddenly in a rage as he realized that every single choice he made seemed to involve a curious penalty. Decisions that should be totally clear-cut had a perplexing double edge. Even now, as enraged as he was by the cattle, he knew he needed their droppings for fuel.

Since the corn crop was in, the cattle weren't doing any harm, but come spring—Jesus Christ—come spring even these three head could do an incredible amount of damage to young growing plants. All he asked, by God, was to be let alone on this land. To work the soil, improve his homestead, and produce food. Just to exist simply by his own wits. Now his days were filled with problems instead of dreams. He was constantly preoccupied with the implications of a town as he broke sod. Pros and cons, pros and cons. Considering Aura Lee, considering himself, angry that they needed the railroad so desperately. Angry with the subtle pressure being applied by his wife. Angry that he needed to cooperate with a silver-tongued son-of-a-bitch who had made his wife act as if she had taken leave of her senses.

He stared at the cattle. Well, he *could* do something about this situation, and he was damned if he was going to be blackmailed by a pile of cow patties. Tugging on the brim of his hat, he raced toward the soddy. The animals had no right on his land, open range or not. He grabbed his rifle and without a word of explanation to Aura Lee, dashed back outside and, taking careful aim, shot one of the tough range steers.

The sweat streamed from his body as he began the strenuous butchering process. It took him all morning, but by noon, the animal had been cut up and the carcass buried. He had carefully confined the work to one area, as much as possible, then covered the tell-tale signs of blood with sod.

"Let's go to the Smrckas'," he said curtly to Aura Lee when he finished his work. "I need to talk to Vensel about the town, anyway, and there's no point in letting good meat go to waste. We can't eat all this by ourselves."

She stared in amazement as he loaded half the beef into his wagon, and then without saying a word, she climbed up beside him. It was chilly and Aura Lee shivered in spite of the blankets she had brought to snuggle in.

"Why are you so quiet?" Daniel asked.

"Just thinking," said Aura Lee. She had not felt this close to Daniel since before Julka's death. They were talking again, as they once did. It warmed her to realize that Daniel's dreams included her welfare. Still, she could not bring herself to tell him in truth about Anton's hand and Vensel's near-death. She wanted to drive the incidents from her mind. This was their first time to visit the Smrckas since her confrontation with Lucinda and she was dreading it.

"Well, Lord knows we have plenty to think about," said Daniel.

The corners of her mouth lifted in a slight smile. If only he knew how much. Sometimes she felt so much older and wiser than Daniel, and today, she felt older than the earth itself.

Lucinda came quickly to the doorway at the sound of the team pulling up. She greeted Aura Lee gleefully, and with secret delight in the dismay she knew her friend felt at the progress she had already made in her work this morning. Her wash was spread neatly over an array of elkhorns to dry. Her body was damp with perspiration. Her hair was drifting into tendrils from the steam of the wash water.

Daniel's eyes were drawn to her breasts, clearly outlined by her damp bodice. He helped his wife from the wagon and was stunned by a sudden violent wave of unhappiness.

"Come in," Lucinda called cheerfully. She looked frankly at Aura Lee as though nothing had passed between them at all. "I've just set my bread. It will be a while yet, but soon we will have *kolaches*."

She led Aura Lee to a chair and settled her down before she could protest. Aura Lee clamped her teeth against the furious feeling that she was somehow being treated as an invalid.

"Where's Vensel?" asked Daniel.

"In the field," said Lucinda, "and the boy also."

She turned to her *kolaches*, cutting the sweetened dough into squares and putting a precious spoonful of dried plums that she had soaked back into their natural consistency into the center of each square, then folding the corners to the center and sealing the dough. Jeremiah Keever had brought her the fruit after one of his trips to town, and she had been possessed by a fierce desire for sweets this morning. Finally the craving had become so strong it overwhelmed her feeling of obligation to save the plums for a holiday. Now she was glad she had done it. The extravagance of sweet dough in the middle of the week, for no occasion at all, would show her royal highness that the Vensel Smrckas too had little things to be proud of.

"It smells wonderful in here," said Aura Lee, searching cautiously for a way to keep from antagonizing Lucinda.

"Yes, in my country, kitchens were always filled with this smell, and others, but out here—" She shrugged, her face clouding just for a moment.

"Your washing looks spotless," Aura Lee ventured again.

"Yes, I use good strong lye," said Lucinda. "When I make my soap I measure it all very carefully. Properly."

For a moment Aura Lee was filled with self-loathing for the Br'er Rabbit inside herself, the cunning trickster who would stoop to such a dishonorable scheme as making the woman believe she could actually cause bad things to happen. But she owed it to Anton to protect him, and this technique was clearly working well.

"My mother taught me," said Lucinda, "and her mother taught her,

to make fine soap. Of course, back home, the water is—kinder." She could not find the word for softer.

Aura Lee nodded. So this woman too, had a "back home."

"Yes," said Aura Lee. "In my home too, the water was kinder." Her eyes were sad and she pitied them both.

"And here," said Lucinda, "and out there, many things are harder, but a woman does what she can, but sometimes, sometimes, what with the water and other things not being so kind, sometimes a woman does things she would not do otherwise." She had paused over the dough, her neck held stiff and high, her brown eyes deepening with the hope she would be understood.

"Sometimes, a woman does things she will never do again." She drew a shaky breath, still not looking Aura Lee in the eyes.

"Yes," said Aura Lee, quietly accepting her confession, "yes, I know this is true. Because of the water." She felt a burden loosen inside of her and was tempted to free Lucinda from her fears. They were interrupted by the voices of the menfolk as Daniel led Anton and Vensel over to the wagon and lifted the tarp covering the beef.

"Is it right?" Vensel asked gloomily. "This does not belong to us."

"No, it's not right," said Daniel. "But it's not wrong either. It is fair. You know what cattle do to a crop. We're entitled to the meat in exchange for the damage they do. But you and I have got to stick together to protect ourselves. There's too many people moving in who I don't trust, thanks to that damn town."

"Not all of them like us homesteaders either," said Vensel.

"No," said Daniel. "And I can see why from their point of view. Cattlemen and drovers are the big-time spenders. They don't care if they ever have a pot to pee in, or a window to throw it out of. It's different with us. We know what we're here for."

"We don't have money to spend," said Vensel. "Drovers do, with the fancy wages they draw."

"Doesn't make any difference," said Daniel. "We wouldn't spend it anyway. The land is what matters to us, not carousing. It's a different kind of thinking, and the merchant knows it. They want to sell things, so of course they're in sympathy with the cattlemen."

"Isn't there anyone or anything that's for the farmer?" asked Vensel in despair. "Sometimes I think God himself must be against us."

"We have each other," said Daniel, clapping Vensel on the shoulder. "And God too. I'm sure he must be on the side of the homesteaders. He gave man stewardship of the earth, and looks like us clodhoppers are the only ones volunteering to do something with it." He curled his hand into a mock fist and tapped Vensel gently on the chest to dispel the man's hesitancy as he stared at the meat.

"In the meantime, there's going to be one hell of a lot of free barbecues, so enjoy your roast beef."

Anton ran inside ahead of the men and settled happily on Aura Lee's lap while Vensel and Daniel continued to talk.

"He's able, Vensel. Chapman bears watching, God knows. But he's no fool, and I'd rather cast my lot with someone who is at least capable."

"If we have a town here, and if it becomes a county seat, will it make it easier to file claims and get the legal work done right?"

"Yes," replied Daniel, "much easier in some ways. We won't have to go fifty miles to get paperwork done, but the big thing is the railroad. That's what's going to make the real difference. It will mean tools and coal. We won't have to burn buffalo or cow chips or worry about a stove overheating with hay cats."

"But if you say Chapman is the right man for the job, why are you worried?"

Daniel hesitated. "Nothing yet, and maybe there won't be. It's that town companies have been known to put counties so far in debt that there's no way for people to survive the taxes and levies, and then too, there's too many times that the damned railroads are the real winners. That's why I want us farmers to stick together. We'll watch out for each other and keep an eye out for anything suspicious."

"Are you going to talk to some of the others?" asked Vensel.

"Yes," said Daniel. "I'm afraid I'm going to *have* to. I don't mind seeing anyone sell their ground if they want to, but I'm not going to sit back and do nothing if Chapman is manipulating people through fears and half-truths. It's not right."

Vensel nodded. Daniel had cleared his mind of the doubts created by Chapman over Anton's welfare. "Just because you're on the land doesn't mean Anton has to be," Daniel had argued. "Point is, you'll have enough money from your crops to finance a truly fine education for Anton some day. If you move to town, you know your income will never rise above a certain level."

"When will you find the time to talk to people?"

Daniel hooked his thumbs in his suspenders and leaned back in his chair.

"After it freezes." He stared at a spot on the ground, suddenly tired. He had been looking forward to being quietly inside, talking to Aura Lee, or reading a book. He was so damn tired some days, the thought of a day just dozing by the stove sounded like heaven on earth.

"What's wrong, Daniel? Is it the man who is upsetting you, or the town?"

"Neither," the homesteader replied. "It's something else." He looked at Vensel, knowing this kind, grave man would understand. "It's just that when we first came here there was not a single person. Not one soul but Aura Lee and myself. I could look for miles and see nothing but prairie. Now there's people coming in, and cattle, and suddenly I need to be thinking about a fence, and I don't *want* to see a fence. Do you know what I mean, Vensel? I just don't want to see one. I want the earth and sky and God and myself, and nothing else at all. Looks like there would be someplace in this world where a man could just be left alone."

Vensel's eyes were bright with empathy but he did not reply.

"And now, I'm afraid it has become necessary to get all of the farmers together. Now instead of getting up and doing the kind of work I like best every morning, I'm going to be split between working my land and talking to people. If I had wanted to spend every God-blessed day arguing I'd have stayed in law." Daniel waved at flies attracted by the blood that had seeped through the tarp. "It's got to be done, Vensel. We've got to be careful who we include in our group, though. It's got to be men who know the worth of the land. If the town comes first, we don't want him. He won't be a part of our group. Doesn't mean we're against the town. Just that we've got to be certain where a man's heart is. In the land or in a town."

Vensel nodded at Daniel. They wanted only stayers, and it was becoming hard to tell a homesteader who wanted to stay from a man who had filed on behalf of a town company.

Daniel began to feel more optimistic. Once he came to a decision, he never looked back. Organizing the farmers was necessary, and he was the best man for the job. Together they would form a bond so strong no one would dare challenge them. They turned at the sound of Lucinda's voice calling them into the dugout.

She pulled the fresh rolls from her primitive oven, and the room was filled with the scent.

"Mrs. Smrcka," Daniel said as he bit into the rolls, "this is the best I have ever tasted."

High color rose to her cheeks. "It is my pleasure," she murmured, "to prepare them. Really, it is nothing."

"It's not just nothing for my wife to bake," he said thoughtlessly, then he was stricken by his blunder. He looked at Aura Lee, but it was too late. Her eyes had already iced to a frosty blue that froze him out.

Lucinda pounced. "You are still feeling poorly then, dear?" she inquired. "You do look tired. Are you ill?"

Daniel flushed brick red under his tan.

"Yes, I am tired from time to time, but I'm not ill. Not really."

"Not really? Then there *is* something the matter then?" she persisted. "Some small problem perhaps?" Lucinda's eyes twinkled with mockery.

"I'm just fine, thank you," said Aura Lee firmly. How dare she do this to me, she thought. Especially when we were getting on so well just a few minutes ago. She's ruining everything. Oh, I was right not to trust her. She's evil to the core to mock me like this. "Daniel, if you are finished with your business, I have things to do at home." At least she would be spared the ordeal of listening to the violin.

Lucinda smiled, knowing she had gone too far. She wanted them to stay longer so she could bask in Daniel's admiration. But never mind, he would be back.

"Aura Lee, I'm sorry," said Daniel after they reached their soddy. "I didn't mean to make you feel bad. It just slipped out."

"Just because it slipped out, you didn't mean it? Haven't you noticed, Daniel, that those are the things we mean most of all?"

He cracked his knuckles and examined his fists. He was tired of being wrong, and sick of being reprimanded by her superior silences.

"Vensel and I need to see Graham Chapman and some of the other homesteaders around here. I'll take Toby and turn the team out to pasture. All you are going to have to do is tether them in a fresh area every day. I'll see to it you don't have any lifting to do. We'll be gone for about three days."

"Surely you don't mean it. You wouldn't think of leaving me out here by myself?"

"Oh, Christ, Aura Lee. You can't go with us. This is men's work. You could stay with the Smrckas," he said. "Would you rather do that? Lucinda's not so bad, honey. I know she'd be glad to have you."

"Glad to have me? That's an understatement. She would be just tickled pink to have *at* me, can't you see that?"

"That's all in your head, Aura Lee," he snapped. "What I see is an extraordinarily competent woman you are unreasonably jealous of. You could at least *pretend* to like her and maybe things would go better for you."

"Pretend? My God, Daniel, just what do you think I've been doing? I've been pretending since the moment we came here. Pretending to feel good when I don't, pretending to stand up under my work when it's about to kill me, pretending in bed—oh, Daniel, my darling, I'm sorry." So the last thing she had intended to say, her most private secret, was out after all.

"And as you said," Daniel whispered, "it's the things that just slip out that we mean most." His eyes were flat and guarded.

"Always?" he asked. "Is it always just pretending?"

"Yes," she said. Her eyes filling with tears. "Yes, always now."

"What in the hell am I supposed to do? Go without? Beg? Spend hours getting you in the mood? Seize my rights like some feudal lord?"

"I don't know. I just don't know."

"I just want to know one thing. Was it real, before?"

"Before Julka?"

"Yes, before that?"

"Oh, yes, Daniel. Yes, of course. Then it was everything it appeared to be."

He nodded, relief flickering across his face. "Thank God for that at least." He stood there for a moment.

"I'm going to check on the horses," he said finally.

Aura Lee watched the muscles ripple in his proud back as he left the room. The peace between them had been so short-lived, and now she had ruined it with a truth she should have kept silent. After he had stayed out much too long, she undressed for bed and huddled under the covers, lonely and chilled to the depths of her soul. Afraid he would never touch her again.

Gateway City attracted people like Lester Farlan. He was a refugee from the Civil War and after the fighting had ended he felt lost and restless. Even though he was far down the chain of command, it fed his sense of power to stand victorious over a whole community.

He was a second-rate crook. He stole everything necessary for survival with a dull cunning that overlooked the greater riches.

When he read the first issue of the *Gateway City Gazette*, he promptly packed his pitifully few belongings, and headed across the prairie. His long greasy hair was held in place with an oily Apache band and he wrapped his bony legs around his worn, unpolished saddle. His horse was poorly cared for and had a dull, mangy coat.

With new towns, there was always an influx of homesteaders, and with the confusion of laws for filing and proving up, Lester always found these men easy picking. He headed for Gateway City like a rat for a piece of cheese. He was a claim jumper.

It was an easy matter to check at the land office to see which plots of ground were filed on and then to set up a tent on the property to await the owner. The area around Gateway City was under the jurisdiction of the land office in Oberlin, and after checking the territorial books, Lester headed for the quarter that lay directly to the north of Daniel Hollingworth. It had been filed on by one Randall Edwards.

Farlan chuckled when he located the property. There were no signs of occupancy. He unloaded his few possessions and settled down to wait. When Edwards arrived a week later, he found the battle-toughened Civil War veteran on his claim.

"Who are you?" Edwards asked curtly.

"The legal owner of this piece of dirt. Who the hell are you?"

"You're a liar," said Edwards. "I've got papers."

"Hell you have." Lester smiled as he saw the man grow pale. "S'pose I told you I had papers too, and you can see who's here first."

"That's a lie," said Edwards. "I was here just a month ago. I left just long enough to get supplies."

"That so! Well, now. No need to get het up. I have a quit-claim deed here in my pocket. Don't like farming much anyway. Won't cost you but fifty dollars. Lessen you want to fight it out like a gentleman."

Edwards shivered. He had no skill with a gun. He would die like a dog out here, and no one would know. There was no one to turn to, and he could just imagine what the chances would be of getting a law officer to come clear out here to oust a claim jumper. Furiously, he dug into the leather pouch on his wagon seat for the money. It changed hands without Edwards saying a word. Farlan chuckled, handed over the quit-claim deed, and tipped his hat as he rode off.

One morning Daniel saw a wagon coming across the prairie. He stopped his work and waved at the man who was slowly working his way East.

"Hello," he called as the man drew up. "I'm Daniel Hollingworth."

"Morning." The man was dejected and grim. "I'm Randall Edwards, and we should have been neighbors."

"Should have been?"

"I've been robbed," the man said furiously. "Fleeced of every damn red cent I own."

"What happened?"

"There was a man waiting for me when I got to my claim. Said the land was his, but I could have it if I gave him all my money. Knew he was lying, but it's hard to argue with the barrel of a gun. I was ruined in the time it takes to blink. Can't afford to leave and can't afford to stay. My wife and two boys are supposed to come out here in six months. Now what?"

"Come on back to my place," said Daniel. "I want to know just how much of this is going on. We'd better put a stop to it fast. The neighbor just to the south and I are going to form a group of homesteaders who'll look out for each other's interests. Up till now we were just worried about the range cattle, but it looks like we've got other problems too."

"I don't have any money. I'd back your group, but I don't have anything to live on."

"It's all right," said Daniel. "I just don't want you to leave. You're the type of man we need out here. We'll work something out. We have plenty of food and I need some help with the plowing. You might as well stay with us for a while. Is the claim jumper still around?"

"I'd bet he doesn't have the guts to stay. But there'll be more like him, you can be sure."

"That's what's worrying me," said Daniel. "It's just not right. We've got to figure a way to put an end to this."

"Count me in," said Randall.

The next morning, Randall took over the plowing, and Daniel set off for the Smrckas'. Clearly they could not afford to waste time in getting the men organized. Daniel reined up in front of the dugout and helloed the house. He knew Vensel would be in the field, and he wanted to get Anton to show him where his father was working.

There was an answering call from within and Lucinda appeared in the open doorway.

"Daniel! Good morning, come in, I'll pour your coffee."

Daniel flushed. "No, thank you, ma'am. I would just like to pick up Anton."

"He's out in the field with his father. Come on in," she insisted. "Wait here. They'll be in for dinner soon."

It was not usual on the prairie for a woman to invite a man into the house for any reason. Daniel looked at her with his piercing dark eyes. Perhaps she would not know that, and would consider the refusal of her simple hospitality an insult.

Deciding quickly, he swung down from his horse and entered the dugout. She poured him a cup of coffee and sliced some bread. She was wearing a coarsely woven dress she had dyed a deep brown. There was a fire glowing in the stove and it was reflected in the sheen of her violin in the corner.

Lucinda went to the window and pretended to scan the horizon for Vensel and Anton. Slowly she raised her arms as if in supplication to the gods of the earth. The sun lit up her hair and for a moment it was the same color as her violin. Her tawny brown eyes glistened with pleasure. Her breasts were taut against the fabric of her dress.

Daniel was acutely aware of all the furnishings in the room. The blue enamel coffee pot, the merry squares of calico in the patchwork quilt on the bed. Her dress hanging on a hook on the wall, and the bed, the bed, most of all, the bed.

"Mrs. Smrcka."

"Lucinda," she whispered, turning from the window, "call me Lucinda."

"Lucinda, then, it is not seemly for me to be in here without Vensel or Anton. I am afraid there are standards here you are not aware of. Forgive me for speaking so frankly," he said rising to his feet. "It's just that you need to know that people, another man, might misunderstand."

"I'm not being misunderstood." A great tear slowly trickled down one cheek and she did not try to brush it away.

Daniel raised his eyes, jolted by longing as she slowly walked toward him. He was revolted by the fierce involuntary trembling that swept his body and was suddenly furious with the woman for putting him in this position.

"I'm not misunderstood," she repeated. "Tell me this, Daniel, what can it hurt? Who is to know? Things are very bad between Vensel and me. Things are not so good between you and your wife either. I can feel it. Life is too strong for her. You need a real woman."

His desire was blunted suddenly by her mention of Aura Lee, and he was swift in her defense.

"My wife *is* a real woman," he said. "In every way. She is simply not in the best of health right now. She will be fine soon."

"She will never be well," Lucinda said. "Not really."

She touched his shoulder and Daniel shuddered with the effort to control himself. He stood mesmerized by her incredible beauty. Aura Lee's face flickered before his eyes and resolutely he pushed Lucinda to arm's length, recoiling at the angry shock he saw in her eyes.

"For God's sake, woman. Your husband is my best friend. It's wrong, and that's all there is to it."

She stood back and looked at Daniel, her face flaming with humiliation.

God damn her soul, Daniel thought savagely. Determined to be a gentleman, to let her save face, he turned toward the door, pretending nothing at all had happened.

"I bid you good day, Mrs. Smrcka. I shall look for your husband in the field."

Lucinda threw back her head, and as she stood in the doorway, her mocking laughter rang through the morning stillness.

"You'll be back," she whispered. "You'll be back."

Vensel's shoulders slumped as he listened to Daniel relate Edwards' experience with the claim jumper.

"It's up to us to put a stop to it," said Daniel. "And we can, if we all act in a body."

"This is bad business and I don't have much taste for it," said Vensel. "Why?"

"When men act as a group, things happen that are wrong. Sometimes the men, they become even worse than the people they go after."

"Not if they've got their facts straight," said Daniel. "I won't let things get out of hand. We've got to organize."

"Farmers don't want to be organized," insisted Vensel. "If we wanted to be part of a group we would not be farmers in the first place."

Daniel grinned at his friend's simple logic.

"There's truth in that, God knows. But we've got to do it just this once."

"You won't have the time, Daniel. Who will take care of your place?"

"Edwards can for the time being. I'll go see all the homesteaders before spring, while it's slack time. I'm going to the land office in Oberlin as soon as I can and get a list of people who have filed claims."

"All right," said Vensel. He rumpled Anton's hair and smiled at the boy. "Your wife is welcome to stay with us as often as she wants to, of course. I think I know a fellow who would be glad to have her."

"Can she, Dad?" asked Anton. Then he turned to Daniel. "Can we keep Aura Lee? We can draw together."

"That's nice of you," said Daniel evasively. "I'm sure she'll appreciate the offer." As he waved to them and started for home he could not look Vensel Smrcka in the eye.

The Homesteaders Union Association was formed the next week in the Hollingworth soddy. It consisted of Daniel, Vensel, Randall Edwards, and two homesteaders who had recently filed. Its purpose was to protect their crops from livestock and to prevent claim jumping. Their weapon would be fear.

"Any range cattle found on our property will be butchered on the spot," declared Daniel. "We're entitled. It's our land."

Randall looked up sharply. "Some of the ranchers are offering big money to anyone who will tell who has been butchering range cattle. That's going to be mighty tempting cash to settlers out here who are starving to death. What can we do about that? Specially when some folks don't hold with butchering other folks' beef anyway."

"We're going to hang any man who tells for money," said Daniel.

"Just for telling who is butchering cattle?"

"Yes. Just for telling who is butchering cattle. The nearest law is ninety miles from here. When we get the law out here permanently, after we're a county, then we can turn this over to the proper authorities. But right now, there's no other way."

Outside black clouds hovered and there was an ominous roll of thunder that dramatically emphasized Daniel's words. His dark, brooding mustache and the angular planes of his swarthy face belonged to a man of power, of action.

"Does anyone here doubt that this group has the right to protect its own?"

"Now I was just wondering," said Randall, "ain't hanging going to be a little awkward, seeing as how there's no trees?"

Daniel flashed him a quick grin.

"We'll use wagon tongues. They're high enough if they're propped up just right."

Hanging alone was considered to be the decent way. It was the proper and legal method of dealing with outlaws. Any other way of administering justice was considered barbaric.

Daniel was well prepared for the meeting. After all the details had been discussed, he led those present through the initiation ceremony. He had made a straw man, clothed in homesteader's clothing.

"Repeat after me," Daniel said when it was time for the swearing of the oath. "If I violate the secrecy of this order, or tell who is in the membership, I can expect to be used thusly." And at that he pulled the retaining rope of the straw man and the men watched silently as he dropped just short of the floor and hung there.

"Jesus, you mean we're going to get hung too?" asked Delbert Marston.

"Yes," said Daniel. "If you cause harm in any way to befall one of our members. This is what will happen to you. Now you know why I am sure people will think twice before turning in their neighbor's name to ranchers when they come upon a little barbecue. You can count on the members of the H.U.A. to hang people."

"How will we know who are members of the H.U.A.?"

"You won't," Daniel said curtly. "Only the recording secretary, Vensel here, will know all the names. No single person will be at every meeting except Vensel and me, so you can't be sure just who's initiated and who isn't. After we get bigger we'll encourage small local lodges."

Randall solemnly aimed a stream of tobacco at a spittoon. "That alone will be a powerful silencer. Not knowing. If a man's afraid his neighbor is a member, he would be scared to say too much to him."

"That's the way I figure it," said Daniel. "As I said, in the beginning our main weapon is going to be fear. And believe me, it will be fear that's justified. We have to be ready to go all the way with this, or nothing will work."

"We're still strangers to each other, out here," Daniel continued. "No one really knows what his neighbor is like, or where his interests lie. He may be an honest man trying to make a decent living, or he may be the agent of a town company or a ranch. Until we get straightened out, it's important to be pretty close-mouthed about our group's activities."

The men were sunburned and hard as rocks from long, back-breaking hours of brutal labor. They were proud and capable of enduring any manner of hardship. They were viewed with contempt by the cowboys, the railroaders, the townsmen, and even the sheepherders, and still they came. And to a man, all other economic groups underestimated their worth. They were the homesteaders, too poor to leave, who by an ironic twist of fate would remain to become rich and someday own huge farms, capable of producing enough grain to feed the world.

"I think you men should know there's another problem out here that we need to keep our eye on. It could be a son-of-a-bitch before it's over. That's the towns coming in around us."

"Towns don't have nothing to do with us."

"Yes, they do," said Daniel quickly. "How many of you know for certain where you're supposed to go to file a claim?"

"Little Beaver."

"That's not true. Oberlin is still our legal land office. That's where you should be paying your taxes too. But no one can keep anything straight. If you ride into a town offering to file or prove up a claim, that doesn't make the transaction legal. And I'll guarantee you there's always someone glad to take your money. They bear watching, and the town companies are promising people the moon. This county will have so many debts by the time it gets organized we'll be the rest of our lives paying them off."

The men listened intently to Daniel's words.

"I just want you men to know that I'm all for Gateway City, a town that's starting up just three miles from here. I think it's going to be a good one, and I have the word of the organizer, Graham Chapman, that he will not go after the land of anyone who is not perfectly happy about selling. Also, he's promised me he will get a decent railroad in this area. Just want you to know where I stand, and that I don't have a thing more to gain from it than you folks do."

The men did not smile as they solemnly pledged themselves to secrecy. The ritual made their duty to one another seem even more binding.

26

Aura Lee watched Charlie Stone Wolf as he knelt beside the well. The big Indian was checking the flow of water. He had measured the length of dry rope when he and Lark left and now he could see that the bucket just had to be lowered to the same depth as when they had first struck water, so the flow was constant. It was a fine well and they had fulfilled their part of the guarantee. He checked the retaining rocks they had put around the walls and the platform and began to assemble the pipe for the pump Aura Lee and Daniel had brought back from Little Beaver.

Randall Edwards was at the far end of the row of sod he was breaking and Daniel was gone for the day, trying to locate some of the homesteaders whose names he had acquired from the land office. Edwards' presence was a blessing to them both. He took the strain off their evenings; the burden of being alone together was eased. The voices had returned again and Aura Lee was so nervous the slightest noise made her jump as though a hand had touched her shoulder. She grimly went from task to task, almost welcoming the fatigue that made her doze off in a chair during the day. At night when the two men were together and talked, Aura Lee felt the tightness within her loosen a little. Anything was better than watching the new grimness in Daniel's face.

Aura Lee wanted to ask Charlie about the word he had used the day she had witched the well. Even now, she was reluctant to think about the strange current that surged through her body as the willow branch dove toward the ground. Stranger and even more frightening was the memory of knowing the moment when her parents died, and that the accident would happen at the Smrckas'.

Charlie was silent, waiting for the white woman to speak, watching from the corners of his eyes as she nervously twisted her apron. Aura Lee drew a deep breath, fearful of what she would be hearing, and her voice trembled.

"Mr. Stone Wolf, I'm sorry I was so frightened the day we found the well. Would you please talk to me about it?"

Charlie froze for an instant. He had learned to live in the white man's world. He had served as a scout in the white man's army to bring the last of his tribe onto the reservation, knowing if his people did not learn to accommodate themselves to change, they would face total extinction. He had learned to assimilate the deep grief over losing his place. He had also come to enjoy the mock raids staged in the circuses, and from time to time felt a surge of the wild power he had once known. But he had also learned that white women were the worst kind of trouble. No matter how congenial the men were, all it took was the wrong look at the wrong woman and all the racial enmity was instantly unmasked.

However, Daniel Hollingworth was a fine man, and he owed this brother a favor. Looking at Aura Lee's pinched face and the nervous tic in her cheek, he nodded without changing his expression.

"You used a word I've never heard. I want to know what it means. What is *shaman?* That's what you called me that day."

"For the Indian, it's our witch doctors or medicine men or the women who preserve our ceremonies."

"I'm not a witch," she whispered. "I'm not."

"No, not like that," he said. "Our *shamans* are the people who seek the sacred. They are the ones the spirits flow through. Our religious men and women."

"But I'm not very religious."

"Yes, you are," said Charlie. "You just don't know it yet. The power is very strong in you. You have been *shaman* from the time you were born. You can't help it. It's just there. No one chooses this."

"I don't even know what you're talking about."

"I know you don't," said Charlie. He looked at her with his fathomless eyes until she looked away. "You would know if you were Cheyenne. When you first began to menstruate you would be shown what to do with the spirits."

She looked away, shocked at the word a white woman never heard used by a man.

"With my people," he said, "there would be feasting and a ceremony when you became a woman, and each month you would be kept apart from the others when the power is strong within you. It is so for all women, but you who are destined to be *shaman*, you would have special guidance and a woman to teach you our holy secrets that have been handed down since Changing Woman created First Man and First Woman."

"Changing Woman?"

"Yes—it's only with the white people that women are not gods too."

Aura Lee listened, fascinated, wanting this strange man to say more, but he was finished with his work now.

"When are you getting the windmill?" he asked.

"Not until spring," she replied, barely hearing the words, her mind still trying to absorb what he had told her.

"Can one of your people help me?"

"No," said Charlie flatly. "We will not even be able to help our own soon. The white men are destroying our gods. If you were Cheyenne, my mother still could help some. But you are not Cheyenne. More than what we would teach you, there are things you would know from the time you were born. You would have memories of what to do handed down from time out of mind, and be guided by the spirits of those who have gone before."

"What would I be doing, if I were a *shaman?*"

Charlie considered the question as he mounted the horse. He held his reins loosely and organized what he knew about the sacred ways of his tribe that were kept by the women. He tried to find the ways for the categories of centuries of tradition. "You must become a teacher, a healer, or an artist," he said slowly. "There is no other way. If you do not, the power will destroy you. And even with our people, the path is very hard and our *shamans* have the worst experiences imaginable. The testing is severe. It is the price they pay for being favored by the gods. It is the price you must pay also."

He turned and started to ride off.

"Who will show me?" cried Aura Lee. "Who will show me?"—realizing that on a deep, primitive level she was accepting what the Indian had said, as though he were verifying truths she had always held.

Charlie spat on the ground. "No one," he said. "For white women there is no way. The power destroys." He rode away, the wind whipping the grass in front of him.

Aura Lee clutched her shawl around her shoulders and looked at the treeless horizon.

"I don't believe it," she whispered fiercely. "I just don't believe it. There must be a way" —she blinked back quick tears—"and I'm going to find it."

27

Jeremiah Keever came to the Hollingworths' homestead to invite Daniel and Aura Lee and the Smrckas to look over Gateway City.

"You should see this new town. I'm proud to have a part in it, Daniel," the man said earnestly. "Hope you don't hold it against me."

"I don't," he said. "Long as it's your own free choice and not somebody forcing you off."

Keever was relieved.

"Come see the place for yourself."

"I'll do just that." He turned to Aura Lee. "Would you like to go with me to see Chapman's town?" he asked. "We'll pick up the Smrckas on the way over."

"All right," she said quietly, injured by the courtesy in his voice. They were like two strangers now.

"See how carefully he handles you," her voices chided. "Aren't you ashamed?" *Oh, stop, stop it,* she protested silently, placing her hands over her ears for a moment. They had come back after Daniel began to treat her so coolly, with rigid politeness.

Daniel was dumbfounded by the progress. He knew Graham had extraordinary abilities, but he had not visualized this transformation. It was close to alchemy. Where there had been empty space, there was now life. Graham greeted the two couples.

"Congratulations," said Daniel, looking around. "I've got to hand it to you, Chapman, I had no idea you could achieve this much so fast."

Graham grinned. A lock of his blond hair had fallen across his forehead and glinted in the sun, giving him a boyish look. His enthusiasm was contagious.

Graham took them on a tour through the maze of stakes setting off an enormous lot. "Here we have our courthouse."

Daniel looked at the row of stakes outlining the building in which all of the business of the county would be conducted, threw back his head, and laughed.

Graham grinned.

"A courthouse," said Daniel. "Now if that isn't something."

"It is important, crucial in fact," said Graham, suddenly sober, "that this particular place be regarded from the beginning as a serious contender for the county seat. That in itself will make the biggest difference in people choosing to settle here. But I want them both."

"Both?"

"A county seat *and* a railroad. All the natural draws are here; there's no reason why it won't work."

"How does a man like you go about getting a railroad?"

"By proving to the officials that there will be enough business to make sense for it to come through here, and that there will be enough shipping for them to locate there. It's got to pay off financially for the big boys. And that's where you men come in. We've all got to work together. The more grain you grow, the more business for the railroad. A railroad will mean less expense for you and less risk. A lot can happen when you have to cart grain over fifty miles to get transportation, not to mention the time lost going back and forth. We've got to get more homesteaders out here as soon as possible. That's the reason this little town is going to have buildings put up first. So newcomers will find something waiting for them when they get here."

"You can almost make me see it," Daniel said carefully, but a warning bell was ringing in his mind. This was no ordinary frontier townsite. There had to be a lot of money behind this venture, and he was suspicious of where it was coming from.

"By the way, Mrs. Hollingworth," said Graham, "may I call on you to aid me in making the incoming women feel welcome? I'm sure you must realize that adjusting to the prairie is very difficult for some, and therefore, the sympathetic ear of another woman may prove invaluable. If you could help make them welcome and offer some type of assurance as to the soundness of the move, until they get settled in—"

Aura Lee stood staring wordlessly at the horizon, and for a moment saw vividly, clearly and realistically, things as they really were. They were standing in the middle of a sea of grass, now rutted with wagon wheels and bravely staked with pegs of wood representing nonexistent buildings. The buildings that had been erected had gaudy false fronts. There were sweat and squalor, and a hot sun scorching their souls and their grain in the summer, and brutal, snow-laden winds in the winter to paralyze their bodies and hearts, and he was asking her to look at her sisters and lie. To deceive another human being. To hypnotize them into believing the "next year" philosophy.

She blinked and the trance was broken. In her heart she had gone from the pinnacle of believing to the depths of despair in a single piercing slide. But slowly, another theme began to make its way into the core of her being, slowly coaxing her along in a tentative melody, incredibly sweet in its clarity and poignancy. Hope had always been the redeemer of mankind, and she above all people should know the effect that the thoughts she allowed herself could have. Nothing had really changed in this last moment, she reasoned slowly, yet just seconds ago she had felt like a different person through the hope that had been given her in the promise of this town. If she could talk to women at the beginning, perhaps they would not abandon courage so quickly. Besides, there was no other alternative. It really came down to adjusting or not adjusting. They certainly could not just go back.

"That's right," her voices encouraged. "You're thinking like Daniel now. It comes down to adjusting or not adjusting." She looked at Daniel, and his dark eyes sparkled with bitter amusement. She looked away, knowing she was hardly the one to help other women find happiness.

"Of course I will welcome newcomers, Mr. Chapman. It will be my pleasure. But how will I know when they arrive, living three miles away?"

"Will there be a boardinghouse?" asked Daniel.

"Yes, and a hotel too," said Graham.

"I have some business to tend to that will keep me away from the farm for several days at a time. No reason for her not to stay here when I have to be gone."

"Live in town? Of course, that won't be necessary," she said, rejecting the ripe smooth fruit he offered. She looked at Daniel, her eyes wide and clear. She too could choose the vinegary tart burden of sweet suffering and be proud. "My place is on our homestead. I will simply come in from time to time if you send for me. We have horses to care for also. Mr. Edwards will soon be returning to his own claim, and of course I must take care of our horses." The mockery in her voice was subtle and masked by a sweet, bland expression on her face. Daniel was aware of the sly undercurrent in her words, and looked at the ground, not trusting himself to reply.

Graham's eyes glittered with curiosity at the nature of Daniel's business and even more with an awareness of the strange tugging going on between this couple. This interplay had not been there the night he called on them. His attention was suddenly diverted to the Smrckas, however. They had not said a single word, and his interest in engaging the Hollingworths' cooperation was laid aside as he became aware of the hostility radiating from the woman.

Lucinda's face flamed, her high, generous coloring making her more beautiful than ever. Graham was again aware of the antipathy he felt toward her. He was keenly conscious of her fury in being slighted in the role he had just assigned Aura Lee, and God knew, he was all too knowledgeable of the trouble women could make.

Years of offering face-saving measures came to his rescue, and he knew he had better come up with some job in this town for Lucinda very quickly or too much of his time would be spent ducking her ill will. He was a total blank right now. He was not positive what she really wanted. Clearly she did not want his town to succeed. He would bet she had her eyes on Daniel Hollingworth.

Helplessly, he turned and began explaining the measurements of the proposed dry goods store to the men, knowing as he did so that he was antagonizing Lucinda even further. She was beautiful, she had abilities and flair, but her sense of superiority to her customers would prevent her from being successful at running businesses. He could see her running a whorehouse and very little else.

Vensel sensed Lucinda's unhappiness and sighed.

He reached for his son, squeezed his shoulders, and resumed listening to Graham's high-sounding plans.

Daniel, too, was aware that Lucinda had been slighted, and as he looked at her broad unhappy face he was moved by pity. It was not right for her to have so many areas of her life go wrong when she was trying so hard. Instinctively, he knew how to console the woman for the rejections she had had to endure. From him, and now this man.

"Mrs. Smrcka, I would be proud to have you look after my Clydesdales in my absence, when my wife would prefer to live in Gateway City."

Aura Lee was split with shock, as though struck by lightning. Oh, how dare he do this to her? How dare he turn those animals over to this woman, as though her feelings did not matter at all? Well, she would not leave for one day now; he could count on that.

Lucinda lifted her chin and trembled with the wonder of this trust. "I will care for your team," she said proudly, rejoicing in her strong body that was capable of a man's work. "I will do this for you."

"No need for you to worry, dear," said Daniel to Aura Lee. "Mrs. Smrcka can just plan on doing the job whether you are at home or not, so you won't be so tied down."

Aura Lee's heart was sucked down into the whirlpool, and she could not have found the words she needed if she had searched for a lifetime.

28

Aura Lee stood in the doorway scanning the horizon. When she saw Lucinda coming across the prairie, she went inside. Her face was solemn and drawn as she peeked around the edge of her curtain, watching the woman carry water from the well to the water tank, and then dip up the measures of oats. She could see Lucinda's lips moving as she went about the chores, talking to the horses, her long legs moving easily in spite of the heavy buckets.

Daniel and Vensel would be home later this evening. Anton had begged to go with the men and when Daniel assured him they would not be gone over one night, his father had agreed, pleased with the chance to treat the boy. Randall Edwards had acquired enough cash to resume residence on his homestead, so she and Lucinda were all alone.

It was getting dark quickly now. Lucinda had delayed doing the chores, because she was uncertain when the menfolk would be back. Clouds had rolled up in black bunches for the last hour, pushing the cold, early winter air before them. The buffalo grass had long lost its color and lay like a low, dry carpet all about the claim, and Aura Lee stared at the barrenness about her, then resumed watching her neighbor.

She heard a dull faint roll of thunder, miles away, and wished it would rain. She hadn't known it was possible for a land to survive so long without rain. She wished Daniel would come home, even with the way things were between them now. She just wanted him home. They were so much closer when Daniel struggled, she thought. When he was making up his mind. But once he had become reconciled to the task of organizing the homesteaders, he proceeded with his characteristic exuberant confidence in his ability to achieve whatever he desired. She had come to accept his deep-seated optimism, she would always admire his strength, but as long as she lived, she would never understand the pride he felt in conquering difficult things.

Even the dry, dull buffalo grass seemed proud to be growing in Kansas, proud of its ability to live without rain. Suddenly Aura Lee was sickened by her own introspection. Sick of dredging up her deep-seated differences with the proud, perverse people who had flocked to this exaggerated state, who welcomed one disaster right after another as though they were privileged and superior because of their capacity for endurance. Kansas was already becoming a byword for the impossible. She knew of the fun being poked at the homesteaders from the bundle of newspapers that Marie Sutton managed to get to her occasionally.

There was an ear-shattering clap of thunder, and it was followed by lightning that lit the room. She heard the frantic squeal of the Clydesdales and ran to the doorway. There was no rain, but wind had increased enough to blow buckets and tools alike, and as she looked across the prairie she saw the bright beginnings of a fire ignited by the lightning. In a flash it took hold and swept across the dry carpet of buffalo grass.

"My God," Aura Lee called. "Lucinda!" Her heart pounded in her throat as she ran toward the corral, stumbling once in the tangle of her long skirt as it whipped about her legs. "Lucinda. Quick. Help me bridle the horses. We've got no time to lose. Oh, my God, Daniel and Vensel. Where are they?"

"What are you doing?" Lucinda cried. "What do you think you're doing?"

"We've got to get out of here. As fast as we can. Outrun the fire."

"You're a fool, woman," Lucinda said sharply. "*No one* can outrun a prairie fire."

"We can't just do nothing. At least we would have a chance."

"No, no. I know a way. Go back into the house," Lucinda ordered curtly, pushing Aura Lee out of the way as she dashed to the side of the corral.

"I'll burn up alive. For God's sake, Lucinda."

"Sod doesn't burn. Don't you know that?" The wind snatched the words from her mouth as she dragged the plow over to the Clydesdales and started to hitch them to it.

"Go inside," she ordered again. "Save yourself. I'm going to plow a firebreak."

"No," said Aura Lee. "No, let me help."

"I don't *need* your help. You are not strong enough."

Lucinda raced through the harnessing. When she tried to lead the Clydesdales away from the soddy toward the fire, Dapper bolted and was prevented from rearing only by the doubletree.

"Aura Lee," she called, her voice shrill with panic, "you must steady the plow. I'm going to have to blindfold the horses and lead them."

Aura Lee immediately took hold of the handles and tried to keep the plow upright, using all her strength to keep the share from digging into the ground until they could begin a row.

"Now," called Lucinda. "Begin, here." Aura Lee trembled as the strength of the horses jolted the blade and Lucinda struggled to calm the team. She did not dare look up but for once she welcomed the presence of this tough wiry grass all about them, whose thick matting did not permit the blaze to leap as quickly as the taller bluestem would have. There was no loose bunch grass to roll and be carried upward in the hot currents. The wind had relented a little and the fire was contained in a high strong wall that was moving inexorably closer. Lucinda talked and pleaded to calm the Clydesdales. She had torn her apron into strips to cover their eyes.

"One row done," she called triumphantly to Aura Lee. "One row." Aura Lee gasped when she saw the furrow gleaming in the light from the flames. "Again," called Lucinda. "We turn them now." Aura Lee struggled to pull the plow out of the ground as Lucinda managed to wheel the panicky horses around. "Now again," the woman called. They were able to plow five rows the width of the soddy and the barn, and then Aura Lee looked up and saw the height of the billowing smoke from the blaze and began to choke from the fumes.

Lucinda's face was dark with despair.

"We can't—it will have to be enough. It is all we can do. Run for the house, run fast."

"What about you?"

"I've got to save the horses. I've got to stay with them. They go crazy in a fire. Sometimes they even run toward it."

Aura Lee began to choke, strangling on her words of protest, dropped the plow handles, and ran toward the soddy. She slammed the door behind her, and then catching her breath, ran to the window and threw the curtains aside.

Oh God, she prayed. *Please, dear God, let her live. We—owe this place to her—if the firebreak works—let Daniel and Vensel—and Anton be safe—please, and let her live—let the firebreak be enough.*

The fire was moving closer, enough to light up the homestead in an eerie red glow, and as Aura Lee watched, she saw Lucinda try to unhook the plow and one of the great horses reared, breaking the doubletree as though it were a matchstick. She'll be killed, Aura Lee thought. The horses will kill her. But as she watched, Lucinda ran to the front of the Clydesdales, who were prevented from bolting from the burden of being harnessed together, restrained by one another's weight.

The woman's hair had come loose at last and was tossed in a stream about her shoulders and her face was smudged with sweat and smoke. Her hands were stroking the horses, her voice appealing to their circus training; coaxing, pleading, cursing, the words blending with the wind.

The night was thick with sparks and stars and the wildness of Lucinda, freed from Hell to ascend to become one with higher flames, wild and swift, and her spirit blended with the night and the fire and the fierce lunging strength of the horses as she tried to lead them toward the sod barn. A part of her soul married the blaze and swept across the prairie in bright fury, soaring high above the night.

"Come on, boys," she pleaded. "Just a little farther."

Aura Lee could watch no longer as the heat around the house made sweat drip from her body, and dipping her apron in the washbasin, she dropped to the floor and smothered her hair in the cold cloth. *Dear God, please let this woman live,* she pleaded in her soul. *If it were not for Lucinda, everything Daniel and I have given our lives for would be gone. I know I have done this woman great injury, in spite of all she has done. I have my sins too. Let me, please, dear God, please, please make amends.*

The firebreak saved them, and when the heat passed over and it was safe to go outside, Aura Lee rushed to Lucinda's side, stopping long enough to dampen a sack at the watertanks. She was hysterical with relief to find her safe, lying on the barn floor; still holding on to the horses' reins. The women clung to each other, then Aura Lee quickly lit the lantern and they both began to talk at once.

"We did it," Lucinda said. "We did it."

"No," said Aura Lee. "It was really you." Her eyes were bright with admiration.

Daniel and Vensel rode toward the billows of smoke, pushing their horses, tormented by dark thoughts. When they came upon the edge of the burned prairie, Daniel caught the odor of the scorched grass and quickly dismounted to place a palm on the ground. The earth had cooled quickly, fanned by the same wind that carried the fire.

"It won't hurt the horses, Vensel," Daniel called tersely. "Come on."

They heard the women yelling to them from the barn and spurred their horses as they approached the homestead. Daniel cursed as Toby's hooves stumbled upon the edge of the firebreak in the dark. He yelled to Vensel to rein in and the two men led their mounts across the newly plowed earth. Daniel rushed toward the faint gleam in the dark cavern and Aura Lee threw her arms around his neck, laughing and sobbing at once.

"It was Lucinda, Daniel, who knew what to do."

The woman turned around and her dark eyes were bright with pain. Her hair hung to her waist in rich locks, damp from sweat. Her body still trembled from exertion. The line from her shoulder to her jaw was as tender and vulnerable as that of a newborn colt, and Daniel was grieved that he could not reach out and touch her neck, stroke her as he did his Clydesdales.

She lifted her head and her voice was raw from the smoke she had breathed, but firm and proud.

"I saved your horses for you," she said.

Jeremiah Keever hurried toward Graham Chapman, carrying a newspaper. The editor stood on the boardwalk in front of his office and was gazing at Gateway City with satisfaction, imagining what it would look like by this time next year. His lots were selling for a fantastic profit. In his mind, the grandiose lines of the courthouse were already rising. He flicked an ash from his cigar and wondered what it would take to find the proper administrator for a normal school. They needed an academy of higher learning in the area.

"You seen this, Mr. Chapman?" Jeremiah called anxiously.

"Seen what?"

"This paper. I thought we was the only town around here."

"We are," said Graham, whirling around. "Let's see." Quickly he scanned the headlines.

"Well, *is* there another town, Mr. Chapman? You promised us we was it. I sure as hell don't want to start a dry goods store here if there's going to be another one a couple of miles away."

"No, there's not another town," he said grimly. "Not yet, anyway. And there's not going to be, either."

"What's this paper talking about, then?"

"That's all it is. Just talk. Someone trying to start one."

He read the opening editorial of this rival paper, then turned to the business cards. Aware of Jeremiah's anxiety, he was careful to keep his face expressionless. The man behind this newspaper clearly knew the ropes. But Graham coolly speculated that the newcomer undoubtedly lacked the financing for his town that he personally had been able to put together.

"Don't worry about it, Jeremiah," he said confidently. "I'll go over right away and see what's up. It's probably just wishful thinking on the part of some would-be editor."

213

"It had better be," said Jeremiah. "Gateway City ain't no damn paradise, you know. We still have to depend on someone going to Little Beaver just to pick up our mail," he grumbled. "At least back East every town had a post office. I thought every town at least had a post office."

"It will be better soon," said Graham. "When we get a railroad through, the mail won't be any trouble at all."

"Well, can't be soon enough to suit me. Hell, I don't even know what's going on with my wife and kid half the time. And it's hell on the women. Wish you could have seen Mrs. Hollingworth's face the first night I was by their soddy. She was yearning for a letter so bad I thought she would die. 'Course then I heard that when Daniel did come back with the mail, she nearly did. It's a hell of a note, Chapman, to hear that your parents have died and been buried and not even know about it for weeks." Jeremiah's blue eyes were indignant. Graham listened quietly and filed the information away in his mind.

"I'll go check on this upstart right away, Keever. In the meantime, just don't say anything to the folks here. No use in getting them riled up."

Graham gave building instructions to the men, and told them he would be back the next day. As he rode out of town, he noted with approval the new meat market that had just been established. The first load of beef and mutton had arrived Monday and the proprietor, Mr. Liter, had already lined up men to harvest ice at the creek to cool his goods during the summer months. Things were going too well now to let anything interfere with his plans.

Locating the new townsite turned out to be very difficult. He had acquired a compass two months ago, but when he tracked through the sea of grass and endless space to the latitude and longitude described in the paper, he found nothing at all. He might have a compass, he thought sourly, but he would bet good money the other editor did not.

The section markers left by government survey teams were cut from blocks of sod from four corners, to raise an earthen pillar in the center. Although the dimpling in the grass was supposed to be a guide to the primitive markers, the columns were often worn away by exposure.

After wandering over the prairie, Graham decided that one of the simplest devices for insuring that newcomers came to Gateway City first would be to leave accurate instructions at Wallace for getting there, even if he had to do occasional staking along the route. The extra time would surely be well spent and save settlers this aggravation.

Frowning, he squinted at the sprinkling of range cattle in the distance. They were getting to be a damned nuisance. Free range was from Texas to Canada, and while the cattle were not numerous, if they happened to wander onto some homesteader's property, his precious crops were lost. There had been a great deal of grumbling lately from farmers coming to

214

town, about their near-misses. Equally hate-inspiring were the yearly round-ups and the attempts of the cowboys to locate their cattle. Their contempt for the homesteaders often led to a sort of premeditated carelessness that resulted in a great deal of damage to both crops and property.

There was not any barbed wire as yet in Western Kansas. It was not available. When the railroad came through, all that would change and the farmers could have some protection, but in the meantime, they were fortunate that the cattle were scattered about in straggly, manageable clusters.

When he rode up over the rise he saw a pair of denim clad legs extending from the flap of a tent.

He studied the printing equipment before riding closer.

The man pulled his long body into a sitting position at the sound of Graham's approach and pushed his hat back on his head. His dark face was accented with heavy peaked eyebrows and he had a tidy, short dark auburn beard. Graham stared into green eyes cold as a snake's. The sun was warming his skin, but Graham felt a sudden chill. His black stallion snorted and impatiently threw back his head to ward off a bottle fly. The breeze rippled the grass at his feet and still the man did not speak, but sat with his arms behind his head.

Graham frowned. He had seen this man before, sometime, somewhere.

"You are clearly our new editor," Graham said finally. "I want to say we always welcome another man of letters to this county. Want you to know that if there's anything I can do for you, just say the word."

"You lying son-of-a-bitch."

Graham stiffened at the words and at the cold contempt in the voice.

"I said, you lying bastard. Don't you remember me?"

"Flynn. Tecumseh Spangler Flynn."

"Yeah."

Graham did not speak.

"I told you I'd get even with you someday. I don't forget my promises. Not like some people I know."

"For God's sake, boy. That was seven years ago. Water under the bridge. Surely to Christ now you're a man you know that what happened was an error in judgment, not malice on my part. I wanted Brookline City to be successful as badly as anyone."

"What happened to mother was your fault."

"No, it wasn't," said Graham.

"It was, and I said I'd get even and I will."

"You can't. You haven't got the wherewithal."

For an instant he was tempted to tell Flynn about the enormous backing he had, but he did not want to reveal the extent of his interests in the U.P. railroad.

215

"Just what is it you think you can do?"

"I can make your life a living hell," said Flynn softly. "I can create doubts in your townspeople where none existed. I can dog you in ways you have never even thought of. I can make your name a laughingstock. I can make you start at sounds that aren't there and turn your bones to water. There isn't a soul in this county who won't be aware of your flattering lips and black, double heart."

"Tem, I deeply regret the events that caused your mother's death. But surely you know I've got years of experience on you." And the backing, he thought. I wish I were free to tell you about the backing. "Son, you're only going to hurt yourself. Come in with me. Don't split the county. You of all people must know what happens then."

"Not a chance, Chapman."

"Is this all you're after, Flynn? Just revenge? It's a two-edged sword, you know."

Tecumseh Spangler Flynn rose slowly to his feet, uncoiling his long thin body as he folded his arms confidently across his chest. He looked at Graham.

"No, Chapman. As a matter of fact, that's *not* all. I owe a debt to my mother and women like her. I'm going to make this desert blossom like a rose, through bright clouds of truth. My pen will slash through lies and injustice, and women like my mother will have a decent place to live."

Graham's eyes were grave as he listened to the archaic, pompous words, but he knew he had just looked into the heart of a fanatic, and fanatics were always dangerous.

"Well, son. I think we've just declared war." He tipped his hat and rode off, regretting the trouble that would inevitably come. When he returned to his office, he sat in his chair and closed his eyes for a moment. Then, clamping his cigar between his teeth, he began to write:

Hats off to the brave pioneer editor, Mr. Tecumseh Spangler Flynn, in the proposed townsite of Plato, due east of here. It is a hardy soul indeed who will agree to be the sole occupant of a town, let alone brave the elements, as this man has done, for he has located miles from water, and there is speculation among our experienced well-borers here in Gateway City that it will be at least one hundred seventy feet to any moisture. His optimism denotes the courage we like to see displayed out here and we congratulate him on his tenacity.

Graham grinned as he reread the type. *That* should take the bloom off any propaganda Flynn was putting out. He made sure this particular issue was distributed to the citizens of Gateway City, to forestall any discontent with conditions in their town.

The next week, Jeremiah came rushing over with the next issue of the rival paper.

"Have you read this, Mr. Chapman?"

"No, let's see it."

"They're getting a railroad. It says so right here."

"Who's getting a railroad?"

"Plato."

"It's just puffery, Jeremiah." He reached for the paper and quickly scanned the headline.

The cords in his neck began to tighten. It was certainly skillful puffery and the farther he read, the angrier he got.

> *Plato Publication* announces with great pleasure that the B & M Railroad is coming through our fair city, Plato, the queen of the high plains.

Graham knew for a fact that it simply could not be true. It was not possible, as E. H. Huttwell would have alerted him to this possibility months ago. It was a blatant lie, but would the people of Gateway know that? He had to convince them of the soundness of his town, starting with Jeremiah.

Looking the merchant in the eye, he handed him back the paper. "It's puffery, Jeremiah. That and nothing more."

He studied the tip of his cigar and delicately blew a smoke ring. "Oh, by the way, are there still rooms available at Mrs. Seaton's boardinghouse?"

Jeremiah scratched his head in confusion. Rooms left? Only one had been taken so far. Surely the editor knew that.

"Uh, sure."

"Good. The Hollingworths are moving to town and they will need a place to stay until they can build their own home."

"Hollingworths? I don't believe it." Jeremiah's eyes quickened with amazement. If the Hollingworths were swinging over, there was no doubt in his mind, this was the winning town. People like them just didn't pull up stakes for nothing. Everyone knew how much Daniel was backing the railroad. And the man was smart. Real smart. If the Hollingworths said the town was going to make it, it would. Folks like Daniel always knew.

He hustled off to spread the good word. Graham grinned at his retreating back.

He had to get that couple into his town somehow. He was still sure the woman was the key and lay awake half the night planning his strategy.

• • •

217

Aura Lee looked at Daniel for reassurance before she could trust herself to speak.

"You want me to be the postmistress? And you are willing to actually pay me money for this?"

"Of course, Mrs. Hollingworth. You deserve a fair wage for the work. It's just temporary, of course," he said, knowing they would reject a permanent position immediately. "Until I can find someone else, you would be helping me out of a bind."

"I can't just ride to town that far every day, Mr. Chapman, and I have my own work to do here."

"I realize that, but since winter is coming on I had hoped you would consent to living in Gateway City for several months. You both said Daniel had some business to tend to. Of course the room and board will be provided. You'll be expected to help clerk in Keever's general store too, as that is where the mail delivery will be based."

"Thank you very much, Mr. Chapman, but I really don't see how this can be managed." Since the night of the fire, she had gained a measure of confidence. Through this near-calamity she and Daniel were becoming closer once again. She did not want to jeopardize the surprising exhilaration she felt at their newly won unity. Even her feelings for Lucinda had changed. The quick fear she once felt in the woman's presence was giving way to a normal sense of caution. She was still deeply grateful for what her neighbor had done.

"Do the arrangements sound agreeable to you, Mrs. Hollingworth? Would they please you?"

"Oh yes," she said quickly, "it's not that at all."

"It would be just perfect for all of us," Graham persisted. "Everyone comes into the general store. It would give you a chance to get acquainted with new women coming in. Think of the good you could do, and I'll back any project you ladies want to undertake. Anything at all."

Aura Lee winked back quick tears at the tingle in her blood, the sudden sense of purpose she felt. Just to think of reliable mail service overwhelmed her. This man was offering her work she was competent to do. What would it feel like, she thought with wonder—what would it feel like to be doing something once again that she was good at?

Graham's eyes never left the woman's face as she looked at Daniel, fearing his disapproval that this offer had even been made.

Hollingworth rose to his feet and silently opened the grate on the stove and poked in more fuel. He went to the window and stared at the scorched area around them before he spoke.

"I think you should do it, Aura Lee."

"What?"

"Things have changed around here since the fire. We just barely had money to get by anyway, but we could have managed. Now we can't. I haven't wanted to worry you, but I'm going to have to find work for at least a month or two to buy enough coal to see us through the winter, and to get grain for the team. The grass will come back in spring, but in the meantime there's not enough pasture. Besides, the fire burned up all the cow chips for miles around. We don't have any fuel." He grinned in spite of himself. His life was being dictated by cow patties after all.

Graham's mouth relaxed. He could not believe his good fortune.

"It's ideal, Aura Lee," Daniel continued. "They are looking for men to help lay the railroad track on past Wallace, and it pays good money. Lucinda will still take care of the horses, and I won't be around at all. There's no reason for you not to move into town for a spell. I'll come back if work gets slack, and just come on in to see you." He also would have a chance to talk to farmers in the Wallace area about organizing, but he still felt reluctant to give Graham this information.

"Vensel? Will he have to go to work too?" Aura Lee eyes clouded with worry at the thought of Anton being left all alone with his stepmother day after day. Her new appreciation of Lucinda did not extend that far.

"No," said Daniel, "he won't. In the first place the fire started a couple of miles beyond his dugout, so he doesn't have the fuel problem, and I'm going to bring back some food and coal in exchange for her taking care of the team. It'll be enough to do them, and that way there will be one man left around here if anything comes up."

"Daniel, how long have you been thinking about all this? You sound like you had it all planned."

"Quite a while," he said grimly. "The only thing I hadn't figured out was what to do with you. We damn sure weren't going to have money to pay room and board in town, and now it looks like it's all taken care of."

"I just can't believe this," she said.

Daniel felt a flicker of sadness at the animation in her face. He resented the fact that it was another man who was giving his wife such pleasure. It should be him. Her own husband. But his heart softened as he studied the light in her eyes. He didn't mind so very much after all. It would be different for them when they got the place built up. In the meantime, if this would let her get by, he was all for it. And maybe the problem of sleeping together would be helped in some way. Maybe with new work to do, it wouldn't bother him so much.

Aura Lee moved quickly from her trunk to stove and back again, fluttering in a distracted manner from task to task. She dished up the food and then with flushed cheeks turned to the men.

"I've finally managed to get a meal on the table. Isn't anyone going to congratulate me?"

Daniel laughed heartily and looked at her. He had not seen any evidence of her self-mockery and quick dry wit since she had left Saint Jo. If that was coming back, the quiet steady core that was so enchanting, then by God, he didn't care if it was this man who helped his wife.

They talked in quick bursts as they ate, interrupting one another, and apologizing with smiles. They were all three well on their way to achieving their hearts' desire.

Aura Lee put her satchel down on the floor. Her face was bright from the ride in the cold air. Graham Chapman watched her from the doorway.

"It's lovely," she said as she looked around the room that was to be her home for the next few months. "Absolutely lovely." There was a large double bed, spread with a cheery patchwork quilt in the flower garden pattern with gay squares of yellow dotted throughout. On the windowsill was a large maidenhair fern.

"That plant needs a stand so it can be turned," she said, "and a geranium. How did you get geraniums to stay in bloom this long? It's too leggy. It needs to be cut back."

She examined each article in the room as though she were a simple country girl who had not been exposed to any luxury before. A large dresser loomed in the corner. It had a marble inset in the middle containing a pitcher and basin. Beside it lay a set of thick folded towels. There was a walnut chifforobe for her clothes, and by the window was a rocking chair with low arms to facilitate handwork. There was a stand next to it with a glass-based lamp painted with yellow roses. There was a small stove just to warm this single room. It was an Acme parlor heater with nickel-plated fretwork and foot rails. The lavish ornamentation had been polished to dazzling brightness, just for Aura Lee.

"There's a supply of coal outside," said Graham. "Just let Mrs. Seaton know when you need your bucket refilled."

Oh, dear God, thought Aura Lee, with sudden understanding. I won't have to gather cow chips any more. I can be as warm as I want to be all the time.

Bright yellow priscilla curtains blazed sunshine into the room. In the corner on a small stand were books. When Aura Lee saw them, she was speechless. There was a complete set of Shakespeare and a volume of

Lord Byron's poems, and a five-volume edition of Rosa Carey's works.

She scanned the titles. They were *Aunt Diana, Averil, Esther, Merle's Crusade,* and *Our Bessie.*

"I haven't read a single one of Carey's books," she said, "not a single one." Seeing a book entitled *The Ladies' New Medical Guide,* she checked herself to keep from crying out. How did you know? she thought. How could you possibly have known how badly I needed this? Struggling for the proper degree of formality, she turned to Graham Chapman.

"This is wonderful. I don't know how to thank you." She was ashamed of the quiver in her voice as she looked at Graham. Ashamed of letting this elegant gentleman gaze this deeply into her soul.

"Is there anything else you will require for your comfort?" he asked smoothly.

"No, thank you," she said, suddenly so grateful for his understanding of her need for a proper distance that it brought tears to her eyes. She quickly turned to hide them and pretended to examine the edging of the doily under the lamp. "Everything is quite satisfactory."

"I urge you, Mrs. Hollingworth, not to hesitate for a moment to ask Mrs. Seaton for anything you would like. Anything at all. You are not to turn a hand in this house during your stay here."

She nodded. Her perfect ease with servants all of her life made it easy to accept this woman who would make her more comfortable.

"Thank you," she said. Regaining her composure, she turned and looked frankly at him, then lowered her eyes quickly again, afraid of the easy knowledge of one another that seemed to flow between them whenever they met. His white shirt sparkled beneath his gray coat and his dark blond mustache was neatly trimmed, and from the time she first met him she found her eyes straying to the curious twitch of a smile that softened his face.

"You may have meals brought to your room, of course, and then you can have your pick of fabrics for any dresses you would like to make."

"Fabrics? No, that's too much. You've done enough already."

"I just assumed from the interest you have shown in clothing that this would please you. I want to do it for you. Naturally, you will feel more comfortable wearing clothes that aren't quite—as—serviceable as those needed on a homestead."

She laughed at his tact.

"Yes," she said. "I would be overjoyed to wear clothes that aren't quite as serviceable."

"Just consider it part of your salary, and naturally, Mrs. Seaton expects to do all your laundry. It's part of the agreement for room and board. I just want you to rest for the first couple of days. Jeremiah isn't expecting you to start until Friday."

"Thank you," she whispered.

"It is I who should be thanking you, my dear. It is a pleasure to have one of your talents and abilities join with others in Gateway City to make this the best town this side of Denver."

Graham tipped his hat and he left the boardinghouse, whistling, his hands shoved into his pockets. He grinned broadly. He had moved heaven and earth to put together the room that Aura Lee had so blithely assumed was standard for town dwellers. He had prowled through all the possessions the town had to offer, paying exorbitant prices for the furnishings he knew would most please a woman of taste.

Mrs. Seaton was being amply paid to wait on Aura Lee hand and foot.

"She is to want for nothing," he insisted, "absolutely nothing. This woman is in delicate health and her first need is rest." He was prepared to tell any lie necessary to quell her quick prairie disdain for pampering, but one look at her concerned face told him her maternal instincts were already engaged.

He waved at Daniel Hollingworth, who had gone to the general store for supplies after he dropped off Aura Lee. He was driving by in his wagon, jolted by the deep ruts that passed for a street. He saw the man pull up in front of the boardinghouse.

Graham smiled to himself. Poor devil, he thought, imagining the pressure Aura Lee would soon be putting on him to relinquish his homestead.

Daniel quickly looked around the room. Since his mind was free at last from worrying about his wife's health, he had thought of nothing but getting a little cash and then organizing the farmers.

"It looks fine, honey. It's clean. That's the important thing," he said, in a hurry to get on with his work.

Aura Lee had been eager to show him the lovely room and wilted under his indifference.

He doesn't see a thing, she thought, he doesn't see what this means to me at all. Oh, Daniel, aren't we *ever* going to share anything?

It was time for him to go now and Daniel was suddenly clumsy and at a loss for words.

"Well, I'll see you," he said. "Probably in a couple of weeks."

"Daniel, aren't you going to kiss me goodbye?"

"Of course," he said, and kissed her carefully and with a wariness that broke Aura Lee's heart. He held her stiffly and his pride kept her miles away.

Oh, I shouldn't have told him, she thought miserably. I wish to God

I had just kept on pretending. Why, oh, why did I say anything?

Daniel's eyes were dark with restrained desire and a muscle twitched in his hard jaw.

"See you," he said lightly, his breath raspy and unnaturally controlled in his effort to sound casual. He had a hand on the doorknob and turned for one last look at his wife.

"Yes," she said. "See you soon. It's going to be all right, Daniel. I just know it."

"Of course," he said. "Of course it is."

She followed the progress of the wagon as long as she could. Then she sat in her rocking chair and stared out the window. Her thoughts were interrupted by Mrs. Seaton's discreet knock.

"Suppertime," the woman said cheerfully. She was bearing a tray laden with thin slices of roast beef, good brown bread, and a full glass of milk. There was a dish of cooked cabbage and carrots that had been stored in her root cellar. And an apple, thought Aura Lee. A real apple. It was her first balanced meal in months.

She accepted the food gratefully, relishing every single bite. After Mrs. Seaton had taken the tray away, she lit her lamp and finally settled on a book, basking in every moment of the luxury. Then there was no doubt in her mind as to what she wanted to do next. She prepared for bed. She studied the violet smudges under her eyes as she brushed her hair. She wanted to sleep and sleep and sleep.

Aura Lee was disoriented for a moment when she woke up in the morning. The sun was shining through the curtains she had loosened the night before.

Breakfast, she thought. I'm late fixing breakfast for Daniel. Then as she saw the comforting red glow of the coals in her stove, she realized where she was and sank back into the deep feather bed. She could not remember the last time she felt so warm and at peace, and when Mrs. Seaton looked in on her later, she was still asleep.

When she awoke again, it was nearly noon. She smiled at Mrs. Seaton and apologized as she brought the tray into the room.

"I'm afraid I'm being a bit of a bother."

"Nonsense. By the look of you, you need all the rest you can get."

"It's true I have not felt well for a long time now," said Aura Lee. "I was wondering, is there a doctor here yet?"

"Oh, land no, child."

Aura Lee's hopes sank.

Mrs. Seaton frowned with concern.

"What ever is wrong with you, dear?"

"I don't know," said Aura Lee. She bit her lip, yearning to confide in this motherly woman, but restrained by her reticent nature.

"We'll just see how you feel after some good food and rest."

Mrs. Seaton's food was all prepared in cast-iron vessels, and as the mineral was absorbed in the food Aura Lee ate every day, she began a slow healing with the iron restoring her blood. The variety of food helped tremendously, but the magic was achieved through the primitive skillets.

She entered the general store three days later, knowing she was over-dressed, but so delighted to wear a decent gown again she could not resist fingering the soft folds of the blue velvet over and over.

Jeremiah beamed when he saw her.

"Am I glad to see you. There's more than I can do to take care of the men, and women ask too many questions I don't have an answer to."

He showed Aura Lee all the stock and gave her a price list.

"Mail won't be in for a couple of days yet," he said. "We just sort it and wait for people to come by and pick it up after Lark Slocum and Charlie Stone Wolf bring it in from Little Beaver."

"What happened to their well-digging business?"

"It's a fair weather job. They both needed something to do this winter and said they would keep it up till it warms up again."

Aura Lee was drawn to the fabrics and after considering the designs settled on a navy serge and a deep rose wool for everyday dresses. She was dazzled by the variety available. Every nook and cranny in the place was stuffed full of merchandise. When Jeremiah left to load lumber for some men, she began to straighten all of the jumbled stock, wondering all the while if she could persuade the Indian to talk to her some more about his people's religion.

She turned at the sound of the door opening and a heavy-set woman walked in, clutching a dark shawl around her.

"Any mail yet?" she asked.

"No," said Aura Lee. "Not yet."

"Land's sakes. Well, I'll be back. S'pose you're the Mrs. Hollingworth Jeremiah's been telling everyone about."

"Yes," said Aura Lee. "Yes, I am."

"Well, I'm Mrs. Karnes and we're all glad you're here. That man is as dumb as a rock about half the things women need to buy. I swear he doesn't know a pullet from a rooster, and some of us want to order chicks from Wallace this spring."

Aura Lee swallowed hard and nodded wisely.

"I'll be glad to help in any way I can."

"Another thing. Not all of us are wild about the prints he gets in.

S'pose you could do something about that?"

Aura Lee smiled at her. Clearly, the fabric department desperately needed a woman's touch.

"Nice meeting you. Come over in the evening and visit for a spell if you've a mind to."

"Oh, I will. Thank you," Aura Lee said.

Her next customer was a small, freckle-faced woman who held a tightly bundled baby close to her bosom. She handed her a grimy list that had items scratched out, then re-added. Aura Lee was embarrassed to be seen in such fancy clothes and moved quickly to fill her order. Clearly each and every item had been mulled over, the value of every penny calculated. She searched her mind for something to say to put the woman at ease.

"How old is your baby?"

"Two months," the woman replied, looking up quickly with shy eyes.

"What is his name?"

"Alfred—it's after my dad. He's the third one now I've named after my dad, but the other two died. They was sickly from the very beginning and now we have this one, and Herman, that's my husband, says he thinks he's going to be all right."

Aura Lee was moved by pity as the woman talked. The words gushed out of her like a torrent. And I'm a stranger, thought Aura Lee. She's telling all these intimate things to a perfect stranger.

As she cut out her first dress that evening, she recalled every detail of the women she had met that day, trying to remember if there was a single one who had said it was her idea to move out here instead of her husband's.

Charlie looked at her with surprise when he came in the next day with a heavy mail pouch.

"Goodness," she said, "are all of those letters?"

"No. There's a whole bunch of papers from Plato, and I've got a feeling the sparks are going to fly when Chapman reads some of this. You are to see that each and every person who comes in here gets one. The postage has been paid."

Aura Lee began to sort the bundle.

"I'll be back after I've eaten," he said.

"All right. The outgoing mail is ready for you."

She finished the job quickly, and then began to read the *Gateway City Gazette* and the *Plato Publication*.

"We are in possession of the most astonishing paper ever to perpetrate schemes upon an unsuspecting county," began Flynn.

The notorious editor has been hounded out of every town he ever resided in, by outraged citizens determined to recover their losses. Now we are in receipt of business cards on the very front page of the *Gateway City Gazette* with the firm of L. E. Gandy, dealer in all kinds of furniture, given a prominent position. The truth of the matter is there is not a furniture store in the county as yet, and not the slightest prospect of one at Gateway City. They are also advertising Chapman and Company, bankers, brokers, and financial agents. The truth of the matter is that the only thing in the county even *resembling* a bank is a small iron safe in Chapman's office. It has never been known to contain more than thirty-seven cents at any one time, being the total of circulating medium among the gambling element, and that is deposited there nightly by the successful gamesters to avoid having their pockets picked by the more unlucky ones.

Aura Lee began to laugh and when Jeremiah saw what she was reading he scowled.

"Better not let Chapman see you reading that. He takes his newspaper pretty seriously."

"But it's so outrageous. I don't see how anyone can."

Jeremiah looked over her shoulder.

"Huh. That's nothing. You should see the kind of stuff Chapman writes."

When Daniel came back three weeks later, he was astonished at the transformation in his wife.

"Looks like town is agreeing with you," he said. "You look wonderful."

"Daniel, I can't *begin* to tell you how much better I feel."

Her eyes sparkled and color was beginning to enrich her pale rims and eyelids. Her fingertips were flushed pink. Her pale yellow hair was regaining its luster and now framed a face restored to its Saint Jo loveliness. The lavender smudges under her eyes had disappeared and there was a faint sweet blush on her ivory cheeks.

"I have just been talking about myself," she said. "How has your work been going? Have you contacted everyone you needed to see?"

"I haven't had a chance to meet near as many as I wanted to," he said. "And I didn't even know it was possible to work so hard. I'm tempted to take my team back next time. I could make a lot more money by hiring them out too."

"Something is worrying you? What is it?"

"I won't get paid until I've worked a month, for one thing. And then

226

too, some of the men I'm running across look so sleazy I don't bother to talk seriously to them."

Daniel had worked his way over the vast sea of grass by tying a rag on the wagon wheel. By counting revolutions he was able to estimate a mile and usually there was a claimant somewhere within the section.

"Why would anyone who wasn't decent even want to file?"

"I don't know," said Daniel. "There has to be a reason."

"How can you tell which ones are the sort you and Vensel want in the Homesteaders Union?"

"I can't, and I would just give my right arm to know what's going on. But enough of this kind of talk. How do you like being a welcoming committee of one?"

"It's wonderful. It's the first time since I came to Kansas that I've felt as though I belong." She was stricken at the pain she saw on his face and tried to soothe his wounded pride. "I mean talking to other women. I can tell by their faces that I usually know the right thing to say. There's just twenty women in the whole town. But more are coming every day, and we all want so many things. We want a church first. Will you help? Please? And it could be used as a school when there are more children."

"Of course I'll help. You know I will."

Daniel watched her face brighten with purpose. Her slender waist was accented by the basque bodice of her rose wool dress. The skirt was draped and bustled into adorable folds in the back.

"Daniel, please come with me tonight."

"Where?"

"To our literary society. Please. I want to show you off."

He looked helplessly at his work-worn hands and stained clothing.

"I brought a change of clothes into town for you when I packed," she said. "The debate tonight has something to do with the War and home-steading. Mr. Chapman is in charge."

Literary societies were second only to dances in popularity on the frontier. They were the first regular activity to be organized in every town and debates were the highlight of the evening.

"Of course I'll come," he said, "if it will please you."

Graham Chapman greeted Daniel with a smile as he came into the room. Heads turned as the swarthy homesteader entered with his lovely wife on his arm.

Everyone in town turned out to hear the noisy debates, patterned after the speeches of small-town lawyers, as the entertainment-starved pioneers never missed a chance to watch a trial. The literaries at Gateway City were held in Graham's office, although in some settlements before there were any buildings they were held under the stars.

The debaters won by their wits and by sheer force of personality. Tonight the topic was "Resolved: Veterans of the Confederate Army Shall Not Be Allowed to Homestead."

Normally the participants knew the subject two weeks in advance, and had time to perfect their arguments, so Daniel was walking into it cold.

"Which side would you care to argue, sir," asked Graham.

"The one that is right, of course," said Daniel. "The affirmative."

Graham raised an eyebrow, surprised at Daniel's choice of cases. He was pleased to have a chance to match wits with him.

"The Homestead Act," Daniel began, "states unequivocally, without a word being left open to misinterpretation, that only those who have never borne arms against the United States government shall be entitled to homestead land. It is unthinkable that a rebel, a member of the Confederate Army, who has conspired to overthrow the United States of America, who sought to fragment this great union for the vile purpose of enslaving another human being, should then expect to receive one precious inch of this beloved soil free of charge, as though no blood had been shed at all, by brave and noble men who know the worth of unity."

Daniel's face was unyielding as his hands rested lightly on the lapels of his coat. Graham's eyes narrowed thoughtfully as he watched the effect the man had on his townspeople. The citizens were swayed instantly, prepared to hang the first unfortunate Confederate veteran who happened into town. Although debaters were expected to argue each side equally well, Graham would bet his life that Daniel could only see one side of this issue. He would have to be very sure indeed of this man's price before he made a move toward his land.

"And now we shall hear the negative," the timekeeper announced.

Graham rose to his feet and began:

"Mr. Hollingworth has cleverly presented a strong case based on punishment for those who theoretically have sought to cause the downfall of our mighty government by creating a divided union. However, the course of action he proposed will perpetuate the very disunity he claims to abhor. My friends, the time has come for healing. The great advances of civilization have been based on compromise, by men of reason. Let us be charitable toward those men who fought for a cause they thought at the time to be right and noble. Let us be generous and benevolent in the final resolution of this sorrowful war. Let us beware of hard, proud men who are unable to relinquish their petty souls' hold on the luxury of righteousness."

The crowd was mesmerized; never had they heard words used with such skill. The tension mounted.

"More evils," Daniel began in his final rebuttal, "more evils have been perpetrated in the name of compromise, which to some faint souls passes as virtue, more evils have been laid on civilization under this guise than by any other single ruse. It was in the name of compromise that states were allowed to choose to remain proslavery or free, and thus continue the blackest practice in our country's history. It was in the name of compromise that the Indian nations have exchanged the rights to their native land for a pitiful existence on a reservation." Daniel's voice was low and controlled. "And it was in the name of compromise that Barabbas was released to the crowds instead of Jesus Christ." The room was hushed as they strained to catch his last measured words. "This then is the result of compromise, death upon a cross."

"Who won, Mommy?" a child asked later on the way home.

Her mother paused for a moment.

"I don't know, honey. I just *honestly* don't know."

The sweat poured from Daniel's body as he strained to lift the heavy iron bar at the command of the section foreman. "Up! Forward! Ready! Down!" The engine backed the flat car with a belch of steam as the six men lifted the massive twenty-eight-foot rail section. He gritted his teeth to absorb the jolt as they dropped it onto the ties. Daniel flexed the muscles in his shoulders to ease their soreness. The men stood to one side to make way for the spikers. He raised his head and wiped his brow, and in spite of the ache in his body, grinned at the cursing coming from the newest spiker.

"God damn yes, nothing like good old Kansas," the man had been swearing steadily for two days. As there was no hardwood on the plains at all for ties, the crews had gathered soft cottonwood, which grew in abundance in Eastern Kansas, and treated it chemically to improve its durability. As the route pushed westward the supply of trees dwindled and when they reached the timberless expanses of the prairie, they were awed by the immensity of miles and miles of open plains. For one tie in five, however, Eastern hardwood was used to add strength and stability. The man's hammer had driven a spike into one of these ties just now and his chest was jolted by the interruption of the easier rhythm of pounding through the softer wood.

"Hell, there ain't no way to get used to nothing in this state," he grumbled. "Everything changes every fifth tie and every five minutes."

Daniel stared at the tie men in the distance. They were working so far ahead that the huge beams looked like rungs on a miniature ladder. They were preceded by the surveying and grading crews, who would have light work for hundreds of miles, and he was still considering renting out his Clydesdales. All around him were teams of horses and men from the area working to get enough money to make it through until spring. He had not realized how many jobs were provided just by laying one mile of track. The amount of material and supplies required was staggering, and the work was pushing relentlessly forward.

A whistle blew, and the string of thirty cars carrying ties, rails, spikes, fuel, food—everything required for the enormous crew—pushed ahead. Daniel took his place on the side of the flatcar and braced himself to lift in unison with the others once again.

He was dog tired as he made his way to the payroll car that evening. The cords in his neck were tight from the strain of the day's work and all he could think about was getting to Aura Lee's soft feather bed in the boardinghouse. He was silent as he waited his turn in line. His crew would be replaced by another team of six for the next five days, while the one he was on rested or did easier work, then they would work again for another two weeks.

There was a farmer in front of him, asking about freight rates for his corn, and Daniel raised his head sharply, all his tiredness forgotten.

"Well, that's what it is. Take it or leave it."

"*Fifty cents* a bushel!"

"Look how much more you can sell it for back East."

"Not that much more. Hell, man, all that would leave me is making two cents a bushel profit, even if the market holds."

The man shrugged. "Next," he called.

"Can't we work something out?" the farmer persisted. "I won't have any money at all till I sell my corn, and I can't sell it here. Hell, we're corn poor. That's what everyone else is trying to sell."

"Go back to Wallace, where they will load you, and they'll help you out. We're offering to loan farmers money to pay freight rates and they don't have to pay us back until the next crop comes in."

"What if the next crop is a poor one?"

"That's the deal we're offering. Stand aside and let the next man in."

"No," said Daniel. "Wait." They both turned to look at the dark-complexioned man with eyes as black and dangerous as a gun barrel. The muscles in his legs bulged from the labor of steadying the plow. His arms and shoulders were knotted with huge iron balls of fiber and sinew from lifting steel day after day. His deep voice rumbled like thunder.

230

"Let me get my facts straight. Are you charging this man fifty cents a bushel to ship his corn?"

"That's the rate."

"And if a man can't pay it, you'll loan him the money?"

"That's the way it works."

"What's the interest?" Daniel asked.

The man flushed and dropped his eyes as he shuffled his papers.

"Thirty per cent."

"*Thirty per cent* interest to ship a crop that is just going to make two cents a bushel profit?"

"We've got to protect ourselves. Not all of these yokels are going to pay us back, you know." The man was watching the section crews starting to collect, attracted by the thundercloud of trouble in the air. Taking courage from their numbers, the station master's voice trembled with zeal and he took the offensive.

"We're doing you all a favor, Hollingworth. Hell, your corn ain't worth *nothing* out here, except for fuel and hitting jack rabbits. Without this railroad, you might as well not even *grow* a crop."

Outrage was mounting so powerfully in Daniel it seemed to glow in the very air around him.

"And what pray tell is the collateral our gracious benefactor is expecting for this financial bonanza? Just our next year's crop, or something else besides?"

"Your land, Hollingworth. We're taking a mortgage on your land to loan you the money to pay the freight bill."

Daniel turned to the group of farmers who were listening intently, and his words rang like a bugle through the cold night air.

"This is wrong. Dead wrong."

"Somebody had better stop that son-of-a-bitch," one of the spikers muttered.

"You're done, Hollingworth. Fired. Get the hell out of here," said the pay master.

Daniel turned from the group and looked at the men who were collecting, with the veteran railroad crews on one side and the temporary laborers from homesteads on the other. Coldly assessing the damage that would be done to either side, he turned to the pay master.

"You can hire and fire whomever you please. It's your right. But by God, I've got wages coming for work done and I want the money right now."

He shoved the cash at Daniel, reluctant even to have his hand touch the man.

"I may be fired," said Daniel Hollingworth, "but I'm not finished. Not by a *long* shot."

Daniel swung by Plato the next morning on his way back to Gateway City. He had ridden all night, too fired up to sleep. Recalling the blistering rhetoric with which the editor had attacked the town, he wanted to meet this man who was giving Chapman such a hard time. His legal training was being put to good use after all, he thought. Uncle Justin had impressed upon him the importance of gathering information before making any moves, and it was time to deal with the intuitive uneasiness he felt about Graham.

The town was still basically composed of tents and temporary dwellings but there was an unmistakable air of energy. He found the newspaper office immediately. The editor unwound his long legs and rose from the chair like a tall, red-headed stork when Daniel came in.

"Sir, I'm Daniel Hollingworth."

"Flynn. Tecumseh Spangler Flynn."

"I'm from Gateway City, and by the sound of your paper, you are more than aware of our existence."

Flynn nodded, his eyes suddenly wary as he studied Daniel.

"I want to know what you've got against Graham Chapman."

Flynn sprang like a snake at the opportunity to tell Daniel his tale. His angry words filled the office and Daniel's eyes grew sober, knowing he was hearing the truth.

"And that was over seven years ago," concluded Tem. "Now he knows tricks that would make a gunslinger run for cover. And worse, he's linked up with E. H. Huttwell and the U.P. railroad."

"What's wrong with the U.P.?" asked Daniel. "We used to own stock in it."

"Nothing wrong with the *main* company. It's the branch Chapman's connected with. Ever hear of a wildcat railroad? Of just lines going nowhere?"

"Why would anyone build tracks going nowhere?"

"Why not? Doesn't cost them a thing."

"What do they get out of it? Doesn't make sense. They won't make money shipping freight."

"Stock." Tem's eyes glittered. "A chance to sell watered stock. After the construction is under way and they have visible evidence of a line being completed, the officers in the company split the stock over and over and sell out completely. Then they're in the clear, and some poor fool is left owning stock in a going-nowhere, useless line, and the residents of a county have raised the money to finance a railroad that isn't going to do them any good."

"Do you have proof of this?" asked Daniel.

"You bet." Tem immediately went over to his safe, and pulled out copies of stock transactions, as well as accounts of ruined railroad towns reported by other newspapers.

"How many farmers have time to read this information? Do you?" asked Flynn. "The problem is you all work too hard and think too little. You're trying to compete against brains with muscle and it can't be done."

"What can we do?" asked Daniel. "We've got to have a railroad," he said, as the implications of Flynn's words saddened him. Even he, with his fine education, was too tired to think in the evening, let alone read. Uncle Justin used to tell him, "The wisdom of a learned man comes with the opportunity of leisure." The only leisure he had experienced since he had arrived in Western Kansas was in memory of sun-filled childhood days and magical Missouri evenings on the Lombards' porch.

"We've got a decent railroad coming," said Tem. "Check out the Baltimore and Missouri. They're going to give us a fair shake, and they're coming through Plato. The B and M will pay for the construction of their own track, and give the farmers a fair rate for their goods."

"How can we fight Chapman?" asked Daniel. "The people of Gateway City treat him like a god."

"With words," said Flynn. "The power of the pen."

"There are other ways," said Daniel, "but you can be damn sure I'll help you with the right words when I can."

Aura Lee looked up as Daniel entered the general store, smiling radiantly at the pleasure of seeing him.

"I was afraid you weren't going to be able to make it back today," she said. Only the presence of customers prevented her from throwing her arms around him. She was glad that her new blue dress enhanced her complexion. Glad to be useful and productive. She was so grateful for the return of some measure of joy and peace that her heart trembled with thanksgiving.

"Does this mean you're getting attached to this place?" she asked.

"Not exactly," he replied, not looking her in the eye.

"I wanted you to be here today so badly, Daniel. It's literary again tonight. Are you up to another round? You were quite a sensation last time. Everyone talked about you for weeks. It made me feel so proud to be married to you. The topic this week has something to do with railroads."

"You bet I'm up to it," said Daniel. Every muscle in his body had tensed at the opportunity.

• • •

"The topic for this evening is," said Graham, "Resolved: The Railroad Will Bring Prosperity to the Prairie."

He was delighted to see Daniel. When the two of them finished tonight, there would not be a single person who would not be overjoyed to vote bonds. E. H. Huttwell would be proud.

"Would you mind taking the negative, this round, Mr. Hollingworth?" he asked with an apologetic smile.

Daniel's eyes darkened with contempt. "Certainly," he said.

"In just a moment then, we will switch sides and then you can make your true feelings known."

Graham presented the affirmative case. "And so," he concluded, "our goods will be shipped back East to the people who need them most, enabling us to command a higher price, and the citizens of the county have a responsibility to bear the initial financial burden. It is only just." He sat down to applause and cries of "Hear, hear!"

"Now, Mr. Hollingworth, would you care to present the negative case. If you can perceive one," he added with amusement.

Daniel rose to his feet and a hush fell over the room. With a flawless sense of the dramatic he waited until every ear was straining. He looked gloomily at the upturned faces, yearning for the hope he could give, desperate for reassurance that they would be able to make a go of the county. He winced inwardly at the lethal blow he was about to deal them. But it was the truth; the iron fact.

"My friends, neighbors, good men and women. You who aspire to a higher life, you who yearn for the peace of mind that comes with economic security and a fair return for your labor—you are rushing blindly into *crushing indebtedness*. The men of the great railroads traversing our country, these men are perpetrating the greatest financial hoax this country has ever known."

The color drained from Graham's face as he removed his cigar from his mouth. Why, the son-of-a-bitch, he thought. The sneaky two-faced son-of-a-bitch.

When they reached her room, Aura Lee turned on Daniel in cold fury.

"Do you know what you did tonight? Do you even have the slightest idea of what you've done? You've ruined, totally ruined the belief Graham and I have tried to create."

"Oh, so it's Graham now?"

"Yes, it's Graham. He knows how women feel, Daniel. He knows how important it is to have just a few material things. He knows—" In her fury she hurled words she would never have said had she not been so angry. "He knows about me, in a way you *never* could."

234

A muscle in Daniel's jaw leaped. For a second they were both silent.

"Aura Lee," he said. "Look at Gateway City tomorrow. Really look at it. Don't lie to yourself. One of the things that made me love you was the way you have always been able to see things as they are. Please, for my sake, walk this town from one end to the other. You'll see, darling, that I'm telling the truth." His black eyes, brilliant with intelligence, begged for understanding. "I'm just telling the truth."

"Yes," she said bitterly. "You always *do*, don't you. You're the one who taught me to see things as they might be, and not as they are. Well, you've taught me well, Daniel."

They lay side by side without touching, without a trace of desire or tenderness between them, and when she woke the next morning, he was gone.

32

Aura Lee sponged the brow of the child lying on the ticking in the tent. The little girl's belly was distended and her eyes stared listlessly at the canvas top. Graham had come to her room at sunrise, to see if she could help this family.

The Carltons had arrived yesterday. Little Mary Kate, the four-year-old lying before her now, played outside with her older sister, exploring the building sites and eluding the distracted eye of her harried mother. Mary Kate was unnaturally flushed as she darted in and out of the tents and her mother thought it was due to the wild bursts of exercise in the cold weather. But by evening the flush became a dull warmth, and in alarm, the mother laid her daughter on the pallet.

She quickly sent for Graham, who glanced at the child, then cursed his luck that there was not a doctor in Gateway yet. In fact, he understood from newcomers who had arrived last weekend that the only doctor in the whole territory had registered for a homestead near Wallace. So he sent for Aura Lee. As far as he knew, she had no professional nursing skills, but she had a comforting manner, and he hoped she had acquired some information from the medical book.

Aura Lee glanced at the now-unconscious little girl and put her arms around the mother. She had known in an instant that this was beyond her abilities.

"I cannot bear this," said the mother softly. "I cannot bear this cup, Lord. Let it pass."

Aura Lee patted her hand in sympathy. "No one expects to bear this, my dear. There's no reason why you should feel like you must."

At this, the woman looked at Aura Lee and began to cry. "My Mary Kate," she said brokenly. The two women knelt side by side and Aura Lee put her arm around the woman's shoulder.

"You would not believe what we promised her," said the mother. "My poor baby. She thought she was coming to some sort of paradise, and now this. We've kept our promise all right. She'll see paradise before nightfall." She began to sob, all pretense of religious courage gone.

Aura Lee's hand tightened on the edge of the quilt she had been clutching. Her jaws were locked in silent prayer.

The little girl's chest rose and fell with torturous breaths. Then there was a faint, delicate rattle as the heavy air left her lungs. She looked the very picture of health. She was slightly plump and had blond natural curls that sprung fiercely from her head, willy-nilly. Tears streamed from the eyes of the two women as the little chest rose and fell. Then the breath broke, faltered, and the rhythm was interrupted. The two watched in horror as the mother stopped sobbing and listened anxiously to her child. There was that miss again, the break in the rhythm.

Quickly she sponged Mary Kate with witch hazel water and again the breath was drawn in a prolonged rattle and the expulsion seemed so slight as to be imperceptible. There was another breath even farther from the last one, and faint as an angel's breath. In the space of a heartbeat, she had simply stopped and would not be any more.

With her trembling hand Mrs. Carlton began to stroke the little girl's forehead.

Aura Lee pushed the tent flap aside. There was a respectful crowd gathered, quiet and anxious to offer comfort. They had heard the rising intensity of the mother's sobs and knew that the little girl had died. Aura Lee said quietly, "The child passed away a few minutes ago. I believe the mother will need all the comfort you can possibly give her."

One of the men nodded, and blinded by tears, Aura Lee began to walk away. Graham came over and fell in beside her.

"What caused her death?" he asked grimly. They were out of earshot of the crowd now.

"What difference does it make?" she asked. "I suppose she was 'feeling poorly.' That about covers it out here, doesn't it? Just feeling poorly. Doesn't matter if a person spends a lifetime dying or goes overnight. Everyone just decides that he always did 'feel poorly,' as though it were his fault somehow, for not standing up. For not being able to take it."

Graham longed to hold Aura Lee in his arms and kiss her eyelids and her lovely blond hair until the hurt went away. He wanted to soften the strained lines in her delicate face, to touch the translucent blue veins visibly throbbing at her temples. Instead he lightly touched her arm and she turned and looked at his face and saw tenderness there. She glanced down at his hand and with wonder her eyes met his and the tears streamed down her face. There was an unspoken current of sympathy between them. He understood her in an instant as Daniel never could in a lifetime.

"The only reason I want to know how she died," said Graham, "is to protect the town, the citizens. Did she die from something contagious? If so, we'll have to quarantine the entire family."

"Quarantine the family! This mother needs all the comfort she can possibly get and you talk of quarantining the family? Don't you have any feelings at all either?" She swallowed quickly in remorse. The "either" meant Daniel, of course.

"Yes," said Graham quietly. "I have feelings. But I have to protect the town. You are an intelligent woman. You must see where my obligation lies. I know this has been a terrible thing for you. But we must protect the community, above all. You've got to keep your head. Did the little Carlton girl die of anything contagious?"

Her emotions worn down, Aura Lee let his words appeal to her sense of reason.

"Yes," she said. "I understand. Let me think."

Carefully she reviewed all she had seen the short time she was there, testing Mary Kate's symptoms against the advice she had gleaned from her medical book.

"I'm no doctor, Graham," she blurted suddenly. "This is not fair, just not fair. I'm not qualified to make this judgment."

"You've *got* to, Aura Lee. There's no one else who can do this."

Slowly her tongue traced the outline of her parched lips and her brow knitted in concentration. There had been no spots, no rash. Not even any vomiting or diarrhea.

"In my opinion," she said slowly. "In my opinion, there was no evidence of any type of a contagious disease."

"O.K." he said. "That's all I wanted to know. I'll tell one of the men to start making a coffin immediately. She needs to have a decent burial. I want you to help me with the service."

"Help you? Why me?"

"Because you are the one all the other women look up to now. You're needed. Get some of the women together and help make a shroud, and we need some pretty material to line the coffin."

"Leave me alone, Graham," she pleaded. "Leave me alone. You asked

237

me to help start civilization out here. Civilization! Do you understand? Not a graveyard."

"You don't think a civilized burial is important?"

For an instant, the bleakness of Julka Smrcka's funeral flashed before her eyes again. For the past twenty-four hours this memory had haunted her. The dirt, the wind, the vast emptiness. And again in all its starkness was the outline of that body in the sheet. Not even a coffin, lowered without ceremony into an undraped hole.

"Yes, of course it's important," she said, tears streaming down her face. "I want that mother to remember that her daughter was buried by decent people who care. I'll help. Of course I'll help."

"Thank you," he said. He tipped his hat and looked at her, his eyes grave and bleak as the cold winter day. "Aura Lee, I know you probably have some doubts about me and God only knows about the confusion your husband has managed to create in everyone else's mind in one evening's time. But it is important to me that you believe this. I *want* a decent town. I want this to be a decent place for people to live." His little twitch of a smile tried to minimize the seriousness of his next words. "And I didn't realize how important this was to me until you came here."

Her blue eyes looked at his, which were so vulnerable that he closed them to protect his soul from the unaccustomed pain of having revealed so much. She knew only too well, from her experience of handling old beaus in Saint Jo, the pedestal on which he had placed her. It was as though for some men, not finding goodness within themselves, their life was spent in a subtle, romantic search for the perfect woman. And she looked at this man with his silver tongue and his winsome ways and knew the woman who won his heart would be very lucky indeed. No men loved harder or more blindly than rogues and sinners. It was as close as they would ever come to experiencing divinity either in Heaven or on earth. The quality of this man's devotion would be awesome.

"Thank you, Graham. And I want you to know that I do believe you."

Aura Lee was racked with remorse as she watched him go. She had exposed too much of her feelings. She had been calling this man by his first name, and now had allowed him to touch her, even though it was just her arm. Every word, every detail of her conversation ran endlessly through her mind and she agonized over her awareness of this man who was not her husband. She was a storm of conflicting feelings, and she blinked back tears as she headed for the comfort of her little room. She had not been proper. She was not a lady. A man had touched her who was not her husband.

Four days later, Graham's column gloomily reported that a citizen of Gateway City had died.

The Angel of Death came to clasp one of Gateway City's fairest blossoms to her bosom. Little Mary Kate Carlton, a recent arrival to our own piece of heaven, was plucked for the Lord's flower garden last Monday evening. The bereaved parents were led through the valley of the shadow by our sympathetic townspeople, who saw to the distressed couple's every comfort as they reluctantly placed their daughter in the hands of her Maker. Little Mary Kate was laid to rest in the finest cemetery between Kansas City and Denver. The severity of the elegant iron fence is relieved by a stand of shade trees, which flourish at the four corners.

The morning she saw the paper Aura Lee was bewildered and sickened by the description of the fine cemetery. She had been so distracted by her sympathy for the mother she could not remember one single detail of the day. She decided to go see for herself. She walked to the area where the Carltons had laid Mary Kate. There were stakes and wire outlining the area, and at the corners four cottonwood saplings drooped in the hostile prairie wind.

She looked back at Gateway City. The courthouse was just a set of stakes. Most of the families were still living in tents. There was no doctor, no minister. The drug store was a glorified saloon. Even though the town had an opera house, a wonderful hotel, and a cobbler, the venture suddenly seemed chaotic and futile.

Her spirit sagged and she was frozen with dismay. Daniel's right, she thought. It's all facade. This is the way things really are. I want Daniel, I want to go home.

"Where is home? Where do you belong?" the voices mocked. She gasped. They had been gone for so long.

"He asked you to look. Really look," they reminded her. She pressed her fingers to her temples to clear her head and stared at the full view of the town from the vantage point of the cemetery. There were pigs rutting in the back yards of some of the frame houses. Every single residence had an area wired off for chickens but most of the fowl wandered freely. Dogs were getting to be a nuisance and the air was often filled with the sounds of their fighting. Tiny seedlings of cottonwood fought the grass for the scarce moisture. The buildings did not have a speck of paint and random piles of lumber added to the disarray.

"Is this what you want?" asked her voices. Panic-stricken, she headed across the prairie, careful to follow the sun for direction, hugging the newspaper to her body. She clutched the shawl around her shoulders and even with the resistance offered by the long waves of bluestem grass, she easily reached their homestead in a couple of hours.

It was high noon. She went inside and sat stunned in her rocking chair, lonely and afraid and chilled to the bone.

Daniel may not be back today, she thought tearfully.

"He may never be back," taunted her voices. She stopped rocking and did not move. They had been banished. There had not been so much as a whisper from them for so long now. Oh, it was not just this place, this house, that had made them come again. They had invaded her mind in town just when she thought she was free of them forever. Nevertheless she yearned for the comfort of her little yellow room. She had never heard them there. She drew a deep breath to regain control and rose to go back to town where there were people and she was at least useful, if not happy. She tip-toed without knowing why. And then there were queer images eluding her and she was in the grip of a terror so heavy she felt as though her heart would explode with each beat. Someone had been in her house. Her quilting hoop had been moved from its usual spot in front of the window, and the lid of her trunk had been opened.

Stricken with terror, she grabbed her shawl. She had just reached the corral when she saw Lucinda Smrcka coming toward her.

"I have come here many times, to feed your horses," the woman began bluntly. "Your man is never home either. He is to bring us supplies in exchange for my work." Lucinda waited for an explanation.

Aura Lee was relieved by the earthy presence, the sheer practicality of the woman.

"He's had problems, Lucinda. He's no longer working on the railroad, but I can assure you he will find the money for your supplies. You can always count on Daniel to do what he says he will do."

"Where is your man then, if he is not working on the railroad?"

"Uh, he's talking to farmers now, while it's slack time," Aura Lee said quickly. Suddenly her relief at seeing a normal person vanished, and she did not want to tell this woman any more about their problems than was necessary to keep her curiosity at bay. Besides, she was reasonably sure it was the truth. Daniel had to be talking to other homesteaders.

"And Anton, how's little Anton?"

"He's just fine," Lucinda said carefully. "The boy often goes to the field with his father now." She studied Aura Lee critically. Her coloring was no longer pasty and unhealthy, the tips of her fingers were red and there was a normal blush to her cheeks and a steadiness to her gaze.

So the little mouse had gotten well without her tonic after all.

"Where do you cook?" she asked.

"I don't," said Aura Lee. "It's done for me."

Lucinda nodded. So even this gap was being closed, this one area in which she was clearly superior. She knew that in time Aura Lee would be perfectly well. She could already see her anemia was being cured.

"And your man?" asked Lucinda. "He is happy when he comes to this town also?"

"Oh, of course not," said Aura Lee. "I mean he's not often in town at all. This is just a temporary arrangement. I'll come back here as soon as Daniel is done."

Lucinda's hands were clenched together under her apron. Her heart leaped with exaltation.

"So he will be coming back here from time to time? Without you?"

"Yes. From time to time. Until we get things straightened out."

Lucinda's pulse raced. She would know when he came. She came over every single day. Lucinda did not look at Aura Lee. Seeing the newspaper, she was grateful for the diversion.

"A paper," she said. "May I see it?"

"Of course, and you can take it home," said Aura Lee. "I was just going back to town when you came. There's plenty more back there. I— I came to get some things I had left. Lucinda, have you been in my house? Someone has, and I was just wondering."

"Yes, I have helped you," the woman replied quickly. "I have done many things for you. The chrome on the stove sparkles now. And your table. It glows from the beeswax I have applied. I have done many things for you and for your man. Within and without."

Aura Lee choked on the bile in her throat. Even this pitiful place was being usurped. She shut her lips against outraged words.

"Thank you. Thank you very much for looking after things so well."

"It is my pleasure," said Lucinda proudly, with a strange formality that Aura Lee heard with dread, knowing it only masked Lucinda's wilder emotions.

"I really must get back to town," Aura Lee said quickly, imagining the barrage of criticism of her housekeeping, her health, her way of life that was about to be unleashed.

"Thank you so very much for the paper," said Lucinda, and she looked about her, inspecting the homestead for work that needed doing. Then she waved to Aura Lee, and set off with her long strides, singing as she went.

Each day after her husband and son had gone to the field, Lucinda went back to the Hollingworths' homestead, and after feeding the horses, she sat in Aura Lee's rocking chair and waited, waited for Daniel.

241

33

The sleet stung Daniel's face as he rode toward his homestead. He pulled his bandanna over his mouth to warm his breath. It was the first winter storm and by the look of it he was lucky to be close to his farm before it hit. "Just one more mile, Toby, and we'll be home." Clouds were rolling in and the patches of bluestem were crusted with ice. The buffalo grass was a slippery carpet under his horse's hooves. His tired mind reviewed the arguments he had been presenting to the homesteaders. He had to make the men understand somehow the enormity of the hoax—the lies that were being told. After the snow blew over, he would consult Flynn.

His patience was beginning to pay off, however. Yesterday he had talked to a man and his wife who seemed to understand the gravity of what Graham Chapman was doing.

"Stocks are a time-honored way of expanding a company," said Daniel. "When people buy stocks they are using their own money. They own what they are trying to build. They have every reason to want a project to succeed. The railroads, however, want to use bonds to finance their construction."

"What's wrong with that? I thought the government was in back of the bonds."

"It is," said Daniel. "But then they sell the bonds to people who can't afford them. Like you and others in your county."

McQuire snorted. "Fat chance of that. I would like to see me finance a railroad. I can barely afford to eat."

"All right," said Daniel, "think about what you just said. That's the problem in a nutshell. You're expected to pay for a railroad when you can't even feed your own family."

"They can't make me do it," said McQuire. "You can't get blood from a turnip."

"Listen, Kevin," said Daniel. "You and Mary here must believe me. They can't make Kevin McQuire as a person do it, but I can assure you that if your county votes to buy bonds to build a railroad, you're going to be slapped with taxes you'll never be able to pay."

"Taxes to build the railroad?"

242

"Taxes to build the railroad." He paused for a moment and the big Irishman absorbed the information.

"If I can't pay, they'll sell my homestead out from under me, won't they?"

"Hell, yes," said Daniel.

"Won't do no good," said Kevin, "if taxes be that high, no one else in the county can afford to buy it either."

"Who will have the money?" asked Daniel, leading the man along.

"Why, the railroads," said Kevin. "Why, Jesus Christ, of course. The railroads will be the ones to buy my land."

"Yes," said Daniel.

"For nothing?"

"Practically nothing," said Daniel. "McQuire, you've got the picture, clear enough. Just tell others about it. You'll be asked to pay for the building of the railroads at a price no one can afford, and they'll be waiting to buy your land for nothing when you go under."

Not everyone was as quick as McQuire.

Daniel drew a sharp breath as he passed over the final gentle swell hiding his house from view. There was smoke coming from the stovepipe. Aura Lee had come back.

With a quick surge of joy he spurred his horse. During the time away, he had brooded over his abruptness with her. If he had used even a fraction of the tact with her he was now using on the men, there would not be this rift between them.

Weeks of checked desire were taking a toll. He was aware of his tormented body in ways he had not been since puberty. He wanted food and he wanted to be warm and he wanted his wife. He hurried into the barn with Toby, ignoring the eager whinny from the Clydesdales as they caught his scent.

He opened the door of the soddy and met the bold tawny eyes of Lucinda Smrcka.

"What are you doing here?" asked Daniel. His voice was coarse with disappointment. "Where is my wife?"

Lucinda did not speak for moment.

"When I finished feeding your horses, I came inside for a moment to warm myself before I went home."

"Lucinda, God knows I appreciate what you're doing for us, but I—you—cannot come here," said Daniel, furious now at his lack of control. "I won't have it, by God."

Still she did not move and looked at him sadly with eyes brimming with tears.

"What can it hurt, Daniel? Who could it hurt?" Daniel reached for her hair, with a hand that trembled—just to touch and nothing more.

She lifted her head and her full lips parted and spell-bound he bent toward her, just to kiss and nothing more.

Once as a boy he had gone swimming in the river and, in spite of Uncle Justin's warning, had gone too far out and been swept along by an undertow, knowing he could be free anytime he wanted, yielding just for the sensation, until he was in the grip of a force he did not understand and could not break free of. He was rescued by Justin just in time.

Now he drew Lucinda to him, just to experience one time the warmth of her body pressed against his—just the warmth, nothing more. Then for the second time in his life he was pulled under by a force he had underestimated, one Lucinda understood all too well. This time there was no one to draw him back, and their bodies swirled down into a fathomless depth. Outside the soddy, the snowstorm hit with full force.

Daniel paced the floor in Tem Flynn's office. He stopped here as often as possible and honed his ideas on the sharp mind of the editor. They often talked late into the night.

"You've been all over now, Hollingworth. And what have you found? Men worn down in body and soul with care and toil in the present and anxiety for the future, I'll wager. They're dogged by debt. They are getting too little for the food they produce and the men who handle it are getting too much. Their wives live in solitary confinement from sunrise to sunset."

"It doesn't have to be that way, Flynn. Folks have got to eat, and we should be able to make a living."

"It's going to come through using your heads. Did you find a single man who could afford to leave his chores long enough to attend agricultural or political meetings where his cause would be heard and understood?"

Flynn was interrupted by a knock on his office door.

"I was told to come and talk to you, Mr. Hollingworth," the man blurted. "They say you are a just man who can help us out."

The man's wife was sitting dry eyed and bolt upright on the seat of their buckboard.

"What happened?" asked Daniel.

"Claim jumper. We wouldn't pay him off, because we heard you have other ways of handling things in the county."

"Good," said Daniel. "I'm glad the word is getting around."

"My wife is taking it awful hard. We traveled two months to get here."

"Tell her to come right on in," said Daniel. "Flynn, I don't want you directly involved in any of this. You folks stay here tonight; I have some work to do."

"No," said the man, "I'm going with you. It's my land, and Harmon Mullholland looks after his own."

"All right," said Daniel, "but this is the first real test of the group and things could get a little rough."

They left immediately and collected the H.U.A.ers. The night was bitterly cold and their breath hung like doom in the frigid winter air. They did not carry handguns, but many had their rifles. There was a luminous shimmer to the prairie.

There was no shame in the men in the beginning. They were exhilarated by their sense of unity.

The claim jumper was dragged from his bed.

"What in the hell is going on?" he asked, looking at the circle of men.

"A hanging," said Daniel. "We don't hold with parasites like you in this county."

The man shook off the hands that were holding him. Seeing the plain denim work clothes of ordinary dirt farmers, he spat on the ground in contempt.

"Don't look like I've got to worry about no hanging out here, lest you boys be magicians that plan to pull trees out of thin air."

Daniel turned and nodded at the men. Quickly they hoisted the wagon tongue upright and fashioned a hangman's noose. The man's skepticism vanished as a gallows, a hangman's tree, was indeed pulled out of thin air.

"God damn," the man said, the color draining from his face. "God damn, boys. Surely you're not going to go through with this. I wouldn't have done this if it weren't for the money they paid me."

The noose was settled around his head and he was hoisted onto a barrel. The rope was suspended from the propped up tongue of the wagon.

"Do you have any final affairs that need to be put in order?" Daniel asked calmly. "Any last words? Anything at all?"

"Jesus Christ," said the man. "You can't possibly get away with this."

"We can and we will," said Daniel. "It's your life or ours. It's as simple as that."

The barrel was kicked to one side. Any man in the group who had not been convinced before of the determination of Daniel Hollingworth was instantly converted. The shame came over them then. They were not men to whom killing came easily. They did not look each other in the eye.

Silently they watched the dying man's final disbelieving struggle. It was as though, to the bitter end, he had thought the whole thing was some kind of a joke. Some of the men themselves had joined casually, not seeing where it would lead.

Tom Nickerson started to ask what they should do with the body, then ruefully closed his mouth as he realized it didn't make sense to hang a man and then become concerned about a decent burial.

They turned and rode slowly back to their homes.

They initiated a new member several nights later, and as the man was led through the secret oath, each word had a chilling effect. The organization had acquired a whole new meaning.

Word of the hanging spread like a prairie fire. The body was mysteriously removed and no one was too sure by whom, and no one wanted to ask either. Someone reported that the drifter was sponsored by a railroad who encouraged him to file on as many claims as possible so that they could buy up the land.

> Never has there been a deed so foul, so unwarranted as the unspeakable crime committed by the loathsome handful of men, self-appointed avengers bent on taking the sacred breath of God from a man who simply moved in error onto a pitiful piece of land. The *Gateway City Gazette* is in possession of proof that he was an honorable man, who intended to rectify his mistake in judgment at the first opportunity.

"It is the right of every human being in this great United States of America to protect his property and his own with whatever means are at his disposal," wrote Tem Flynn in the *Plato Publication*. "We salute the courage of the fine, brave men in this county, who with stalwart hearts could steel themselves to a task that admittedly went against the grain of some of our farmers, but it was necessary, and again I say, we salute them."

Aura Lee read each paper over and over. Each customer who came into the store spoke of nothing else. She wanted to talk to Daniel, yearned to hear his side of it. He had not been back to Gateway City since the night he had debated Graham. She wondered what was becoming of the man she had married.

Charlie Stone Wolf stamped his feet to shake off the loose snow as he came into the general store. He blew vigorously on his cold hands to warm them and set the mail pouch on the counter. He looked at Aura Lee, seeing the taut lines at the sides of her eyes. She was beginning to lose weight again. He turned to the stove and waited for her to speak.

The store was rich with odors. Jeremiah had freighted in dried fruits for the coming Christmas season and there were even oranges available for the few families who could afford the luxury.

They were alone and Aura Lee's hands nervously sorted the letters.

"Charlie," she said. "I'm having a terrible time again. It was so much better for a while. You've heard about the hanging?"

He nodded.

"I don't understand how this could have happened. Things aren't— right between Daniel and me anyway, and now this. Suddenly he seems a stranger. Nothing makes sense any more. I'm not like I used to be," she said quickly, knowing he would understand that the intense mental torment had eased again. "It's not that bad. It's just that I don't know where my place is. Where I belong. We're a pair, now, aren't we, Charlie?" she said with a wry smile. "A white woman asking an Indian to help her figure out what to do."

He grinned, his white teeth flashing in the store's dim interior, then was startled by the wave of sadness that swept over him. In his tribe, where he had taken his rightful place with the wise men, the learned ones, the old ones spent hours on long winter nights reciting the holy legends that preserved the tribe's soul. Everyone knew where he belonged within his family and tribe and the land around him. His life had been ordered by the seasons, and the rituals that entreated and placated the gods century after century. He too had lost his place, his people. He had learned to accommodate to the white man's ways, but most of all he missed the exchange of wisdom, the testing of paths. White men just decided what they would do, then asked the gods to bless their endeavors. This frail woman was the only one he had met who was alive to the whispering of the gods.

"Daniel is right," he said abruptly. "My chiefs waited too long. Men must do whatever is necessary to preserve their own way of life. We listened to too many lies, and we have been destroyed. The women no longer keep the sacred. Our men have replaced seeking visions with the white man's reasoning. Daniel is right to do what must be done."

"Is there no peace, then, Charlie? I'm trying so hard. Did you hear about the Carlton girl dying?"

He nodded.

"You told me I must be a healer, or a teacher, or an artist, Charlie. I wanted to heal her so badly. I prayed and prayed and nothing happened."

"Then those demons have not yet picked your bones," he said quietly. Seeing the flicker of fear in her eyes, he searched for words. The Indian words and stories were so clear, so vivid, but they were his people's words and he could not find a parallel for white men.

"When you are favored by the gods," he said, "and are *shaman*, you

247

are carried away to the underworld and during the three days you are there, you are torn limb from limb and your bones are scattered. The demons come and devour your flesh. Then the gods put your bones back together again, and when you ascend, you will be able to cure the ills caused by the demons who have stripped your bones. And only those ills. No one is capable of healing all."

"I will only be able to help those who are experiencing what I have gone through myself, then?" asked Aura Lee.

He nodded, relieved at her swift comprehension of this difficult myth.

"You must be cured of that illness to help another. It is not enough just to have gone through it, you must be *cured*. You bear the wound of God, Aura Lee, and you must seek the touch of Changing Woman."

Another customer was entering, and she turned from Charlie with reluctance, wanting to hear more from this unlikely ally. She watched him leave the store and shut her eyes for a moment against the unasked question, which she placed in the blinding circle of white light. She had been through hell out here. Surely she had endured the worst suffering God could inflict. Had she made the last terrible descent? Been carried away to Charlie's dark underworld? Suddenly she did not want to know or even think about the agony he had suggested was necessary for the cure.

Daniel glanced at his wife, his eyes dark with pain, and waited for her to assemble supplies for Mrs. Karnes.

When they were the only ones left in the store, Aura Lee turned to him, and seeing the deeply etched new lines in his face, she was in his arms in a flash.

"Daniel, where have you been? I've been so worried."

"Have you heard about the claim jumper?"

"Yes."

He gave her a long, hard look.

"Am I the kind of man you want to be married to?" He averted his eyes then, to disguise other guilt, and, picking an orange from the display, slowly began to remove the peel.

"I can't believe you would doubt me, Daniel. We always knew it would come to that for the H.U.A.ers. You know how much I love you. I'm sorry I flew into a fury the last time you were here. I just love working in this town and store so much, but I want to be with you. I want to come home."

He turned to her with a burdened heart. "In another month or two, Aura Lee, my work will be done. We need to be back together again," he said abruptly, and at the hoarse sound in his throat she looked at him

248

in amazement. Never once before had he told her he needed her. Her body quivered in wonder. She reached for his hand, proud to comfort, and ambushed by joy, she was so gloriously sure of her place she felt as though she were on the new earth.

"It's going to be all right, Daniel. Thank God everything is going to be all right." The words gushed from her in a flood of relief. "Christmas is coming, Daniel. My first Christmas away from—from—" Her head was on his chest as she began to cry. "They're not there any more, they're dead and I can hardly bear it. And not to be around Marie—and the lights—and the parties—and the singing—and my wonderful church— and I just could not bear it without you. And now it's going to be all right. I can feel it in my bones."

Daniel's double heart beat as heavily as the footsteps of a firing squad. He shuddered as he stroked her hair and did not reply.

"Daniel, we're having a program at the literary, and an oyster supper and a play, and we want everyone to come. I want Anton here, Daniel. Could you please talk to Vensel and Lucinda? It won't be so terribly far for them to walk. And he needs this so badly. He needs to have a merry Christmas. Not just another day in the dugout. And, oh, just think. To give Anton a present. He'll be beside himself."

Daniel nodded and his mouth was grim as he firmly suppressed the treacherous need to confess that crawled like a lizard from his dark soul. She must never, never know.

"I'll talk to the Smrckas, sweetheart," said Daniel. "And we'll all have one hell of a good time."

Lucinda reread the paper Aura Lee had left from first page to last. The edges were ragged now from constant handling. All of her work was done and time was hanging heavy on her hands these cold January days. Her days were filled now with thoughts of Daniel. She yearned to be with him again. She was too distracted even to let the boy get on her nerves. Anton had the sniffles and wanted to stay home all day.

She read and reread the little item saying that the young people were gathering nightly for singing at various homes. None could sing as sweetly as she, she wagered. None had the range or the breadth, and yet she had not been invited once to any of the social activities. Not once. But then how could she be? No one was aware of her existence out here in this miserable hole. And her violin! If she could take her violin into town, wouldn't people be surprised?

She carefully read the social items one more time and they were filled with Mrs. Hollingworth this, and Mrs. Hollingworth that. How Aura Lee had begun a literary group, and Mrs. Hollingworth proudly announced they had been able to obtain the promise of a touring Shakespearean troupe to come to Gateway City. It would be the first troupe to perform at the new opera house.

Touring Shakespearean performers indeed! And who was this woman anyway, to think she was so high and mighty she would decide who was to come and who was to go within a town. Lucinda knew she was being deliberately ignored by Aura Lee. The truce that existed between them ever since the night of the fire had ended in a moment when she refused to let Anton come to the Christmas party. Even Daniel was angry with her. Well, they could see clearly now her scorn for such unnecessary frivolity. And the boy, too, did not need to be encouraged in his giddy streak that made him want to draw all day.

Vensel was over at the creek. He was going to cut some blocks of ice to use for cooling food in the summer and put them in the straw-lined pit he had dug. She could hardly stand her husband now. She detested the earthy odor of his body and his clumsy, dangling hands. She was revolted by the fear in Anton's eyes.

Her extreme discontent had begun when the attention had switched from homesteading to town-building. She was no longer the victor, the star, the wonder of the plains. In fact, if there were really any star at this point, it was Aura Lee.

Abruptly, she decided to go into town, to see for herself this marvel that Graham Chapman described so eloquently.

"Anton, get dressed."

The boy lifted his head and protested weakly.

"I can't."

"Nonsense. Of course you can. Hurry now, we're going to town."

"Town? Does Dad know?"

She did not reply.

Anton was torn between a chance for a rare, wonderful excursion and a yearning just to lie in his bed. He bit his lip, then slid from beneath the warmth of the quilts and dressed, his body trembling all the while. He folded his arms across his frail chest, attempting to still his chattering teeth.

His coat was too light to give him enough warmth. Even the sun looked pale and unfriendly as he and Lucinda set out into the bitterly cold winter weather.

The main street had mushroomed true to promise. Now many of the stakes were being replaced by buildings. The pace of the town, the quality of vitality, of hope, made Lucinda smile. She delighted in the men she saw, with their joyful optimism, and intensely disliked their pinch-mouthed little wives with their deeply lined faces.

She went with wonder from shop to shop and examined the attractive array of goods. It was terrible, the way she had to pinch and scrape. She smiled slyly when she thought of the anxiety Vensel would be feeling at even the possibility of spending his hard-earned money in any of these places. Oh, to have the ready cash to be able to buy one of these bolts of calico to brighten her life.

Anton was silent.

"For God's sake, boy, hurry up. Quit dragging your feet."

"I just don't feel good," he said.

"That's because you don't want to. You are deliberately trying to ruin my day."

Tears sprang to Anton's eyes. He just wanted to lie down where it was warm.

"Come along, boy."

Grabbing his hand, Lucinda started down the boardwalk. She stopped and listened as she passed the door to one of the town's three saloons. There was singing inside and joy and laughter. She hesitated only a second before she turned around, then pushed through the bat-wing doors.

For a moment, the clientele was frozen as they looked at the apparition in the doorway. The sun was highlighting her abundant auburn waves. Her lush sweet curves were outlined provocatively in spite of the severity of the cut of her dress. Her light brown eyes were aglow with pleasure. She loved men, she needed men, she drew her vitality from their admiration. She had unwittingly found the perfect forum.

"Jesus Christ," someone said. "I must be dreaming."

"If you are, let's both don't wake up," said his companion. "I won't pinch you if you won't pinch me."

Jake McIntyre, who was considered the authority on females, said solemnly, "I believe that's the most beautiful woman I've ever seen." No one argued.

"Come right on in, ma'am," he said with mock chivalry. No one believed for a second she would. All saloons were exclusively masculine territory. Only "soiled doves" were ever seen inside, and usually the working life of a prostitute was short and dismal. So when Lucinda walked in, a hush fell over the room and all the men were uncomfortably speechless.

Only Lucinda was totally in control. She walked proudly over to a table and sat coolly down in a chair.

"Bartender, I want a bourbon and water."

The men continued to stare.

"Well," she said softly. "Is anyone buying?"

"Hell, yes, we're buying. Whatever's for sale."

No one paid the slightest attention to the slender little boy at her side. No one had seen her before. Jake's eyes were gleaming.

"Do you live around here, ma'am?"

"Yes, my husband homesteads." She enjoyed even more the consternation the last statement brought.

"Married, huh?"

"Oh, yes."

Jake's eyes narrowed. There were problems here. Not the least of which would be the husband. But the right kind of woman could make a fortune in these parts. Any prostitute who was managed properly did extremely well, and true beauty was such a rarity she would be able to name her own price.

"What happened to the music, boys?" No one spoke. "Am I going to have to make my own?" she asked teasingly. "I believe the song went something like this."

She picked up the strain of the song they had been singing and her rich contralto filled the room.

"My God," muttered Jake. "Just what is it we have here?"

Aura Lee was passing the saloon door and stopped abruptly as the sound of Lucinda's voice spilled out into the street. Her feet were rooted to the ground. It simply could not be. Swallowing her pride, she timidly pushed the doors apart enough to peep inside.

Lucinda was standing now, one arm stretched toward the men in a curve of invitation. The other was casually braced on her waist. Aura Lee's cheeks flamed with shame for her neighbor. Then she froze as she saw the miserable face of Anton Smrcka, his eyes wide with despair. Oh, how could she do this to this child? She pushed the doors aside and stepped inside. The note died in Lucinda's throat and she stared coldly at Aura Lee.

"Mrs. Smrcka," Aura Lee said evenly, struggling to control her anger, "would you please come outside with me for a moment? I have a matter I would like to discuss with you."

Anton jerked to attention. His chin snapped up and his face flooded with relief when Aura Lee spoke. Lucinda shrugged and wordlessly left the saloon, her head high.

Once outside the saloon, Aura Lee fell on her instantly.

"What in the world do you think you're doing?" she blazed. "Lucinda, just going into that place brands you forever in this town. *Surely* you know better. How could you possibly do this to Anton? Think of the disgrace this will be to your husband."

Lucinda smiled. She had gone in on impulse, without thinking, and now she realized the blow this would be to Vensel. He had a deeply ingrained Czech pride in his good name, and his reputation for decency was priceless to him. She could imagine the hang-dog sense of tragedy that would appear in his eyes when he heard his wife was not the epitome of Czech respectability.

"Yes," said Lucinda mockingly. "Think of the disgrace this will be to Vensel."

Anton had instinctively pressed against Aura Lee.

She knelt, alarmed at the unnatural warmth of the little boy and pressed a hand to his forehead.

"Lucinda, this child is burning up. He needs to be in bed. You're supposed to be his mother now. Just what kind of a woman are you?"

Lucinda's eyes darkened. "A real one," she said softly. "A real one and I think that's more than you can say for yourself."

The color drained from Aura Lee's cheeks. Her eyelids blinked furiously at the stinging tears that were threatening to spill over. What did she mean? What could she possibly mean? But in her heart, she feared that Lucinda *knew* what the situation was between her and Daniel and was going to use it against her.

"You're wicked," Aura Lee said slowly. "You're one of the most attractive women I've ever seen, and you're rotten through and through. But then, Satan has always appeared as an angel of light. You've hurt Anton and you're killing Vensel."

Lucinda's eyes narrowed at the last. "There's more ways than one to kill a man. But I think *you* should know that by now."

Aura Lee flinched as though she had been struck. Her sensitive blue eyes were cold with wounded pride as she thought of her failure to be the wife she wanted to be to Daniel. How could she know? Lucinda loomed before her, ten feet tall. Aura Lee could not bear the humiliation. The weight pressed on her heart like an anvil. How did she know? The dark thoughts swooped at her like bats. Was the agony in her husband's eyes that obvious?

"Anton will come home with me," said Aura Lee.

"He can't," Lucinda said crossly. "I would not know what to say to his father."

"I'm sure you'll think of something," said Aura Lee.

Lucinda walked home with proud strides. There was a hum, a vibration under her feet, and she was so full of wonder at the sights she had seen she was able to put her irritation over Aura Lee's concern for Anton out of her mind. One thing was for certain: there was a place for her in town. She wished for a second that she could call back her words to Aura Lee, however. Not because she had wounded her, but for fear that Daniel would find out. Once home, she brooded over her folly in leaving the boy, but when she saw Vensel coming across the field, the right words came quickly enough.

"Where's Anton?" he asked.

"Thank God, you're home," said Lucinda. "The boy was running a fever. So I was worried and carried him into town. He's with Mrs. Hollingworth and will be there where medicine is available until he is better."

"Will he be all right?"

"Oh, yes," said Lucinda. "The fever came down very quickly when she gave him one teaspoon of the cold cure concoction she keeps. I told him he could stay with her a while."

Vensel let out his breath. "You did a wonderful thing."

"It was nothing," murmured Lucinda.

"Nothing? To carry a boy two miles?"

"He was very light."

"Lucinda, I know things are not as we want them to be between you and the boy, but I thank you from the bottom of my heart. Thank you for caring for my son." Vensel's eyes shone with gratitude.

"It was nothing," said Lucinda. "Really nothing at all."

Aura Lee pressed her hands to her temples to still the throbbing in her head after she had laid Anton on the bed. She had to pull herself together to deal with the boy's health. The other thoughts could wait. He was so hot. Given a chance to rest, Anton had sunk immediately into a deep, labored sleep. She pulled out her medical book. What good will it do, she thought bitterly, to know the remedy when there's no drug store to supply it.

"Mrs. Seaton," she called, her voice quivering with urgency. "Run get Mr. Chapman, please, as quickly as you can find him."

The housekeeper peered through the doorway at the little boy lying on the bed, and her lips clamped together in a line. Without a word, she ran from the house.

Graham Chapman listened to the labored breathing of Anton Smrcka. His mind raced furiously. He could not look Aura Lee in the eye. The child clearly needed a doctor, and Gateway City did not have one.

"Tell me what to do," said Aura Lee.

"He needs drugs and he needs a doctor," said Graham flatly. "And there's not a one near here—not for a hundred miles."

"Mr. Chapman," Mrs. Seaton hesitantly took a step toward him, her wide cheeks reddened from the heat radiating from the stove. "Sir, that may not be true. I know you don't hold with the man, sir, but according to the editor of *Plato Publication*, there is a doctor in their town."

"Lies," said Graham. "All lies. Plato is nothing."

Aura Lee looked over Mrs. Seaton's shoulder at the paper.

"Dr. Lawrence McVey," she read. "General practitioner in medicine," she whispered. "Oh, Graham, a real doctor."

"Nonsense, it's puffery."

"You don't know that for sure," she said. "Just because you—" She bit back the words, still bitter over the contrast between his description of where they had laid Mary Kate Carlton and the stark reality of the actual cemetery.

Graham lifted his head, sensing what she had been about to say, and cursed his tendency to rush matters in Gateway City. It was a mistake he did not often make and it would be fatal with Aura Lee.

"All right," he said. "I'll go check, of course."

"Oh, thank you," she said. "Thank you."

He looked at the small blond woman in her immaculate maroon gown with the skirt draped sweetly about her petite body. The black piping on the fitted bodice seemed to be the same texture as her velvety eyelashes. She belongs in a mansion, he thought, surrounded by the very finest the world has to offer. He wanted to comfort her and pamper her.

The contrast of her soul here instead of on a miserable homestead claim should be obvious to even her self-righteous, self-centered husband. She needed servants and flowers and a fine home to reflect her exquisite taste. And he couldn't give her one of the most basic of human rights, that of decent medical care.

"Mrs. Hollingworth, I'll go at once. Just don't get your hopes too high."

"All right." Her blue eyes were wide with hope. "All right, I won't."

Graham tightened the cinches on his saddle, with no doubt in his mind that he would find an empty prairie, no doctor, and a vindictive conniving editor to meet him at his journey's end. He leaned his head against the side of his horse, suddenly filled with sorrow for all of them.

On the way over to Plato, he saw several dimpled places on the prairie, and rode over to see what was causing the break in the sea of grass.

Maggots were already working their cleansing effect on the remains of two steer carcasses. The heads were intact and fleas buzzed about their glazed eyes. Puzzled, Graham dismounted and examined the remains. On the right hip where the brand was normally displayed, there was a hole. The brand had been crudely cut out. Graham wiped his hands and rode on toward the town. It was just two head of cattle, not worth mentioning.

He slowed his horse to a trot as he came up to Plato. Some twenty tents dotted the landscape, and squares of stakes spread across the plains. There were four buildings: a dry goods store, a blacksmith shop, a hotel-cafe, and the store housing the *Plato Publication*. He immediately rode to the paper office.

"I came to see if you have a doctor," Graham announced abruptly.

Startled, Flynn swung around to meet him. He nodded curtly and Graham kept his eyes expressionless as the man began to walk toward the second tent from the east.

Graham was flooded with conflicting emotions. Relief that Anton would be getting proper care and despair that this little cracker box of a town had managed to attract a doctor when Gateway City hadn't.

"I need help," Graham said. He quickly described Anton's symptoms and the doctor went into his tent and came out with his bag and mounted his horse.

They left for Gateway City, and then what he saw made him bring his horse up short for a moment.

There was a set of stakes driven across the prairie for as far as the eye could see. He suspected that Flynn himself had driven them to give the appearance that Plato had been surveyed and designated a railroad site.

Still, the man had managed to find a doctor. He knew in his heart that it was impossible for this man to have procured a railroad, but still if these stakes were enough to cause doubt in his mind, the effect on ordinary citizens could be very troublesome, indeed.

He was overcome by a savage sense of urgency. He wanted his railroad right now, before anything went wrong. He had the buildings, he had the people, the water, and the potential. All he lacked was the railroad.

He looked over the range cattle straying in the distance, and began considering another approach. There had to be a reason for people to assume the financial burden of issuing bonds—and that came from iron-clad assurances that there would be a railroad. It was a vicious circle of cause and effect.

The range cattle were like money in the pocket. Thousands were attracted to the lush, level prairies. The same unbroken pasture that had been the grazing ground for millions of buffalo was like a beacon to them. Ranchers could save a fortune if there were railroads up in this area of the country, which would save them from having to trail cattle all the way back down again to Dodge City to ship back East. Gateway City was not that far from ranches in Nebraska and Wyoming. It would be the natural location for a cattle shipping point.

There was a soothing breeze blowing. It softly teased his clothes and rippled his horse's mane. Somewhere a cow bawled and he had never felt more alone in his life. In his heart, he knew that the decision he was about to make would be the most important one of his life. Once made, there would be no calling it back. He sighed heavily. He would court the cattle trade. There was no other way. Cattle men spent so much money in a town the merchants would be glad to vote in the bonds. He *had* to protect the life of his town.

He frowned as he recalled Daniel's warning that no one would be allowed to have his land or ever threaten his land. After all, they were merely a handful of dirt farmers. What could they do? In time they too would be persuaded to go into ranching. It made a damn sight more sense than breaking up perfectly good land for nothing but a few sheaves of wheat.

Dr. McVey had reined in too, to see why Graham had stopped. Graham waved at him to reassure him, then spurred his horse, and wheeling around, they raced toward Gateway City.

Dr. McVey's forehead was beaded with sweat as he came from Aura Lee's room.

"Would you boil some water, please?" he asked Mrs. Seaton. Aura Lee sprang to her feet.

"Is he going to be all right?" she asked.

"I think so," said the doctor. "It will be a bit, though, before I know for sure."

Aura Lee sat back down and resumed her wait. She and Graham were rewarded by a big grin on the doctor's face when he stepped from the room an hour later.

"The fever has broken," the doctor said. "He'll be fine."

Aura Lee turned to Graham with relief and without thinking gave the man a hug. "You were wonderful. Oh, thank you for bringing the doctor. Thank you."

Graham evened his breathing as the woman touched him, but his body was afire. The doctor gathered up his medical supplies and followed Graham out into the street.

"I want you to move to Gateway City," said Graham without any preliminaries. "Name your price."

"I don't have one," grunted McVey. "Plato suits me just fine."

"I'll give you a lot—no, two—here in town, and a stipend."

The doctor's eyes flickered with attention at the last. He would like to have money once in a while for drugs and equipment. Most of the folks paid in goods, and you could only use so much butter and eggs. And those who could pay cash sensed his high-souled resolution to help wherever he could and meanly withheld payment, knowing he would come to their aid. Sensing his interest, Graham fished for the magic combination.

"I'll set you up in an office," Graham promised, "the likes of which has never been seen before out here. It will have the finest equipment of any doctor's office between Kansas City and Denver. No expense whatsoever will be spared."

"You've got yourself a deal," said McVey.

Graham walked briskly back inside the boardinghouse, and grinned broadly as he told Aura Lee that Gateway now had a doctor.

"How wonderful," she said, "that you were able to persuade him." Her eyes were bright, dazzled by the magic of this handsome elegant man who could bring about such miracles.

"Such a vile, loathsome deal has never before been perpetrated in the annals of prairie history," said the *Plato Publication*. "Never has there been a deed so foul as to lure our coveted physician away with a handful of empty promises to a gullible impressionable man, whose expertise in the medical arts had already been called into question, however, by the citizens of Plato."

Lucinda recognized Jake McIntyre as being one of the men in the saloon. Her heart beat a little faster as she watched him ride toward the dugout.

"My husband is not here," she said as she opened the door a crack. "He is in the field."

"Don't want to talk to your husband. I want to see you."

Lucinda shrugged and let the man inside without saying a word.

"Do you remember me?" asked Jake.

"Yes. How did you know where to find me?"

"I remembered the name the Hollingworth woman used, then checked at the land office for the location of your homestead."

"What do you want?"

"I want to talk business. We can make a fortune out here, you and me. The fact that you were even in the saloon tells me you want something more than this—" His arm gestured around the dugout. "And you deserve it. Have you ever had dresses made specially for you? Or perfumes to select from? Fine furniture? Furs?"

"Of course not," said Lucinda. "If so, why would I be here? Get to the point. Just what is this business proposition?"

"I would like you to manage some women who have chosen to make their living in a manner commonly misunderstood by the run-of-the-mill citizen."

Understanding immediately, Lucinda let her laughter ring across the room.

"You want me to become a whore?" she asked bluntly.

"Uh, no, not exactly. I want you to look after them." Then losing all caution, Jake continued. "My God, woman, you're a natural entertainer. No, of course, *you* won't be available. Just your girls. But your beauty, your voice will be a draw, and some men keep coming back to see what they can't have as much as what they can. Of course you won't work. You're just the drawing card."

Lucinda's eyes widened. A madam. He was asking her to become a madam. She, who had the love of Daniel Hollingworth.

"You've made a mistake," she said. "I'm not that kind of a woman." But she did not look him in the eye.

"Just think it over. That's all I ask. I'll be back someday soon and we'll talk some more."

She watched his horse for as long as she could trace it with her eyes, then panicked as the universe seemed to be spinning wildly away from her, twirling her feet off the soil.

Daniel pushed open the door to their soddy and he braced his shoulders as he walked inside. It was a raw, chilly day and the wind moaned outside. His numb hands fumbled with the cow chips, but at last he coaxed the prairie fuel into a warm glow.

He started at a movement in the corner and the muscle in his jaw leaped at what he saw. A snake, attracted by the warmth, had dropped through the ceiling. He eased out the door and grabbed his hoe. Coming back inside, he attacked the snake, relieved it was a common bullsnake. But it could just as easily have been a rattler.

Seized with a sudden rush of fury and hopelessness, he chopped the snake into fragments long after it was dead. He was sickened by his lack of control, yet powerless to stop his desire to destroy.

His hands trembled as he sank into the chair and sat with his hands between his knees and his head bowed, filled with self-loathing.

He had worked furiously since the time he had made love to Lucinda, but for all that, his infidelity was like a stone in his heart.

So many parts of his life were splitting off into fragments over which he had little control. There was a sour uneasiness to the H.U.A. The farmers understood the need for uniting against the claim jumpers, and a few of the braver ones certainly did not hesitate at whatever measures were necessary to keep their crops from being trampled, but convincing them, educating them to the necessity of protecting themselves against the railroad men was going to be a very delicate business indeed.

He got up, stretched, and poked a few more cow chips into the stove. The furrow in his brow deepened as he looked at his dwindling pile, and he remembered the conversation at the last H.U.A. meeting.

"If we chase off all the cattle, what will we do for fuel?" asked Kevin McQuire. "Ain't no more buffalo."

"We'll get a good supply of coal in," said Bert Hensley.

"Can't get no coal without a railroad," said Kevin.

"We'll have a railroad," snapped Daniel. "But it's not going to be a line that will bankrupt the county. It will be the one we want."

"Ha," said Bert. "*They're* the ones who choose us. We don't choose them."

Daniel stopped by Tem Flynn's office at every opportunity. During his last visit, the young editor was all fired up over papers he had received.

"Ever hear of the Grange, Hollingworth?"

Daniel shook his head.

"It's worth looking at. There's a national organized movement of farmers who have declared war on all the monopolies that have paralyzed this country."

"If we can't get a few men in a county to act as a group, how can all the farmers in the country organize?"

"I don't know," said Flynn slowly, "but the Grange is spreading like wildfire, and I'm checking on all the information I've been getting. It's a *decent* movement, Daniel. Run by decent men. It goes far beyond what you are trying to do with the H.U.A. And, Hollingworth, there's a place for the women in this group. The local granges meet once a month. The society is open to both men and women except for the secret ceremonies that precede the meeting, which are for full members only."

Daniel's face was gloomy, recalling the secret ceremony of the H.U.A. that had created a fearful bond.

"Not secret like your group, Hollingworth. It sounds Masonic as near as I can tell. On the local level the chapter confers degrees of Laborer, Cultivator, Harvester, and Husbandman on the men, and degrees of Maid, Shepherdess, Gleaner, and Matron on the women. Don't know what is done in the ritual, but one thing is clear, the women are side by side with their husbands. You know yourself that when the women are included it tones things up."

"Women should be protected," said Daniel. "They should not have to worry about trying to keep their heads above water."

"It's not that kind of a group, Hollingworth. The meetings consider social and moral questions. My God, Daniel, the man who started all this is trying to get farmers to *think*. That's what I've been trying to tell you all along. You all work too hard and think too little."

Flynn glowed with enthusiasm as he read from the charter of the organization. He was alight with zeal as he pulled random phrases from the constitution.

"Individual happiness depends upon general prosperity. The prosperity of a nation is in proportion to the value of its productions. The soil is the source from whence we derive all that constitutes wealth; without it we would have no agriculture, no manufactures, no commerce. Of all the material gifts of the Creator, the various productions of the vegetable world are of the first importance. The art of agriculture is the parent and precursor of all arts, and its products the foundation of all wealth."

"They are seeking knowledge, Daniel. And they understand the worth of the farmer. The group is also known as the Patrons of Husbandry. Women read papers at the meetings and learn to be better housewives. The men discuss the proper crops for particular lands and the best methods of cultivation."

"Sounds lofty all right," said Daniel, "but just how do they plan to stay alive long enough to get to these meetings? They still can't do a thing about the railroad robber barons. All they can do is make people feel a little better for a very short time."

The soddy was warming, and Daniel dug the latest issue of the *Gateway City Gazette* out of his saddle bag and began to read. Graham's editorial was on the front page:

261

> The editor notes with satisfaction the sleek heads of livestock
> wending their way into our fair country. The cattle industry has long
> been the backbone of the West, and we welcome their growing
> numbers into our territory. It is with deep regret that we note the
> lack of a railroad out here. 'Twould make shipment easier.

Daniel slapped the paper down on the table. The fool was playing up
to ranchers and ignoring the homesteaders.

The H.U.A.ers had butchered twenty-five head of beef in the last week
alone, but it was not mentioned in the paper. By cutting out the brand,
the homesteaders were advertising that this was man's work. They wanted
people to be aware. Daniel could not believe the man was oblivious to
the farmers' mood. Their strength was growing in spite of their apprehension over violence. New members were added to the H.U.A. weekly,
as the rush to acquire homesteads continued.

Daniel was suddenly aware of a racking hunger and he had begun to
rummage through the cupboards when he heard a sound at the door.

He drew back the bolt and looked into the eyes of Lucinda Smrcka.

"I thought I smelled smoke," she said. "I came to see."

"Yes, you did," he said slowly. "I have a fire going."

"Yes, I see."

She came inside and without another word they were in each other's
arms.

Later, Lucinda collected all the food she could find, cutting strings of
dried vegetables and putting it to simmer with some jerky.

"It's not right," she blurted, "that you should come home to a place
so cold, without a woman."

"I *have* a woman," said Daniel, not looking her in the eye.

"Not the right one. We're the ones who belong together. You and I.
She's all wrong for you." Her voice was hard with spite. As she turned to
set the table she was stunned by the fury in Daniel's eyes.

"Don't you ever speak that way about my wife again," he said. "She's
one of the finest human beings I know, and neither one of us is decent
enough to wash her feet."

"What have we done that's so wrong?" asked Lucinda. "I need, you
need. It's as simple as that. We're the ones who should be together," she
said stubbornly. "Us."

Daniel looked at her as though he were seeing her for the first
time.

"We could get divorces," she continued, digging the pit deeper and
deeper. "Start over. Just think of what we could do together."

Daniel was standing now, every sense focused on this woman. How
could he possibly not have been aware of what she intended?

"This was the last time today, Lucinda. And I swear to God I'm not going to let you do anything to hurt my wife. We had an agreement, you and I. You were the one who kept saying, 'What can it hurt?' Well, it *has* hurt. More than I ever imagined possible. For reasons I cannot expect you to understand. Now leave. If one word of this ever gets to Aura Lee, you'll regret it in ways you've never dreamed of."

Lucinda's eyes were wide as she clutched her shawl and backed toward the door, bewildered at what she could have said to make him so angry.

Daniel watched her head across the prairie and he felt as though the earth had opened up beneath him. Suppose Aura Lee found out? Suppose through his wrong choices he lost his wife? The chance at a fine law practice and a comfortable place in society suddenly seemed attractive. Had he lost it all, and gained nothing in exchange? Not just a wrong choice, he thought. Deliberate and willful sin. He could have pulled back. The words from Aura Lee's prayer book echoed in his mind. "By my fault, by my fault, by my grievous fault."

Aura Lee smiled at Anton as he looked through the picture book for the hundredth time. She was so jubilant at seeing the child's health return she could not wait to get up in the morning. He slept on a cot at the foot of her bed and the sun's rays on his black tousled hair were the first thing she saw.

Today his face was troubled as he put down the book and looked up at her.

"Aura Lee, I want my dad."

Vensel had come to check on Anton immediately.

"Your mother told me what happened," he said, not seeing the fright in his son's eyes at his use of the word "mother," a term they had always used between them by unspoken agreement for Julka and Julka alone.

"Anton, we must try harder, you and I. Lucinda is a strong, brave person. I shudder to think what would have become of us the night of the fire if she had not been around. And now this fine thing she has done for you in seeing that you get the right care. We will be kinder, and she too will be a kinder person. It always works that way."

Anton trembled like a rabbit pursued by the hunter, waiting in the soft warmth of a little hole, waiting to be discovered. He wished Aura Lee were in the room with him. He was drowned in confusion. He wished—he bit his lip to stay the tears. He wished his *real* mother were alive. Seeing the pleading in his father's eyes, and hearing a new firmness in his voice, Anton knew he must go back.

"Can I stay for one more week, Dad? Aura Lee is letting me draw and reading to me."

"Of course, son." Vensel's eyes shone with pride and tenderness. "Of course, and then we will all begin together again. A clean slate."

The week was up now and he had promised.

"Aura Lee, I want to go home. I want my dad." His voice quavered, belying his mock bravery, and his huge gray eyes held the look of an old man.

"Oh, Anton. It's so unfair." Aura Lee's eyes filled with tears at the burdens this precious child was bearing. "Sweetheart, I can't let you do that."

"Yes," he said quickly. "Yes. It will be all right. I know what makes her mad and what doesn't, and Dad says if we try harder, she will change, too. I want my dad," he said simply. "I promised him I would try."

"All right, Anton, but this time I must speak to your father. You both can still try to work things out, but his eyes simply must be opened." They had been living in a fairytale and she had known this moment was coming. She would take the boy home. But now she knew she must talk to Vensel. He must know of Lucinda's enmity toward the boy.

"Let's go today. There's no point in putting things off. You're fine now. But I don't want you to walk. It's a good two miles to your dugout and I think it would be a good idea for us to ride, don't you?"

Anton beamed.

She rented the horse and buggy from the livery stable and set off. Aura Lee was dreading the talk with Vensel Smrcka.

They saw the man working in his field and Anton ran to throw himself into his father's arms. The dugout was beyond the next rise and Aura Lee was relieved she would not have to see Lucinda at all.

"Anton. Tomorrow, I was coming to get you myself."

"I wanted to come home today," said Anton.

"Mr. Smrcka. I need to talk to you about your son. Alone. For just a moment."

Bewildered, Vensel touched his boy on the shoulder.

"You run on now, Anton, and say hello to Lucinda. She will be relieved to see you."

"Vensel, believe me, I would do anything to keep from having to say this to you, but you simply must know that your wife must not be left alone with your son."

She watched the expression on his face change from disbelief to acceptance, and then his fine dark eyes reflected a sadness so deep she would have given anything in the world to dispel it.

"She did not carry the boy to you when he was sick?" Vensel asked finally.

"No, that's not the way it was at all." Quickly, she told him about Lucinda dragging Anton to town in the freezing weather. Then, seeing his despair, she decided to say no more. There was no point in telling him of the scene in the saloon, and the hand, the burn, was in the past now. Vensel knew just enough to protect the boy, and if he knew too much, if she told him everything Lucinda had done, there would be no chance of their reconciling. She really believed Lucinda would be very careful not to hurt Anton again. He was warned, and that was all that was necessary.

Vensel's eyes were moist as he looked at her.

"The boy will come to the field with me from now on. Always," he said flatly.

Aura Lee grieved for the childhood that was being cut short.

She decided to stop by their homestead and pulled up in front of their soddy. She would be living here again with Daniel in just one more month. For a moment she felt as though she had never seen the place before. She went inside and the room did not seem to belong to her at all. It was a habitation of strangers. Poor people, she thought, who would stoop to live in this strange earth home.

Her hand traced the design on her patchwork quilt as she tried to regain her familiarity with the house's contents. She would be back here soon, day after day. Her hand froze as her fingers fumbled across a bronze hairpin. As bronze as the gleam of a violin.

Her breath turned to ice, and the blood in her veins dropped in temperature. So that is how the terrible, evil woman knew. What she had thought could never, never be was true, then. The dark thoughts she had shoved to one side when she was nursing Anton, the very ones that seemed so foolish after he regained his health—*every one was true*. He had lain with her. It was the only way this hairpin could have gotten into her bed.

She rushed outside, wanting to be free of this house, this life, this land that had the power to corrupt a character as fine as her husband's.

She drove back to Gateway City in a daze. I don't belong anywhere any more, she thought wildly. Now I don't have anyone either. Not a soul in the world to turn to. I've lost Daniel.

"You never had him, my dear," the voices cried in triumph. "He never did really love you."

Not true, her heart cried in protest.

She paid the man at the livery stable, and then walked blindly to her room. Her sense of loss was so deep she was afraid she would die.

She looked up then at a flock of geese headed north, intent on their flight, and recalled what she had read about their mating habits. They were together for life. Forever. She knew that some of her beloved composers' feelings went so deep the emotions could never be rechanneled, and she knew her own heart lay at that fathomless depth few would plumb or understand. She could only love once, and that love had been given to Daniel. Her love was cursed with the weight of "for better or worse" that she had spoken such a short time ago. A meaningless combination of words then, a holy freight of innocent hope, cancelled by grief now, and the knowledge that no one was pure—not one, not even her Daniel.

She cried for hours, refusing Mrs. Seaton entrance to her room when she tried to serve the evening meal.

"Leave me alone, please. It's just a headache," she lied. "I'll be fine when morning comes."

The headache became real and she lay motionless on her bed. Rage rolled through her like a cymbal clash, beating down a yearning to see Daniel. She hated, hated, hated them both. They were welcome to each other. Welcome to their lust. Welcome to this fierce state that killed the melody existent in its victims' hearts and forced newcomers to dance to a wild, discordant song. She had thought Daniel Hollingworth was the finest man she had ever met, and he had betrayed her in every way possible. He had lied about the land, lied about his love, and even taken her money. She was stripped in every way a woman could be. He left her with nothing. As the supply of tears she had been born with, the allotment that should have seen her through a lifetime, was used up in one night's orgy of weeping, a residue of tiny ice crystals took their place.

Her mind was giving birth to twins again. The double demons of hate and love stood side by side and beckoned to her tormented soul, and she chose coldness. Her heart frosted with layer upon layer of ice until it was diamond hard and created anew. But at its core was a center of molten lava, ready to erupt.

Two days later, when the swelling in her eyes had receded enough for her to be seen in public, she walked into Graham's office.

"I would like to apply for the position of postmistress on a permanent basis," she said. "I'm going to be living in town."

He quickly removed his feet from his desk and offered her a seat by the stove.

"You know, of course, the job is yours."

"Yes, I know." Her voice quivered. "I know, and, Graham, you know me all too well not to know that something is terribly wrong between Daniel and me, and I can't bear to talk about it, so please don't ask for a long time, and maybe I will never tell you and maybe I will." And then she hurled the words out in spite of her pride; the ancient grief-laden words spoken by millions of wives before her since the beginning of time, without one syllable's variation. "He has another woman."

Graham looked at her solemnly, knowing instantly who that other woman was. He did not move for a moment, afraid that if he said the wrong thing, did the wrong thing, she would shatter into little pieces.

"You must know, of course, my dear, that if there is anything at all I can do to help you through this difficult time," he said carefully, feeling his way, "if there—"

"No," she said curtly. "No. I just want a job. That's all. I've had all the help from men I can stand."

Daniel rode toward Gateway City. He was more at peace with himself since he had broken off the affair with Lucinda. In one more month, Aura Lee would be home again and he would make amends.

He entered the general store with a letter to Uncle Justin in his hand. It contained detailed questions about the Grange movement that was so exciting to Tem Flynn.

His wife was alone in the store and as he entered her face paled and she did not move.

He looked at her in shock as she put a stamp on the letter and trembled, turning her face away.

"What's wrong? Aura Lee, what's wrong?"

"Do you even have to ask, Daniel?"

"What? My God, what?"

She looked at him long and hard then, and the silent accusation crushed his heart. His blood froze in his veins, leaving him incapable of any movement. Knowing, knowing, that somehow, someway, someone had told her. He could not speak.

"I found this, Daniel," she said simply, handing him the hairpin. "Give this back to Lucinda the next time—the next time you are together." Her voice was like little seeds rattling inside a pod, and as barren of hope as the dead of winter.

"There won't be any next time. I swear to God. Aura Lee. I'm telling you the truth. It meant nothing, absolutely nothing, and now it's over. She won't even be taking care of the horses any more. I've asked Charlie to take over for me on the days I have to be gone. She won't have anything to do with any part of my life at all. I promise."

His wife was tall with injured pride.

"Save your promises, Daniel. Save them for someone else. I've heard enough of them for one lifetime. I don't ever want to see you again."

He sat like lead on Toby as he rode toward Tem Flynn's office, the gray wolf of guilt tearing at his guts, until it left only a shell.

Graham turned over the cards one at a time, placing red on red, black on black, but his mind was not on solitaire. It was on Aura Lee. Abruptly, he gathered the deck together and went down to the general store as he did several times a day now, just to see her. It would take time and more than a little patience, but he was positive that healing would begin and she would see how infinitely precious she was to him. Her place was so clearly in a town. She was shaping the soul of Gateway City as though she were a sculptor.

There was a quiet dignity in Aura Lee now as she went about her work. She bore her sadness like a cloak she had worn all her life. She had been wrapped in its protective folds all her childhood days. She was home again.

She smiled at Graham when he came in. How was it possible, she thought for the hundredth time since she had left Daniel, that there could be a man who always knew so clearly what was in her heart. To the townspeople, nothing had changed. She had always worked here by herself, while Daniel lived at the soddy, and she was delaying letting anyone know the arrangement was no longer temporary. It would be for her whole life.

"There's a Chautauqua program at Wallace next week," said Graham, "and I wondered if you would like to go with me? I think it will do you good to have some diversion."

"Oh, Graham. You do so much for me all of the time. Really, I'm fine, just fine."

Graham's mouth twitched in his mocking smile and he looked at her tenderly, his eyes filled with compassion. He did not reply.

"I can never fool you, can I, Graham?" she said with a laugh. "No, I'm not just fine. But I think I'm going to live." Then despair rippled over her and she hid her face in her hands and willed back the tears. She was jolted by a sudden fierce longing to have this man hold her, comfort her, and dear God, for an instant, just for an instant, before she banished the desire into the circle of white light, she had wanted him to make love

268

to her. This wonderful, marvelous tender man who was not her husband. Not her husband.

She did not trust herself to speak and swiftly guarded her eyes behind a misty curtain of tears. But Graham saw, and his heart beat with triumph; and knowing the importance of not rushing this fragile, adorable woman in any way, he too looked away.

"Well, give the Chautauqua a little more thought," he said, not blurting the words that were on the tip of his tongue. Words that would heap confusion on her tormented soul. They would be spoken at the right time, and he was prepared to wait as long as would be necessary.

"All right," she said. "Will there be others going?"

"Of course," he said quickly, knowing she did not want to risk the censorship of the community by being alone with him on a long drive, understanding her need for a chaperone for other, more subtle reasons. "We'll take a whole wagon full."

Graham watched Aura Lee's face as she cut the ribbon on the long box. Her blue eyes grew bright as she drew the dress out, and she gave a little cry of delight. Graham had it made of the finest silk, and it gleamed with a soft luster as it reflected the lamp light. The pink fabric was the shade of wild roses that grew so profusely on the roadbanks back in Saint Jo. The dress contained yards of material, draped into intricate folds that reminded her of her bridesmaids' dresses. Mrs. Seaton had constructed a magical dress, the kind women looked for all their life, a Cinderella garment. The dress highlighted the sweet blush in Aura Lee's cheeks and deepened the blue in her eyes.

"Oh, Graham." She stood up and held the dress against her. "Graham, it's absolutely lovely. It's just gorgeous. Graham, I'm going to keep this dress," she said firmly, and laughed in spite of herself.

"Well, I should hope so," he said, relieved that at long last she was actually going to accept one of his gifts. She had resolutely turned down every single one.

"I just can't resist it. Look at it. Just look." Aura Lee turned to him, ashamed of the pleasure she was taking in something so frivolous. "You know, Graham, I've heard all my life that material things don't matter. That it's just what is inside you that counts. But they *do* matter to some of us. I want to keep this dress." There was a new stubborn note in her voice, and she laughed as she looked at him, bright with defiance against the part of her that observed all the proprieties. "Just *because* I want it."

"Good," said Graham. Through her acceptance of his present, he knew the time had come to speak what was in his heart. "Good. Would you try it on for me, please?"

He went into the parlor and waited for Aura Lee to change. He could not remember another night in his life that was more important. Aura Lee entered the room and her lovely pale face held a trace of shyness. Her white shoulders were bared above the sweetheart neckline and her small firm breasts were outlined by the pink bodice. The silk rustled softly as she glided toward him. He slowly rose to his feet. She hesitated and trembled for a moment, then drawing a deep breath she walked toward the great love radiating from Graham Chapman's eyes.

"My God, my God," he whispered. "You are so incredibly lovely. You are—"

Aura Lee smiled in delight as his words failed. She was washed with pleasure at being back in a gentle world she knew so well—a world where men were polite and courteous and colors were paler and days rippled slowly by in decent order like a minuet and women were beloved and shielded and cherished and her heart had ease and peace. She had lived her life under the protection of such men. She paused again, then her eyes never left Graham's face as she shuddered and reached for his extended hand. Oh, under the protection of men, like her father and her beloved Professor Brock and her marvelous old beaus who had anticipated her heart's desires. Sheltered by the shadow of their steadfastness, her life tinkling by in a harmless tune, played at a lovely, undemanding tempo.

Graham loved her, she thought with wonder. He loved her. It was so painfully evident in every word he said, everything he did. Graham was restoring her slowly day after day. She suddenly wanted to turn her whole life over to him. Wanted to be protected and cared for by this marvelous, graceful man. He was helping her to become once again exactly the woman she had been back in Saint Jo. She was no longer torched by hate or numbed by her iced heart. Her lovely trace of self-mockery gentled her days with a soft witty gleam.

Her fingers were inches from Graham's hand now, when the breath was suddenly slammed out of her body by a longing that overwhelmed her in its intensity. The room was filled with Daniel. Daniel with his head thrown back in laughter, his white teeth gleaming in his swarthy face. Daniel with his love of the morning and his strong arms firmly gripping the handles of the plow. Daniel joyfully calling out, "Scudda hoo, scudda hay!" as he guided the Clydesdales. Daniel with his strong colors and his mighty voice crying like a warrior for people to follow. Daniel with his joy of combat and his maddeningly unreasonable sureness of right and wrong. *I don't want to be exactly as I was in Saint Jo,* she thought, her heart tripping in panic. *I want to be the way I was again when I first married Daniel.*

"You can't, my dear," the voices reminded in a reasonable tone, "you've lost him to another woman."

Slain by grief, she swayed toward Graham, and his arms were around her instantly. He pressed her to his chest and Aura Lee quivered from head to foot, so assaulted by conflicting feelings she was faint.

Stiffening, suddenly, she took a full step backward, and turned away, not wanting to risk looking into his eyes.

"Thank you for catching me. I—I tripped."

Graham grinned at her confusion and was silent for a moment; then looking at the rigidly proud line of her neck, he said politely, "Of course, my dear."

She turned then, her eyes thanking him for letting her save face, and was deeply grateful for his exquisite sensitivity.

"It is the most wonderful gown I have ever had, Graham. But I really don't know what came over me earlier. I cannot keep it. I think we both know that."

"I understand perfectly," he said, with his graceful half-smile. "And of course you are quite right. I apologize for putting you in this position."

"Thank you. Graham. For everything."

He nodded, accepting and seeing all. He was a very patient man. Virgins and spinsters and banked fires always took a little longer. Well, he hadn't played his hole card yet.

"Charlie, would you mind giving these letters to Daniel?" asked Aura Lee. Her voice was brisk and businesslike, as she handed him the material from Justin Hollingworth. "He said you are taking care of the horses now." She held her breath, waiting to hear if it was true. "You can just put these on the table where Daniel will find them. It will save him a trip to town."

"All right," he said, looking sharply at Aura Lee, wondering what had caused the flicker of relief on her face. "Be glad to." But she clearly was not inviting any conversation today, and he was disappointed. He had begun to look forward to talking to the woman.

Aura Lee tidied up the stock at the end of the day, and walked home to her room, her cloak wrapped firmly around her to keep out the cold, late February air.

Graham and Mrs. Seaton were waiting for her and she smiled at the editor as he opened the front door.

"We have a surprise for you," said Mrs. Seaton, and her eyes sparkled with delight. "I could hardly wait for you to come home."

Aura Lee looked at Graham and was touched by his persistence. Another present she would have to refuse.

"Close your eyes," ordered Mrs. Seaton.

Laughing, Aura Lee obeyed and allowed herself to be led toward the parlor.

"Now open them," the woman commanded.

Aura Lee burst into tears. Dear God, dear God, she thought with wonder, what ever am I going to do? In the corner was a parlor upright piano. The rich mahogany finish gleamed softly in the early evening light.

"Graham," she whispered softly, "I can't possibly accept—"

Her words were quickly cut short.

"It's not yours to accept or decline, my dear. It's a gift from me to the town. And Mrs. Seaton's boardinghouse is the logical place to put it."

"Oh, Graham." She knew it was not true, that the piano had been purchased for her and her alone. "Well," she said with amusement, "I guess you've fixed me, haven't you?"

He grinned quickly and extracted a cigar from the pocket of his jacket.

"Thank you, Graham. Oh, thank you." She spun the top of the stool around, adjusting the height, and then began to play.

"I'm very rusty," she said with a quick apology. "I think I had better do lots of technique and scale work first." Her hands, still slightly numbed from the walk from the store, were awkward, and she winced as they hit a wrong note. Graham and Mrs. Seaton said good night and quietly left the room as she struggled to recall so much that had been lost.

Aura Lee sought the piano every morning before she went to work and each evening when she got home. Slowly, firmly, she advanced through scale after scale, and then progressed to more difficult technique work. Her fingers were regaining their former agility, and at last they were in condition to attempt her favorite concerto. She fumbled though the first measure, stopped and tried it again. The music was coming back to her, she could hear it clearly in her mind just as she used to play it.

By the second week, her frustration had become so great it was no longer a pleasure to be able to sit down at the instrument. It had become an ordeal.

I can no longer play, she thought. I can no longer play the piano. I can hear the music, but I can't—make it work for me. Tears rolled down her cheeks as she firmly lowered the lid. It's Daniel, she thought. It's Daniel. I can't play because of him. He and my music are fused together somehow and I can't keep them apart.

Dr. McVey stopped in the store one morning and invited Aura Lee to ride to Plato with him.

"The ride will do you good, my dear. I need to pick up some of my instruments, and you need to get some fresh air," he said firmly. He was very much aware of her potential for melancholy.

Aura Lee held the latest copy of the *Plato Publication* on her lap, and smiled at Dr. McVey, grateful he did not insist on talking. It was lovely just to ride for a while, and the fresh air truly was doing her some good.

The past week had been very unsettling. A cow herd trailed down from Nebraska had passed through their town. It had taken nearly three hours and the amount of disruption the animals caused was staggering. They were headed for the railhead at Little Beaver. It had taken hours more for the dust to settle, and the air had been filled with the wild cackles of chickens and other poultry as they protested the invasion.

She glanced at the newspaper again and her lips thinned as she read the business cards, wondering what she would actually find when she reached the rival town.

Dr. McVey helped her down from the buggy and she studied the scene before her. There was a general store as had been promised, and a land office, a drug store, a blacksmith shop, a hotel, a livery stable, and the ever-present newspaper office. A crudely lettered sign was in the window of the editor's office advertising a meeting of farmers in the area. It was open to the public, and she decided to go.

She went into the lobby of the hotel and squeezed into the group that had collected. A door to an ante-room opened and Daniel walked out. She drew a deep, quavering breath as her husband began to speak.

"I am here to tell you about a farm organization," he began, "so mighty in its concept and so pure in its ideals that it is bringing hope to its members throughout this mighty land. The Patrons of Husbandry is sweeping the nation like wildfire. In any community where the farmers form a Grange, the members prosper and their burdens are lightened. The Order seeks to cultivate and enlarge the mind and purify the heart."

Daniel's eyes found Aura Lee at the back of the crowd and his voice faltered. "The information I have received has come from an impeccable source, my Uncle Justin Hollingworth, whose integrity is well known back in Saint Jo. The Grange is *different* from other organizations," he said, his eyes firmly fixed on Aura Lee, wooing her, persuading her. "The Grange admits women to full membership, because every husband and brother knows that where he can be accompanied by his wife or sister no lessons will be learned but those of purity and truth."

"Oh, Daniel," her heart cried, remembering an enchanted evening in Saint Jo when he had spoken of the role of True Man and had won her heart forever. No, not forever, she reminded herself. Not forever, just look at us now. Daniel stood before the group, his thumbs hooked in his suspenders, and paused; his black hair gleamed in the light and his face shone with purpose. And with wonder she found herself once again hypnotized by his ideals.

"Thought you was pushing another kind of farm organization,

273

Hollingworth?" a man called. There was a ripple of nervous laughter, as Daniel's activities in the H.U.A. were talked about a great deal. "Are you calling it quits?"

"No, not yet," said Daniel. "The H.U.A. will remain in effect until there is law enforcement in this county."

"Why should we talk about the Grange when the other group is doing the job?"

"Because I have been from one end of this county to another during this winter," said Daniel. "I have talked to the men and I have talked to the women. I have seen how they live and I have seen their tears. I have seen women so worn down with labor they are little better than beasts of burden."

Daniel looked directly at Aura Lee, and a muscle in his jaw twitched.

"I'm telling you about the Grange because I am now convinced that if the calling of agriculture will not enable you and yours to escape physical degradation and mental and social starvation—if it does not enable you to enjoy the amenities, pleasures, comforts, and necessities of life as well as other branches of business—it is your duty to abandon it at once and not drag your family down in misery. I'm telling you about the Grange because it's just not right to ask a woman to live this way." He swallowed painfully as he said the last words, and only Aura Lee, who knew every square inch of his body, noticed the quick bobbing of his Adam's apple as he worked to suppress his vulnerability.

Aura Lee sat entirely motionless, with her hands folded neatly in her lap. Her heart was overflowing with joy. He knew, he really understood now. She was washed with pride at being this wonderful man's wife. In spite of all the attention Graham had given her, and in spite of his marvelous sensitivity, she had spent her whole entire life under the pro-tection of men of honor. And it was this quality of honor that was so lacking in Graham Chapman. She looked squarely at Daniel and saw the pleading in his eyes, and knew she would follow him wherever he wanted her to go.

The men were pressing around him asking questions and she had to fight her way through the group to get to his side. She touched him lightly on the arm, and he swung around to hear the soft words she whispered.

"I'm coming home, Daniel. Wait for me. I have some business to take care of first."

He nodded slowly, his eyes never leaving her face.

"Thank God, Aura Lee. Thank the good God."

Her eyes misted as she withdrew her hand reluctantly and hurried off to find Dr. McVey.

. . .

She went into the newspaper office, dreading telling Graham of her decision. He knew at a glance that something was terribly wrong and he carefully ground out the stub of his cigar before he spoke, his eyes never leaving her face. Aura Lee stood stiffly before him, and her thoughts ran so swiftly she could not contain them all. She was desperate to get Daniel back before it was too late. How far could you go with people, she wondered, or with fate, before you could never get back at all. How far? Had she crossed over the line where she had lost it all? She had let another woman steal his heart and soul. It never would have happened if she had been at his side where she belonged.

Realizing what must be done, for all of them, she looked him squarely in the eye and drew herself to her full height. "Mr. Chapman, could you come talk with me in about an hour? There is a matter I would like to discuss with you, and it requires privacy."

"Certainly," he said, bewildered by her formality. He did not like the tone of her voice at all.

She began to pack immediately and the job was done by the time Graham knocked at the door. "What is going on here?" he asked.

"I'm going back to my homestead. My husband needs me."

"Why? What has happened?" His voice was raw with shock.

She did not speak.

"I need a reason," he persisted.

"Oh, Graham, don't you know I cannot exist apart from this man?" Her voice was tender, begging him to understand, but knowing he never would. They lived by different codes. He would never understand the security she felt in living with a man who was honest. It made her feel that the world was in order and controlled and the rules were ones she understood. "Let it be enough for you, please, to simply know that I now see that my place is with my husband and I shall have the man at the livery stable take me home at once." Her voice was trembling and she bit the inside of her cheek in an attempt to check the tears.

"Forgive me for speaking so bluntly," said Graham. "But if there ever were more clearly a place for anyone, it could not be more obvious that yours is here in this town. I cannot begin to tell you of the effect you have had. You belong here, doing the things you do. At one time I thought you belonged in a great city, surrounded by luxury. But it's not true. I know that now. You belong right here. I've watched you teach the women coming in to adjust. I've watched you heal their spirits and guide their path toward beauty. Don't leave," he pleaded. "I need you and this town needs you and surely you must know by now that I love you. Let me take care of you, Aura Lee. You must know in your heart that I'm the kind of man who will understand you in a way Daniel never could."

Aura Lee was facing the window, and her face was perfectly still as he spoke.

"That's true," she whispered. "Oh, dear God, I do know in my heart that you are the one who will understand me best."

"Leave him, Aura Lee," Graham coaxed. "I'm going to be a very wealthy man someday. I can give you things he will never be sensitive enough to see you need. A piano, books. Just look what this room has meant to you. I want to marry you. Why do you want to link yourself to such a fanatic?"

"Because since the beginning of time, women have been attracted to a man with a cause. By being a part of that man's life, we feel as though we too are greater, finer, making a mark on society, and because this kind of man is always so sure he's right, so sure that he alone has been handed the stone tablets, it makes us feel secure, Graham." And that is the part of me you cannot understand that Daniel does, she thought quickly, her need for a totally stable framework. Dear God, was there no man on earth she would be totally safe with? No middle ground? Even now, with full knowledge of the consequences, she was choosing to leave a life she was beginning to love for a man who had chiseled away at the core of her. And her choice was again based on words, on illusions.

"I want to go back to the homestead," she said. Then as the fuller meaning of all Graham had said hit her, she quickly turned and grasped his hands and held them in front of her, but kept him at a distance. She was not surprised by his declaration of love, she had always known; her eyes asked for forgiveness.

"If you leave," said Graham, "I want you to be aware that your husband and I are going to be on opposite sides of the fence. Not *because* you are leaving—*I'm* not that small a man—but there will be many developments in the coming months that we will be at odds over. Aura Lee, he'll always want hard things. He always will."

Aura Lee nodded.

"Oh, don't you think I *know* that, Graham? And you're right. He always will." Her wonderful stubborn pig-headed Daniel, chasing rocks instead of rainbows.

Then as she turned, in a single anguished moment she whirled back around and blurted out, "If it's any comfort to you, Graham, a part of me *wants* to stay here with you. A part of me would just love to have you take care of me forever. You deserve to know that. It's just that I can't. I honestly can't. Graham, I don't expect you or anyone else to understand this, but some women, some of us can only love once. Just once. And for us it really doesn't matter how things work. We simply aren't able to take our love back."

He raised his head and never before had she seen a man's soul so nakedly revealed. His mouth twitched in his little smile as he looked at her with eyes full of so much sorrow she was condemned by their grief. And in that instant, she knew he understood. He too was just such a person.

The wagon carrying her belongings pulled up in front of her homestead, and she rushed into the house and into Daniel's waiting arms. Her tears soaked his shirt as he kissed her over and over again. His hand trembled as he stroked her hair.

"No more lies between us, Daniel. Not ever again. There's been enough pretending in this house to last forever. No more pretending problems don't exist." He nodded his head.

"And Lucinda Smrcka is never to come in this house again. For any reason."

"Don't worry," he said grimly. "That's one promise I won't have a bit of trouble keeping."

"And I don't want any of this brought up ever again. Beyond what we say to each other right now. We're going to start with a clean slate."

He picked her up as if she weighed no more than a feather and cradled her against his body, and continued to kiss her until she was breathless with desire.

"And I want to be back in your bed, Daniel. I want you to accept what I can give you for a while. Will that be enough? No more pretending."

"Yes, darling. Oh, my God, yes." His voice was harsh as he carried her across the room. As she clung to his chest, basking in his warmth, a single sustained melancholy note from a violin ripped through her heart like an arrow.

Graham's columns had taken on a new bitterness since Aura Lee left. You are in debt to me, Hollingworth, the editor thought. If it were not for me, you wouldn't be getting your wife back in the shape she is in right now. It was through his care and attention that she had been able to rise above her grief. Graham furiously denounced the hanging in the *Gateway City Gazette,* and no longer gave offending the homesteaders the slightest consideration. He and Flynn slashed and jabbed at one another every week and Chapman came down square on the side of the cattlemen.

The merchants who read the column agreed readily enough. They certainly preferred the spending habits of the cowboy. The homesteaders' reluctance to part with any money at all was legendary. Even their store-bought lunches consisted of just enough cheese and crackers to get by on the rare days they were forced to go into town. The cowboys were a different sort. They could be counted on to spend every cent in their pockets with a dashing nonchalance based on the belief that they were a lasting breed and there would always be plenty of money.

However, no more hangings were needed. When word of the one spread, it was all it took to dissuade other claim jumpers. They were a notoriously cowardly group. The cowboys were something else again. They thrived on excitement. And as the activities of the H.U.A. spread, with more cattle found dead on the prairie with their brands cut out, a delegation of ranch hands arrived in town and began asking questions.

Aura Lee walked down the street to the general store to collect the goods she had ordered an hour before. It was not her town any more. New people were arriving daily, and there were many she did not recognize. She made her way down the boardwalk with a growing sense of unease as she coldly ignored the eyes of the men lounging against store-fronts who watched her progress.

Suddenly the saloon doors flew open and two bodies sprawled into the street. She was horrified at the violence that was calmly observed by the bystanders, with a few bets placed on the outcome.

After picking up her supplies, she drove back to her soddy. The sun was setting and the sky was paint-stained, containing the hues of spilled inks as it washed over the approaching twilight. Her team plodded willingly toward their evening oats and easily pulled her buckboard.

She heard the sweet notes of the meadowlark in the distance. Normally it would have lifted her spirits, but this evening she was troubled.

She no longer felt safe going to town. Gateway City was not developing in the direction she wanted it to at all. Her wonderful town was sprawling out of control and attracting people who made her fearful and apprehensive.

Aura Lee stared at the menstrual rags she kept hidden in the drawer underneath her bloomers. Always now, she dreaded getting her period. At home there had been maids and professional wash-women to discreetly whisk away any mess. The pieces of cloth were returned to her drawers promptly, bleached immaculately white.

Out here on the prairie, even the monthly ritual of washing the rags seemed overwhelming and somehow shameful. First came the cold water soaking, then heating the water to boiling and the scrubbing with the caustic lye-based soap suds that had ruined her hands months ago. Then came two rinses to rid the rags of the irritating residue that would chafe her skin if every trace was not removed.

She had thought it would be easier when they had the well. When water was available on their own property. But now she had to lower a twenty-pound iron-rimmed bucket to an enormous depth and it took all her strength, even with a pulley, to raise it to the top.

Each step involved lugging in, then lugging out, masses of water. Even this, she thought with dismay, this most natural function of women, takes physical strength. Her shoulders ached with the memory of the bucket's weight and the tiresome rhythm of scrubbing, scrubbing. Then the drying for all the world to see. Would there never be any privacy in this god-forsaken place?

Today, however, she knew she would give her soul to get to perform that particular washday chore this month. She slowly closed the drawer and like a sleepwalker found her chair and sat down.

I'm pregnant, she thought, with terrible certainty. How could I not have noticed? I'm nearly three weeks overdue. Her heart went cold as the image of Julka enshrouded with her dead baby in blue membranes came before her eyes.

"That which I have greatly feared has come upon me," she whispered. Where did that come from? Shakespeare? The Bible? It didn't matter. Someone had said it first, before her. Did they understand her fear? This chill absorbing horror that turned her bones to water?

The voices, banished for so long, now were back in a flash; taunting, chanting with ghostly echoes in her numbed ear.

"You'll die, of course."

She sat totally motionless, unable to respond.

She told Daniel that night. He hugged her to him and stroked her hair.

"I've been wanting to start a family so badly I didn't know how to tell you. Children are so important to me I can't imagine a life without them."

"I'm glad you're happy, Daniel."

"You've got to take care of yourself. I don't want you to work any harder than you have to. I'll have Charlie come over to take care of the horses again if I have to be gone, so you won't have to pitch hay."

He held her at arm's length and searched her face.

"Are you going to be all right, Aura Lee? Are you happy?"

"Oh yes," she said. "Why wouldn't I be?"

"Traitor!" her voices cried triumphantly. "You were the one who said there would be no more lies in this household."

40

E. H. Huttwell stood on the boardwalk and watched the activity. Gateway City had become a beehive of enterprise. Every essential service was provided for, and it even offered a few luxuries.

"Well, Graham, you've done yourself proud. Any man who can put together an operation like you've managed here deserves a pat on the back."

"Well," said Chapman, "I am proud of this town. I admit it."

"Now," said E.H., "back to business. You're absolutely sure you can deliver the bonds? Then we need the cattle business. We'd starve to death trying to come out on the few bushels of grain the farmer can produce."

"I'll deliver," said Graham. "All the townspeople know we need their business." Everyone prospered, except the farmers, when the cowhands came through. They bought boots and leather goods, dry goods, clothes, groceries, and many other supplies.

"O.K.," said E.H. "You've got yourself a railroad. I'm counting on you, Chapman. I don't mind telling you we got a copy of *Plato Publication* down home, and they are reporting some mighty funny goings on up here. We don't like the sound of it."

"It's nothing," said Graham. "Believe me. Just a handful of dirt farmers, raising hell, that's all. Don't amount to nothing." Inside he was seething. How in the hell could the financier have gotten hold of that paper?

"They are killing too damn many cattle to call it nothing," insisted E.H. "According to the *Plato Publication* there's been a hanging. It said this group of farmers you are pooh-poohing could be the ones who did it. And worse, this editor makes it sound as though they had a right to."

Graham slapped the newspaper he was holding into the palm of his hand.

"All lies, I tell you, made up by the spineless puppet who edits that rag. I admit there was a hanging, but no doubt there was a hired gunslinger involved. The farmers themselves are too damned stupid to do it, and too yellow. I'll manage the farmers," he said curtly. "They'll come through on the dotted line as promised. Frankly, I'm surprised you even bring this up."

E.H. thoughtfully puffed on his cigar. "Well, they sure stand in the way of progress. There's other places that are beginning to take a closer look at the homesteaders, however. I'm not worried about a simple claims club. They generally die out fast. But the Grangers are causing a lot of trouble. The courts have not paid any attention to their attempts to regulate railroad rates or control the activities of elevators. Every single law they've tried to pass has been struck down as an infringement on private property. But they're still trouble, Chapman. I don't want to see a Grange started in this county," he said flatly. "Keep these homesteaders under control."

"They're plodders," argued Graham. "Men who can't imagine eventually die. They'll go on forever trying to grub a living from their miserable little plots of land. Working themselves to death for nothing."

"They have to have some sort of vision," said E.H. mildly. "to imagine they could get a crop at all out here. I'm telling you, they'll bear watching. Men who are that relentless always do."

"There's nothing to watch. You'll have the support of the people for your particular branch of the Union Pacific."

The two men were participants in the most enormous transfer of wealth in American history. For in addition to being financed by towns, desperate for reliable transportation, the railroads were given by the United States government 12,800 acres of land for each mile of track that was completed.

"Nevertheless," said E.H., "I want your paper to continue paving the way for the cattle market. Don't let up."

Graham nodded. He was very blunt in the next issue:

> Towns that have become shipping points for our vast beef industry are models of prosperity and longevity. It is a fortunate city indeed that is a vantage point for this business.

When Daniel received this particular copy of the paper, he read it with amazement.

"He wants to make Gateway City into a cow town, Aura Lee. I know it for sure now."

"Oh, surely not."

"Here, just read this. People won't even know the danger in this approach until it's too late."

She reread the item, then burst into tears.

"Daniel, I want something more for Gateway City than whorehouses and gunfights. I want churches and schools for our children."

He pulled her onto his lap.

"I know that, darling, but all the merchants are going to worry about is lining their own pockets, and cowboys are good for business. They won't stop for a second to think about the future for the womenfolk and children."

"Isn't there a way to stop them?"

"I don't know," he said slowly. "People usually vote their pocketbook and we are talking about a hell of a lot of money." He gently kissed her lips and said, "You'll have a decent town near here. I promise you."

Daniel went into the saloon. In the corner sat Clem Mayhew and Isaac Minton, both staunch H.U.A.ers. Good men. Sensible and trustworthy.

At the opposite end of the room, with their elbows braced on the bar, were three strangers. They were of slight build and compensated for it by wearing clanking gunbelts and broad-rimmed hats. Daniel's jaw tightened. No need for cowboys to be this far north this time of year. They were arrogant and noisy, and Daniel continued to watch in silence as they asked the bartender about the availability of women for the night. Gateway City did not have the atmosphere that had attracted professional prostitutes. Even this bar was a totally masculine domain.

The doors opened and Graham Chapman walked in. He spotted the cowboys immediately.

"A round of drinks for my friends, bartender."

Daniel's hand tightened around his glass and everyone stopped talking.

Graham turned to face the men in the room, measuring their reactions with casual elegance.

"On second thought," said Graham, "how about a round of drinks for everyone. I want you all to meet these men. They're part of E. H. Huttwell's band from Alabon, Texas. They're here to site the easiest trail for their cattle to these parts."

His eyes challenged Daniel.

"E.H., as you know, is the major stockholder in the Union Pacific Railroad. He plans to see that the line goes through Gateway City if it looks like it's going to make sense to drive cattle this way. It'll make sense all right. There's absolutely nothing to stand in his way."

Daniel felt a quiet rising of rage inside as he realized that Chapman had so badly underestimated the farmers.

"Hell, no, nothing will stand in our way," said one of the cowboys, "except a few sprigs of wheat here and there, and we'll make damn short work of that."

Daniel saw the muscles in Isaac Minton's forearms tighten. He shook his head with a barely visible movement to warn Isaac off.

Hollingworth had a mature pragmatic control that was above being drawn into a fight for ego's sake. It was nevertheless galling that the farmers would be this consistently misread. These were the men who had grit enough to dig down one hundred seventy feet for a well and to walk miles for water or to obtain supplies. These were the men capable of withstanding the deadening cold of winter and the ever-constant wind, and still stay. These were the men who were as resistant and unchanging as granite cliffs that had withstood centuries of erosion.

Daniel nodded to the other two men. They rose together and quietly headed for the doors.

"Air getting a little sticky in here, sodbuster?" one of the cowboys taunted.

"We'll meet tomorrow night," said Daniel tersely when they were outside. They did not discuss what had been said in the saloon. There was no need to. All three knew what a cattle route in this direction would mean. What the cattle would not eat would be destroyed by the trampling of the loosely herded animals.

"There's twenty-five separate groups of H.U.A. ers by now," said Daniel. "Some just have two or three members each because of the distance between claims. I want every last one of them to meet at my house tomorrow night."

"How many members then?" asked Isaac.

"We've got over a hundred by now, I guess," said Daniel.

Isaac immediately took heart. "Looks like the farmers are going to have some clout after all."

"'Clout' is putting it mildly. We're going to run this county. But we've got to get together, and there's a fellow I want everyone to meet."

All of the homesteaders assembled at the Hollingworths' soddy the next evening. It was too crowded to get more than a handful inside, so they settled for spreading out into the open prairie.

"You men all know what a cattle route through Gateway City will mean," Daniel began. "Our crops will be ruined and our property damaged. You know full well the agony inflicted by claim jumpers." Several nodded their heads at the last statement. "Well, we've solved the last problem. No one dares try to steal a man's property in this county now. The group we formed, the Homesteaders Union Association, handled claim jumpers effectively. Now we are left with two things to deal with. The damage cattle will do, and being robbed by the railroad men. There's a man I want you to meet. He says we are going about things the wrong way. He says we use too much muscle and not enough brains. He says we work too hard and think too little. Gentlemen, I present Tecumseh Spangler Flynn. I want you to hear him out."

All eyes turned to the fiery, red-headed editor as he emerged like a gangly stork from the doorway of the soddy.

"You're being lured into mortgaging your souls to the devil," began Flynn. "No other class of people in American history has had to endure more suffering than the farmer. I'm here tonight to urge you to abandon violence and start using your heads. You all know the saying, 'Out of debt, out of danger.' Well, the amount of debt you are being asked to assume as a county is staggering. I call you to organize in a manner that will be effective. You cannot kill every cow and every cowboy. Throw your energy into the Patrons of Husbandry and you will be united with a body of intelligent men who seek justice."

The men were listening intently. Flynn paused for effect, and then: "The remedy for these evils lies in our own hands. We must obtain the enactment and enforcement of just and liberal laws to protect our rights."

"How do we stand a chance to do that?" Kevin McQuire asked. "Hell, I can't leave my work long enough to take a leak, let alone go galavanting off to twist some senator's arm."

Flynn grinned. "The unified voting power of the farmers is awesome. I'm speaking about the body of farmers as a whole, not just here in Kansas. One-fourth of the male population of the entire country is engaged in farming. Can you imagine the weight that gives at the polls?"

"I've heard of the Grangers," Isaac Minton said, "and all the laws they've tried to get through have been struck down."

"True," said Flynn. "True enough, but we're not through yet. And while we're working for legislation, the Grange will raise the standard of living in all your homes. It will provide educational and social outlets for your children and wives. We'll show you how to get out of debt and stay out."

Daniel's face was gloomy as he listened to Tem's words. He had heard the man's arguments often enough and knew he was right on target. At last he tapped the editor on the shoulder.

"I think the men are ready to decide which direction they want to go. I'm calling for a vote," said Daniel. "All those who would disband the Homesteaders Union Association and seek membership in the National Grange say aye."

The prairie echoed with the affirmative vote, and more than one man was relieved he would not be called upon ever again to participate in a lynching.

"And now," said Flynn, "you are faced with an important decision. Who would you have as your Grange Master? The position is one of great responsibility and calls for the exercise of top executive abilities. He must be firm, possess great tact, and be a practical man devoted to his farm and to the interests of our Order."

The chant began immediately. "Hollingworth, Hollingworth, Hollingworth!" The sound drifted toward the heavens and every eye was on Daniel, who stood arrow straight, and looked solemnly from face to face. Inside the soddy, Aura Lee glowed with quiet pride. Her heart overflowed with gratitude. And he's my husband, she thought, basking in the warmth of secure integrity that surrounded Daniel.

"I appreciate your confidence," Daniel began. "But this is not your decision to make. I have studied the constitution of the National Grange until I nearly know it by heart. This is not your decision alone. The women are full voting members in your organization."

"You mean the women get to vote too?" asked Kevin. "They don't even get to vote in national elections, and you are saying you think they are smart enough to know how to run a lodge?"

Aura Lee was outside now and stood looking at Daniel with adoration. He reached for her hand and she stood by his side.

"Yes," said Daniel. "That's exactly what I'm saying. I think the women are smart enough to know what they want and need. It's one of the platforms of the Grange Constitution. So you're going to have to wait to select your Grange Master. The womenfolk may not want me."

The men were stunned by the novelty of letting women help make decisions.

"We have a very serious item of business to consider now," said Daniel, "and that's the changes occurring in Gateway City. Tem here has come up with a plan to deal one Graham Chapman the most lethal blow of all—to his pocketbook."

"His pocketbook," snorted one of the men. "We're the town joke now. Everyone knows we ain't got no money to spend. None of us has a spare nickel, so how can we control anyone through finances?"

"Think for a minute," said Daniel. "What does Chapman want more than anything else in the world?"

"A cattle shipping town?"

"A railroad town," said another.

"A town period," said Isaac. "Hell, yes, back of this whole cattle thing is the desire to build a town. If we stop Gateway City from becoming a town, it will stop the railroad and the cattle both. Dead cold."

"How can we stop a town?" asked Harmon. "Gateway City is a nine-day wonder. We can't just make it disappear."

"Oh, yes, we can," said Daniel. "It's happened before. The way you make a town disappear is to start a bigger and better one. It's happened before," he repeated. "I'm asking you men to back Plato as the county seat."

There was a round of clapping.

"You can count on my support for the farmers," said Tem. "My printing press will be in back of you, as it has been all along. I pledge that Plato will be a model of decency and integrity, but I'm not going to say anything more. You men have all heard too much talk as it is. The B and M coming through our town has agreed to pay for its own construction, and I have proof. The rails are getting closer every day. Come and see for yourselves. And the proof that you are not going to have to pay for it lies in the fact you haven't been asked to."

"Doesn't there have to be a county before there's a county seat?" asked Isaac.

"Yes. Chapman has taken care of that. He's already petitioned Governor Martin to organize a county. It's just his foregone conclusion that Gateway City will be the county seat. They're wrong. It's going to be Plato," said Daniel.

"How in the hell can we get people to vote for a town that's just barely there? Most of the people in the county live in Gateway City. They would be voting themselves out of house and home."

"We don't want a cow town," said Daniel. "I don't want one. You don't want one. There's bound to be others and I'll bet more townspeople feel that way than we know. We are the ones who have the most say in the end. I know it doesn't seem that way now, when we seldom go to town or meet others like ourselves, except through our little lodge meetings, but we actually outnumber any other kinds of group here in the county. But we're going to have to campaign hard to persuade the citizens of Gateway City."

"How are we going to keep all this a secret, Daniel? Over a hundred men slipping up on people to try to get them to switch towns is bound to attract attention."

"Yes, and how can we stand up to that newspaper?"

"I'll take care of that," said Flynn. "In fact, I'm looking forward to it."

"We're not going to keep anything a secret," said Daniel. "Not any more. We've got the *Plato Publication* on our side. I'm counting on there being lots of decent people in this county who will want things done properly and in order. Everything we do and every idea is going to be up front. I'm even going to ask Chapman to publish the minutes of this meeting, announcing the formation of a local chapter of the Patrons of Husbandry."

Graham looked over the minutes of the meeting to organize a lodge, hooked his thumbs in his belt, and reached for a cigar. He had promised E. H. Huttwell this was one organization that would not be let into his county.

"Hollingworth," he said. "Why don't you give this all up? Take a decent job where you can make a living and amount to something?"

"Just publish the minutes, Chapman."

Graham snorted with contempt.

"By God, now, don't you men think you're something."

There flashed through Daniel's mind the faces at last night's meeting. He thought of Vensel, who had lost his wife in childbirth. Tim, whose children had died when the ridge pole supporting his sod house had collapsed. Jake, who had returned after finding work on the railroad, only to learn that his wife and baby had starved to death. And his own beloved Aura Lee with the perilous grip on her sanity that was shared by thousands of women out in the country. More women were eventually driven mad by the wind and loneliness than people dreamed. Yet they stayed. And this man, who claimed to have vision, dared to laugh.

Daniel tipped his hat. "I bid you good day, sir," he said mildly, and turned and left the office.

Graham stared at his back. This was the one man among the homesteaders whom he truly admired, but he could not believe he was expected to take this farmers' alliance seriously.

A mouse trap sprang at that moment. Graham swiveled in his chair to see the dying kicks of the little gray body, and swallowed uneasily. He had felt a cold coming on for a couple of days now, and all at once he was depressed by the demands of keeping his town developing.

The announcement of the formation of the local chapter of the National Grange was published that week in the *Plato Publication*. It was coldly omitted from the *Gateway Gazette*. Quickly copies of the paper were passed from hand to hand. Even in Gateway City, the merchants were uneasy.

"There is nothing to fear from this new alliance," Graham assured everyone.

The following week, there was another article with the minutes of another Grange meeting. This time there was a brief report of the business followed by the announcement that two weeks from that day, the Grange would be in session to hear offers from towns desiring to have the coveted honor of becoming a county seat.

An issue of the paper was given to one of E. H. Huttwell's hired men, who immediately wired his boss about the contents. Graham received a wire back, the same day.

RECEIVED TELEGRAM FROM TOMBLY CONCERNING GRANGE REQUEST TO SUBMIT WRITTEN TOWN PROPOSALS AT NEXT MEETING. WHAT DO YOU INTEND TO DO ABOUT THIS?

Graham crumbled up the wire and drafted a reply.

NOT A THING. THEY ARE POWERLESS. THERE IS NO TOWN OUT HERE BUT GATEWAY CITY.

Several days before the meeting to hear the town proposals, Graham strolled into the saloon. As he downed his whiskey, he mentioned to the bartender that he was leaving for Denver the next day on business.

"You're not attending the meeting?"

"The what?"

He grinned at Graham's arrogance.

"Oh, come now. They deserve more attention than that. Seriously, won't Gateway City have a proposal there?"

"No," said Graham firmly, "under no circumstances will this town kow-tow to a handful of dirt farmers. This is the county seat. There *is* no other town. And I'm not going to lend this group any credibility."

A newcomer, who was unaware of Graham's position, added to the talk.

"Lots of womenfolk here in town are agreeing with the farmers. They think the town is getting too rough. Things have gotten out of hand."

Graham looked at him coldly. He did not bother to reply.

41

Lucinda's eyes darkened as she thought of Daniel Hollingworth, and she swallowed painfully. She was still stinging from his rejection. The humiliation was like a weight in the pit of her stomach.

Since she could not have Daniel, a peculiar lassitude crept over her from time to time. It was as though the vibration under her feet and her unity with the universe had been suspended. She found she could no longer stand her life on the prairie. It was not enough. Her awesome energy could not find an outlet.

Her absence of joy was translated into a fierce directionless anger; dishes were broken and ingredients carelessly left out during her baking. Restlessly, she looked around at her spotless dugout.

She would go mad, she thought, if she had to stay much longer with Vensel and Anton. She had grown to detest the sniveling child. She was enraged by his flinching each time she extended her arms toward him. Just the sight of Vensel made her sick.

She conjured up the image of Aura Lee's frail face and briefly focused her hatred on what she saw. It was that woman's fault to begin with that she had lost the respect of Vensel and Anton. It was Aura Lee's doing that she did not have any place in the new town. It was certainly Aura

Lee's fault that Daniel had rejected her. She hated her superior ways.

Lucinda's reverie was broken when a speck in the distance caught her eye. It was becoming larger and soon she could see that the three men who were approaching were cowboys, not homesteaders.

She watched uneasily as they rode up to the soddy. Only one man dismounted. The man's basic character was clearly written in the cruel line of his mouth which was distorted by an ugly scar that ran from one corner nearly to his ear, and in the unbalanced gleam in his eyes.

Lucinda's heart beat rapidly. She held her breath as he approached the house. Vensel would be in the field until sundown. She drew a quick breath and made her decision. She opened the door and greeted the men. The man's eyes flickered at the boldness of this gesture.

She did not speak, but stood in the doorway, one hand firmly gripping her shawl about her shoulders.

"Afternoon, ma'am. Are your menfolks about?"

"Yes," she lied skillfully. "There's several beyond that draw, just over the next rise. They are within shouting distance. Do you want me to call them in?"

The man laughed at the brazenness of the lie. His eyes wandered over her lush curves.

"Well, well," he said. "Now, ain't you something? Any others about? Settlers, I mean?"

"No, yes," she said in rapid confusion. "Yes." All of her hatred of Aura Lee focused on this sudden opportunity.

"Yes," she said. "There's others around here. Just over the rise, three miles to the north, there's another soddy. Don't know if there's any menfolks around or not. He's gone a lot. More than likely there's just the woman at home. He's a homesteader," she blurted quickly, as though she and Vensel were not. As though the fact that the Hollingworths were homesteaders justified the information she had just given. "I think you'll find what you're looking for there."

The man silently studied her for a few minutes. In spite of her beauty, it would be like taking a whore and he fed on helplessness, on the pathetic fluttering of trapped birds. He turned suddenly and mounted his horse and they headed for the Hollingworths' soddy.

Aura Lee watched the men ride up. Her fingers traced the wild flutter of her heartbeat at the base of her throat. She willed herself to still her apprehension. So many men came now. So many came out on business to see Daniel. It was surely this and nothing more. And yet, from the time she had moved here, the sight of an approaching rider still filled her with terror.

They loomed larger and as the three rode up, without bothering to hello the house, she knew deep in her heart that it was this she had feared from the very beginning.

All three looked around and then, as if satisfied they would be uninterrupted with their prey, they moved toward the door.

She stood like an animal mesmerized by a snake, her heart sinking. But there was no place to run to, no place to hide.

Suddenly the door burst open. Tears of knowing despair began to trickle down her cheeks. Still she did not move. Not a word had been spoken. All her fears were concentrated on this moment, all the night terrors, all the voices she had struggled so hard to suppress during the daylight hours. All were coming to fruition.

Her eyes were drawn to the cruel mouth of the man in front of her. She smelled the stench of his unwashed body. On the mantel, next to her blue Dutch pitcher, sat her clock, steadily, relentlessly ticking out her fate.

As they started toward her, she had a sudden last vision of her piano in Saint Jo—one perfect day from her childhood when she had been wearing a pale blue dress that made her look like a Dresden shepherdess and the roses had bloomed beyond the doorway and her kitten had curled sweetly on her lap.

"Momma, Papa," her soul cried out. The yearning for her parents was so intense her eyes stung with the pain. And then they were there, calling to her, coaxing her, drawing her toward the light and sweet reunion and an infinite blissful peace. She was being drawn ever closer to the light.

"Daniel," she whispered as a hand clamped over wrist. "Daniel, oh, my God." Suddenly in a fierce blaze of strength she wanted to live, to find a place for herself in this harsh prairie.

I want my baby, I want to live, she thought. Then the light was there again, fierce and blinding, and Charlie Stone Wolf's words seared through her mind. "The price you must pay for being favored by the gods is terrible beyond all imagining." And she felt herself being hallowed with a tremendous heat and as it vibrated through her body, she was purified, cleansed, all her fears lifted. She was no longer afraid to have a baby, or love, or even die.

I want to live, and dear God, I want to have my baby. I want to live! And the light is there to show me my path; my own path, my own way. And this knowledge gave her courage and a blaze of strength possessed her and opening her eyes, she began to fight.

Charlie Stone Wolf was chilled to the bone as he rode through the grass. He would be very glad when he no longer had to care for the

Hollingworths' horses. Soon it would be spring and Daniel would be back on his own homestead.

Seeing the horses in front of the soddy, he supposed that Hollingworth had gotten home after all and had some visitors. The trip was for nothing, then; but he could use a warming cup of coffee before he started back. He went toward the house, then stopped as he heard the woman scream.

Quickly he ducked behind one of the horses, and seeing a Winchester strapped to the saddle, loosened it and crept toward the window. The men's coarse laughter filled the air and as he watched, one of them grabbed her arms and pinned them behind her back. His stomach lurched as one of them drew back his hand and slammed it into her face.

Propelled by fury, Charlie crashed through the door, shooting while he still had the advantage of surprise. The men fell to the floor, and Charlie gave the one nearest him a vicious kick. He knelt beside Aura Lee and felt for her pulse. It was there. Faint and erratic, but it was there. He needed to get her to a doctor at once. He ran to the corral and hitched up the Clydesdales to the wagon.

Daniel rode toward his homestead, and as the house came into view, he spurred Toby. Winter was beginning to lift. There was a new moist scent in the air, a quickening to the landscape.

Puzzled, he looked at the three strange horses in front of his soddy. He dismounted and patted Toby on the rump and started to lead him toward the barn. He stopped and looked around, his mind whirling with confusion. The Clydesdales were missing. God, had someone stolen his team?

He ran toward the house and flinging open the door he stumbled over the nearest body. He reeled with shock. Aura Lee, he thought wildly, Aura Lee. He looked around desperately. The air was driven from his body as though squeezed from a blacksmith's bellows. There was no note. He backed out and closed the door on the macabre scene and, mounting Toby, raced toward Gateway City.

He found her in the boardinghouse. A grim-faced Mrs. Seaton met him at the door and led him to the little yellow room where Aura Lee was being attended to by Dr. McVey. Daniel trembled as he knelt beside her. He saw the deep bruises on her face and his own grew stern and cold. He reached for her hand and patted it over and over again, hoping she would sense his presence, his love. Finally he sat in the chair beside the window and buried his face in his hands. He was going to leave this goddamned country. Give it back to the grass and the Indians. But before he did, he had one last chore to do. Rising quickly, he swallowed as he looked again at the battered, unconscious body of his wife.

He found Jeremiah at the general store.

"See what a damn cow town leads to?" he asked. "I tried to tell you. I want to know when Chapman will be back. There's going to be one last chore performed by the H.U.A. I want all the men to meet in front of the boardinghouse in three days."

Jeremiah paled. "I thought you was through with hangings, Hollingworth."

"Just spread the word," Daniel said tersely as he left the store.

The news of the attack on Aura Lee swept the town like wildfire. Have you heard? Have you heard about Mrs. Hollingworth? The details were discussed in shocked whispers on the street corners and a fear gripped the town.

"They say terrible things were done to her."

"But not the worst, she was spared that at least. The Indian was just in time."

Each stranger was looked upon with suspicion. The streets were emptied of women.

"Will she live?"

"They aren't sure yet."

Vensel Smrcka heard the news when he came into town with Anton for some supplies. He looked intently at his son, who adored this woman, then rode immediately to the Hollingworths' to comfort his friend. Daniel had come back to get extra gowns and clothing to take to Aura Lee.

Daniel met him at the door. They did not speak. Vensel clasped his shoulder and awkwardly touched his face. He twisted his hat in his hands.

Vensel did not ask any questions. "If we can help, the boy and me," he said, "let us know."

They left the silent house together. Beside the pile of elkhorns, where the men had hitched their horses, there were hoofprints. Vensel pointed out that a single horseshoe on one of the horses was undersized, as though it were a make-shift job the rider planned to correct later.

Vensel started toward his dugout. He wanted to get home while it was still light enough for him to finish his chores. As always, Anton was glued to his side. He watered his livestock and headed back to the dugout for supper. He stopped. There were hoofprints on the ground in front of him. He traced the faint pattern with his finger. All about their dugout was a vast sea of grass. Just this small broken plot around the watering tank could bear a trace. His hand trembled as he ran his fingers around the indenture made by an undersized horseshoe. The same pattern—he was sure of it.

He ate supper in cold, terrible silence. Finally he examined the ridges on his hands, the calluses, the broken nails, the cracked and brutal evidence of back-breaking labor. Lucinda watched him uneasily. At last he spoke.

"Were there men who passed through here yesterday?"

"No," she said quickly. "I would have said so. Why?"

Like a wary animal, she sensed she would have to be very careful in what she said to Vensel at this time. She felt the warmth in her cheeks fade as though drawn out by a syringe. Ever since the men had left, she felt as though she had lost her center, the core of her being. Still he did not speak. She was anxious for news. Had the men reached the Hollingworths' soddy? If so, what had happened? She shied away from asking the question, even in her mind.

Still Vensel sat in brooding silence, nearly motionless except for the intermittent examination of his hands. She could not ask anything without revealing that there had indeed been three men through yesterday. She went to bed and left her husband sitting silent in the darkness.

It was cold the next morning—made colder by her fear of Vensel. She had slept poorly and her limbs had twitched spasmodically many times during the night, waking her repeatedly in the clasp of an icy terror.

Still he sat in heavy silence. He had not gone to bed or even moved, the entire night. He did not eat breakfast, but marched stoically to the field on an empty stomach.

That evening he looked her full in the face and demanded once again.

"Lucinda, were there three men through here?"

"No," she said weakly. "No, I swear to God there was no one here."

Nervously, she watched as he finally stood and got their Bible from the corner shelf. She, who had never been afraid of any man before, was now absolutely terrified of her own husband.

He thumbed to Second Samuel, and in his heavy guttural Czech tongue began to read the story of David and Bathsheba. Her face went white and she sat perfectly still as his voice droned out the ancient words that sealed David's sins: "Set ye Uriah in the forefront of the hottest battle, and retire ye from him, that he may be smitten, and die." Vensel closed the book.

"You knew," he said heavily. "You always know. You did it on purpose. Put her in the front line and withdrew to let her die."

Lucinda defended herself fiercely. "I did *not* know. I swear to God." She swallowed as she realized that through her attempt to deny, she had admitted her guilt.

"Anton," said Vensel, "go on outside."

She wanted to call him back. She watched the boy leave with growing apprehension. She wanted the presence of his innocence to protect her.

There was a quiet, terrible rage within this man. He waited for a few minutes after Anton left, then turned to Lucinda. He did not look her fully in the eyes. It was as though he could not stand the sight of her.

"You knew, and as your husband, I swear to God, you are never going to hurt anyone again as long as I live."

Lucinda screamed with fear as Vensel approached. She screamed again and again as his hand clamped over her wrist. The sound echoed into the empty moonless night and there was no one to hear except a pale, terrified little Anton, whose soul was so scarred with the effort of survival that he had nearly become insane.

Lucinda's screams reached a new intensity as Vensel methodically smashed her fingers with a hammer. Before she fainted, she looked at her violin case with a sudden blaze of grief.

Vensel looked at her lying at his feet, then said again softly, "Before God, I swear you are never going to hurt anyone again as long as I live."

He paused with his hand on the door, silent and sickened by her words as she whispered through her pain.

"Vensel, you know what is so terribly, terribly wrong? I am the only one of us who belongs here. You're all wrong. All of you. You're not equal to this life. You shrink before it. Daniel and Graham want to turn it into something different. Oh, lord. . . ." The pain washed over her again. "Oh, my God—" She was silent for a moment. "I'm the only one who just loved—it—" As she drifted into unconsciousness, Jake's face swam before her eyes. Jake and the temptation of jewels and luxury, now the only door open, and she heard her voice soaring above her grief to a high place where the despair of ruined hands was eased, and a sob caught in her throat as the light glinted on her violin.

Vensel called out the door to the panic-stricken Anton. They rode into town in silence, and he presented his son to a stunned Mrs. Carlton, whose child had been the first person to be buried in Gateway City.

"This child needs a mother," he said simply, without further explanation. He turned and walked away as Anton was gathered up into her arms, sobbing as though his heart would break.

42

Dr. McVey tapped Daniel on the shoulder. He had fallen asleep, and jumped to his feet at the doctor's touch.

The doctor was finally able to reassure him. "Yes, she's stabilized now. There are massive bruises over her body. They beat the hell out of her, but no internal injuries. And did you know your wife is pregnant?"

"Yes, and I was afraid something would happen to the baby. Maybe we would be better off if she had lost it," said Daniel bitterly. "It's not right to bring a child into this kind of life. I see that now."

Dr. McVey looked at him sharply.

"Unless something changes, there's no sign she will lose the baby. They are both going to be just fine. Why don't you look in on her? She was awake when I left her a moment ago."

He tip-toed into the room, sickened at the sight of her slight, battered body gleaming with ointment. He choked back tears, then took her hand resting gently on the quilt and pressed her fingertips to his lips.

"Darling." He broke off with a muffled sob and let huge, quiet tears drop on her nails.

"Daniel." Her voice was very faint and he bent closer to catch every breath. "Daniel. Those men. Is the baby going to be all right?"

"Yes," he said, holding his breath. Would she be glad to be carrying it, or after this ordeal would she want to lose it?

"Oh, thank God, Daniel. Thank God."

His heart jumped with relief. He felt a surge of adrenaline.

"Just get well, sweeetheart, and when you can travel we'll leave this country, I promise you."

"You would do that. For me? Leave your land?"

"I was wrong," he said. "Wrong all along."

"Daniel, I've lived through the worst—the very worst. It's all happened to me now and I've made it. Something has changed inside me. But oh, darling, to be back East again. Oh, Daniel, it's like a dream come true."

"You just rest," he said. "Just rest and I'll be back a little later."

Aura Lee drifted off into a deep sleep and her dreams were filled with soft summer evenings, and sweet melodies that beckoned her back to tree-lined streets and banks of wild roses perfuming the air with a delicate scent. She was going home again. Going home.

Mrs. Carlton carried the silent boy to the boardinghouse. He had not spoken once since the night his father had brought him to her.

"I've done everything I can, Doc," she said. "I don't know how to reach him."

Dr. McVey patted Anton on the arm and led him to a bedroom for an examination. There was not a bruise or sign of injury on the boy's body. Just the alarming blank stare was the only indication there was something very, very wrong.

Aura Lee was up and around now. Daniel was making arrangements to sell their farm, but she had stayed in town, under Mrs. Seaton's motherly attention. She came to the doorway when she heard Mrs. Carlton and Dr. McVey talking.

Seeing Anton, she gave a little cry of dismay and rushed to the boy's side.

"What is the matter, sweetheart? What's wrong?"

Dr. McVey sighed with relief as huge tears started down the child's cheeks. Anton had not withdrawn so far that he could not come back.

"Please," Aura Lee begged. "I want to talk to Anton a minute. By himself. Come into my room, sweetheart."

The boy blinked his eyes at the flash of yellow as she closed the door firmly behind them and pulled Anton onto her lap.

Still he would not speak.

Tears stung her eyes and she kissed him over and over again.

"Anton, you must tell me what is the matter," she said. "You must talk to me. Please."

Finally through clenched teeth he was able to speak.

"I want my dad," he sobbed as though his heart would break. "But I can't go back to her—there—something happened." He reconstructed the terrible night, and Aura Lee felt as though she had dropped off the edge of a cliff, knowing that this boy's mind, his whole life was at stake.

What was it Charlie had said? You would only be able to heal the illnesses caused by the demons that had picked your bones during the time you were stripped of your flesh in the underworld. Something inside her leaped in recognition of the new truth. She knew all about healing this kind of illness. She had come back from this particular hell with a sure, clear understanding. Suddenly the room seemed to grow brighter and was filled with light and tears stung her cheeks and she hugged Anton over and over again.

I don't want to leave, she thought with wonder. I can't leave Anton.

He'll die if I do. No one else will understand him at all. She was giddy with power now. And the others. The women coming in. Who would help them? Who would show them if it were not her? No one else could take her place. She was washed in the light and her joy was so intense it was nearly unbearable.

"It's going to be all right, Anton. Really all right. And you can stay with me. And I'm going to have a baby and we'll teach it together. We'll start a school, Anton, and a library. This town needs books. And music. This town needs music. This country *needs* women. And next year—" Her voice quavered as she heard her own words with trembling wonder. "And next year—" she whispered. "Oh dear Heavenly Father—and next year—"

Anton's face softened with the beginning of hope. She could feel him listening with every fiber in his body.

"You'll get to paint and draw, Anton. And in other ways than just on paper. This land is a huge blank canvass. And we can use any colors we choose. We'll make our own culture. Shape it any way we like."

Dr. McVey appeared in the doorway and he watched the two cling to each other, knowing a tremendous healing was taking place in them both.

She looked over Anton's shoulder at the doctor. Then her face was filled with anxiety, and she said to Anton, "You stay here, sweetheart. I'll be back as soon as I can. I've got to stop Daniel before he finds a buyer for our land."

The boy nodded and she bundled up in her cape and bonnet and went out into the early spring air. Her steps faltered as she headed toward the livery stable. A crowd was gathered in front of the hotel and at its center was Daniel. His face was grim as he listened to the men.

"Let's gut-shoot the son-of-a-bitch," said Kevin McQuire. "Hanging's too good for him."

"No," said Daniel sharply. "Hanging's the decent way. We're going to do this right."

Graham. They're talking about Graham, thought Aura Lee with despair. She pushed boldly through the crowd of men until she had reached her husband's side. He turned with alarm when he felt her hand on his arm.

"Aura Lee, you should be in bed. Go back. You have no business here."

"No, Daniel. This *is* my business, if anything ever was. It's my turn to give a speech now."

The men grew solemn as she stood before them and began to talk.

"Please, I beg of you. Do not blame what has happened to me on Graham Chapman. For that matter, I don't believe that the three men who—" Her voice quavered and she drew a deep steadying breath. "I am sure the three men are not typical of cowboys. What you are planning on doing is wrong. It's blind reaction, and I can promise you that if you resort to violence yourselves, you'll lose the support of every decent person in the county forever. I thought we had given up the H.U.A. I thought the Grange and its ideals were taking its place. I thought you were going to pay attention at long last to what the women want too. Well, we *don't* want a hanging. I can promise you this, gentlemen. The decision you are making right here and now is the most important one you will ever make in your lives. It will shape the community for years. Will it be the H.U.A. and its vigilante justice? Or will it be the Grange with its foundation of order and decency? And civilization! Civilization!" Her voice was clear as she swept the crowd with her eyes. "I am asking you to decide what you really believe. That's what it boils down to. What you choose here today is a decision that can only be made once. What do you really believe in your hearts? Can we make this into a decent country? Can we impose the same laws out here that preserve society over the world? Do you have the strength to do it? If not, if not—then there's no place for any of us."

The crowd was silent and she turned to Daniel. His face was an iron mask.

"I mean it, Daniel," she said softly. "I want to stay here if we can do things right. I want to know what you really believe." She turned and went back to the boardinghouse.

Daniel came into her room later that evening.

"Well?" she said.

He gave a quick grin. "The Grange won. Hands down. That was quite a little speech you gave. I don't know what all has happened, but I'm still willing to go back if you want me to. We can still sell out."

"No, I'm staying."

His eyes were brilliant with gratitude.

"Chapman will be back next week according to Jeremiah. We'll be waiting for him. The Patrons of Husbandry have arranged a little surprise."

It had been a long, hot trip and Graham looked forward to the time when the train would come directly into Gateway City. He was dog-tired and covered with dust. After telegraphing Jeremiah Keever he would be returning that evening, he picked up his horse at the livery stable in Wallace. The last miles home seemed to take forever. All he wanted was a change of clothes and a hot bath.

"What the hell," he muttered as he drew closer to town. He was still too far away to make out details as he squinted at the gathering of people on the street.

Something was up. His sudden unease was sensed by his horse, who shied nervously when a rabbit bounded at their feet.

He rounded the corner of the livery stable and rode down the main street toward the newspaper office. There were tight, silent clusters of people watching, watching. The crowd was solemn, as though they were gathered for some grim occasion. The hostility to him was so tangible it made drops of sweat break out on his forehead.

"Jesus Christ," he said softly. "Just what in the hell has happened?" He was trapped as the crowd surged around him and knew he had ridden into a mob that was capable of lynching him.

His black stallion pranced nervously in the soft evening air. The people parted on each side as he rode through the silent corridor. Jeremiah Keever grabbed the reins of his horse to keep it from rearing.

"Couldn't get ahold of you to warn you, Graham," he said. "They've been waiting ever since you telegraphed."

"What the hell has happened here?"

Jeremiah quickly told him of the attack on Aura Lee.

Graham was miserable as he looked at the people before him.

"Is she going to be all right?"

"Yes—but—" Keever's voice broke off as Daniel and Aura Lee Hollingworth emerged from the boardinghouse, accompanied by Tem Flynn.

"What's that bastard doing here?" asked Graham.

Flynn walked to the front of the crowd. His voice rang over the group as they all turned to face him.

"This first meeting of the Patrons of Husbandry is now duly called to order. The first order of business this evening shall be the election of our Grange Master."

"I nominate Daniel Hollingworth," a voice rang out.

"I second the motion," said another quickly.

Then the people's voices were all united and began to chant, the words becoming louder and clearer with each beat of their hearts.

"Hollingworth. Hollingworth. Hollingworth." The words rolled like thunder through the air, and Daniel jumped lightly onto the platform beside Flynn. He stood for a moment, unable to still the uproar. The rays of the setting sun outlined his body as they had on the evening when Aura Lee first saw him. A quiet giant of a man. With steel to conquer the prairie, led by his fierce iron star that beat firmly in his body. Aura Lee proudly smiled through her tears as his eyes found hers. The women's voices were added to the men's as they called his name. "Hollingworth.

Hollingworth. Hollingworth." And the noise swelled up to the heavens themselves and the plains were filled with the sound of victory.

"And now," Flynn said. "Now nominations are open for the post of Ceres, the woman who is the equivalent to the Grange Master. What is your pleasure?"

"Aura Lee. Aura Lee. Aura Lee."

Daniel reached down and pulled her up to the platform, and her joy was so intense as she buried her face in her husband's chest that her soul shot to the moon.

Suddenly hands reached for Graham and pulled him from his horse and he was racked with terror as he was dragged to the front of the crowd. His throat was too dry to swallow. "We want you to be able to hear this, Chapman," said Tem Flynn. "Every single word." Flynn's arms were folded across his chest and his auburn air blazed in the evening light.

Daniel turned and his voice rang out.

"The first item of business this evening will be the selection of the town we desire to be our county seat."

"Plato," a voice cried out. "Plato, Plato, Plato."

Tem jumped high, elated and victorious.

Then the cry of "Hollingworth, Hollingworth," began to swell again and with his arm around his wife he addressed the crowd.

"The work of our Order is just commencing," he began, "and you all know the hardships we have endured. I know you have doubted the ability of the Grange to act in true unity. But I have an announcement for you." Daniel looked squarely at Graham and he could not restrain the trembling victory in his voice. "You know I have been in close communication with my Uncle Justin Hollingworth regarding the activities of the Grange nationwide." Every ear strained to hear him. Aura Lee looked at him in alarm, bewildered by the underlying emotion in his voice.

"I received a telegram from Uncle Justin today. And the Supreme Court of the United States of America—" His voice broke and for a moment he could not continue. "The Supreme Court of the United States of America," he said again, each word standing separately as he spoke, "this great good body of men agreed to hear a case presented by the Grangers, and have ruled in a landmark decision that the government can regulate the rates of all those transportation industries affected with a public interest. There will be a national interstate commerce commission. The rates the railroad will be allowed to charge will be fixed in Washington. Ladies and gentlemen, let us begin. Let us begin this land."

They went wild. Graham looked up at Daniel and he was stricken with despair. It was all lost in a moment, with a single turn of the cards—his town, Aura Lee, the people's trust, everything. Graham's eyes flickered over the faces of the homesteaders and he saw for the first time the anguish of living with the harshest of realities day after day, and the quiet resolution shared by the men here. His soul was drowned in their unity, and for a moment he wished he too were a part of them. As lonely as Adam yearning for the lost Eden, he looked steadily at Daniel.

Daniel looked down at him. This will not be the end of Chapman, he thought. He will go on and in another section of the country he will be the forerunner of commerce and industry. But not if it involves working with people like this breed of men. And Graham's eyes never left Daniel's. There passed between them in the gaze an admiring acknowledgment of one another's worth.

"Let us begin," Daniel said again. And the people began to pack and plan for the move to Plato. Teams of horses began to move toward the buildings with their giant prairie sleds and Graham knew Gateway City would vanish in a week's time.

As the crowd dispersed, he was left alone and chilled and silent as he had been throughout the whole evening.

"Graham," said Aura Lee. "I just want you to know—"

But he turned abruptly, his face a smooth mask to disguise unbearable anguish.

"Graham," she called softly as he began to walk away. "I just want you to know that in another place, another time, it would have been you."

He stopped and she could see his back stiffen and he hesitated for a moment, then continued to walk without looking back at her even once.

Charlie Stone Wolf slowly drank his cup of coffee and talked to Aura Lee for the last time. He sat at the table in the Hollingworths' soddy and waited for Daniel to come in from his day's work.

"I'll miss you, Charlie," said Aura Lee. "More than you'll ever know. You've taught me so many things. I still don't understand why you would want to perform in a circus or a Wild West show." She did not say what was in her heart, that this type of exhibition seemed somehow degrading.

What Aura Lee could never know was how the blood of chiefs surged through his veins in his wild rides around the ring. War cries of a mighty, vanishing people echoed in his ears, and occasionally his gods visited his performances and suspended reality and he was transported in time to a proud past and in those brief magical moments it all seemed real. He looked at Aura Lee and shrugged with a slight, sad smile.

"Are you no longer keeping the boy?" he asked.

"No," said Aura Lee. "No, we're not." Vensel had come for him one evening, carrying Lucinda's violin under his arm.

"The woman is gone," he said simply. "This is for you." He had come home from the field one night and found the dugout deserted. She vanished as mysteriously as she had come to him, leaving no trace of having been there at all, except for this instrument.

Aura Lee stared at it, remembering the night of the fire when she and Lucinda had worked together to save their homestead. Remembering Lucinda's proud, strong body braced against the wind. Remembering Lucinda laughing, challenging the prairie, with her wild exuberance as she thrilled to the morning. Remembering the great strength of the woman's hands. And tears stung her eyes as too many other memories crowded in. Painful beyond all endurance.

"I don't want it, Vensel. I'm sorry. I don't care what you do with it."

He nodded, understanding.

"I think we have a little boy here who needs his father."

Anton took his Vensel's hand.

"I want to come home, Dad."

Aura Lee had watched as they departed in silence, moving across the prairie toward their lonely dugout.

"Charlie, there's still so many things I don't understand," said Aura Lee quietly. "So many things. But I don't think it matters. We don't have to know it all, not in this lifetime. I don't know all I want to know about the light. But it's there and that is enough."

He nodded. She had come a long way if she was able to live with mystery and still trust.

"I think there's a fourth way, Charlie, for women. You said I must become a healer, or a teacher, or an artist. But women are also the keepers. We keep the light."

"There were those women in my tribe who were keepers," he said. "They sought the sacred and preserved the wisdom of my people, passing the knowledge from generation to generation. They are gone now, and took our medicine with them."

"Here comes Daniel, Charlie," said Aura Lee.

The Indian rose to his feet and the two men grasped each other in a hug as they said goodbye, knowing they would never see each other again.

Charlie smiled as he turned and looked back at the couple, still waving from the doorway, standing side by side now. Each in the rightful place. His horse lowered its head and tugged at a bunch of buffalo grass, and in the distance, the eternal bluestem seemed to beckon to him. His eyes swept the horizon as he said farewell to his homeland, his earth that was being slowly stolen from his people, acre by acre. He sat a long while just looking at the changes sweeping the vast prairie.

Aura Lee was still in the silent protection of her husband, transformed by bearing the mighty wound of God into a new person, and Charlie

302

knew she was whole now. She had endured the purification of the *shaman*, and through her strength she would bring powerful gifts to people who came into this raw land. She had received the touch of Changing Woman, and once given it could never be denied.

He gave a slight tug on the reins, and turned the horse's head away, always away now, from his natural place on the earth. There were fences and railroads and the white men's earth homes constructed from the mother herself, who struggled valiantly against each block of sod torn from her bosom. There would be no end to it, he knew that now. At the forefront would be Graham Chapman, Coyote, the Trickster, a powerful figure viewed with fear and awe by his people. For Coyote always bore the twin gifts—one light and one dark—of creation and destruction. The one could never be received without accepting the other. But he would always emerge again, time after time, having been created by the gods themselves, to bring about the changes they had ordained.

Sadness swept over him in a great wave of grief and he stopped and looked back once. They too were still looking across the vast prairie. Then the woman went back inside and Daniel Hollingworth stood alone, and his rugged body was in dark silhouette in the doorway. He stood on the land where Charlie's people had once reigned supreme and his dreams would be mixed with those of the Indians as he worked the land and received the imprinting from the soil, for once a people's blood was spilt on the land their souls became part of the earth and could never be removed. For a moment the gods lifted their veil and the future blended with the past and the present and Charlie saw the Great American Desert changed into golden fields of wheat as far as the eye could see. Enough grain to feed the world, and at the vanguard of the men who would become masters of the earth was Daniel Hollingworth, the homesteader. It was his moment in history. His time had come. He was a Kansan.

Author's Note

The Interstate Commerce Commission was established as a result of "Granger Laws" passed in 1887, not 1881, as is implied in this manuscript. The time sequence was accelerated for fictional purposes. The Grange was the only truly effective national farm organization in this nation's history, and I employed direct quotes from old Grange speeches when they could be used appropriately in the book.

An organization called the Homesteaders Union Association once existed in Sherman County, Kansas. The oath and declared purpose of the group was identical to that of the men in this book. Half the counties in Kansas had county-seat wars, and this group once took the county records from a rival town at gunpoint.

Kansas has always been a hotbed of political activity. There were once more newspapers per capita in Kansas than in any other state of the Union. Again, when the words could be worked into the story, I have quoted from old Kansas newspapers. No writer of fiction could possibly devise rhetoric more inflammatory than was actually printed by our pioneer editors.

I want to thank Marion and Betty Parker, Evelyn Walden, and Marilyn Carder for the countless hours they gave to collecting and preserving regional history.

Words will never adequately express my gratitude to three people who encouraged me during the development of this manuscript. They are Jeanne Williams, Damaris Rowland, and Don Worcester.